A NOTE ON THE AUTHOR

Jack Fernley is the pen name of a leading British television executive. Over his career he has been involved with programmes as varied as *Strictly Come Dancing*, *Top of the Pops*, *Dragons' Den*, *Top Gear*, *Doctor Who*, *Dancing with the Stars* and *The Crown*. He lives in London.

Also by the Author

The Babylon Revelation

America Über Alles

Jack Fernley

Unbound

This edition first published in 2018

Unbound
6th Floor Mutual House, 70 Conduit Street, London W1S 2GF

www.unbound.com

Text Design by Ellipsis, Glasgow

A CIP record for this book is available from the British Library

ISBN 978-1-78352-474-7 (trade hbk)
ISBN 978-1-78352-475-4 (ebook)
ISBN 978-1-78352-473-0 (limited edition)

Printed in Great Britain by Clays Ltd, St Ives Plc

1 3 5 7 9 8 6 4 2

MIX
Paper from
responsible sources
FSC
www.fsc.org   FSC® C018179

With special thanks to Super Patron, Keli Lee

Dear Reader,

The book you are holding came about in a rather different way to most others. It was funded directly by readers through a new website: Unbound. Unbound is the creation of three writers. We started the company because we believed there had to be a better deal for both writers and readers. On the Unbound website, authors share the ideas for the books they want to write directly with readers. If enough of you support the book by pledging for it in advance, we produce a beautifully bound special subscribers' edition and distribute a regular edition and ebook wherever books are sold, in shops and online.

This new way of publishing is actually a very old idea (Samuel Johnson funded his dictionary this way). We're just using the internet to build each writer a network of patrons. At the back of this book, you'll find the names of all the people who made it happen.

Publishing in this way means readers are no longer just passive consumers of the books they buy, and authors are free to write the books they really want. They get a much fairer return too – half the profits their books generate, rather than a tiny percentage of the cover price.

If you're not yet a subscriber, we hope that you'll want to join our publishing revolution and have your name listed in one of our books in the future. To get you started, here is a £5 discount on your first pledge. Just visit unbound.com, make your pledge and type **America5** in the promo code box when you check out.

Thank you for your support,

Dan, Justin and John
Founders, Unbound

CONTENTS

PART 1

BERLIN, GERMANY

26 April 1945

ONE

The second round of anti-aircraft fire almost did for them.

The first burst had flown harmlessly wide of the left wing, but the second hit the lower side of the Fieseler Fi 156 Storch's cockpit. The round of armour-piercing bullets cut through the machine's flank, catching Robert Ritter von Greim's right foot and leg, peppering him with hot shrapnel. He screamed out, involuntarily letting go of the joystick and frantically attempting to stamp out the burning metal that had struck through the boot leather and was torching his foot and calf.

Hanna Reitsch immediately recognised the danger.

Unstrapping herself from the jump seat, she leaned over von Greim and seized control of the plane.

Already the plane was making a desperate, right-sided lurch to the ground; within seconds it would be crashing on to the streets of Wilmersdorf below them.

Using all her strength, she pulled the Fieseler out of its sudden descent, parlaying to the north-east, and avoiding the smouldering ruins that ran to the edge of the Grunewald. She was little more than a kilometre from the Heerstrasse. Out of the forest, more ground fire came at them, bullets popping off the fuselage. Ahead she saw the line of the Heerstrasse and banked right to follow it, leaving the enemy fire behind.

Von Greim moved to take back the controls, but without looking at him she barked, 'I have this, Robert.' Then, more softly, 'Sit back and enjoy the ride.' Groaning, he slumped back into his seat.

As the street gave way to the Siegessaule, she saw the open expanse of the Tiergarten to the left. Spring was the best of times for the Tiergarten, the lush canopy of its trees sheltering marble monuments and furtive lovers, the streams along which cygnets and ducklings took their first rides, the lush flower beds springing to life – but not this year. Those once magnificent trees had been reduced to ugly, charred stumps by months of bombing and shelling; statues, bridges, all lying in ruin, the streams and flower beds polluted and filthy, the swans and geese long eaten by a starving city, young lovers separated by war and death.

She was heading for the east–west axis, where the Unter den Linden crossed Friedrichstrasse. In the distance, the Reichstag loomed to the left, and before it the Brandenburg Gate. She eased the joystick up, straightened the plane and then gently moved the controls down, readying for her landing. The plane wobbled slightly. She knew she was moving a touch too fast, but there was little she could do. She had limited room to land and no chance of pulling up and attempting a second approach. Reitsch gambled to get it right.

Pushing her body tight against the back of the seat, she jammed down the stick. The wheels of the Fieseler touched earth, immediately bouncing back up. With great effort, she pushed down again. This time the plane hit the ground and stayed there. The Unter den Linden was full of rubble and the wheels of the plane threw up stones and bricks into the air. She was braking hard, but her ability to control the landing disappeared when the right wheel struck a large chunk of concrete. The wheel collapsed. Immediately, the Fieseler banked to the right and the undercarriage began to rip along the road, sparks flying out.

The plane started a wide spin; Reitsch went with it. She had no

4

control over the Fieseler now. The momentum of the circle was pushing the plane towards a reinforced sentry post. The right wing of the plane smashed the sentry box into splinters before detaching itself. Now the plane tipped to the left, the remaining wing throwing up a cloud of mud and rocks, illuminated by sparks as it ran along the ground. Through the murky window, Reitsch saw the Brandenburg Gate coming closer and closer, until finally the nose crashed into the masonry. It crumpled up, a concertina of metal, but just as she thought it would swallow up both her and von Greim, it stopped short.

There was a low moan from her companion and a weak whisper: 'And that, my darling, is why you will never get to be in the Luftwaffe.'

The three boys had watched the plane fall from the sky in their foxhole on the edge of the Tiergarten. From the insignia, they saw it was one of theirs, but as they scrambled towards the smoking remains, they were surprised to see a woman pulling a man out of the cockpit.

'It's Hanna Reitsch!' the oldest boy shouted.

'Who?' asked one of the others, as they ran towards the wreckage.

'The greatest girl pilot in the Reich. It is you, isn't it, Frau Reitsch?'

She eyed him up. He was no more than thirteen, and the other two looked even younger. They wore street clothes, dirtied by months of aerial bombardment, a swastika armband the only nod to a uniform. So these were the last defenders of Berlin, boys who should have been at school. The Volkssturm in all its glory.

'I am, well spotted. Boys, I need your help. The general has been injured. Come, let's not mess about, I need your help here.'

The boys ran round the plane and did their best to help her pull von Greim out of the Fieseler.

'I saw you when you flew that Fa-61 in the Deutschlandhalle, in thirty-eight, my papa took me,' the oldest boy said.

'Yes, I remember. That was a glorious day. Robert, let me take this boot off.'

Von Greim winced in pain as she unbuckled what remained of it, most of the leather having been burned away. His foot was badly scorched, almost charred in places.

'My papa was a pilot too, in the Luftwaffe. The English shot him down. We've never seen anyone land a plane on the Unter, have we, lads? Did you land it, Frau Reitsch?'

She nodded her assent.

'Can you walk?' she asked von Greim.

'I, ah, it's just some small burns, I'll be fine,' he said before putting his blackened foot on to the ground. 'Aagh!' The scream was involuntary – so too the buckle of his body as he fell towards the ground, stopped by Reitsch's outstretched arms.

'It's not just burns. There's shrapnel in there. We need to get it out. Before you lose the foot. No, you can't walk.'

'Then I'll crawl to the Chancellery.'

Reitsch turned to the boys. 'You boys, you're members of the Volkssturm, yes?'

'We are Frau Reitsch, the Volkssturm Mitte Group. We're here to defend the Reichstag from the Communist barbarians. We will fight to the death!' said the oldest boy.

'To the death!' echoed the other two.

'What with?'

They looked at each other.

'With whatever we can get our hands on!' shouted the oldest again as the other two cheered.

'That's the spirit. The Reich will triumph if everyone has your attitude. What are your names?'

'Karl, Karl Dahrendorf. And this is Wilf, my cousin, and our friend Paul. Are you going to the Chancellery to see the Führer?'

Reitsch looked at von Greim and he replied, 'We are. The Führer sent a telegram asking us to come to see him and – as you know – we always have to obey the Führer.'

'Heil Hitler!' Wilf said, shooting his arm up.

'Heil Hitler,' von Greim replied, a thin smile across his pained lips. The smile was interrupted by the explosion of a shell in a neighbouring street. Reitsch noted that none of the boys flinched, let alone paid it any attention.

'Boys, we need to reach the Chancellery as soon as possible, but we need to help the general, he can't walk.'

'We have a car!' said Karl proudly. 'We captured it yesterday.'

'You captured it?'

Paul spoke up. 'It was our reward.'

'Your reward?'

'Yes, our reward for telling the Feldgendarmerie about Gen-scher the grocer's son; he was a deserter and his father was trying to protect him. They gave us the Volkswagen.'

'Where is this Volkswagen?'

'Outside his store.'

Reitsch and von Greim exchanged a smile. 'And where might that be?'

'Oh, just off Friedrichstrasse. Come on, I'll take you there.'

'Won't be long,' she said to von Greim.

'Don't worry, Paul and Wilf will protect me,' he said with a further smile.

Reitsch and Karl jogged down the pockmarked street. The light was lowering now. It must be about seven-thirty, she thought. For the first time she was able to get a sense of Berlin as it was, a city under siege. She had last been here a little over a year ago, just after the terrible bombings of March 1944. Then she had thought that there was not much more the city could take, but the bombs had continued to fall for a year, night after night of devastation, with barely a break. And then the last month had brought a fresh round of annihilation. Nothing had been spared, it seemed. But it wasn't the ghostly half-destroyed buildings that struck her; it was the acrid, fume-laden air, dark with smoke. As they ran through the streets, jumping over rubble from fallen buildings and the debris of homes long lost, she realised that the constant grittiness in her mouth was because the air was thick with masonry. It seemed as if the buildings were dissolving into the atmosphere, taking the life of the city with it, soon to leave nothing but memories and apparitions behind. A falling shell rudely interrupted her reverie.

'They'll be coming again soon,' Karl shouted. 'They send Katyusha rockets first, then the proper shells come. But there's no planes now. Not for five nights. Because the British and the Americans are letting the Russians in. Cowards. Wait till we get them here, on our streets. Look, there it is.'

The boy pointed to a grey Volkswagen. Amid the rubble and the destruction, it was oddly perfect, the thin sheet of dust across it like wrapping paper around a present. It was parked outside the grocer's store with its windows broken, its shelves empty. It had been looted. Outside, from a lamp post, two bodies hung, just a few feet off the ground. From one a hastily written sign hung from the neck: '*Wer kumpft kahn sterben. Wer sein Vaterland verrat mufs sterben. WIR MUSTEN STERBEN!*': 'Whoever fights can die. Whoever betrays his Fatherland must die. We had to die!'

'The Genschers,' the boy said without emotion. 'Look, the keys are still here!'

'Then we better go for a ride,' she replied, barely giving the Genschers a look.

It was only a matter of a few minutes' drive to von Greim. They put the general in the front passenger seat, the three boys squeezed into the back and Reitsch drove. Shells had started to fall intermittently in greater numbers, the roads were strewn with everything from fallen masonry to upturned carts, but it did not take long to drive from the crash site to the Reich Chancellery on Vossstrasse.

'Will you introduce us to the Führer, General?' Paul asked.

'The Führer is always busy, he has little time for niceties. He has the Army, the Navy, the Luftwaffe, the defence of the Reich to organise. I can't think any other man could handle such responsibility,' von Greim answered.

'Tsch, General. I am sure the Führer would only be too honoured to meet such brave defenders of Berlin as these boys.'

'They say that General Wenck and the Twelfth Army are no more than a day away from breaking though the Russians and then we'll see the Communist swine off for good,' Paul again.

Reitsch stared straight ahead. Von Greim hesitated. 'He is a great general and the Twelfth Army is one of our finest armies . . . if anyone can do it, it will be General Wenck. The Führer tells us he will be here soon, so we must believe he will.'

Reitsch stopped the car abruptly to the left of a heavily sand-bagged gun placement in front of the Chancellery's large brass doors. She swung open the car door and called out to the four troops manning the post: 'Heil Hitler! I am Hanna Reitsch, holder of the Iron Cross First Class. I am here with Generaloberst Ritter von Greim, ordered by the Führer himself to come for an urgent conference. The Generaloberst is injured. I need you to come quickly to help him into the Chancellery!'

The soldiers looked at each other, confused. They had strict orders not to abandon their post, but the insistent tone of the woman intimidated them.

'What are you waiting for? Come on!' she screamed, getting out of the car.

The men now ran forward and made to pick up von Greim, carrying him quickly from the car into the Chancellery, Reitsch following. As they reached the doors, Reitsch stopped. Karl, Wilf and Paul were standing by the Volkswagen, mutely.

'Hey, boys, I thought you wanted to meet the Führer, what are you waiting for?'

She saw the smiles break out on the boys' faces, but her pleasure was disturbed by a low, whining sound. She knew what it was. She threw herself to the ground before the shell arrived. There was a torrent of noise, and then dirt and concrete formed a heavy cloud, small remnants of the street paving dropping on her body, a cruel hailstorm. She slowly raised herself. The Volkswagen had disappeared, replaced by a five-metre-wide crater. Of Karl, Wilf and Paul, there was no sign they had ever existed.

TWO

'Dear Generaloberst, Hanna!'

They were in Ludwig Stumpfegger's medical room, deep in the bunker underneath the Chancellery. Von Greim lay on a canvas bed, his wounded foot had been treated by the surgeon, painkillers had given him respite. The door flew open and the ermine-clad figure of Magdalena Goebbels entered. She embraced Reitsch warmly.

'Magdalena, how are you? The children, are they with you and Joseph?'

'They are, dear Hanna. They are the pride of the Reich. They take it all so well; they understand the sacrifices that have to be made. If the rest of the nation were so bold and brave, we would not be in this terrible mess. Cowards, cowards everywhere, those old Prussians in the army have betrayed the Führer. There are even' – her voice moved into a softer register – 'traitors here in the bunker. Some of them have started to run already. We haven't seen Fegelein for two days.'

'Probably holed up with one of his whores in that place he has over at Charlottenburg,' von Greim joined in.

'Generaloberst, I heard you had been wounded. You are always so dashing, so brave. You have raised everyone's spirits by coming here. The Führer will be overjoyed. But your leg?'

'Ach, these are nothing,' he replied, addressing his bandaged leg and foot. 'Scratches, my dear, mere scratches. Herr Stumpfegger and his nurses sorted it. You should thank Hanna we're here; she landed the plane.'

'Really? You landed it? Hanna, you must tell me everything, and the children, they will be so excited to see you again.'

There was a sudden commotion outside the door. The door opened again, there was a pause, and in came a small, shrunken figure. It took a second before both von Greim and Reitsch recognised the man standing before them.

'Mein Führer,' the general said, attempting to stand.

'Dear Generaloberst, please, stay. It should be I bending my knee to you. You came. You both came. Dear Hanna,' he reached out to take her hand and kissed it.

She noticed his shaking left arm, the result of the treacherous assassination attempt the previous July. His voice sounded weak, exhausted, his face ashen, his eyes rheumy, with pain running through them. Such sadness, she thought.

'My Führer.' Reitsch felt tears welling in her eyes.

Hitler slowly eased himself into the chair next to von Greim's bed.

'You are both the epitome of the ideal German. Even a soldier has the right to disobey an order when it is futile and hopeless. But you, you came here, risked everything. You have never wavered in your love for the Fatherland and for its poor servant, Adolf Hitler. If I had a hundred legions made up of Greims and Reitschs, ah! We would have seen off the Slavic hordes. But the German people have shown themselves to be weak, Herr Generaloberst, weak!'

'My Führer, we are as honoured as ever to be with you. But, let us lead you from Berlin. If you were to fly south, there you can command our forces safely once again. There is too much risk in Berlin, the Bolsheviks are too close. You must leave. The German

12

people need you safe. We must leave for Bavaria, to carry on the war for civilisation.'

'Generaloberst, I am only the Führer as long as I can lead. And I can't lead my troops and the German people while sitting remotely on a mountain top. I have to have authority over armies that obey me. I must be at the centre of the struggle. I'd regard it as a thousand times more cowardly to commit suicide on the Obersalzberg than to stand and fall here with a pistol in my hand. Let me win a victory here, however difficult, however tough, however impossible, it may appear in this moment. Then I hold the authority, the authority to do away with the sluggish forces that are holding us back. Then I'll work with the generals who have proved themselves. Generals like you. And we will be victorious.'

He stood up, slowly, painfully, and held von Greim's hand in his.

'Only here can I attain that victory. Even if it is only a moral one, it's at least the victory of winning time. Only through a heroic attitude can we survive this hardest of times. If we win the decisive battle, I would be proved right. And even if I were to lose—'

'No!' screamed Magdalena Goebbels.

'And even were I to lose, then I will have perished decently, not like some inglorious refugee sitting in Berchtesgaden and issuing useless orders from there. If we leave the world stage in disgrace, we'll have lived for nothing. Rather end the struggle in honour than continue in shame and dishonour a few months or years longer. I am not made to run. My victory will come here in Berlin – or my honourable death.'

Again he slumped back to the chair, a faraway stare coming across his pale face. Von Greim studied Hitler. The complexion deathly, sweat pouring off him, the relentless shaking left hand, this was not the man he had known since 1920, when von Greim had flown a then unknown thirty-year-old army propagandist to Berlin to observe the Kapp Putsch. Nor the man who had entranced him from the beer halls of Munich to the fields of Nuremberg. Now that man seemed finished. But Adolf Hitler suddenly snapped alive, once again there was that unmistakable passion in his voice, an echo of the furious oratory that had transfixed von Greim in Munich twenty-five years earlier.

'But everything is not lost! The situation in Berlin looks worse than it is. Wenck's army is outside Potsdam, they are coming. It will be here, perhaps tonight, tomorrow or at the latest, in two days. They will join with the Ninth Army and then we will see the Bolshevik behemoth for what it is! We will hold Berlin and then the Americans and the British will understand there will be only one way to defeat the Russian Moloch – an alliance with Nazi Germany. And the only man to lead such an alliance is me. So, you see, victory is still in our destiny.

'And we have one more card to play, the ultimate card, the product of our scientific superiority, the card that will demonstrate to the world that National Socialism is the greatest vehicle for harnessing the powers of the human imagination. In this, our darkest hour, when our enemies surround us, mock us, humiliate us, in this hour when darkness seems to be total, we shall emerge into the light triumphant!'

Von Greim raised his head, 'So it is true? We have it, the weapon to end this war, as you promised we would?'

'We do, we do. And here lies the reason I ordered you to Berlin, both of you. For I am frail—'

There was a low murmur of dissent from Reitsch.

'No, I am frail, my dear, my body is disappointing me. This weapon may have arrived too late for me to harness its powers. But I am blessed with having the perfect agents for its delivery and with it the delivery of our triumph. Generaloberst—' Hitler rose to his feet once more. 'In the name of the German people, I give you my hand. A traitor must never succeed me as Führer. You will ensure that does not happen. I can no longer trust the Army. The Luftwaffe yes, but the army – traitors, cowards, idiots, all of them! Even the leadership of the SS, they have proved themselves unfaithful – cowards, scum! This is why I turn to you. I am promoting you to Generalfeldmarschall. You will lead a group of our finest men on this mission. They have been training for six months. Our finest, most loyal SS division. Our pride. They are the very finest of the Reich and they are waiting for you to assume leadership.

'There is little time. You must travel now, with Reichsminister Goebbels, to Dahlem, the Kaiser Wilhelm Institute. The Russians are desperate to capture the Institute, but you will get there before them and unleash this weapon. Goebbels will explain the details of the plan to you. And you, Hanna Reitsch, it is important that you go as well. All will become clear when you arrive.

'There is an armoured car waiting for you. Generalfeldmarschall, I know your wounds are painful, but you must leave, this instant.'

'My wounds are nothing, mein Führer. I shall take this commission with pride. I believe we will meet again in the future and celebrate our eventual victory.'

'Ah! So do I, Robert von Greim, so do I!'

And with that the leader of the German people turned on his heels and walked as sharply as he could out of the room, no longer the forlorn figure that entered it.

Magdalena Goebbels pressed something into Reitsch's hands. 'Dear Hanna, take this. Please. A symbol of my affection for you. Please, always think of me when you see it.'

It was a striking ring, gold with a large blue sapphire cabochon, surrounded by a ring of ten perfectly cut diamonds. Clasping both hand and ring, Magdalena looked into her friend's eyes and said: 'I wish I were going on this journey. Both Joseph and I wish we had been chosen by the Führer. You and Robert, you are blessed.'

THREE

The drive to Dahlem was perilous. The city, a roaring monster of flash and explosion. Constant bursts of detonation, shells raining down from every direction, tongues of orange, red and white flames licking buildings and sending them crazy, into a burning, exploding and collapsing fever. Bricks and debris bounced off their armoured car, the driver weaving between falling buildings and burning vehicles on roads pitted by craters. The closer they got to the Kaiser Wilhelm Institute the more intense it became.

To von Greim it was no surprise: since the 1930s, the Institute had been the centre for experiments with nuclear fusion under Werner Heisenberg and his team. The Soviets were hoping to take the Institute and with it the secrets of Germany's atomic-bomb programme. He had been under the impression that Heisenberg and his team had been moved in January to the Black Forest to ensure that such a capture could not happen. But then the Führer had hinted that the building did indeed house a weapon. He was perplexed and wanted to ask Goebbels, but, under the cacophony of explosions, conversation was impossible in the car.

Outside the Institute, a group of troops had dug deep trenches and built barricades. The building was pockmarked from incendiaries, but the huge white Blitzturm – the tower of lightning where the key experiments had been done – was intact. Now, however, it was simply serving as the perfect marker for the Soviet artillery.

The armoured car thudded to a halt and Goebbels, without a word, threw open his door and marched off towards the entrance of the Institute. Von Greim struggled out of the car, Reitsch handing him the crutches he needed to walk. He surveyed the scene.

It was clear that this defence of the Institute must have been planned for months and involved vast numbers of manpower and materiel. There were numerous concreted pillboxes, now pitted with shell marks, metres and metres of barbed wire, many sandbagged gun emplacements. Yet for how long could it hold back the Russians? A group of exhausted troops lay with their backs to the wall of the Institute, their faces smeared black with the dirt and sweat of the struggle, their eyes hollowed out by exhaustion.

'Soldier, why are you here and not in the battle?' Von Greim gently kicked the boot of one man.

A shell exploded overhead, briefly illuminating the soldier's face. He was expecting to see a veteran, but it was just another dirt-stained boy defending the Reich.

'What?' the youngster looked up, angry. 'We've been fighting the Russians, house by house, building by building, retreating all the way from Potsdam. We haven't slept for three days, haven't eaten for just as long, the schnapps is the only thing keeping us going. In an hour we'll be back out there. Holding someone's parlour, falling back into someone's bedroom, before it all turns to shit like every house we've been in. And where will you be, General? Will you be with us? Or will you be tucked up in bed or eating bratwurst and drinking champagne?'

Von Greim thought about striking him for his insolence, but looked past him to the huddled ranks of his comrades. He could see from their exhausted faces, they had given everything. What right did he have to tell this teenager he should work harder? In an hour he would be back in the fire and he might not last beyond that. Without saying a word, von Greim pulled up on his crutches and hobbled towards the Institute's entrance.

Goebbels led his charges through the corridors of the first floor. The impact of the Soviet assault was increasingly felt inside the building: broken windows, fallen masonry, discarded books and files strewn across the floor, a small huddle of exhausted men wrapped around a staircase which had come away from the floor above. Goebbels clearly knew the route well, taking them to a metal cage lift.

'We have several floors to travel down, I'm afraid. I'm sure that will be not be a problem for the two finest aviators of the Reich?' he smiled, a grin breaking out of his hollowed cheeks, the dark, sunken eyes that carried a strange power of their own.

They travelled for what must have been several hundred feet until the lift came to a halt. Down there, it was unearthly quiet, sterile and virginally clean. The tumult, the havoc of the world above seemed improbable. In the Führer's bunker, it was impossible to forget what raged above: the smells, the dirt, sweat and filth that everyone brought with them saw to that. Not here. Not down the whitewashed corridors they walked, the lab-coated technicians they passed; there was no sense that the world they had come from seconds earlier even existed.

Through several corridors they moved, until finally they entered what von Greim and Reitsch took to be some form of control room full of metal cabinets, dials, electrodes and metres of colour-coded cabling. A bank of chairs stood in front of a long window which looked down on to a larger room, a hall almost, in the centre of which was a large cylinder of highly polished steel; along its front edge ran embedded green lights, flickering intermittently. The centre of the cylinder was hollow, with a slightly raised platform in the middle. It stood about two and a half metres in height and was close to forty metres in length. It was an impressive construction and von Greim and Reitsch exchanged looks of awe.

'Only the Reich could build something as marvellous as this,' Reitsch mumbled.

'Yes, only a Nazi state would have the imagination and desire to achieve such things, Hanna,' Goebbels agreed. 'Come, let us take a closer view.'

They exited the control room and walked down a metal staircase to the floor of the hall, von Greim's crutches clanging against the metal railing. Several technicians were busying themselves around the cylinder.

'Herr Doktor Bewilogua,' Goebbels addressed himself to the group. 'I have arrived with Generalfeldmarschall von Greim and Frau Reitsch. Let us begin their briefing immediately.'

Ludwig Bewilogua, a small, owlish man, spectacles perched on his nose, turned to the group, clipboard in hand. 'You are late. We have been waiting on you for too many hours.' He handed the clipboard to an assistant. 'Come, we have little time for your briefing. We cannot miss this window.'

Without further acknowledgement, he left them, walked past the cylinder and out of the hall, beckoning them to follow. Goebbels raised an eyebrow to von Greim. 'Scientists. They lack finesse. Which is why we keep them in laboratories.' Another hollow smile and then he gestured for von Greim and Reitsch to follow him.

They went out of the hall and back down another corridor until they entered a final room, an enormous hall, in which over two hundred men stood immediately to attention. They were dressed in a peculiar form of the field uniform of the SS: grey-green, four-pocketed, five-buttoned jackets, with the SS emblems on the collar replaced by silver swastikas, and on each sleeve, an eagle. And on their right arm, a red armband with another swastika. A belt pulled the waist in, accentuating the powerful chest and shoulders of each man. Slate-grey, straight-legged trousers and black leather jackboots finished the uniform. They looked magnificent. It was a long time since von Greim had seen such well-finished uniforms, a long time since he had seen such fit, healthy and well-fed soldiers.

Goebbels stepped forward.

'Gentlemen, I give you your new leader Generalfeldmarschall Robert Ritter von Greim.'

'Heil Hitler,' they responded as one, each raising a perfect Nazi salute.

Von Greim returned the salute.

Goebbels continued: 'This is your special force, General-feldmarschall, hand-picked men from elite SS units. They are all, as you would expect, most excellent specimens of Aryan superiority. They have been trained especially for this mission for the last six months. Each has expert knowledge of the terrain, the enemy, the weaponry, the tactics. Aside from these fighting men, you will also be aided in your mission by a number of experts from the highest levels of the Reich.

'You know, of course, of the work of Hugo Schmeisser, the finest weapon designer in the world, creator of the Sturmgewehr 44, among many others.'

A balding, suited, bureaucratic-looking sixty-year-old man stepped forward, gave an awkward salute and a mumbled 'Heil Hitler.'

Goebbels paid him no heed, moving on to another suited man, 'And, of course, you know only too well Alfried Krupp von Bohlen und Halbach, our most respected Reichsminister für Rüstung und Kriegsproduktion.'

'Alfried, of course, what a surprise to find you here in Berlin. I had thought you might have been captured in Essen.'

A tall, confident, patrician figure, Krupp was only thirty-seven and yet the leading German industrialist of the age, a supporter of the Nazis since the 1930s. He brushed past Schmeisser, warmly grasped both of von Greim's hands and then kissed Reitsch on both cheeks. 'Dear Hanna, Robert. Such a joy to see you both. I left the city the day before the Americans overran it. We at Krupp's have been heavily involved in helping Doktor Bewilogua realise his vision here; it has been something of a special pet project for me. I came directly from Essen and begged the Führer to allow me to take part in this mission. Fortunately, he agreed and here I am. Unlike yourself, Robert, I lack military training, but my background in manufacturing, well, I hope it can greatly assist you.'

'Ah, I beg of you to hold that thought, Herr Krupp,' Goebbels interjected. 'As yet, the Generalfeldmarschall has not been briefed. Before we do so, one more introduction. I especially wish you to meet the finest young historian of the Reich, Doktor Werner Conze of the University of Vienna.'

An elegant young man, with a handsome face set off by a Roman nose, stepped forward and pushed out his hand towards von Greim.

'Generalfeldmarschall, it is a honour to serve under you. And Frau Reitsch, I have long admired and thrilled at your aeronautical feats.'

He leaned over to kiss Reitsch's outstretched hand, a waft of cologne escaping from him.

'Doktor Conze has played a most important role in developing our thoughts on *Lebensraum*. You may have read his pamphlet "Die weissrussische Frage in Polen", highly influential among the young members of the Bund Deutscher Osten?'

Von Greim shook Conze's hand.

An intellectual. Von Greim despised intellectuals, especially those who had jumped on the bandwagon just before 1933 when the Führer's ascent to power was all but confirmed. A cancer on the party ever since, with their political infighting and machinations. He recalled no intellectuals standing shoulder to shoulder with them in November 1923 when they marched out of the Bierkeller in Munich. No doubt this Conze had been shirking from military service while pontificating in Vienna.

'You praise me too much, Reichmaster Goebbels.'

21

'Nonsense. Since he was injured during the invasion of France, Doctor Conze has been researching both the realities of social life in the American revolution and the details of George Washington's campaigns and staff.'

Von Greim looked again at the younger man.

'You served in France?'

'Yes, 19th Korps under Guderian. I was wounded at Sedan, during the crossing of the Meuse.'

'One of our greatest triumphs.'

'It was an honour to serve, Generalfeldmarschall. My only regret is that I could not continue with the push on to Paris. My injuries were slight, but others decided I should not continue, but return to convalesce. I see that you have had better luck in persuading the doctors that you should be allowed to continue to serve.' He pointed at von Greim's bandaged foot.

'A recent injury of little importance. We didn't have an especially warm welcome into Berlin. But we cannot allow small obstructions to distract from the wider goal.'

'I hope you will find that I can be trusted on that score.'

Perhaps I am wrong about this one, thought von Greim.

'I am sure you will be proved correct, but I don't see the relevance of studying George Washington. What does a historian know of the atomic bomb?' asked von Greim.

'The atomic bomb? My dear Generalfeldmarschall, there is no atomic bomb. So the Führer did not sketch out your mission? Yes, we were experimenting here with Heisenberg and his team to harness the atom, but so far we have had no success. It was Doktor Bewilogua here, while researching the area of low-temperature physics – you'll have to excuse my layman's ignorance, I am afraid I may understand the passions that motivate an entire nation, but for the life of me I cannot fathom the science of this project – who, I hope this does not insult you, Doktor, *stumbled*?'

Bewilogua nodded his head, 'I will accept the initial discovery was a stumble. So much of science begins with a stumble. The skill is knowing whether the stumble leads us to a dead end or a new vista.'

'Ha, indeed, and what a vista you opened up for mankind, my dear Doktor! You were looking for divine power and instead you found an even greater power, and we are about to unleash it.'

Von Greim opened his hands, a silent question playing across his face.

Goebbels read the expression and asked: 'Generalfeldmarschall, why are we losing this war for civilisation? The barbaric Slavic hordes from the East may have greater numbers, but sacrifice on the scale they endure is unsustainable. They are barely civilised, nothing they create will survive. Given time we would easily outwit them. The British, perfidious Albion? Untrustworthy, weak, immoral, they have thrown away the greatest empire the world has seen, grown soft, too easily seduced by those they rule. The French, the French we can easily disregard. No, the reason we are losing this war is because of the Americans.

'Their *Lebensraum* is far too great for us. A land of almost unlimited resources. Imagine if that was our land, populated by our people. Free of all the limitations of the past, free of the Jew, the Slav, the Gypsy, the scum that has weakened all of Europe. Imagine a German America. Imagine an America infused with the same principles, beliefs, spirit that our Führer has given us. Imagine how history would have been written! How different mankind's story would have been if the first free Americans had been fired by the ideology that has made us so strong! By now our people would be living with the fruits of our manifold destiny. That is your mission, Generalfeldmarschall. That will be your lasting achievement.'

PART 2

BUCKINGHAM TOWNSHIP, PENNSYLVANIA

20 December 1776

FOUR

It was the worst winter anyone could remember. The snow and ice had come early in December and showed no sign of retreating – rivers frozen for weeks, blizzards blocking roadways, bitter winds sucking up all hope. It was the worst winter at the end of the worst year. The war seemed lost. Freedom seemed lost.

Washington's army had suffered defeat after defeat, retreating from New York, through New Jersey to Pennsylvania; only the Delaware River kept away the British and final destruction. The Continental Army, they called it, but it defied such a description. It was made up of all kinds of the new America: the urban elites, the country folk, the freed slave, the slave owner, the mechanic, the labourer. This was no proud army; the main body of the army was little more than a ragbag of bootless, homesick civilians, all looking for an excuse to get back to their families. Within days the annual enlistment would be up and Washington feared the worst. He would lose the majority of his men just as Lord Cornwallis's army was being supplied with fresh German mercenaries, Hessian troops heavily experienced from war in Europe. Even Washington's closest confidants talked openly of suing for peace. Congress had fled from Philadelphia, two of its members had crossed to the British and scores of citizens were signing the British Proclamation of 30 November, pledging loyalty to the crown. The Revolutionary War was all but over. This harsh winter would finish it.

And the year had been harder on no man more than Edward Hand.

In the glorious summer of 1775, no one symbolised more the hope of the coming struggle than Hand. A first-generation immigrant, from Clyduff, Ireland, he had joined the British Army as a surgeon's mate, which in turn had brought him to the colonies. America offered Edward Hand a dream of advancement that even he, a fully trained surgeon from Trinity College, Dublin, could not see in a pauperised Ireland in hock to Britain's imperial interests. Once in America, he soon resigned his commission and set himself up in Pennsylvania as a doctor, practising in and around the Irish settlements of Lancaster County. There he had fallen in love with Catherine Ewing, a second-generation Scot from Philadelphia. They were both enthusiastic supporters of the rights of the colonies, and when war had broken out, he had assumed a role as a lieutenant colonel in the 1st Pennsylvania Riflemen. He was just thirty that summer, of moderate height, strong cheekbones, his high forehead showing the first suggestions of a fading hairline, a handsome man with a taste for glory. In that year, Hand had been one of the heroes of both the siege of Boston and the battle of Bunker Hill, coming to be noticed and highly regarded by Washington. At the end of that most tumultuous of years, Catherine announced she was with child, a child due in August 1776.

And then the tide had turned and all Hand's hopes and dreams were washed away.

First came the defeats of the army. The sudden and dramatic change of affairs that placed the impetus with the British and led to people disparaging the ability of the Colonists' army and the incompetence of its leader, Washington. In August, Hand played a major role in ensuring the Colonists' army's successful retreat from Brooklyn Heights with no casualties. No sooner had his feet landed on Manhattan's soil than came the letter that crushed him.

A simple note: 'Your wife's confinement has ended early. She and your son both lost.'

Hand broke that night from camp with Washington's blessing. He reached his home in Trenton, the candles burning dimly, a hearth barely heated, his sister Sarah waiting for him, Catherine and the baby Edward cleaned and dressed. He buried them the following day and entered a period of fog, of drinking, of simply getting through the days to hit the bottle at night. Anything to avoid the grief that threatened to swallow him whole.

He returned to the army, Sarah coming to the camp with him, to serve as a cook and a nurse. She and his best friend, Patrick O'Leary, proving himself to be more than the Irish oaf he pretended to be, provided comfort and support, trying to minimise the damage he was wont to do to himself. But the failures of the Colonists at Fort Washington, Fort Lee and elsewhere in the autumn only seemed to illustrate the hopelessness of everything. And yet, without the war, what did he have?

Tonight, as on so many recent nights, Hand sat in a nameless tavern with Sarah and Pat, arguing with anyone who cared.

'I'll say it one more time: what would be the point in going back to Lancaster now? We have nothing and we'll have even less if the English win. Their revenge will be pitiless.' They were debating whether now was the time to face the truth. Give the war up, Hand was adamant. After all, he had nothing else now, now Catherine was no longer there to return to. 'They'll dig out all us bogtrotters and any rights we might have will disappear. We'll become like Cromwell's people, slaves.'

Hand pointed to Oliver Cromwell, former slave, now a freeman fighting alongside them.

'And that'll be a true disaster,' replied Patrick, shouting over to Cromwell. 'Oliver, what'll it be like for us poor Irish boys when the English put us to work alongside you Negroes down on those cotton farms?'

29

'What? You think you redheaded boys with your puny white skin will last more than a few days wi' that sun beating down on ya? "Oh, mister, please get me out of the sun, have you got me a parasol I can use while I pick this here cotton?"'

Cromwell gave a large belly roar, so much so that even Hand felt happy to join in.

'I'm no redhead, that's Pat you're talking of. And you're right, he wouldn't last a day.'

'I'd last longer than you, they'd end up putting you in the scullery, dressed up in a maid's outfit, fella.'

'There's freshly laundered maid's uniforms, fresh linens as well? I'll have some of what those Brits are offering!' shouted Sarah to more laugher.

Cromwell left his group and walked over to the Irish. 'You Irish, anyways, you be so beaten down, you'll be slaves to us niggers by sundown on the first day! You'd be the lowest of the low! It'll be a good day for the African man. At last we'll have somebody to master!'

'That's my point: we'll be slaves to these idiots, and our children will be slaves if we give up this fight.'

'You might be right, Eddie Hand, you might be wrong, but I would say it's not a question you would like to put to the challenge. In which case I would say that we shouldn't much bother to find out, but keep to this struggle for as long as we can muster arms.'

The two men splashed their pewter tankards together, drowning another gulp of warm, foaming beer.

'A happy Christmas to yer, Cromwell!'

'And to you, Hand. And to a good year to come. You've suffered more than most this past year. We all know that.'

A little later that evening, just past the time when the songs had been sung and thoughts of drink were being overwhelmed by tiredness, the door of the tavern opened to a new group of men.

They were members of the Continental Army, but unlike many of the men who had joined the army, these four were gentlemen from the slave-owning lands of Virginia. Their fancy coats underlined their prosperity.

They came in, the four of them, more swanky than the northerners – not for them beer but rye and whiskey – different in taste and attitude. As they threw back the drams, their leader spied the now sleeping Oliver Cromwell.

'What have we got here, a nigger in our camp? Boy, what are you doing here with these fine gentlemen?'

He kicked the sleeping Cromwell's foot.

'What? What you playing at?' Cromwell awoke confused.

'I'm asking what a nigger is doing drinking in this bar.'

'My name is Oliver Cromwell and I'm a free farmer from New York and I have every right of a freeman to drink here, among my fellow soldiers.'

'Not in my book, you ain't. We don't need any niggers to win this war. King George may be wanting slaves to run from their masters and take up arms, so why don't you take your black arse over to Howe and beg for your freedom, boy. But first, take that nigger arse outside and find some drinking place more suited for ya, get cha now, boy!'

'I ain't going nowhere.'

'You'll go where I tell you to go.'

'I was born a slave, but I won my freedom squarely and rightly, ain't no man, white or coloured, going to tell me where I rest my head.'

'Is there a problem here?' Hand came to stand firmly by the side of the southerner. 'Who are you?'

'Sir, Lieutenant Harold Penny of the Virginian Rifles. I have a problem with your drinking companion. I don't like to take my drink where there's niggers.'

'I see no such thing. I see one of the most loyal members of the

2nd New Jerseys. One of the best, most honest fighters in the Continental Army. A man I have been proud to fight alongside. A man free to drink wherever he pleases. If you don't like that, well, you're free to go find your drink somewhere else.'

'I don't intend taking my drink anywhere else but here, but I do intend to take this nigger and any nigger lover with him outside, so I can have my drink and not be contaminated. You understand, Paddy?'

'I understand perfectly.'

'Good.'

'You better pay up and leave then.'

'You Irish bogtrotter, you're the one that'll be leaving.'

Penny swung a fist, missing the Irishman who stepped sharply back, but then Hand moved forward and threw a punch to the southerner's stomach. As Penny reeled back, his three friends joined in and so did Cromwell, O'Leary and a few other regulars from the Pennsylvanian Rifles. Now a proper fight had started. Penny came back at Hand, striking him a blow to the right temple and then pushing him over a table, scattering glasses and bottles to the floor. Hand fell to the floor, Penny's boot striking him in the side. Rolling away, he tried to get to his feet, but the Virginian was on him, pinning him to the ground, punching him in the side and then the face. Dazed, Hand groped around him for anything that might serve as a weapon. He found the neck of a bottle, grabbed it and swung at Penny.

Only when the bottle sliced open the artery and blood began to spurt across them both, did Hand realise it was a jagged broken bottle.

FIVE

'You know my rules, Hand. Discipline in an army is everything. Once discipline breaks down, you lose the army. This incident is especially ill-favoured. The Continental Army is a confederation, an alliance of different parties. If we are to win this war and gain our independence, I need to keep all the interests aligned. North and south, aligned together. God damn it, sir!'

General George Washington grimaced in agony. The constant pain from his teeth made him irritable at the best of times, but the events of the previous evening at the tavern had tried his patience beyond reason. It was symbolic of the near disaster he was facing: his army was falling apart. He sensed that on his daily walks around camp: he could hear it in the low murmurs that grew the second he passed; he saw it in the men who avoided eye contact where once they would have raised a 'Hurrah!'; and he smelled it, that unique smell of defeatism, that was starting to pervade the camp and growing stronger each day.

The evening's conference with his generals Henry Knox, Hugh Mercer, Horatio Gates and Nathanael Greene had started badly when a messenger had brought news that Charles Lee, supposedly his most senior field officer, had been captured by the enemy in a tavern in Basking Ridge; the victim, it was said, of some contrivance involving the British and a local woman. He smelled a rat. He had endured enough disloyalty from Lee and his friend Gates.

Their allegiance to himself was questionable at best. He could ill afford further bad news. And now he had this issue with Hand to deal with.

Washington had come to hold Hand in high regard; he was one of his most trusted men in the field. But now the general had the wrath of the Virginian officers to contend with. It had taken so much energy to bring them into the main body of his army in July. He had pushed his closest friend, Hugh Mercer, to breaking point almost in getting these troops integrated, to ensure the British could not claim the Continental Army was an army only of the northern towns and cities. It was the kind of problem he had foreseen when he had opposed free Negroes fighting in the army. Such conflict was inevitable.

'Whatever moral impugnation we might share regarding the institution of slavery, has to be set aside against the greater good of maintaining our alliance. Your efforts in killing one of the most regarded southern officers just made that even more difficult to maintain. And if I do not act swiftly and be seen to act appropriately, there is a possibility that our great alliance may fall apart. The Lord knows it is struggling as it is.'

'Sir, Lieutenant Penny wronged one of the best regarded northerners, someone who has proved himself many times over the last year. It was Penny who started the brawl. There are many who will bear witness to that. His death was an accident. One I obviously regret, but it was an accident, caused by his own reckless behaviour,' countered Hand.

'You, sir, were equally as reckless. My understanding is that you were drunk. You have ambitions, sir, to be a true leader of this army, yet you wallow with the lower ranks in the taverns. Drunkenness, the worst vice men can have. A vice no senior officer can partake of. Enough, you know the charge for the murder of a fellow officer?'

'Murder? It was not murder, General, it was—'

34

'Silence! It was murder in my book. You unnecessarily started a brawl with a fellow officer that ended only with his death. It's murder and the penalty for such a crime is death itself. You'll be up before court martial at first light.'

'What?'

'Sir, may I intercede?' General Nathanael Greene stepped forward, putting his hand out towards Hand, hoping that would stop the Irishman from saying anything further.

'What Hand did was unacceptable, and I understand only too well the strains that it will put upon on us as we look to hold this fragile coalition of interests together, especially given the unfortunate events of these past months, yet—' Washington now raised his hand in dispute, but Greene continued, 'This is a man who you and I have come to respect and depend upon. We have few such characters around us at this moment in time. At Boston and Bunker Hill and on the retreat from New Jersey, this is a man who has fought with pride. This is also – and I freely admit to appealing to the sentimental aspects of your character – a man who lost his wife and unborn son just a few months past and yet is still within our camp. That is testament both to his loyalty to the cause and to the sacrifice he has endured.'

'Greene, I know of this. You are the most humane of men. The individual pain of such circumstances is something that I would expect all of us to bear with heavy fortitude and deep sadness, yet it does not excuse his behaviour and the problem he has presented us with. We run the risk of our army being reduced still further to a rump. I cannot lose the southerners.'

'And what a rump it will be if we keep the few southerners who would leave and lose the large numbers of northerners who would flee the camp if you follow through on this penalty,' Mercer pointed out.

'What do you mean?'

Mercer continued: 'Our Colonel Hand here: do not under-estimate his popularity, not just with the Pennsylvanians, but with the greater body of our men. They are itching for an excuse to leave the camp, to return to their farms, their families. There is but a week or so before most of them are free of the bond created by their annual enlistment. We need them to sign up again, not to flee the camp. Put Hand under court martial, even worse on the gibbet, and you may face an empty camp. Frankly, the northerners from our towns and cities are far more valuable to our cause that those from the plantations. It is those militia who remain loyal and firm. Do not give them cause to think otherwise.'

Mercer moved closer to Washington. He placed his hand on the general's shoulder, a degree of intimacy that no others in the room could share, an intimacy born almost twenty years earlier when they had both served the British at the siege of Fort Duquesne. In almost a whisper, certainly in a pitch none but the general could hear, Mercer said:

'George, Nathanael is correct. And there is your own personal reputation to consider. You know there are, even within this room and our closed ranks, those who argue that you have failed to lead this war competently. Do not give them an excuse to seed further discord. For they will seize such an opportunity and we will all be damned. A house divided falls. Do not be the architect of your own division. By all means we should punish the man, but do not make him a martyr to provide excuses for others to desert our cause.'

With that he pulled back to stand with the ranks of the other generals, and then said loudly:

'We have need to dispatch a proper person over the river to make the necessary enquiries of Trenton and its surrounds. What guards are posted upon the different roads leading into the town, the number on the mill bridge, where the enemy's cannon lay and their number. Indeed, to ascertain the number of enemy forces in

Trenton, whether reinforcements have latterly arrived or indeed marched out of the town, where they lay and the general defences that have been established. This and other intelligence we have failed to procure in the necessary detail. Despite the efforts of those brave souls who have perished attempting to do so.

'For that, knowledge of the town would improve our chances of good fortune and Hand here has knowledge of the town. Did you not practise in Trenton before joining the cause?'

'I did, sir. I practised as a surgeon in the town for a period of time. Myself and O'Leary continued to live there until my family were . . .' His words trailed off. The memory of Catherine, barely a year earlier, her face so radiant, a wide-open smile, kneeling before him, telling him she was carrying their child.

Mercer, embarrassed on Hand's behalf, continued: 'I would respectfully suggest that, as a consequence of his unfathomable actions of the night last, Hand be stripped of his rank of lieutenant colonel, and be sent to scout the town and its surrounds. The knowledge he returns with can be used to ascertain whether the policy you so recently brought to this table should be acted upon. There is, of course, not an insignificant amount of risk attached to such an assignment.'

Washington stared at the man, not unsympathetic to his pain. But there was only one thought occupying his mind: could he be seen to back down?

As he thought, Henry Knox spoke up: 'Sir, a man from Jersey came into our camp this past hour. He crossed at Howells Ferry further up river. Our man's news was that Rall this morning had a local farmer shot, accused of spying. A fresh attachment of Hessians appear to have arrived in the past few days, straight from Europe. My man believes the Redcoats have heard wagons going all night and may have notice of the boats that we have brought down to McKonkey's. They appear to have information, sir, information regarding our every movement. We have little time before us. If we hesitate for too long, we may be surprised in our camp. Once the ice is formed across the Delaware, Howe will move those Hessian troops, invade Pennsylvania and aim to take Philadelphia. We may not be able to stop him.

'We must guard against his designs, but how are we to do that? Sir, we must strike and strike fast. On the question of Hand, I agree with you. He has behaved as a fool and should rightly be punished as such. But in war, pragmatism is always the best card a player can be dealt. If our spies are correct – that the town holds significant numbers of Hessian troops, yet remains unfortified – now may be the time for us to launch a surprise attack. But we require the highest quality of evidence. Just as we cannot afford not to make a significant breakthrough at this juncture, equally we can't afford another disaster. If we send Hand on this mission this evening, we will know by this time tomorrow how likely either scenario is. I would agree with these gentlemen: commute the sentence and send Hand on a journey that may be equal in peril, but far more satisfactory to our ends.'

'Thank you, General Knox, thank you all. But you are all northerners. I need to understand how this plays with our men from the south.' Washington fixed his eye on the only commander yet to express an opinion. 'In the absence of General Lee, I am indebted to you, General Gates, for your thoughts on this matter. How would this play with your Virginians?'

Gates, the English army veteran who had established a plantation in Virginia only a few years earlier, at first maintained his silence. He felt little loyalty to his Virginian troops, in his eyes little more than a godless rabble, incapable of discipline, but he felt even less loyalty to Washington, whose prowess in recent months he had openly started to mock. It was evident to any halfwit that a far more competent general to lead the army in the field was available. He, Horatio Gates, could win this war, could have won this war in a matter of months, but no, he had to play second fiddle to this amateur. Any opportunity to undermine Washington's leadership was too good to pass on.

'I am not surprised by General Knox's interpretation. This camp – as I have often insisted – is riven with Howe's spies. We continue to create our own misfortune. The men of Virginia will do what I as their commander command them to do. I have little faith in these plans for this proposed attack on Trenton. To my mind, as I have said, it is folly. We should retire at once for the winter to Philly and plan for the spring. By all means send your Hand to Trenton. I would hope that he comes back with certain intelligence that would disabuse you of an attack.'

Washington refused to follow the bait, and simply turned to Hand, and said: 'You have made an unlikely escape from an early grave.'

SIX

The snow had been falling for several hours. The night was bitterly cold and dark, every misstep and fumble reminding Hand and O'Leary how ill-suited their clothes were to this weather. They had crossed the Delaware by boat, rowed by Old Tom who kept the ferry, his face furrowed and turned to leather by fifty-odd years of winter and summer crossings. From there they had made it on foot across farmland, stumbling over frozen, rutted fields, making the most of a weak moonlight and their shared memories of the lay of the land. They walked with their muskets ready, for at every step they expected a British scout.

'This is a grand adventure you've got me into, fella, I don't think. I should be under cover, dreaming of girls from County Kerry, not freezing my arse off out here. For Christ's sake!' He had stumbled over a frozen cart rut, almost falling to his knees.

'Keep it down, Pat, you'll have them on top of us before we know it. I'm not going to apologise any more. Besides which, you don't mean it. You would have done the same for me. Did you get Cromwell out of the camp?'

'Yes, Sarah took care of that as soon as we saw those Virginians running off to tell their bosses. He should be safely in Philly by now. Lucky sod. Wish I were.'

They spoke no more after that. Moving quietly, their senses attuned to every foreign sound in the muddled darkness. On the edge of a copse they saw it: no more than a silvery flash in the early dawn light, something that might have been nothing, but something that could have been the faint movement of a well-polished inch or so of steel, something to signify immense danger.

They halted.

Slowly they started again and almost immediately stopped. In the dull light, Hand brought his right hand to his temple and discreetly pointed left. O'Leary faintly nodded. And then, suddenly, they were off at speed. Ahead of them a bush erupted in frenzy and there was their game: a man, a soldier, a scout now being scouted.

The chase was on, across bramble and thorn, to the edge of the woods, over extended, gnarled, grasping roots and under low-hanging, fingering branches. The two Irishmen, in a pincer move, gaining on the man heading through the woods and back down towards the river.

O'Leary was closer and he took the decision to bring the man to ground. Throwing himself over a thorn bush, he flew through the air at the man's midriff. The two fell heavily to the ground. But O'Leary had no grip on the man, who fought to free himself cleanly, kicking the other in the forehead. A powerful kick. A well-heeled boot.

Hand ran closer to them, the opponent now free of O'Leary and on his feet once more, finding his way along a little-travelled path, but a path, nevertheless, that brought him quickly to the end of the woods, and running along the edge of the buffs. He was running north, towards the town. He had to be stopped.

Hand was just a few inches from the man. He would have felt the hot breath of the Irishman on his neck before he felt the heavy weight of his body, knocking his legs from him. They stumbled to the ground together. The pursued, screaming out at the top of his voice in an accent Hand could not decipher, but took to be German, scrambled to his feet, disorientated.

Hand also got to his feet and saw in the breaking light that in his disorientation, the man was teetering on the very edge of the bluff, at its highest point above the river. Without knowing where he was, the man turned and stepped out on to the blank canvas of the drop. Hand moved quickly and with no little luck, was able to grab the collar of the man's jacket. But the force of the man's fall pulled Hand to the ground and he lay on the edge of the rock face, his right arm over the precipice holding on to the collar, the man dangling above the icy waters of the Delaware.

There was something odd about this jacket. It was neither a Redcoat nor the blue coat of the Hessian, let alone the calico smock of a scout. A grey-green jacket, shorter than the usual military cut, with pockets on the buttoned tunic. The man was struggling, which made Hand's hold almost impossible, even as he added his left hand to the jacket collar.

'Stop your kicking and struggling, otherwise I won't be able to hold you! Stop it, damn it!'

He looked down at the man, whose eyes burned fiercely. There seemed a dark hatred to the man, a harsh defiance. And then, most extraordinary, he started to hit out at Hand's arms, as if he wanted to fall.

There was a tear in the fabric of the jacket, so Hand had a clear view of the man's neck. There was an odd tattoo across it. Numbers, as if a code. And then the jacket tore apart. And the man fell silently to his death, crushed by the rocks below on the bank of the river.

Hand pulled himself to his knees, still clutching the remnants of the grey-green torn collar. O'Leary was next to him now.

'What happened, Ed?'

'He kinda . . . he kinda refused my help, like he threw himself down. He didn't want me to pull him up.'

'What's that?'

'The collar of his jacket.'

'No, what's that silver thing on the collar? I've never seen that on a Hessian before.'

Hand looked at the cloth in his hand. He had never seen the marks before, different to anything he had seen on a British soldier or a Hessian mercenary. A silver cross of sorts, four arms, each bent at ninety degrees.

SEVEN

Dawn had given way to a frosty, but clear morning. After the incident on the bluffs Hand and O'Leary had moved quickly, skirting the edge of the River Road to Trenton, wary of running into any other Hessians. Reaching the edge of the town, they heard the typical sounds of a camp rising, men coughing, pissing, murmuring, complaining. Hand turned to O'Leary.

'There's a couple of sentries to the left over there. If we make a quick run for the wall to the right, that'll get us to Helen O'Flannery's. Fancy some eggs and coffee for your breakfast?'

O'Leary nodded. Of course, he knew what also lay to the left – the town cemetery, where Hand's Catherine and their child lay. He noted that his old friend could not bear to look towards the picket fence of the graveyard. So they moved off to O'Flannery's cottage.

Helen O'Flannery, a Limerick girl by birth, had come to America twenty years before with her new husband, Seamus. Settling in Trenton, they had set up a grocery and hardware store, and raised a family of eight girls, the last three of which Hand had brought into the world. Seamus had died a few years earlier, one of the victims of the 1770 cholera epidemic, along with three of the girls. Tough, rough and a bitter enemy of the British, Helen supplied food and drink to both sides of the conflict, 'But there's never a pound of apples I've sold to the Brits that I haven't pissed on beforehand.'

'Doctor Hand and that wastrel Patrick O'Leary, now what could bring you here this morning at such an early hour, your clothes all wet and dirty?' she asked, a twinkle in her eye, as she opened her parlour door, a broad fire already burning.

Walking in, the immediate warmth of the room a more than welcome respite, Hand replied: 'And I might ask what would you be doing up at such an hour with this fire already so well established, Helen O'Flannery?'

'You've a lot of questions for a man who I would wager is looking for some eggs, bacon and coffee, Edward Hand. Many more of those and I'll send you back out of the yard and into the warm embrace of those Prussian soldiers who look so pretty in their blue coats and breeches, unlike scruffy monkeys like youse.'

'I wouldn't mind getting meself one of those coats, Helen, you know, to keep the cold out.'

'Yes, and it'll be typical of a stupid lad like yerself that you'd pick one up and then get shot by a Yankee soldier looking for an easy mark, Patrick.'

'You know the boy too well, Helen.'

'Aach, if it kept me bloody warm, I'd run the risk of getting shot in it. We're supposed to be an army, but we've no uniforms. Some of the lads are barely shod. The British know how to look after their boys, so they do,' said O'Leary.

'They have to, otherwise they'll bugger off back to Germany. That's the price we pay for being a free army of lads, Pat,' Hand said, taking his place at the table.

'From what I hear, there'll be no lads left come this New Year's,' said Helen, stoking the fire. 'Out of New Jersey and hanging by a thread in Pennsylvania, what the hell are youse playing at? You had the bloody Brits on the run; now all the talk is of begging for forgiveness and Washington being taken off to London in chains.

45

Marie, get your arse out of bed and get some eggs scrambling for our gentlemen callers, and some bacon frying while you're at it.'

'You wouldn't be having some chops would yer, Helen? I'd die for a chop.'

'If you want, you can have porridge and damn the bacon, Pat O'Leary. Chops? Who'd you think yer are? King George and Lord North come a-visiting?'

Marie, thirteen years of age, entered the kitchen, mock bowed with a 'Doctor Hand, Mister O'Leary, pleased to see you both' and immediately started to work the food.

O'Leary joined Hand at the table, while O'Flannery began to pour three cups of warm black coffee.

Hand took his and said, 'Thank you, Helen. Good to be seeing you. Been a long few months.'

'Aye, all the best men in Trenton are camped with yours on the other side of the river. Just some of the Tories left here. The girls around these parts getting mighty itchy though; those Germans are a very handsome band, believe me.' She paused. 'I've had the girls keep an eye on Catherine's grave. You'll find it as sweetly manicured as it could hope to be.'

Hand looked away, his eyes scattering around the room.

'Thank you, thank you all.' Then an urge to find something else to discuss. 'So, tell me, how many are there?'

'The Germans?'

Hand nodded.

'They bring in fresh troops regular. Last group came in, what, three days ago. Smaller group, maybe two hundred or more, led by a proper general an' all, von Steuben they call him; right bastard, I'd say. Seem a different bunch to the rest. Most of them are the kind, as you say, mercenaries, been around, fight for anyone, would fight for the damn Indians if they had money to give 'em. This lot. This lot are different. They are what you'd call disciplined. Proper discipline. They shave, their hair is short and well kept, their uniforms ironed and different to the others. And such uniforms, like none you've seen before.'

'Grey-green, short, buttoned up?'

'That'll be them. They have some very nice boots as well. You'd be snug with their boots, believe me. Proper cowhide, them. If I didn't know better, I'd be thinking the British have paid these to come and finish the job off. And they look like they could, believe me.'

'Where are they settled in?'

'Well, they're with most of the troops, camped out back of Morgan's field. Their general, this von Steuben, he's not like Rall, the fella in charge. He's a lazy arse, make no mistake. Living it up in Pott's house on King Street like King George himself. Nothing he likes more than entertaining himself with some of the finer ladies of Trenton, as it were. To bed late, up late. I ain't got none of your military training – look at me, I'm just a poor grocer from Limerick with no sense whatsoever – but even I might be a-thinking: the Continental Army – what's left of it – is parked outside across the river. I'd be looking to make some fortifications. Not him though.'

'We passed through their lines with barely a muster.'

'Aside from one fella who must be with this von Steuben. The same uniform and a silver mark I've never seen before,' added O'Leary.

'Like a spider's legs?'

'Like a spider's legs, yes.'

'They're fond of that one, make no mistake. They march behind a banner with it, black and red, quite fetching it is too. You can see for yourself this morning.'

'This morning?'

'Aye, there's going to be some kind of parade in the town this morning. A presentation of the new troops to Rall. If he can get out of bed in time.'

'How many troops you reckon in the town then?'

'Two thousand, might be a few more. Town can barely cope with any more. Mind you, there's hardly any of us locals left. Most of the families left for Philadelphia. Those of us still here are here because we have something to sell to the soldiery.'

'Sure you're not complaining about that, given the prices you'll be charging these British and Germans?'

'A woman's got to make an honest living, especially when the menfolk are away. Men gonna lose out, mind you. Ain't forgot, Patrick O'Leary, that you were sweet once upon my Olivia. An' she's still not betrothed. Not keen on seeing her being swept away by some fine Prussian, but a girl's gotta look after herself.'

O'Leary shifted in his seat. There was a memory of a summer's day and what might best be described as an indiscretion.

'We ain't got no time for matchmaking, Helen O'Flannery,' interrupted Hand. 'We're here to do some scouting. How easy is it for men like us to take in the town?'

'Well, on account of all the able menfolk running off to parry with the perfumed General Washington and his merry men, two boys like you striding around town is going to cause some attention and controversy. So you best have a story and a good one at that, or I'd suggest you stay here low. My Olivia will be around, so that may be pleasing for you, Patrick.'

O'Leary squirmed once again.

'Helen, come on, there's a time and a place. What time is this parade?'

'Eleven. Listen, Doctor, I make no jokes about this. Trenton isn't what it was. All the good uns have left; the men left behind are loyalists, true Tories. In their eyes, youse are all lawless rebels, ready to be taught a lesson. Look what happened to poor Nathan Hale up in Manhattan. Then the other night they strung up some boy not even old enough to have a shave, accused him of being a Washington spy. They'd like nothing more to have a hanging party in Trenton for someone like you who made such a big name for themselves up at Bunker Hill.'

Her eyes now lacked their usual humour, they were imploring Hand.

'Keep safe, Edward Hand. We've lost enough good men. We can't afford to lose you.'

EIGHT

Trenton, a town of no more than a hundred houses, ringed on the edge by orchards and farmland, a single mill for grinding corn and an iron furnace, owned by Stacy Potts, the host of Colonel Rall. A town barely started. Two main roads crossing the centre, King Street and Queen Street, running parallel to the River Delaware. In the centre, a two-storey courthouse, an Episcopal church and a marketplace. It was in this marketplace that the Germans had decided to hold their presentation.

The troops far outnumbered the citizenry that morning. But the seventy who had turned out had done so in their Sunday best and in good spirits. Many had come from the farms and settlements outside Trenton, evidenced by the carts and carriages resting in the square. The morning had something of the festival about it. A day of celebration, a precursor to the Christmas celebrations to come later in the week.

Hand and O'Leary held themselves back, on the very edge of the marketplace. They recognised many of the characters. Courtney Conte, the schoolteacher; Wilfred Wallace, the blacksmith, who had refused to shoe horses of any man he suspected of being a rebel, and who kept a portrait of King George in his forge; Peter and Ella Prop who ran an English dry goods store and a grocery store. All of them second- or third-generation immigrants, all of them resolutely loyal to King and Country.

It was Wallace who saw the Irishmen first.

It was the first time that Hand had seen him without his black-smith's smock, and, although he had made an attempt to scrub the dirt away, his hands and face still bore the taint of the forge, his neck scarred with scratches of black. He was with his wife – Amanda, Hand thought she was called – and their two young children, a boy and a girl, both of whom Hand had brought into the world.

'What have we here? Have yer deserted your General Washington and seen sense, Doctor Hand? Brought back your Irish hound, I see?'

Hand ignored the blacksmith. 'Good day, Mrs Wallace. Your wee ones seem bonny and well.'

The woman nodded silently back, but her husband was not to be stopped, 'Come to see the Hessians who will finally put an end to your madness and return this land to a benign and tolerant government instead of lawlessness? Had enough of starving out on yonder riverbank with that fool Washington and his gang of cowards and criminals?'

'I fear there are more criminals on General Howe's army than there are in General Washington's. Your king cleared out all the drunks, debtors and rapists from the slums of Bristol, Liverpool and London for his army to come and take our common rights away.'

'Our common rights! Pah! It is you, sir, and those brigands you call an army who are looking to take away the common rights of the hard-working people who have carved and clawed a civilisation out of this hard land! Look here, Thomas—' He lifted up his small boy, no more than six. 'Look upon this creature. The man who delivered you into this world, but who now would throw you to the wolves. You are not welcome in Trenton any more, Doctor Hand. But I will implore you to stay for this morning, and look upon the troops who will render your cause worthless. Come, children, Mrs Wallace, let us move away, the stench of these Papists is overpowering. I fear for the health of our young uns.'

Wallace pushed away, his wife passing an apologetic look at Hand.

'Charming as ever,' said O'Leary. 'I would have you notice, Ed, how I refused to allow myself to engage with the fella, even when he called me a hound.'

'A newly discovered reticence that demonstrates rare maturity.'

'Nah, I just didn't want to embarrass him in front of his bairns. Otherwise I would have knocked him down flat. The cunt.'

There was a sudden commotion on the edge of the square. To applause from the citizenry, first came a small marching band, with pipes and drums, and then, on a chestnut mare, came what Hand took to be Colonel Rall. To the Irishman he bore the unmistakable gait of the mediocre military man he had come across throughout his time in the British army. Overweight, arrogant, late fifties, plump and preening his way into the square on a wave of obsequiousness from the yapping Tories.

He pulled the horse up, two young lads ran to hold it, and with no little difficulty, Rall dismounted, stumbling as he did so. In Boston, New York or Philadelphia, there would have been plenty in the crowd jeering and mocking him; in Trenton, he was only met by applause, as if he were Julius Caesar returning in triumph to the Roman forum.

Rall adjusted himself, bowed in the direction of the local ladies and in halting English, declaimed, 'Lords and ladies of Trenton, the warmth of your hospitality to myself and my soldiery, the munificence you demonstrate us, touches my heart. It, ah, it demonstrates strong passion for King George . . . beating throughout the Americas . . . Today we wish to advance those strong feelings of pride and belief in victory that lie deep within your hearts.

'Three days ago our opportunity for a swift cessation of the present difficulties was enhanced by the . . . ah, arrival in Trenton by one of the finest military generals in all of Europe. By now, there will be few citizens in Trenton, and I hope in other towns and villages throughout Pennsylvania and New Jersey, who have not marvelled at the tales of General von Steuben . . . Ah, he arrives on this continent fresh from a period as the Chamberlain of Fürst Josef Friedrich Wilhelm of Hohenzollern-Hechingen. Before he served in the service of his most excellent King Frederick of Prussia and was involved in the many triumphs of that most magnificent of kings during his campaigns in Pomerania, Silesia and Austria . . . Ah, just as the ancient Emperor of Rome would have around him the very best men of the Empire in the Praetorian Guards, so too Baron von Steuben has brought with him the finest regiment to be found in the whole of Europe! Yes, the finest from Europe!

'This regiment will unleash themselves on the usurpers like a mighty and powerful winter! The rebels will soon be shivering and cursing von Steuben's men! Today, we celebrate General von Steuben and with him the beginning of the end of this bloody conflict!'

With that, the drums began to roll once more, and into the square came another charger, a white mare, proud and strong, and on it rode a man very different to Rall.

Von Steuben seemed magnificent to both Hand and O'Leary.

He sat upright in his seat. In the cold winter air, he had neither hat nor wig, his greying hair cropped short and tight. His physique was trim, muscular, highlighted by the cut of the grey-green uniform. Decidedly, this was a man of great character, whose mere bearing set a standard for his troops in how they should look and behave. Now came those troops.

They numbered around two hundred and fifty, and again there was something different in the way in which they followed their leader into the square. Their lead man carried a huge flag, red with a white circle and within it the unmistakable spider-legged symbol. The manner in which they held their muskets, marching with a lengthy, loose-limbed and pacey stride, was very different to the usual parade style of the age. Their faces were firm in a jaw-locked countenance; their uniforms, tight, clean, belted grey-green jackets, slate-grey trousers and the leather boots so admired by Helen O'Flannery. They seemed much superior to the regular Hessians, previously admired as the finest fighters on the continent. Hessians were the most experienced, most weather-beaten and most disciplined troops in the Americas, but set against these men, they seemed almost of a different age altogether.

'You gotta say, fella, that's as smart a band of Prussians as you'll ever see.'

'Aye, but what good is what, two hundred, hired hands against twenty thousand freeborn Americans?'

'Well, if we could count on twenty thousand that'll be an argument we might like to have,' Pat passed a frustrated smile at his friend. 'Put those buggers in the field and most of our men will feel beaten before a single musket gets fired, even if there are only two hundred of them.'

Hand did not reply. He didn't much care to. Pat was right.

Von Steuben sat atop his horse while his men paraded around the square. The response from the townsfolk bordered on the hysterical, one teenage girl swooned and fell to the ground, her clothes ruined by the soft mud underneath, her mother chiding her. Others threw perfumed, paper roses while the men watched in awe, applauding. Von Steuben's men never broke a step, never looked anywhere but straight ahead, with a determined precision.

'These are how I imagine the Spartans at Thermopylae would have appeared,' mused Hand, the Trinity scholar.

'What's that?' asked O'Leary.

'The most acclaimed fighters of the ancient world, disciplined in iron since their infancies. They numbered but three hundred and they all but held off the entire Persian army. It wouldn't surprise me if these lads were taken from their mothers while still in swaddling and left on some rocks to see if they could survive.'

'I don't know what the hell you're talking about, fella, but I'll say this: we saw off one of them just a few hours back. They may look the part, but they may not act it. These could be but preening peacocks.'

And then they noticed a further surprise.

At the rear of the troops was a woman. At first they took her to be a short man, but as the parade continued and passed close by them, it was clear. She was a blonde, her long hair pulled back into a ponytail, slim and attractive. They would have been no less surprised if a mountain gorilla were marching in formation.

'That's a woman.'

'Yes, Pat, that's a woman.'

'And she's a regular soldier by the looks of things. And a very fine-looking woman at that.'

Hand did not respond, but he did not disagree either.

Their parade around the square completed, the troops came to a smooth halt in front of the courthouse and Rall. Von Steuben dismounted from his horse and threw a javelin-like salute into the air towards Rall. The smaller man fumbled a reply. The crowd moved itself forward. There were some formalities in German between the two generals and von Steuben passed some kind of pennant to the more senior man.

As von Steuben stepped back towards his men, he had a noticeable limp. The ceremony was broken by a sudden tumult from outside of the square and with it came two civilians, shouting, carrying behind them a cart on which lay a grey worsted blanket, covering something. Clearly nervous, the two men nevertheless brought the cart to the generals.

'What have we here?' thundered Rall. 'Our celebrations interrupted!'

'Please excuse us, sir, but we were down on the Delaware, looking to do a spot of fishing, and we came across this broken body and we thought best to bring it to you. The uniform is of one of your new recruits. Looks to us as if a Washington spy has beaten him to death.'

Von Steuben strode forward and pulled the blanket off.

'This is one of my men, Neuville. He had been out to scout positions.' He pulled the blanket over the dead figure and spoke to the crowd: 'People of Trenton, we came here to aid you in your struggle and now I see that the opposition we face are cowards, hiding in the shadows, looking to pick us off one by one. This man, Neuville, he came from a small town in Bavaria, Munich. It is very far from here, his parents will grieve for him, but they will understand his sacrifice. We will look to avenge his death.'

'Avenge it now, sir! Avenge it this minute!' It was Wallace the blacksmith. 'Two of those cowards are among us this very minute, fresh from Washington and his camp. I'd wager they be the cause of this outrage!'

The big man let loose his children's hands and pushed his way towards Hand and O'Leary. The crowd around them started to part.

'Ed Hand! Pat O'Leary! Those traitors to our King and our Land!' Now the schoolteacher Conte, pushing his way towards them, joined Wallace.

'Time to run, Pat,' Hand said, and the two of them hightailed it out of the crowd towards Queen Street. The blacksmith and the teacher and several others gave chase, but they were soon overtaken by six of the new Hessians, who had immediately broken rank on command from von Steuben.

'Where the hell should we be heading, Ed?'

'Make out to the orchards, then the woods. If we get there, we may just have a chance.'

Down the iced track that was Queen Street they ran, past the houses marking the edge of the town, down the still frost-hard pathway and towards the orchards and the cemetery. But their flight was pointless. The blacksmith, the teacher and the other citizens had fallen away, but the Hessians were too fast, too fit.

Vaulting over the picket fence of the cemetery, Hand stumbled to the ground and could see the Germans were gaining on them as they came through the open gate. As he scrambled to his feet, he was aware of O'Leary shouting behind him. They had caught his friend. He began to run on, but spotted a Hessian standing before him, Hand darted to his right and weaved in and around a number of headstones. But another stood in front of him and as he turned around, he saw he was surrounded. He went to charge one, but before he could strike him, a huge blond man let out a single punch that felled him. As his head fell to the cold earth, he was already unconscious, so he never saw the simple engraving on the wooden cross: 'Catherine May Hand, 1753–1776, Edward Thomas Hand, 1776'.

NINE

When Hand regained consciousness, his face and hair were soaked from a bucket of cold water that had been thrown over him. Coming to his senses, he found his arms bound to the back of a chair in an empty room, dimly lit by candlelight. He was alone; the bucket thrower had no sooner deposited the water than he left the room. Unable to turn, so tightly was Hand bound, he became aware of footsteps behind him: more than one person he thought, and a few steps later a figure appeared in front of him, dragging a chair into which he then sat.

Hand studied the face of von Steuben up close. The closely cropped grey hair, the smooth face, freshly shaved, a small cut on the underside of the jaw where the blade had gone awry.

'What is your name?' The accent was almost perfectly English, a slight German hint, but he could have passed for an English aristocrat.

'I asked, "What is your name?"'

Hand resolutely stared back at him, refusing to give his name.

'You see, you have made a mistake there, because my question is rhetorical. I already know the answer. You must know I know the answer. The people of Trenton were queuing up to tell me about Edward Hand, the traitorous Irish doctor, even those whose children you brought into the world, even those who you saved through your professional skill. The traitor Edward Hand. So what would be the point of wasting your energy on refusing to answer something I already know? You see, Doctor Hand, you have much to learn if you are to survive an interrogation.'

Interrogation? Hand was unsure what this man was suggesting. Survive an interrogation – what did he mean?

'So please, let us start again, Doctor Hand. Let us not waste each other's time. Life is too short for that and we have much to get through. I know who you are. I know you fought with distinction at Boston and Bunker Hill, played a major role in the army escaping from New York. No losses on that retreat. Most impressive. I know that from my men. They are very knowledgeable about this war and they respect great warriors. You recently lost your wife and child. I heard that from the townsfolk who would have me hang you as a spy. For that is what you are, I suppose, a spy. A spy sent here to find the lay of the town before Washington launches a crossing of the Delaware, attacks Colonel Rall and wins a famous victory.'

Hand blinked. He knew nothing of Washington's plans. 'I am no spy, sir. I am a proud and honest member of the Pennsylvanian Riflemen, a free man of a free America.'

'Indeed, of course you are. In my experience, spies are worms who slither on the ground unnoticed, hiding themselves, living in the shit. Spies do not distinguish themselves on the battlefield. Now that we have agreed on that point, perhaps you would like to ask me about myself.'

'I know who you are.'

'But do you? You know my name, Baron von Steuben, you may know of my past exploits, my service for the King of Prussia, you may even know of my reputation for military strategy and training, but what do you know of me? Why I am here?'

'To crush us for a few purses of gold no doubt.'

'There you are wrong. Totally wrong. You see, you know some facts, but you know nothing about me. Just as if I only knew the basic facts of your time as a doctor or as a surgeon's mate in the British Army and then fighting the same army you once served in, as if I didn't know about the tragedy of Catherine's death—'

'Don't speak of her.'

'Why not? Are not her death and that of your son at the core of you? The man you really are. Does it not give colour to your character, meaning to your actions?'

Hand eyed von Steuben, unsure of how to respond.

'Yes, I have arrived in America with a small force of the finest soldiery you could find in Europe. Killers like no others. Men trained beyond the capabilities of most ordinary men. But you do not know what really motivates me. You should look to what spurs me into action.'

Wearily, Hand said, 'And what would that be?'

'Revenge. I too had a wife, and two daughters. I married young, at seventeen. I was a junior officer in an infantry unit during what you call the Seven Years' War, and was with King Frederick. The English were our ally, but King George's uncle, the butcher the Duke of Cumberland, refused to defend the Rhine, his priority was to protect British Hanover. So our armies abandoned Wesel, where my family were living. My wife decided to leave the town and take refuge in Hamelin. She thought the British, our allies, would protect her and our children. It was a fantasy. Cumberland was defeated by the French at Hastenbeck, and in their retreat, the British did what the British always do. Murder. Rape. None of my family survived their retreat.

'So, you see, you would need to know this to understand why I am here in America.'

'I don't understand: you're here with the British.'

Von Steuben came off his chair and crouched in front of Hand.

'That is what I call my "cover story". All good spies need a cover story, Edward Hand. I have sailed with no little difficulty here, offering General Howe my assistance to bring this war to a quick close. In doing so, I have been able to learn close at hand his strategies, his strengths, his weaknesses. I have behaved like the filthiest of worms to get what I want. I have been prepared to do what it takes to gain the advantage. And now I have that advantage, I am here to offer myself to General Washington. Not just me, my troops as well. We can transform the Continental Amy into the finest fighting force since the days of Charlemagne, win America the freedom it deserves and create a new society based on those principles of freedom you hold dear.'

'You are here to fight with us?'

'Of course. Is there a more noble cause in the world today?'

'And yet you hold me, tied like a prisoner.'

'Well, I cannot allow the people of Trenton, who would wish to see you hanged, see me treat you as an honoured guest. Besides which, I have to be sure of your commitment.'

'My commitment?'

'Your commitment. How am I not to know that yourself and Patrick O'Leary have not joined those others who are leaking from Washington's camp on a daily basis?'

'Ah, I understand your trickery, sir. I see your plan now for what it is. You attempt to comfort me with the soft balm of your story, hoping I will reveal myself as a spy, and then you will have me. And I will be hanging from one of those trees in Morrison's yard by nightfall. I would prefer an honest trial to one conducted here amid the shadows of your duplicity.'

'Bravo! Very good!' Von Steuben laughed aloud, sat back on his chair and clasped his hands across his lap. 'Let us parry no more. Let me come straight to the point. I wish to offer my services to General George Washington and I wish for you to act as my ambassador. I will come with all the men in my service and I suspect that I may be able to win over all the Hessians employed by Colonel Rall. They are mercenaries, but they are not stupid. The possibility of defeat does not interest them. The possibility of success excites them.'

'You wish for me to introduce you to General Washington?'

'I do. As soon as possible.'

'What, shall we just ride to his camp together? Here's a German general I recently met, he says he wants to come over to our side. He would hang me for stupidity, or rather I hope he would. What kind of knave do you take me for?'

'I take you for no such thing. Why would you, let alone the general, trust me to enter your camp without evidence that I am to be trusted? So I have a plan.'

He sat back in his chair and continued.

'I will entrust you with the details of the layout of the troops and artillery here in Trenton. I will suggest a plan of attack for General Washington. The attack should be made on the evening of Christmas Day. Any later and Rall will be ready. He refuses to set up defences for the town, but even he must realise that he must sooner rather than later. Regardless, the town has to be taken before reinforcements arrive. And those reinforcements are not too far from here. They should be at Bordentown, but they remain at Mount Holly, a few days' march. Their leader, Colonel von Donop is apparently much taken with a doctor's widow in the town and is . . . well . . . one should be polite and leave it at that. But Rall's patience will soon break and he will demand von Donop and his troops come to Trenton. Once they arrive, you will have no chance of breaking this army. With this damned weather, the river will permanently ice over soon and then Howe will have Philadelphia open to him.

'Washington will be aiming for three crossings. From a military point of view that makes sense. He will want to cut off any possible retreat and stop von Donop from moving to support Rall. But he has no need. As I have said, von Donop is distracted and I will ensure he does not need to worry about a retreat from Trenton.

Besides which, the river will be unbridgeable around the Trenton Ferry, or below it at Bristol. The weather is not for turning, believe me. The perfect place to cross will be at McKonkey's. He should place all his forces there. The ice will make any other crossing impossible.

'He should advance on Trenton in two columns, along the River Road and the Pennington Road. He will meet little resistance on the way. I shall see to that. Once in Trenton, he should aim to place his cannons at the head of King and Queen Streets. The fighting will be bloody there. It needs to be bloody. Your army needs a famous victory and you shall achieve one.

'I will sit apart from the fighting. I will assign the men under my command to hold the Assunpink Bridge. We shall not enter the fray. No matter what orders I receive from Rall, my troops will remain steadfast. Once the battle is won, I will present myself to General Washington and offer our services.'

He held out a sealed parchment. 'Here. These are the plans, but in greater detail. I ask you to present them to the General and stay with him when he opens it. I believe he will find them satisfying.'

'Sir, he will be suspicious. This has the making of some trickery, only a fool would agree to this.'

'Of course, which is why you are going to take with you the most precious thing I have as proof of my honesty. Let me introduce you to Frau Hanna Reitsch.'

TEN

O'Leary could not be sure whether it was Reitsch's strength and fortitude or her beauty he admired most on the haul back from Trenton to Buckingham. He had never come across a woman like her.

Von Steuben told Rall he was sending the spies, along with Reitsch and a few covering troops, to Howe at New York. The colonel was happy with this, especially when the baron said Reitsch would report the capture of the agents was Rall's work. As it was, Hand, O'Leary, Reitsch and half a dozen men left on horses at nightfall. The clear sky of the day had given way to a night of intermittent snowfall, the paths were hazardous, the horses slipping, on several occasions they were almost thrown. The crossing at McKonkey's was slow and painful, yet at no stage did Reitsch demure. And then when they presented her to Washington, Gates, Greene, Knox, Sullivan, Mercer and Alexander Hamilton, the aide-de-camp, she was astonishing. O'Leary liked strong women, but he had never known such a woman as her, standing in front of these high and mighty generals and delivering a strategy for an attack on Trenton that was bold and to his ears unarguable. Sullivan, in particular, was affronted to be addressed in this manner by a woman, making no attempt to disguise his contempt, but as she spoke, with clarity and forcefulness, the others appeared to concede her qualities. Hand remarked to

O'Leary that it must have been similar when Joan of Arc had appeared at Orleans. It was another of his historical analogies, part of what he called his education of Pat O'Leary.

After Reitsch finished, Washington asked to retire with his coterie and welcomed her to make the full use of his officers' mess, along with Hand and O'Leary, which was how they came to be sat on benches, feasting on pork and cabbage, fresh bread and brandy.

'Miss, that was a mighty performance back there. Is this a common thing in Hesse, for ladies to address military commanders as equals?'

'I don't come from Hesse. I was born in Silesia, in a town called Hirschberg. You know what that translates as, Mister O'Leary?'

'Aach, I'm afraid my German is a little scratchy, miss,' he laughed nervously.

'It means "Deer Mountain". I grew up outdoors, on the deer mountain, hunting, trekking, climbing.

'When I was eight and my brother twelve, Father took us away from our mother for an expedition to the mountain. Not in the summer, when the days are long and the sunlight comes pouring down through the pine trees, when every creature underfoot appears as your friend in the warmth. No, this was February. February in Silesia is worse than December in New Jersey. We had jars of pickled cabbage, wurst wrapped in oily paper, and a rye bread that you had to chew and chew again, hard as the rocks we fell against. We drank only schnapps. We must have had water, but I remember only the schnapps. We were deep into the deer mountain. There were no paths, no roads, of course, no other people. Just isolation. Just wilderness.

'On the third day, we tracked a deer, a doe. All day we followed her, silently. There would be a moment when my brother or I would disturb her, we would snap a twig or send a small rock down the mountainside. Her ears would bolt upright, she would turn her head and those beautiful eyes would shoot straight at us,

boring into us. The look of disdain she had, no human can compete with that look of contempt! And then she would skip away.
All Father said to us was, "Did you see her face? See what she
thinks of you?" And we would start again.

'Just before nightfall, we killed her. My father said we had
played enough and he shot her, with his . . .' she hesitated, 'with
his musket. One shot. Father led us to her, had us look at her,
crumpled on the ground. Even then she wore that look of contempt. "Children," he said. "she is the queen of this mountain.
Men named the mountain after her. This is her dominion.
Remember that look she gave you when she caught us prying on
her? That pride did not last a day. You proved yourselves, you
overcame her, you conquered her and her lands. If you can overcome the Queen of Deer Mountain, there is nothing, no one, you
can not overcome."'

'And that was the lesson you took away from that trip?' asked
O'Leary.

'No, it was nonsense. We didn't beat her, the gun beat her. Science beat her. I learned that machinery is everything, without the
guns, without the food that came from a pickling factory or the
schnapps from a brewery, we would have been two dead children
up a mountain, probably a dead father as well. I believe, Mister
O'Leary, in science first. With science as your partner, there is
nothing that the human cannot achieve.'

'But that doesn't explain why as a woman you have such confidence in the presence of these great men. Your deportment is a
rare thing, Frau Reitsch, you must acknowledge that?'

'Doctor Hand, I do. And there perhaps you are right: Father's
behaviour did create in my mind a belief that I was equal to men.
But not by design.

'The morning after we had killed the doe, my brother and I
woke up to find father had left our camp, with the deer. By the
small fire we had made, he left a note, a note to my brother.

"Hans, I have returned home. You will return home with Hanna. Ensure her welfare and prove yourself as a man. Father." I can see that note clearly today. I was furious. Furious that he had left us and furious that he thought that I needed the protection of my brother. My brother was not furious. My brother was – is this how you say this – he was "shitting his breeches"?'

Hand laughed, 'Yes, ma'am. It's something that Pat here is a master of.'

'My brother had no idea. He had been following our father blindly, where I had been thinking throughout, "Where are we? How do we get back to Hirschberg?" I had never stopped planning, I was prepared for it. My brother, my brother started to cry and I had to comfort him. And I told him that I would lead him home.'

'And you did?'

'I did. My brother was terrified that we did not have enough food to survive the journey – we had been on the expedition for three days – but actually Deer Mountain is not so big. You can trek to its summit in a matter of hours. We had simply moved around the mountainside. If he had been more alert, he would have seen that. We were home within a few hours.'

'And your father, he was proud that you brought your brother home?'

'He never knew. My brother was terrified that my father would be angry with him for failing the test. He begged me not to say anything. I was happy to say that Hans had been strong and led us back to the hearth and Mother. What good would it have done for me to have said anything else? Men, I realised, are prone to weakness. But help a man cover his weakness and they are for ever in your gratitude. Would you not agree?'

She looked at them with her piercing blue eyes. Hand had an image in his head. The haughty disdain of a doe on a German mountainside.

ELEVEN

'Sir, we cannot be certain that this is not a trap. That is the cause of my reticence over this plan. That and that we appear to be taking instruction from a handmaiden. Not so many years ago, a woman like that would have met her natural end at Salem.'

A furious debate had broken out as soon as Reitsch had taken her leave. For weeks, Washington had been planning an attack aimed at turning the tide. Two days earlier, he had confided in his command staff. Reitsch's dramatic appearance suggested that the plans had leaked, that the enemy had them.

There were two sides to the debate. Greene, Knox and Mercer led the faction supporting Washington's plan, but prepared to make subtle changes in line with the information brought by the German. Sullivan, Stirling and Gates opposed. Sullivan argued for a very different course, an attack from the north on Trenton, and believed it was insane to even listen to the German. Gates, as gnomic as ever, repeated his view that any attack under present conditions (by which he implied Washington's leadership) was doomed to disaster.

'Enough, John, such talk of Salem is contemptuous. The plans she has brought from von Steuben do not alter our general course of action, they merely give us some cause for refinement as Knox and Greene have argued.'

'Sir, that her plans are so close to your own suggests to me that your designs have in some shape been released to the enemy. I will repeat this: we will be walking to an entrapment that will ruin us all,' Gates said furiously. 'You know all too well my feelings on this issue as it is. Our men are shoddy, ill-equipped and unprepared to take on a well-trained body of soldiers such as these Hessians. Of your commanders, I have the greatest experience of the field, yet you prefer to listen to the prattlings of a boy, a Boston bookseller, over the considerations of a renowned man of action! Now, you contemplate carrying these plans through, even though the evidence suggests the enemy has full knowledge of them. Pray, what has to happen to alter you from his disastrous course of action? Will you not be satisfied until General Howe sits in this room, warming his feet at your hearth?'

There was a snort of indignation from Henry Knox, the Boston bookseller himself, but Washington moved quickly before Knox could find words.

'Gates, your patronising of the deliverer of the Ticonderoga cannon ill becomes you. But, please explain to me how if only the commanders in this conference were given any understanding of my designs, they fell into the hands of the enemy? Sir, you cannot be suggesting that someone here passed my thoughts to the enemy?'

Gates snorted in derision and Mercer, in an attempt to prick the mood, said, 'I am afraid that Horatio's opposition is really that he cannot bear the possibility that a woman may possess a military mind.'

'Hugh, she has no military mind, she is a messenger girl. The architect of this mischief is this Baron von Steuben, if not Howe himself. This is madness, sheer madness. If Congress were to understand the nature of these events, they would not countenance this attack.'

'Then perhaps we should be grateful that Congress are not here.' Now Brigadier General Stirling joined in the debate. 'Let us discuss this no more. The debate has changed my view. The general's mind is set, we should proceed with the plan.'

There was a small murmur of assent, only Gates and Sullivan stood opposed.

Washington, buoyed by the confidence of others, looked directly at Gates and Sullivan. 'Gentlemen, I did not hear your assent, but I assume you retain your discipline.'

'You can have no doubt of my allegiance to you and our joint cause, sir. You will not mistake my passion for anything other than a hearty debate, I hope?'

'I do not, John. Horatio?'

Gates stared back and then, 'The die is cast. We proceed in unity.'

Washington moved back to the centre of the long table on which sat their rudimentary map of Trenton and its environs.

'So, gentlemen, let us make our plans clear to all before we depart. We aim for three crossings, one to the south under John Cadwalader—'

'Sir, you pay no heed to the reconnaissance provided by Frau Reitsch that the river will be impassable around the Trenton Ferry and even at Bristol?' asked Greene.

'I heed her advice, Nat, but we will need protection from the south. Without that second front, I gravely doubt we will be able to take Trenton; without such a loss that victory will be no more than a defeat in disguise. We'll have Ewing hold the Assunpink Bridge to stop any retreat. If General Gates is correct and these Hessians prove foul, we will need that bridge held by our own. Cadwalader is to bring his forces across at Bristol to distract the brigades of Hessian grenadiers and Highlanders encamped at Mount Holly. My message to John Cadwalader is simple: "If you can do nothing real, at least create as great a diversion as possible." We don't want these troops racing to Trenton in support of Rall.'

'And if they fail to make these crossings?' Greene asked.

'Then we must hope that our incursion in Trenton is swift and decisive,' replied Washington curtly. 'Our most difficult challenge is ensuring the safe passage of the main party of our forces and a successful attack on Trenton. We will have an advance party, who will form roadblocks and seize any persons going in or out of the town. Major General Stephens' Virginians will form that party. Alexander, ensure they provide themselves with spikes and hammers to dash the enemy's cannons if they cannot bring them off to our side. Make sure his men have plenty of drag ropes for that purpose.'

Alexander Hamilton, writing down the orders of the day, nodded his assent.

'We muster the forces one mile back from McKonkey's Ferry and embark on the boats under the supervision of Colonel Knox. I trust our experiences at New Jersey will ensure we have a successful crossing of the river. But we must maintain a profound silence, both on the crossing and the march to Trenton. The men must understand this fully. Any soldier who breaks that silence will be summarily executed on the spot.'

'Executed on the spot?' Knox expressed alarm.

'Indeed. Inform them of this consequence and they will understand the necessity of silence. The first execution, if there are to be any, will render the point forcefully.'

Both Knox and Greene made to oppose, but Washington lifted his right hand to stop any protest.

'I can see from your response that you find this extreme. However, this is a day of extremes. Should we fail in our course, we will find ourselves at best shackled and bound in one of King George's warships heading for a treason trial in London or, more likely, hanging from a gallows on Boston Common.'

'I trust then our men will understand the necessity for such severity,' Knox replied. 'In what order should we embark for the crossing at McKonkey's?'

'General Stephens to embark first, with his advance party. General Mercer, you next, then General Gates, followed by Lord Stirling. Stephens will appoint a guard to form a chain of sentries round the landing place at a sufficient distance from the river to permit the troops to form. In silence.'

'In silence. And what time would you wish for all the troops to be across.'

'At midnight. No later than midnight. We will then march on to Trenton and arrive to surprise the enemy as they are still abed,' Washington answered.

'Then the crossings must start tonight as soon as the sun sets, not long after four o'clock.'

'You have the required boats, John Glover?'

Glover, a grizzled mariner, one of the famed 'codfish aristocracy', ran one of Washington's most disciplined units, the Massachusetts Continentals, or the Marblehead Mob to others, named after the fishing port in which he had raised them. He had kept his counsel throughout the discussion. He maintained a simple view of matters military: his role was to ensure the plans of others came to fruition. As he was fond of saying, 'I would no more trust George Washington to lay my lines across the Newfoundland coast than I would trust myself to lay his lines across the fields of New Jersey.'

'Aye, the Pennsylvanian navy have proved their mettle. We have fourteen Durhams, several ferries and some smaller vessels. What with my old sea-dogs, dock hands from Philly and local pilots, we can get all the men, horses and artillery across, whatever storm is thrown at us. But we have to start as soon as that sun goes down if you want everyone shipshape and lined up by midnight, sir.'

'They'll be there, have no doubt of that, John Glover. Now, we'll set off as one line, but when we get to the crossroads at Birmingham village, I want us split into two factions. Nat Greene, you will lead the brigades of Mercer, Gates and Lord Stirling, and march on the Pennington Road.' Washington thrust his finger onto the map, tracing the route into Trenton. 'John Sullivan, you are to march by this river road, acting as the first division of the army and the right wing. General St Clair, your brigade will form the reserve of the left wing. These reserves are to form a second line to each division as circumstances demand. May God help us and each of our men.

'Now for the artillery. I require four pieces at the head of each column, three pieces at the head of each second brigade, two pieces with each of the reserves. We will aim to place our cannons on the high ground at the head of King and Queen Streets—'

'As requested by the Germans.'

'As makes most military sense, General Gates. John Sullivan, we will require your artillery to bombard the town from the River Road at the same time. We wish to give Rall a belief that he is surrounded.

'Now, let us ensure each man has three days' ration of bread and his flints are fresh. Officers should wear white paper in their hats to distinguish themselves. Gentlemen, may God through his grace provide us with sufficient courage and luck. May we depart hopeful and meet next as victors. Our password shall be this: "Victory or Death!"'

TWELVE

Hand had never felt such cold.

The temperature had dropped to beyond freezing, driving sheets of iron sleet, thousands upon thousands of icy pinpricks that cut through clothing and stung the skin. The river itself appeared tormented by the cold of the night, thrashing wilfully, protesting against the ice forming by throwing chunks of it into the air. There were about thirty men and half a dozen horses on the flat-bottomed Durham boat, still filthy from its usual job of moving pig iron from the works up in Philadelphia. In silence, the old boat inched slowly across the raging Delaware, propelled by oarsmen cursing under their breath. The only sounds, the thwack of huge lumps of ice buffeting the sides of the boat and the occasional moan of a horse driven to distraction by the pain of the weather and the rocking of the boat.

'This cold is total, yet he stands there, aloof, proud, leading the way. And there she is with him, as insensible of the conditions as if she were taking a pleasure punt down the Charles River,' Hand marvelled to himself at the sight at the prow of the boat.

Washington, stood tall at the front, jaw jutting into the abyss. A single lantern on the prow, lighting him, guiding the boat. Just behind him, Reitsch, as firm as any sentinel, eyes fixed on the darkness ahead. The general had asked for her to be kept close to him throughout the expedition. If the plan was proved a trick, he would seek immediate redress. But to Hand's eye, there was already something else there, some form of bond between the two of them. An intangible trust.

It was clear that the crossing was taking far longer than anticipated. They had arrived late at McKonkey's, the first embarkation not starting until well after six that evening. Each crossing took thirty minutes, without the loading and unloading of men, horses and artillery. And the conditions were steadily deteriorating, so that each trip was harder, riskier and slower than the last as the storm grew wilder, more dangerous with each beat.

Their late departure was partly explained by the failure of Gates to attend at the head of his men. He had sent a message that he was suddenly taken ill. Few believed that. They preferred the rumour that Gates had left camp for Baltimore, where Congress was sitting. The suspicion was if the Colonists were defeated, he would be ready to make the most of it for his own benefit. Washington had heard the messenger out and simply turned to Hamilton and barked, 'Put his men under Mercer.' There would be a reckoning with Gates, but that would be determined by the success or failure of what was to shortly unfold. And if it was failure, well, he would have bigger concerns than Horatio Gates to consider.

In the darkness, the Durham inched forward, jolted by the chunks of ice still throwing themselves at the boat, unsteadying the oarsmen battling to keep their oars to a steady rhythm. They were halfway over, Hand could see the dim light of Knox's landing point on the other bank, when a giant slab of ice hit them.

It came with no warning, struck the left-hand side of the boat, wedged itself under and stubbornly stayed put, lifting one entire side of the Durham up and out into the air. Horses neighed, oars crashed into each other, men fell about the deck amid muttered gasps and moans. Then the unmistakable splash. Man overboard.

From the spluttering 'Help!' Hand immediately knew it was Pat O'Leary, but he had no way of helping. He was half buried under a pile of bodies, all frantically trying to right themselves. The lantern was out. He had no sure way of knowing even where the gunwale of the boat was. He struggled to free himself, but he knew he was too late to help his friend.

O'Leary had been standing behind Reitsch and the lifting of the boat had been so unexpected and so great, that he found himself thrown over the lip of its gunwale and into the darkness before he had any understanding of what was happening. He hit the Delaware, a peculiar mix of free-flowing water and hard ice of all shapes and sizes, the cold immediately terrifying. He went down, but came up quickly. Thrashing around, he seized on the stern heft of an oar and tried to hold fast to it, screaming out the 'Help!' that Hand had heard.

But O'Leary's weight only pushed the oar back down into the water and him with it. He freed himself and broke through the water again, but already he knew that if he went down for a third time, it would be his last. He struggled, his fingers failing to stick to the edge of the Durham, his coat acting as a murderous weight; he started the descent into the depths, the cold water sucking all sense from him.

At that moment, when he had given up hope, he felt the pull.

Someone had got hold of his collar and was pulling him up and over. Vaguely, he could feel more hands grabbing him now, at his midriff, at his legs, pulling him up and out of the water, until he was over the boat's gunwale and being thrown to the deck, so that the only hands that remained were those on his collar, those that had saved him. He looked up to see Ed Hand's face, but it wasn't Ed Hand. Even in this inky darkness, he knew Hanna Reitsch had saved him.

Five minutes later, the Durham came to a halt.

Hand heard hushed whispers from the dark vegetation in front of them, followed immediately by disembarkation. On the riverbank, it was a state of organised chaos. Knox was in total command. From atop of his horse, his stentorian voice barked at the men, regardless of rank, to immediately leave the boat and assemble in the holding area just beyond the bank. His was the only voice permitted to be heard.

Moving to the assembly point, there were men, horses and field cannon placing themselves in line for the route march to Trenton. The quietness, the stillness that pervaded among the necessity of urgency, impressed Hand immensely. And then he remembered why: they had enjoyed far too much practice over the last few months in the dismal trade of retreat. No army in the world was better at crossing rivers with minimal loss as the Continental Army. In their abject failure, they had become masters at something. Now they were using that skill to attack. Perhaps the last attack of the war, especially if they were walking into a Hessian trap.

But he had O'Leary to attend to.

Reitsch's saving of O'Leary had not ended by dragging him back on to the boat. Once she had him on deck, she insisted on his throwing off his wet clothing and wrapping him in her own coat, blankets that had been protecting the horses and Washington's cloak. In doing so, she had saved him from hypothermia – that and the brandy they had poured into him.

Now he sat in the clearing, swaddled like an infant child, murmuring, 'It was a miracle,' while Hand and Reitsch attempted to dry his clothes around a makeshift brazier.

'We best be quick, the general will be wanting his cloak back before we set off for Trenton. We should make the move soon.'

'No, I think not. While I can see your General Knox and the boatmen are doing their very best, we shall not be leaving here until around three in the morning. We will not have the troops over in sufficient number until then. We have time,' she spoke knowledgeably.

'Hopefully, this weather will have given up by then.'

Reitsch raised her eyes to the sky. 'I think not. The worst is yet to come.'

'The worst you say?'

'The worst. There is a snowstorm coming.'

She was right. At around eleven, the sleet gave way to an enormous snowstorm, a white devil of razor-sharp wind and lumps of hard snow that fell to the ground and looked to cover anyone who stood still in their place. And yet, still they had to wait.

Finally, at around three, as she had predicted, the final load of weary troops made their way from the Durham boats. At once, Washington paraded along the line of men and in a distinct voice above the flurry of wind and snow shouted: 'We advance! For God's sake keep with your officers! Forward to the enemy!'

That thought of taking the fight to the enemy once more appeared to sustain every face Hand saw on the long march through the night. This may have been an ill-equipped army, lacking discipline and materiel, but it was an army of volunteers sprung forth on guiding principles, and on that cold, painful night many recognised this for what it was: one last chance to damn the English and reaffirm both those principles and their own capabilities.

But the march was terrible. First there was the upward climb from the Delaware, hundreds of men trying to pull themselves up through the thorn bushes and trees, falling on each other, the air thick with curses and recriminations. Then came the long tramp down primitive paths, the fallen snow turning immediately into treacherous ice that pulled down men, horses and cannon. Few of the men had lanterns, almost all would find themselves slipping on the rock-hard ground or stumbling into the man ahead as yet again the line inexplicably stopped. That was the worst of it: when the line halted and men were left standing for ten minutes or more. The lucky ones had wrapped themselves in worsted

blankets or had taken women's shawls. For those who had ven-
tured out in clothing more useful for a summer stroll, the march
was unimaginably terrible. The lack of boots among the men now
became a source of disaster for some, their cowhide moccasins not
fit for the extended march across the iced fields and paths. There
was no need to enforce the code of silence: men kept their own
counsel, their own thoughts and fears. They plodded on, heads
down, bristling with a mixture of cold, determination and fear.

South of the crossing, the army of fewer than two and a half
thousand men divided itself. Sullivan took his troops off down the
River Road and Greene, with Washington on his fine white mare
Betty alongside him, set off on the Pennington Road. Washington
turned to Hand and barked: 'Hand, I pass Frau Reitsch into your
safekeeping. I trust in your judgement as the situation plays out.'

'Yes, sir,' Hand replied.

'I take it he means that if there is a trap, you have the necessary
authority to deal with me as you see fit, Doctor.'

Hand looked at Reitsch. 'That would be my interpretation,
madame.'

'Then we must both pray that my baron is as good as his word.'

'I save my prayers for other matters, madame.'

At that moment Alexander Hamilton rode up alongside Washington. His face, pinched white by the cold, bore an unmistakable
anxiety.

'Sir, I bring painful dispatches.'

'Cadwalader?'

'He and General Ewing. Ewing reports that there is a massive
ice jam below the Trenton falls. It is impossible to cross, neither in
boats nor across the ice on foot. The ice is chopped up and unstable.'

'And the same at Bristol?'

'Yes, there the ice was so broken and the swells so great, that
Colonel Cadwalader moved on to attempt to cross at Dunk's Ferry.

79

But there, even though they overcame the currents, the ice was jammed 150 yards from the shore. The boats could not get close to the shore. Some of the light infantry made it across on foot, but there was no hope for the artillery.'

He paused, the words stuck in his throat.

'They are now bringing those who crossed back over the river and from there will go back to camp. He says he has no other recourse.'

'No other recourse? Does he think we have been making merry on our crossing? Our attack on Trenton depends on him and his men! If the Assunpink Bridge is open, Rall and his Hessians can escape and in turn if they meet up with von Donop's forces, they will turn upon us immediately and we will be cut to ribbons in the field. Our odds of success have been bitterly reduced!'

'General, do not hesitate.' Reitsch stepped forward. 'You have no alternative. You can and will still make this victory. The plans I came to you with made no account for Cadwalader or Ewing being successful. My baron predicted the crossing would be impossible, I am sure you will recall my insistence on that matter. More importantly, he pressed there was no need for them to succeed. You will have the forces to prevail at Trenton. And he will show you the value of his word by holding the bridge.'

Washington held his horse steady and looked deeply at Reitsch. Should he have listened to her and brought Cadwalader's forces with him as she had suggested? Damn Cadwalader and his failure! Damn Gates and his insubordination! He was hesitating. The tribulations of the past few months had grievously affected his confidence. Was this another disaster into which he was leading his men? Was he a fit commander after all? He had spent much time in an earnest search of his own strengths and weaknesses. He was not much of a gambler, he abhorred gambling among his men, and in his own life he preferred rational weighing of certainties. But now, he had to take a chance. On this throw of the dice everything rested: his ability to remain as commander-in-chief, the safety of the men under him, the course of the war and the lives of a million Colonists. Should he pull back now, lead the men back across the river safely and hole up for the winter, or proceed and gamble on one victory?

Around him, his generals awaited his decision. He looked across at them: Mercer, Sullivan, Greene, Knox, St Clair, Glover and Stirling, all awaiting his decision. Troops passed, still marching towards Trenton, unaware of what was playing in his head. 'Damn it!' he said under his breath and then aloud so everyone around him could not be mistaken:

'We continue, on to Trenton – and victory!'

And he led off, leaving Hand, Reitsch and O'Leary to fall in with the rest of the privates of the line to make their way down the Pennington Road, a road in name, but in truth a rutted track useful for little more than delivering cattle to Philadelphia. As he watched him go, Hand thought that might be the last he would see of George Washington.

It was just before five in the morning when they reached the outskirts of Trenton. Snow was still falling, the wind whipping it into a frenzy of excitement. They lined up carefully, officers attached white paper ribbons to their hats so as to distinguish themselves, men readied their muskets, bayonets fixed where possible. Hand cursed that he was unable to be leading his beloved Pennsylvanian Riflemen and was on little more than nursery duty with Reitsch. All he could do now was stand and wait.

The silence of the early morning was broken by the enormous roar of the field cannon opening up on Trenton from the River Road. From their position, Hand, O'Leary and Reitsch could not see the ball laying bare the walls of the two-storey barracks, but after its noisy discharge, they immediately heard the sounds of men surprised and then alarmed by the assault, followed quickly by the repetitive ping of Sullivan's musket line advancing on to the town.

A cry came up from Greene, immediately passed on by the men themselves, and the second detachment of the army moved at speed across the open ground before the town. Where before they had been united by their silence, now it was their noise, their clamour for battle, which united them. Men played down their fear of what was to come by screaming, most often impenetrable oaths that were senseless to all but themselves. They trotted, and then they ran, straight towards the centre of the town. Hand held Reitsch and O'Leary back.

'Ed, come on, we'll miss the fun, fer the sake of Christ!'

Hand gave a small look of approval at O'Leary and said to Reitsch, 'Miss, let us see whether your General is as good as his word,' and they gave chase to the army running rampant into the town.

THIRTEEN

'General Washington, may I present to you His Excellency the Baron von Steuben.'

The baron had delivered on his word as Reitsch had said he would.

Whereas the main body of Rall's troops were unprepared when the assault had come, some still asleep, others breakfasting, lamenting Christmas hangovers, few of them at arms, von Steuben and his men were dressed and ready. At the sound of the first artillery, he had led his troops out of the town and straight up to the Assunpink Bridge. There they had set a firm line, their muskets aimed at the town. As Hessians attempted to flee out of Trenton, they were surprised to find their exit route blocked by their fellow mercenaries who, politely, told them to drop their arms and fall in to the rear.

In the town itself, Washington's battle plans proved to be accurate. In all, the Colonists suffered but three fatalities. As for the mercenaries, by the time their leader Rall, himself fatally wounded, surrendered, they had lost twenty-two men, with around a further hundred injured. The Colonists had captured over two hundred Hessians. It was barely a battle.

And now, at its close, the moment when Washington and von Steuben came face to face.

'General Washington, I come to you as your honourable

servant. Congratulations on your victory this morning. A great victory. You have routed Rall and the shock of this loss will be felt most deeply by Howe and King George alike. I trust it may be the start of an even greater victory, one that brings forth the liberation of these colonies from the tyrant himself. I come to you now to offer both my services and that of the small band of men behind me. They are few in number, but you will find that for quality they cannot be matched. They are especially well trained. The finest troops from the European theatre, using the latest weaponry and tactics. They are a new form of army ready to serve a new form of country.'

'Baron, I owe yourself and the estimable Frau Reitsch a debt of gratitude. I am not afraid to admit that at first I looked at your plan with scepticism, but you have proved yourselves to be the greatest of friends to the people of these colonies. Our victory today was in no small part aided by both your insights and your constancy in holding back your troops as you promised. I hope you will dine with myself and my fellow officers this evening, and we may plan how best to use you and your forces in the present struggle. But for now, I'm afraid we must return across the Delaware. I had hoped to push on to Princeton, but we lack the forces necessary.'

'Ah, I take it that not all the crossings were made?'

'You are correct, sir. General Cadwalader and his forces were unable to make the fording at Bristol, nor General Ewing at the falls below Trenton. As was predicted by Frau Reitsch. Who also informed us we would not require those crossings and we should bring all our forces together at one point. Unfortunately, we failed to heed all her advice and now we find ourselves lacking in sufficient numbers to make further advances. But no matter, we have a scalp for the day and that is more than we had before daybreak or have indeed had for some time.'

'If I may, sir, I have some thoughts on how you might maximise the weakness of the British and achieve another victory before the year is out.'

'It will please me to hear your thoughts, Your Excellency. Let us make haste in our return to Newtown for a victory supper! Baron, it would please me if you were to ride alongside me.'

And with that the victorious Washington and his new ally made their way back down the River Road. Watching from a few yards away were Knox and Greene, exhausted by the march and battle.

'Nat, I was under the impression that we were not going to rely on foreign mercenaries to help win our freedom. Our beloved general appears to have had a change of heart.'

'Yes. And what thoughts for John Cadwalader? While he was freezing his bollocks off downriver, a Hessian mercenary was taking the plaudits for this victory, and his failure to cross the river is blamed for our inability to press our advantage.'

'We will have ample opportunity to tease old John. Poor bugger, he will have hated to let Old George down like this. More seriously though, do you share my concern? When a man has proved himself disloyal once, can he ever be trusted? A man comes from Europe pledged to one side and as soon as his feet have landed in our colonies, he pledges both himself and his men to the other.'

Greene lifted his hat and scrubbed at his head. 'I'll withhold judgement on this baron for now, Henry, I wish to see a few more scenes of his performance. But I am looking forward to the return of that other supporting actor Horatio Gates. He dallies with Congress, I suppose, waiting on word of our anticipated defeat to agitate for a leading role in the next act. His disappointment is going to be great, but I suspect Old George will demonstrate the wisdom of Solomon and bring him back into his bosom once again.'

'That fucking viper. I'll be looking forward to his return if only to hear the variety of excuses he will manage to conjure up between here and Philadelphia. He is the turd in the bathhouse that one.'

'The what?'

'The turd in the bathhouse. You only need one turd in the bath and the bathhouse is finished for the day. To my mind, that's our friend Gates.'

'What a splendid image, I'll be using that one, Henry.'

'Of that I have no doubt, dear Nat, no doubt at all.'

FOURTEEN

The return across the Delaware seemed much easier, although the weather had yet to lift. Men who had drudged through the snow and mud with their faces downward on the way to Trenton, now had them lifted to the skies. Where the march out had been conducted in total silence, now there was singing, joshing and shouts, all aided by the brandy discovered in Trenton and liberated for the victors. This despite frostbitten hands, lacerated feet and exhausted bodies.

By the time the main body had reached Newtown, night had fallen, but the snow had ended and the township was lit up by an array of torches. Before the victorious army were the women, children, peddlers and suppliers who were as much a part of the army as the troops themselves, and – in truth – glory seekers who had heard word of the triumph and come running from hamlets and villages in the area to join in the celebrations.

Sarah embraced Hand and O'Leary. Their festivities were ended by a messenger, who asked, 'Lieutenant Colonel Hand?'

'That's no longer my title.'

'That is who General Washington asked me to collect and bring immediately to the Widow Harris's house where he is holding a conference.'

For Hand, the meeting at the widow's house was an entirely different experience from his previous visit. The mood was relaxed.

Nathanael Greene lay on a chaise longue, boots off, his hand around a glass of something dark. Hugh Mercer and Henry Knox were in deep conversation with Hanna Reitsch and another German. John Sullivan was involved in a passionate discussion with Washington. As Hand entered, the first to notice him was von Steuben.

'Colonel Hand, we meet again, in far better circumstances, no?'

The German gave Hand a large clap on the back. 'General Washington, I am afraid I had to make something of an example of your colonel here. I hope there is no ill feeling towards me on your part, Colonel Hand?'

'On the contrary, sir. If I should have to suffer a few personal humiliations for our cause to win such a victory as today, then pray, visit more on me!'

'No, I promise no more humiliations, Colonel!' replied von Steuben, wagging his finger.

'And I too must thank you, for ensuring my safe delivery both to the general and to Trenton, Colonel.' Hanna Reitsch left Knox's side to approach Hand, extending a hand.

'Ah, I'm not sure whether I should shake or kiss your hand, Frau Reitsch,' he replied.

'Whatever your pleasure may be, sir,' was her coquettish reply.

'In the barracks, a handshake seems the only pleasure allowable,' he said, shaking her hand firmly. 'But it is I who am indebted to you. Or rather, my dear friend O'Leary, who would have been carried down the Delaware if you had not acted so swiftly.'

'What's this, more heroics, Hanna?' asked von Steuben. 'She has made a habit of rescuing endangered men, isn't that so?'

Reitsch looked sternly at him. 'Only you, dear General.'

'Do tell us more, Frau Reitsch,' said Greene, still lounging on the chair. 'We enjoy stories of heroism among us here, especially so when they are of petticoats saving the breeches.'

'I would hope that in future, General Greene, many of your American womenfolk would have stories the equal of their men.'

The other German now spoke up, 'Frau Reitsch is something of a radical when it comes to the rights of women. I am afraid that she and I have some profound disagreements on the issue. While I appreciate there may be among their number a few splendid Amazonians capable of equalling men in their courage and imagination, to my mind, most women's role in society is to sustain future generations.'

Greene replied, 'Sir, I'm afraid I have yet to be acquainted.'

'Doktor Werner Conze, General Greene. I consider myself a philosopher soldier. I believe wars are fought not just in the physical sphere, but also in the mind. We are in a battle for the hearts and minds of those we lead, while at the same time the physical destruction of those who do not agree with us.'

'If you want to win the hearts and minds of women, Werner,' Reitsch retorted, 'you may wish to reflect on how best to achieve that, how we differ from the opposite sex. We are more complex than you men. What works for you does not work for us. Your propaganda is too simplistic for us women.'

'Propaganda, what does that mean?' asked Knox.

'It is a new term we have in Prussia,' replied Conze smartly. 'Frau Reitsch should have known better, that it probably has not reached the Americas yet. Put simply, it is the use of words to convince people of the rights of a cause. So you might say that your Thomas Paine is a propagandist for your cause.'

'Paine. Too much bloody trouble, that man,' Sullivan shouted. 'We have to be careful. This revolution of ours at times threatens to rouse the passions of those who might otherwise find it difficult to discover an audience. The Thetford tailor I would put among them.'

'You are correct, sir,' enjoined Conze. 'However, your cause is such that it will – already has – stoked up the fires of those who will look for utopias at this time.'

'Utopias be damned. We just want our freedom and then to return to our farms and our families. I'll leave the utopias to those squawking hens in Philadelphia.'

'Huzzah to that!' cried Greene, raising his glass.

Washington now took the floor. 'Now, Hand, Baron von Steuben and myself have been considering what role we might find for you and we have an offer. I have asked the baron if he will accept a commission and lead his troops as an auxiliary to our main body. I have agreed that they may continue to wear their insignia.'

'This strange insect-like symbol?' asked Hand.

'It is called a swastika. We have a sentimental attachment to it. We came together under the swastika. It reminds us of our homeland, the sacrifices both ourselves and our comrades made in the past. I am obliged to the general for forgiving us such sentimentality.'

'Not at all, Baron. We have plenty of colours and symbols ourselves. As fighting men we understand such sentimentality. Hand, the baron has asked if one of our true patriots could join the unit and he wants you.'

'Sir, I am greatly honoured, but I must beg that I return to the Riflemen. I have a degree of attachment to them equal to you for your own men. Especially so as I will be returning to the ranks.'

'Ah, stop the tarrying, Hand. I will be pleased to restore you to Lieutenant Colonel if you accept this role. And Baron von Steuben would also be obliged to accept the Pennsylvanian Riflemen into his unit.'

There was a snort of derision from the direction of Sullivan.

'Colonel Hand.' Von Steuben placed his arm around the Irishman's shoulder, a degree of intimacy noted by all the Colonists in the room. 'We have a great opportunity to work together to win this damn war and settle the question of America forever. A great opportunity. My men are clever and sharp, they have a degree of military training and knowledge that surpasses those of General Washington's army. They are the best. But they – and I – lack an understanding of the lay of this land, the villages and towns, the roads and paths, the hidden dangers of the Indians. A coming together such as this will only help both sides. I beg you, help us to help you.'

'General, how can I refuse? Myself and the Pennsylvanian Riflemen will be pleased to join you and – you must excuse me – what designation do you give your platoon?'

'Ah, we call ourselves the Stormtroopers.'

At which point Greene stumbled from the chaise longue and raised his glass with a shout that was picked up by the rest of the room: 'Huzzah for the Stormtroopers!'

FIFTEEN

After the conference with Washington, Hand returned to the tavern where he found O'Leary and Sarah deep into the rum. The mood was raucous, an impromptu band was making mayhem in a corner, the chatter was loud, a smattering of the Hessians already forming close links with the Colonists.

'Now, will you be joining us fella for a rum or two?'

'Last time I took to the drink, I killed a man and nearly had myself hanged, Pat. I would be wise to leave off it for now.'

'Aye, but if you hadn't done that, we might not have our Trenton victory. And I would never have met the delightful Frau Hanna.'

'Ed, our Pat is obsessed with this lady. Apparently she's the most beautiful, most tender, most fierce woman in all the colonies. He's all doe-eyed when it comes to Frau Hanna Reitsch. I'd say he's lost all his senses,' Sarah teased him.

'She's certainly something different, I'd agree with him on that score. But she can't be that clever, given that she risked her own life saving this simple oaf's life and all.'

'Ach, she's wonderful, like she's from a different age like. If all women had her strength and character—' Pat caught Sarah's strong and characteristic response; she was not someone who regarded herself as inferior to any man in any way. 'What I mean is, she takes men as her equal. Like yourself, but with more . . . I

92

don't know with more confidence perhaps. Perhaps all European women are like her, forthright and bold. I don't know, but she's different. Ach, what am I saying? You'd like her. When you meet her, you'll see what I mean.'

'I've had this the past two hours, Ed. I would be insulted if I didn't think our Pat was drunk with unspent passion for this madame.'

'He hasn't mentioned she's quite the looker as well then?'

'Oh, is that the case? Now you mention it . . . no.'

'I can't deny she's a right honey. That's true. But I was first attracted to her character.' Ed and Sarah burst into laughter. 'No, listen, that's true as the day is long.'

'So do you have designs on her honour then, Pat?' Sarah could barely control her laughter.

'I might. She clearly has some sense of affection towards me or she wouldn't have pulled me out of the water. Who's to say we couldn't become confidential, like.'

Hand snorted. 'Confidential? You've no chance of that happening, you fool. She's far too sophisticated for a bogtrotter like Paddy O'Leary. Besides which, I would hazard she and Baron von Steuben have an arrangement of sorts.'

O'Leary appeared crestfallen. 'You think so? You can't be sure of that. You can't be. You're just playing with me, fella, no mistake. Besides which, you know these sophisticated ladies, what they really want is some of that old Irish charm – and I've plenty of that!'

A cheer from the far side of the bar drowned out their laughter. One of the Stormtroopers was taking all comers on at arm-wrestling – and winning all, much to everyone's amusement. It could be no surprise, the blond Prussian seemed twice the size of every colonial in the room.

'I have some news. I am restored to my former glory of Lieutenant Colonel.'

'Hurrah!' shouted Pat and Sarah in unison.

'And I have agreed to bring the Riflemen in with von Steuben's troops. They call themselves the Stormtroopers.'

'I like that, Stormtroopers. That's a good name. That's the kind of name that'll put fear into the enemy straight away, "Look ahead, boys, the Stormtroopers are coming for yer!" They'll be shitting their pants and heading for their mamas before a shot is fired. Stormtroopers, that's properly fearsome. The Riflemen doesn't have the same ring to it.'

'I sense there's much we can learn from them. They are far more advanced than our farmhands and clerks from Boston. If we're to make the most of this recent success, we need to become more disciplined, more thoughtful in our approach. Our militia have to become soldiery like them,' Hand replied.

'They also be easy on the eye. I don't know what they feed them in that Prussia, but none of us ladies are complaining about the size of these boys. Or their teeth. Have you seen their teeth, Ed? You don't get teeth that white and gleaming in America.'

The door of the tavern opened and Werner Conze strode in, stopping at the door, to survey the scene.

'See what I mean. Look at him,' Sarah drooled.

'That one's called Werner Conze, speaks very good English.'

Conze spotted Hand, gave a cheerful wave and walked towards the group before asking, 'Colonel Hand, may I join you and your comrades?'

'Werner Conze, may I introduce you to Sergeant Patrick O'Leary, the finest friend a man could have, not to mention the finest gunsmith in the Americas, and my sister, the dearest sister in the world, Miss Sarah Hand.'

Conze reached out for Sarah's hand, before elaborately bowing and kissing it. 'Charmed to make your acquaintance, Miss Hand. Sergeant O'Leary, a pleasure to meet in person a gentleman of whom I have heard only praise from the esteemed Frau Hanna Reitsch.'

'She talked of me?'

'She has spoken of little else since her return from Trenton,' replied Conze with a hint of good humour that the Hands noticed, but flew straight above the head of O'Leary.

'Did she now? You see, you two, I told you there was something there. Would you share a drink with us, Mister Conze?'

'Please, call me Werner, we must be less formal. We are friends, comrades on the same journey. Of course, I'll have whatever you're having.'

'On a night as cold as this, it has to be rum, hot-peppered rum.'

'Then hot and peppered rum it will be.'

'This chair is free. Won't you take it and join me here, Werner?' said Sarah forwardly.

'Ma'am, it will be a pleasure.'

'Please, call me Sarah. I agree that allies should be less formal with each other.'

Hand raised an eyebrow at O'Leary.

Conze sat down as O'Leary left for the drink. There was another shout from the corner. Conze looked over.

'Ah, I see Scharführer Lothar Kluggman is entertaining everyone in his usual polite manner.'

Hand looked over. 'Who's he?'

'Oh, a prized fighter of the Reich. There are few people who can take on Kluggman. Well, I don't think there is anyone alive who can. He is a phenomenon. If we had a hundred Kluggmans, we could win this war in days. I'm afraid he is lacking in English, or German for that matter. A man of very few words, but extraordinary action. A wonderful tool.'

'Where do you come from, Werner? Are you Hessian?' Sarah asked.

'Ah, I'm from Heidelberg originally, to the south, but I have been living for most of the last decade and more in Berlin, the capital of our Prussia.'

O'Leary placed the drinks on the table and pulled up another stool. Conze picked up his toddy, raised it and announced: 'To our new-found friendship and the coming victory. To America!'

'To America!' they all repeated, even Hand without a drink.

Conze winced as the rough, flaming toddy went down his throat. 'You say you're a gunsmith, Sergeant O'Leary?'

'Pat or Paddy, please. Yes, I have the unfortunate role of keeping Ed's Riflemen armed in the field. Not the easiest thing in the world, believe me.'

'I must introduce you to a friend of mine from Germany, Schmeisser. Schmeisser is a genius, his guns will change the world, believe me. He will soon make your muskets irrelevant.'

'Is he with you in camp?'

'No, he is travelling about New England with someone else we brought over with us, Alfried Krupp. He is equally revolutionary. They are studying the iron- and steelworks of Jersey, Boston and so on. We have plans you see. We have ideas that may bring you victory sooner than you might have imagined. This has already been a long and difficult war, has it not?'

'Indeed, sir. This past year has been especially difficult; today was our first victory for some time,' replied Hand.

'And this year has been very hard for our Edward, he lost his wife and a bairn,' said Sarah, stroking her brother's head affectionately.

'I cannot imagine such a loss,' said Conze sympathetically.

'I don't wish to dwell on my losses tonight. I have had plenty of time to do that and will do so again. But not tonight, tonight we look to the future, with good cheer and grace.'

'Indeed. Today is the turning point, the day from which in a thousand years people will look back and say, "The world changed then. On that day, man set forth on a new path."'

'Why have you come all this way from your family in Europe to fight our war for us?'

'Your war? Sarah, this is not just your war, it is our war, a war for everyone who hopes for a better world. This war is not simply about making King George pay for taxing a people with no representation. This is a war that will shape the course of the human race for a thousand years. This America of yours is not yet half-formed, the lands to the west are yet to be civilised. When they are, when this America stretches from the Atlantic to the Pacific, you will have the greatest *Lebensraum* of any nation on earth. The land is rich in minerals, it stands ready and willing to make the most of technologies the likes of which you cannot imagine. The age of the machine is almost upon us. It is coming faster than you might think. Soon there will be iron horses that can transport men from city to city in hours rather than days or even weeks. There will be a time when we will launch machines that fly in the air. Imagine a time when you can fly like a bird from New York City to Spanish missions in Las Californias! That world will soon be in our grasp, within a century or two, for our children's children.

'How best to achieve that? How best to ensure the best possible world for those children not yet imagined, yet conceived? To ensure light over dark? We at this moment in time must lay the foundations for such a society, for an empire that will last a thousand years and propel mankind to fulfil all its potential. That, my dear friend, is why I am here. To ensure that the soon-to-be-born America is a wholly new world, without the prejudices and follies of the past. To create a new world, for a new man!'

'It's like Tom Paine said in that pamphlet you gave me Ed,' said Pat excitedly. '"The cause of America is the cause of all mankind."'

Hand looked stunned. He had no idea his friend had actually read the battered copy of *Common Sense* he had given him.

'Indeed, Thomas Paine,' snorted Conze. 'I have issues with

Mister Paine, but that is for another day. Another toast: To America!'

Conze raised his glass once more, clinking with Sarah's and Pat's glasses. Hand looked upon them. There was something of a fury in Conze's eye, madness perhaps, but in Sarah and Pat he saw the growing embers of something worse, a kind of worship, as children before a teacher.

Then a fiddler started playing and a hornpipe began, pairs of men and women pushed back their tables and chairs to clear a space and began a raucous, chaotic dance, the music almost overwhelmed by the cheers and whoops of the dancers. The celebratory mood was intoxicating.

Conze turned to Sarah, 'Miss Hand, would you care to escort me to the dance floor.' Then, checking himself, 'If that is acceptable to your brother, *natürlich.*'

'I long ago gave up looking after Sarah, or rather trying to. If she wishes to partner you, then so be it.'

'Werner, it will be my pleasure. We are commonly lacking in gentlemen in these parts. It's a rarity to be asked and not to be dragged to the floor.'

'Then, please, take my arm,' said Conze, and within moments they were part of the whirlwind that had so suddenly erupted around them.

'It's a rare old night this, Ed, what every Christmas should be, I'd say. Fair forgotten the storm outside,' smiled the slightly drunk Pat O'Leary.

SIXTEEN

While his men caroused into the night, Washington was dealing with his own affray, mostly a torrent of abuse from Sullivan.

'Sir, I am astounded by your lack of compunction about placing such trust in this Hessian. We know nothing of him. Well, we know he is a mercenary and a mercenary is motivated by one thing, that which can be weighed in a purse. How do we know that he will not betray our cause, as he has the British? What . . . what if this is all a British ruse, to place a viper in our bosom? What if we have a spy active at the heart of our enterprise?'

For once, Washington responded with his own form of fury.

'A British spy? A British spy who provides us with such intelligence as to give us our first victory in so many months? A British spy who holds back his troops, sees the death of a British general and then brings most of his force over to our side? The British are prepared to pay a heavy price if they sent him as a spy. No, if the baron is a British spy, I'll congratulate him for the complicated web he has spun these last two days.

'You above all others, John Sullivan, will remember the disarray, nay, the shame of Long Island. What was it, sixty British infantrymen we counted turning two of our brigades on their heels? That day we understood the chasm between the British army and our own forces. From that day, I understood our militia required the tactics, the training and the discipline that the British possessed. I believe that the baron and his two hundred and fifty Stormtroopers will swiftly give our boys the very essence we lack. Or would you prefer to be held captive once more by the British and sent to Congress as a mere messenger boy again?'

Washington held Sullivan's ferocious stare. The others in the room stood silent, surprised by the lack of control Washington had demonstrated, a lack of control at odds with his usual bearing.

It had been just a few weeks since the British had returned Sullivan, captured amid the chaos of the Long Island debacle. Howe had agreed he could return to the American side only if he took a message to Congress offering to open negotiations for peace. Sullivan had been humiliated, John Adams calling him the 'decoy duck'. Others pointedly asked if the British sent Sullivan because he would do more harm to the Colonists' cause in the field rather than without. The general was more than aware of the whisperings against him in Philadelphia. Now he felt Washington turning against him.

He replied in a quiet voice: 'That, sir, is a low observation, unbecoming of you. I have served you loyally and well. After Trois-Rivières, I was content to oversee the retreat from Quebec, when others would have baulked at such a mission. Did I complain when you placed Putnam over me at Long Island? No, I did not. I have borne these and other humiliations with stoicism, always remaining loyal to the cause and yourself. And for what? For petty insults it would appear.'

Now Washington paused. He had allowed his temper to get the better of him. He was tired, he wanted to rest, but he could not let Sullivan depart feeling bruised. He had enough enemies without creating another one. He deliberately softened his tone.

'John, you and I have been through too much together to have things fall apart when we are at last seeing the fruits of our endeavours. This war cannot be about the vanity of any one of us, this cause is greater than that. If you damn me for taking whatever opportunities come our way to ensure success, well, then you must damn me, but know that I do so because I believe it will be to our benefit, our eventual success. You have proved yourself on so many occasions to be both able and loyal. I have dispatched to Congress news of our victory and I have placed your efforts at the head of those deserving the greatest appreciation from the delegates. My hope is that it will go some way to silencing those who stay by a warm hearth yet think nothing of directing calumny towards you.'

The fury drained from Sullivan's face. His reply echoed Washington's tone.

'I thank you, sir. I do not damn you; I would never consider such an abomination. But I say this: we know nothing of this gentleman, aside a vague understanding of his reputation in Europe. It is true, he helped us achieve a famous victory, but my concern is plain: a man has to earn the right of trust. He has betrayed the English, it would appear, for what? What gain does he perceive? Would he not equally betray those he barely knows if such a gain was to twofold?'

And now Mercer joined in with his soft Scottish burr: 'I too share some of John's reticence on this issue, George. I urge caution before holding the baron too close. I would observe him for a period of time. You have made an excellent choice in having Hand join with these Hessians. He is a man we trust. I would encourage you to ask him for reports on the true nature of von Steuben and his ambitions. Then you will be able to determine his purposes and indeed his usefulness to our cause.'

'Thank you, Hugh. I will act upon those reflections. Nat Greene, what do you say?'

From the chaise longue came a languid reply, 'I'd like to provide you with some honest reports on Frau Reitsch, sir. Now there's a woman.'

SEVENTEEN

Von Steuben, or as he still preferred to consider himself, Robert Ritter von Greim, lay stretched out on a canvas bed in lodgings that had hastily been found for him. Hanna Reitsch sat on a small stool, untying her boots.

'My dear, our victory seems to have been achieved with greater ease than I envisaged. If there were any champagne available in this backward country, I would order a magnum and drink it immediately.'

'I'm afraid you're unlikely to taste champagne again, Robert, certainly not the kind of champagne you love so. Has it even been invented? Besides which, victory is still a long way off, you must know that. This is just the start.'

'Ah, but look how easy it has proved to be. Conze's analysis of Washington was correct. What did he tell us? "A simple man, used to prevarication, his position so weak at this moment, so frustrated with his generals, he will soon turn to a new ally." Excellent. Excellent work. He is something, our professor.'

'He is too much of an intellectual for my liking.'

'No, you much prefer some animal brawn, my dear,' said von Greim, stroking her hair from behind. 'I know you adore me because I lack such finesse.'

Laughing, she replied, 'I adore you because you are twice the man he will ever be. But there will come a time when Werner Conze will look to push himself at your expense.'

'That may be true, but by then, I may be ready to retire to one of these southern plantations, serviced by young Negro women. Did not most of these "revolutionaries" father several children by slaves? I too could be the father of such a nation!'

Reitsch smarted him with a soft punch, pushing him down on to the bed and undoing the buttons on his shirt. 'And I thought you were a stickler for *fassenschande*? Perhaps we need to introduce our own Nuremberg Laws on racial purity sooner than I thought. By all means go find your self a few negresses, but none of them will be able to satisfy you like your dear Hanna.'

'Now, that is true.'

Moving down, she started to unbutton his trousers, pulling them off and revealing the scars from the flight to Berlin, scarlet and enflamed against the whiteness of his limbs. 'How is your leg? I was always worried that such a long and primitive trip from Berlin would only open up the wound, but it seems to have healed almost perfectly.'

'Ah, it is nothing. Little more than a dull ache now. I count it as just one addition to the growing list of small insults that old age brings. It certainly doesn't stop me from performing my favourite form of exercise.'

With that he rolled over, taking Reitsch with him, and furiously began to unbutton her white blouse.

EIGHTEEN

By the following morning, the storm had finally broken. As the camp slowly stirred, those awakening were met by a clear sky; the freezing winds replaced by a still cold. The ground was firm once more, which was just as well, because the Continental Army was on the move again: Washington had made the decision to recross the Delaware to establish a more permanent camp at Trenton, where they would be joined by Cadwalader's and Ewing's forces.

While the Colonists packed up their camp and started their move, a different conference was taking place in the small lodging room in which von Greim and Reitsch had spent the night.

'So let us once again rehearse our strategy.' Both von Greim and Reitsch were beginning to tire of Werner Conze's schoolmasterly approach. They had often spoken of this stage on the long journey from Berlin to the Americas, had run through the plan only two days earlier in Trenton, yet he was insistent on a further rehearsal. It piqued Reitsch in particular. The designated führer was Ritter von Greim, but Werner Conze clearly felt he was more than his equal.

'I'm not entirely sure this is necessary. I am not some dolt who can't remember anything, you know,' von Greim expressed his annoyance.

'I'm not suggesting you are, Generalfeldmarschall. But this is vital. If we play our cards well over the coming days, we will have achieved the first stage of our plan. Remember: stage one, infiltrate, win the Americans' confidence by bringing them previously unknown victories—'

'All of which we know they would have achieved without our help.'

'Hanna, that makes no difference. The important foundation of myth creation is not the truth, but what people perceive to be the truth. What is truth? What people take to be the truth. The story is everything, not facts. Our aim is simple: to make it appear that we – or rather, the Generalfeldmarschall here, is responsible for both Trenton and the forthcoming victory at Princeton. This creates the conditions for our ability to start the second stage: the ideological battle for the very soul of this revolution – or rather, to put something into the soul of the new America beyond these half-baked, flimsy concepts of liberty and freedom. Generalfeldmarschall, humour me, how do the events of the next few days play themselves out?'

Grudgingly, von Greim gave the answer Conze was awaiting.

'Today Washington will receive news that General Cornwallis has departed New York with a large force, the aim to restore Trenton and crush him. There will be discussion in the war conference of a response. There will be those who suggest that the army should immediately retreat and avoid conflict. The leader of that cause will be Mercer, especially now Lee has departed to Congress, where his attempt to have Washington removed from the leadership will fail once news reaches them of the victory at Trenton. Washington will receive full authorisation from Congress to direct the war as he sees fit, which almost gives him dictatorial powers, although he will not realise their full implications or perhaps not want to. But we shall. He also has to convince his men to stay with him for a further month, rather than keep to the terms of their contract. He will bribe them to stay.'

'Good, very good.'

Reitsch could not hide her disdain for Conze's patronising tone, nor for that matter, could von Greim.

'I'm pleased you think I can remember so much, Werner,' he said with a sting. 'At this war conference, I allow the debate to begin, but crucially – you see I do take in all your details, Conze – crucially, I have to make a stand before Washington outlines his thoughts. I will suggest that we keep no more than a skeletal resistance in Trenton. That we first prepare for an assault by Cornwallis on Trenton by organising defences to the north of the town, but we take the main body of the Continental Army south by the Assunpink Bridge. I will argue that we use the Pennsylvanian Riflemen and our Stormtroopers to hold up Cornwallis, so that he is unable to take the town before nightfall. We retreat across the river. Then, using the backwoods, we launch an offensive against the British forces at Princeton. From there we immediately move on, although, and this is different I believe to previous . . . what would you say? The previous time when this event happened? This time, we will raid the British supplies at New Brunswick and make off with them. That will be your job. To secure those supplies.'

Conze nodded his assent then asked: 'And the battle?'

'Well, if the battle follows the previous battle – this is all very peculiar, sometimes I find it very difficult to understand how all this works, this notion we are changing a past we already know. I wish the science was a little clearer.'

Conze shrugged. 'It makes no difference. You need not understand it.' That derogatory tone again.

'The battle will be fierce on the outskirts of Princeton; there will be a time when the Colonists in the rear will panic and start a retreat. At that stage Washington assumes control on the field and saves the day. I must engineer a situation where instead I rally the troops before he has that opportunity, to win the acclaim for myself.'

'Excellent. Very excellent. But there is a further—'

'Mercer. Mercer must perish. He is Washington's key confidant. He will throw himself into the battle around that time, but he will be isolated and receive multiple wounds. We must allow him to die. The loss of his closest, and earliest, confidant will hurt Washington, who, surrounded by those young men, Knox, Greene and Hamilton, will look to Baron von Steuben for experienced advice. We shall make an ally of Gates, who is already alienated from Washington. We will need him to bring the north-east colonies to our side.'

'Excellent! Our Stormtroopers are ready to play their part. I would say they are itching to see battle. I have a number of small improvements to better the original American plans to harass the British along the Princeton road. In the next few days, we will firm up our reputation for valour and for tactical cleverness. The first stage will be well on its way to completion.'

'And the second part, Werner? How goes the fight for the soul?'

Conze could hardly miss Reitsch's sarcastic tone now.

'As you will understand, Hanna, the battle for the soul is far more difficult and longer than any physical battle. One has to have the cunning of the fox, but the stamina of a lion hunting its prey. The battle for the soul is underway.'

'Is it? Or have you simply found some girl you want to fuck?'

Conze smiled. He was a handsome man until he allowed himself a smile, when his face appeared crooked. He was not a man much given to good humour, and his smile undermined the charm that he was so keen to use on others.

'I was unable to bring my own sandwiches to this picnic, unlike yourself, Hanna.' He cast an eye over the hurriedly made bed. 'I see no reason why I can't look to find my own pleasures. Besides which, we say we look to win the hearts and minds, don't we? My plan remains the same. We use the Pennsylvanian Riflemen as our entry point. This fellow Hand, as our research suggested, will be the perfect foil. We shall win him over and through him, his men. Then over the next few months our ideology will spread, like a virus, through this army and on to the Colonists' townships and villages. It will be a contagion, like history has never seen before.'

'No further word from Alfried Krupp?' asked von Greim.

'No. I suspect he is still moaning about the quality of accommodation. By the time we reached New York on that boat, I was close to wanting to kill him. Such a bourgeois dilettante!' roared Reitsch.

Von Greim laughed out loud. 'I'm afraid that three hundred years of luxurious living has not left the Krupps with much of an understanding of how most people live in the twentieth century, let alone the eighteenth.'

'It's that poor chap Schmeisser I feel sorry for,' said Hanna. 'Alfried has decided him unworthy of any role aside from his manservant, when he is possibly the true genius of this entire campaign.'

'Yes, you're probably right, my dear. It is Schmeisser, his understanding of weaponry, that will change things here for ever. Forget our plans, our tactics, no matter how modern, if he can find the way to give our troops the Sturmgewehr 44 or the Maschinengewehr 42, we will have victory within two years, if not sooner. From there, we no longer have history to follow. From that moment on, we will be writing history anew.'

'Indeed, we are the masters of the future now,' Conze said in agreement.

'And now we are at war, we must give you a suitable rank Werner. This Herr Doktor, philosopher, warrior may play well in the salon, but you require a proper rank for the battlefield and to establish your position among the men. So, I award you the title of Obergruppenführer.'

Conze blushed, 'That is—'

'Indeed, that is the senior most rank of the Stormtroopers. It indicates to all that you are second only to myself in command of the troops.'

'This is a most wonderful honour. I am truly indebted sir.'

'Congratulations Werner, sorry Obergruppenführer!' Reitsch said before kissing him warmly.

'There is one other appellation I have been considering. It is time for us all to say goodbye to our beloved friend Robert Ritter von Greim. From now I can only be addressed as Friedrich von Steuben. Even in private, my dear.'

'That may prove difficult, darling. Friedrich. It lacks a certain . . . a certain something.'

'Although more noble sounding than Robert, and more fitting to the age, I would counter,' said Conze.

Von Greim pulled his bottom lip up, 'I know nothing of that. This is our age now. We cannot return to the lives, the world we left behind. We understood that when we entered Bewilogua's infernal machine.'

'Ah, do you think often of that moment, Generalfeldmarschall, when we took that step into the unknown?'

Von Greim paused. He did. He often thought of it. There had been so little time to understand the implications of the journey. By necessity they had to agree to the mission almost immediately. No time to question Bewilogua's obscure calculations and insistence they would land perfectly in Berlin in 1775. The scientist confident because he had sent a scout ahead (or rather back) with a mission to leave a message in a steel canister buried at a specific point in Dahlem, a canister newly discovered, close to a hundred and seventy years after it had been buried. Not until he found himself standing in the green fields around the eighteenth-century village of Dahlem, welcomed by that very scout, had Robert Ritter von Greim begun to understand what he had left behind or the risk involved. There were still times when he would awaken in a wet sweat, his dreams punctured by the memory of the violence of the travel, the noise, the nausea, the bone-crushing pain of the transition, the headaches they all suffered in the weeks that followed. He did not understand the science, all he knew was they could not return and he was glad only because he would never again have to experience such agony.

Sensing her lover's discomfort, Hanna broke the silence: 'I think only of the feeling of nausea from that journey. That and the sanitary sacrifices we have made!'

NINETEEN

Washington was flushed. He had been addressing the troops in the same square in which Rall had paraded his men before Christmas. As he entered the house on Queen Street now serving as his head-quarters, Washington's colouring was caused less by moving from cold to warm, and more by the news Alexander Hamilton had just delivered: Cornwallis was on the march from New York.

The commander-in-chief entered the main dining room to find Mercer, Sullivan, Knox, Greene, Cadwalader and von Steuben awaiting him.

'General, were you successful in persuading the men to stay their leave?'

'Aye, Nat, I was. I begged them to stay to our cause for another month. I gave much flattery about their efforts over the last few days and the forthcoming triumphs we will enjoy. However, I am not convinced it was my flowery rhetoric that convinced them, more the bounty of ten colonial dollars per man.'

'To be paid at month's end?'

'If only. Hard cash up front is required. That much was made clear. Given that most of them seem to be without winter uniform or even boots, I am a tad sympathetic. I hope the funds will arrive tomorrow, or the efforts will be in vain. That said, the news from New York may render everything achieved worthless.'

'Cornwallis? He marches?'

'He does indeed, Hugh, he is already on the road. The question, gentlemen, is how we should respond.'

'His force is much greater than ours?'

'Alexander has the details,' Washington signalled for his aide-de-camp, hovering in the background as usual, rarely keen to voice an opinion, preferring to record events for posterity. Always nervous in the company of the generals, he cleared his voice before saying huskily, the tone betraying his anxiety.

'Our report, a good source from the city itself, is that he leads close to ten thousand men. He aims to leave some at Princeton, under the command of Colonel Mawhood to bulwark the town and the sizeable supply depot he has settled there. At our roll calls this morning, we have fewer than eight thousand men under our command, which includes the Hessians the baron brought to us.'

'The numbers are against us then,' murmured Cadwalader.

'What of his artillery, Alexander?' asked Knox.

'We believe they have twenty-five cannon. Each bigger than our six pounders.'

There was shaking of heads among the assembled staff.

'Gentlemen, we have a number of opportunities before us, but we have little time to dither. What are your thoughts?' asked Washington.

Mercer opened the debate. 'We have to avoid the possibility of an open engagement between our forces and Lord Cornwallis's. We are not prepared, in number or ordnance, to succeed in such a task. Nor are our men any match for the British Army coming at them in open formation. They will be cut to ribbons. As painful as it may sound, I believe, we must recross the Delaware and take our army towards the safety of Philadelphia.'

'Sir, if I may,' responded Nathanael Greene. 'I agree that we cannot sustain a force in direct combat. However, we have recently achieved a great victory. With Trenton we have established ourselves as a force to be reckoned with. I would argue we stay this side of the river and prepare for the spring here, right here at Trenton. Stay here and men will return to us, new men will join us. I would also argue that we can defend Trenton, through earthworks and other devices, and hold the town.'

'We have little enough time to prepare the necessary defences. We will still be digging them when the enemy is upon us.'

'But, General Mercer, if we fall back again, we will lose any advantages our recent exertions have provided us with. We cannot keep crossing and recrossing the Delaware like some half-wit who has lost his map.'

'Nat, Cornwallis's forces will not be the unprepared garrison that awaited us at Trenton.' It was Sullivan, moving to support Mercer. 'This will be the English army in all its glory, with Cornwallis at its head. Ten thousand men. Hessian Jägers. English Dragoons. Infantry and cavalry. Twenty-five cannon, Hamilton says. They will pound us into the ground. The enlisted men will flee, regardless of the extension the General has achieved today. The war will be lost.'

'I agree that the risk is too great, sir.' Knox now entered the debate. 'May we reflect for a moment on the outstanding good fortune that we enjoyed at Trenton. We crossed under terrible conditions that for once worked to our advantage. The garrison was, as Nathanael says, unprepared and, of course, we had the added benefit of Baron von Steuben and his men holding the bridge. Our men remain unproven when such favourable conditions do not exist, and I fear for what might occur if we engage the enemy directly.'

'We are all in agreement with that, Knox.' Mercer was exasperated with the younger man's gift for platitude. 'The question is what to do.'

'Well, your plan for a further recrossing of the Delaware has a flaw: the boats we used have already been sent upstream. Many of them returned to their rightful owners. It would take a day, maybe two, to get enough Durhams and the like downriver again. There is only a small chance we could evacuate all the Continental Army before Cornwallis arrives.'

Washington turned to Cadwalader. 'John, you are a man usually spoiling for a fight, what say you?'

'Indeed I am, sir, and my men are spoiling even more than ever after we were unable to join the attack on Trenton. But my usual desire for engagement has been softened by the arguments I have heard. We stand to gain little by holding fast in Trenton. We are ill prepared to deliver a knockout, and I fear we may only be inviting Cornwallis to deliver just that to our own side. He will be smarting after Trenton. The British will hit us with everything they have and we could lose an army before we have even fully savoured the victory just won. On balance, I would agree with our General Mercer. We should begin the evacuation immediately, boats or no boats. We could return by way of Crosswicks, from which my militia has just come to Trenton. I say, let's hasten to Philly.'

'Baron von Steuben, your thoughts?'

Von Steuben stood up from his chair at the back, paced around the room, paused for maximum effect and then strode to the map table, placing his palms flat on the table, before saying:

'First, war is the art of the unexpected. Warriors win when they do what their opponents think is impossible. What is Cornwallis expecting from you? He expects you to run. Because that is what you have been doing for, for how long? Running. Running away. At the very best, he might imagine your pride is bursting after Trenton, and you may defend the town against him. As we speak, he is probably ordering all the supplies necessary to start a siege of Trenton, or planning the laying out of his cannon around the town. I suspect that may be what he hopes you are planning to do, given the new confidence among you. But I must agree with General Mercer, it would be foolish to look to hold this town. I have overseen and been part of many sieges in Europe, and

Trenton is not in a state to hold out. One whiff of grapeshot, let alone a fusillade of cannon, and the town will be lost. It is, I'm afraid, General Greene, indefensible.

'However, I cannot agree with Generals Mercer and Sullivan that we should therefore retreat to Philadelphia. I have not yet visited Philadelphia. I am sure it is a fine city, but I have no desire to visit it yet. Take the army to that city and it will disappear among the populace, ten-dollar bounty or not. An army must maintain itself in the field. Moreover, by retreating to Philadelphia you create the paradox of weakening the city while appearing to strengthen it. You will lay open the road to the city. Cornwallis will simply march past Trenton and attack your capital, his troops fresh and ready for the fight. The best you could hope for is that you force him to lay siege for the winter. The likelier outcome is that he will seize the city and scatter you to, well, the Indian lands, I presume.

'The Englishman expects you to do one of two things: retreat or hold out. In either case, he sees a victory for himself. So, why do as he expects – no, *wants* you to do? Why not do what he would never consider you capable of? Why not attack him?'

There was a theatrical gasp from the six generals and a mutter of 'Madness' from Sullivan.

'Victories follow victories, General Sullivan. When one is achieved, you must act quickly to achieve another. Momentum is everything in a campaign. Once men have a taste for victory, they become greater and they want more victories. If you want to keep your enlisted men, show them victories. Victory has a far greater value than a few dollars. A great general does not rest on his laurels. A great general seizes the moment and strikes hard, strikes hard at the enemy. Maintain momentum. That is what you must do.'

'Sir, how do you suggest we do that? Cornwallis's forces outnumber us. Our men are exhausted, ill equipped and ill shod.

They lack the tactical discipline of the British,' protested Cadwalader.

'You do not engage Cornwallis's army in battle, that I agree is madness. Not the whole army. But you look for an engagement that will shatter his arrogant assumptions about this war. Sometimes an army can be defeated off the battlefield. You do something so audacious that it undermines Cornwallis's supreme confidence in himself, and the confidence of his generals and men in him and their cause. So while Cornwallis comes here for you, you attack one of his prize assets, which will suggest nothing is safe any longer. You attack the garrison at Princeton.'

'We attack Princeton!' exclaimed Mercer. 'How should we do that when he will be coming directly from Princeton towards us?'

'We take the back roads. Look here,' von Steuben planted his finger on the map. 'These roads here, the one marked Quaker Bridge Road. You follow this stream—'

'Stony Brook, we had it reconnoitred last month,' added Cadwalader.

'Stony Brook, which leads you to this unnamed road across what appears farmland and takes you directly to the town, through an area I would wager is unguarded. At best, there will be a few outlying sentries.'

'As I said, we had this approach reconnoitred in early December. It is not easy. It passes through woods. Those woods are no more difficult than what you passed through the other night, and give the benefit of much cover. I daresay there will be treacherous parts, but this road on the farmland has the benefit of not being visible from the Post Road. If our forces could move swiftly and quietly, there is the possibility they would not be spotted.' Cadwalader drew his line to the Post Road on the map, the main highway between Princeton and Trenton. Contemplating his work, he whispered: 'It is not unfeasible.'

'It uses some of the very skills we put into practice on the march

116

to Trenton,' said Knox. 'The men managed those manoeuvres under the strictest quiet. We have learned how to muffle the sounds of moving cannon and infantry most effectively. We are masters at this subterfuge.'

'But if we give up Trenton completely and march out, Cornwallis will soon become aware of our plan. We'll either be slaughtered on these back roads or he will about-turn and see us off at Princeton,' replied Mercer.

'We do not give up Trenton. Or rather, we do not *appear* to give up Trenton. We immediately start preparing fortifications as if we are preparing for a defence and siege. Then we place Hand's Pennsylvanians and my own Stormtroopers, who are well trained in the art of guerrilla warfare, to hold up Cornwallis's advance.'

'Guerrilla warfare?' asked Knox, puzzled. 'What's that? I have read all the military textbooks and I've never heard of it.'

Von Steuben checked himself. Damn, he thought, of course they've never heard of it. It hasn't been invented yet. To Knox he replied, 'No, I would think not. It is a recent phenomenon. It comes from the Spanish word for a small war. It is perfect for the conditions we face. Indeed, many of your militia, with their apparently random attacks on the British these past few months, have been practising a form of guerrilla warfare.'

'Tactically ill disciplined, they create more problems for our side than for the enemy,' countered Mercer.

'At times, yes, I am sure. The key is to embrace such tactics within an overall strategy. But that is for another day. Let us move back to this particular battle. Cornwallis will be coming down the Post Road, which, as I have witnessed, is surrounded by woods, ravines and many bends that make it easy to defend, but difficult for him to organise his men in battle formation. We continually fall back, until eventually we stand here at the Assunpink Bridge and the high ground on the other side of the creek.' He planted his forefinger on the map. 'Here General Knox's artillery can start firing on the English, slowing them still further. It will allow Cornwallis little time to set up his positions. By then the night will be falling and the English will have little option but to fall back. Then comes our master stroke for the situation.

'We leave at nightfall with the main body of our troops, which allows us to leave, say, five hundred men in Trenton. That will give the enemy the appearance of our full complement. Light enough lights, stoke enough fires, and they will believe the entire army is camped out, especially if occasionally we offer up cannon shot to keep up the pretence.

'In the morning, as the English begin their attack, these five hundred men also slip away. We may keep a few sharpshooters here until the very last. By the time Cornwallis has entered and realises the ruse, we will have taken Princeton, scored another victory and seized all the stores that we can make off with.'

'Their winter stores are at New Brunswick, I think,' Hamilton interrupted. 'I'm confident that's where they are.' He came to the map now. 'New Brunswick is no more than, what, fifteen miles from Princeton. If we could seize those quarters . . .'

'Your youthful enthusiasm is getting you too excited, Hamilton,' replied Mercer.

'No, perhaps the young gentleman is right. Why not make a raid on them? The stores are indeed at New Brunswick. My men and I passed through it on our march to join Rall at Trenton. It is very well stocked. If we seize it, we will create a crisis for them. They will be unable to push on, or even to give chase, and have no option but to retreat to New York for the winter. An excellent suggestion, Mister Hamilton. So along with the proposal I outlined, I add to it the thought that we send a raiding party on to New Brunswick and pick Cornwallis's pocket. That, sir, is the plan I suggest.'

He stepped back from the table. There was silence around the room.

Washington nodded his head quietly. Greene, Knox, Sullivan and Cadwalader were taken aback by the detail, the precision and the sheer effrontery of the plan. Mercer attempted to find a flaw in von Steuben's plan.

'The baggage. Are we to take all our own supplies with us on this route march, Baron? I cannot imagine that we can strike camp and have all our necessary supplies following us through this backwoods.'

'Ah, a good point, Your Excellency,' replied von Steuben, temporarily lost for an answer, thrown by the peculiar question. He had outlined an astonishing, audacious plan and all Mercer could bring up was the baggage?

'Burlington,' Washington interrupted. 'We shall send the excess baggage to Burlington and from there to Pennsylvania and our proposed winter camp at Morris Town.'

From the tone alone, Mercer understood the die was cast.

TWENTY

'Here they come, boys! Shoulder your firelocks. Steady as they come. On my order, first volley. Hold yourselves just now!'

Hand and the Pennsylvanians lay nervously behind the low, muddy embankment they had thrown along the Five Mile Run. Some of the men had planted short wooden sticks along the edge to hold their rifles in place; all had loaded powder in their pan, flints sharpened, shot in the barrel, ready for the British. It was largely open on this part of the Princeton road, and the Colonists formed a V-shaped funnel some twenty yards behind the rutted track that passed for a highway. Down it, in a single column, came the British Army: mounted Hessian Jägers, followed by green-coated Hessian foot soldiers, drums banging to maintain a steady march, two troops of light dragoons, two battalions of British highland infantry and a number of six-pounder cannons. It was Cornwallis's vanguard to his full complement, which was faltering behind, as the narrow road had been churned into a quagmire by the weight of men, horses and cannon passing along it.

Conze lay next to Hand. His Stormtroopers were not on the line. They were waiting in position in woods along the Shabakunk Creek, the fall-back position for when the Pennsylvanians could no longer hold Five Mile Run. He had suggested this part of the plan to Hand, who had eagerly embraced it, but had left the

Stormtroopers there. Conze wanted to witness at first hand how ready, how able Hand and his Riflemen were.

The English came further down the line, the first few stepping into the mouth of the American trap.

The tension among the Riflemen was unbearable. Hand cast an eye up and down his line, looking at the faces of his boys, hoping to stop any of them from firing too early. Some of them had been with him since the forming of the Lancaster militia two years earlier, had been through the retreats in New York and New Jersey, were battle-weary, hardened and exhausted, their clothes ragged. How much more would they, could they, give to the cause?

The British drew further into the ambush. The mounted Hessians first, then the foot soldiers, finally the red British troops, Hand, waiting until the moment he thought his boys could maximise the impact, swivelled his head around to cast his eye over the bank. Immediately satisfied, he screamed, 'Let them have it, boys!' and as one the Riflemen raised themselves up the parapet, took aim and fired off a volley of shot. The crack of gunfire was loud and quick, scattering the vanguard, forcing the green and red jackets to flee back towards the main body of Cornwallis's forces.

Within seconds the Colonists recognised the discipline and battle readiness of Cornwallis's troops, for almost immediately, they lined up outside of the funnel in a line three deep, ready to return fire. Hand screamed out: 'Second volley!'

Conze had no sooner heard that cry than the whistle of shot passed him. Battle had begun in earnest.

This was a different kind of fight to that which he had become accustomed in another age. The ponderous nature of loading and reloading of both the American long rifle and the English infantry rifle, created a strange, almost balletic atmosphere. Technology did not allow for the rapidity and brutality he had become accustomed to. Accuracy seemed rare. After the opening rounds of both sides, Conze could see no evidence that any men had been struck on either side. He reflected on the fighting he had undertaken in France, wounded by a sniper shot to his left leg, and the brutal hand-to-hand fighting in the streets of ruined Russian cities in an Eastern Front winter that was far more treacherous than the New Jersey winter of 1776. How different to what he was witnessing, how much easier, he considered, for this theatre to bend to his will.

Then he became aware that men were falling along the British line. As the Colonists got their range, so accuracy improved. Nevertheless, fearlessly, the British line started to advance, slowly, but confidently, returning fire.

It was something to behold, Conze thought. The manner in which the British and Hessians strode purposefully forward and stopped, the front row firing, the second row readying, the third row preparing, then the second row and the third replacing the first. Hundreds of men, shoulder to shoulder, elbow against elbow. Total discipline while under fire. Boom! A synchronised line of fire. Over the din, he heard a voice of authority: 'Rear row – make ready! Second Row – load and prime! Front row – present, fire!' Another volley, another boom. Then repeat commands and a further volley and that sharp boom again. Men moving expertly in front of the preceding line, a perfect rhythm, moving inexorably towards the Americans. Within a minute, each row had fired a volley. Now along the Colonists' line came screams and shouts, followed by low moaning and a singular cry of 'Mother!' Wherever battle took place it was always to the sound of young men in pain screaming 'Mother!', Conze reflected.

'Fire at will!' shouted Hand, but the line had already started to do just that, as the different loading speed of the Riflemen began to undermine their synchronicity.

The British line halted. Hand understood what was happening. 'Preparing for cannon, boys!'

Shot continued to pepper from both sides, wafts of smoke drifting dreamily together in the middle of the field. For an instant, the British were covered in a thin mist. Then came the whoosh of the canister. It flew over their heads and buried itself twenty yards further down the field. 'Getting range, lads, they're getting range. Keep your firing.'

Conze began to feel the heat of the battle, such as he had never experienced before, a different kind of brutality. The enemy here was closer than in the battlefield warfare he had known. Little more than fifty yards separated the two sides. Some of the smells – old sweated clothes worn for months on end, foul breath, nausea, shit and piss, fear itself – he recognised, but there was a different layer rising to the top, not the lubricated, mechanical stench of 1945, but the bad-egg stink of gunpowder. It pervaded everything, tickling his throat, making him gag. Conze gasped for something fresh in the air, but all he found was more sickly egg.

And his ears were burned by the din of the battle. The popping of the American muskets close by him, the drumming and thrumming of the cannon shot, shrieks and cries from the wounded, confused and contradictory shouts of command; he even thought he heard drum, bugle and pipes in the melange. The cacophony of hell itself.

A gust of wind raised the mist of spent gunpowder, the Redcoats appeared once again. Their line still held firm, the magnificence of the tomato-red coats shining brilliantly against the grey pallor of the day.

'We keep holding! Daniel Jones, back to your post!' Hand screamed at a young man, panic scribbled across his mud-lined face. The boy was no more than sixteen, Conze thought, his face smeared with dirt and grease, mouth black from chewing the wrap off his powder, ragged fingernails blackened by the powder, thumbs callused from constant cocking, checked himself, threw himself on to his back on the ground and shouted, 'Fresh flint! My flint's no good!'

Then an explosion to their right. The British guns had found their range from the embankment on the other side of the road. A huge tower of mud and water flew into the sky; in its midst the white blouse of a man, the torso detached from its legs. As the dirt fell back, Conze could see the explosion had taken at least three men with it. These primitive cannon, he thought, should not be underestimated.

The British line inched closer. Soon they would be near enough to use their bayonets, an advance over the Pennsylvanians whose long rifles could not hold a knife. Hand gave a quick look around to his far left; the English had slightly wheeled their line and already Redcoats were preparing to run, their bayonets at the ready. The Colonists were in danger of being overrun, so Hand cried out, 'Fall back! Back to the creek!'

At that moment Hand was worried that he had left it too late, but the men were ready and as one they turned their backs, stooped low and ran away from their earthworks and towards the trees that marked the end of the Five Mile Run. They had the benefit of a few moments before the British would reach the top of the embankment and get a free view of the fleeing Colonists. Earlier that day, he had some of the men make the run, so he could have a good idea of how much time they needed to be safely within the woods before the grenadiers could open fire from the top of the constructed ridge. Had he timed it right?

His heart thumping, his rifle stretched out before him, Hand made it into the pine copse, and took sanctuary behind the second line of trees. Around him his Riflemen flew in. Conze was by his side once again. Hand had timed it well. As the Redcoats ascended the ridge, not one of his men, aside from those injured in the opening exchanges, was left in the field. The British troops stopped as they reached the top.

Their enemy had vanished into the woods. The failure to engage in open combat frustrated the British. For a time there was quiet on the battlefield. The British began to reorder themselves into the single line they had held coming from Princeton. The wounded, including two Colonists, were taken to the back of the lines to be treated.

Hand and Conze watched all this from the edge of the copse.

'A good start, Edward,' said the German.

'I'd rather not have lost those men to that cannon, and two others wounded by the looks of it. I thought I saw George McCarthy lying out; I don't want to have to explain to his father the Brits have his boy. He may never see him again.'

'But the tactics worked as planned. You held them back. They appear disorientated. Your men did well with their long rifles. Now we need to let loose Forrest's artillery to hold them still longer.'

'And then we'll see if your Stormtroopers are as good as their name suggests, Werner,' replied Hand. Looking about him, he saw Captain Thomas Forrest, his six guns ready. 'Tommy Forrest, in your own time, open fire. Hold them here for a while yet and then fall back to Trenton. Don't lose any of the bloody cannon. I'd rather you leave earlier than wait too long. Obergruppenführer Conze tells me his Stormtroopers can pick them off.'

'Colonel Hand, we're going to let them have a blast any moment now. We have them in range. We're loaded and ready for 'em.'

'What you waiting for then? Give 'em hell and now!'

And within seconds the American artillery was peppering the British line with howitzers. It had the immediate impact they had hoped for: further confusion in the British lines and a delay while Cornwallis called up his own guns to train and then fire back on the Colonists' arsenal. As their shot came screaming through the woods, bringing down branches and trees, Forrest immediately gave an order to pull back. Thick ropes appeared and with them tough men from the Pennsylvanian coal mines, hauling the guns through ready-made tracks in the undergrowth.

For twenty minutes, the British cannonry threw everything at the woods. Then Cornwallis halted the firing and sent a dozen scouts ahead to the trees. They gingerly made their way through destroyed trunks and battered stumps, coming to the line where the trees were unharmed, and slowly entered the forest, rifles pointed ahead of them, bayonets fixed.

There among the treetops awaited a further surprise for these British grenadiers.

As the scouts moved in, there was a sudden crack and two fell to the ground. The others looked around them in confusion. They barely had time to figure out where the firing was coming from before they were all cut down. The Stormtroopers had their first kills in the war for American independence.

In the open field, Cornwallis watched for the return of his scouts. For ten minutes or more, he held firm and then cursed aloud: 'These woods need to be cleared!', before sending in the Jäger infantry to do just that.

Again the Hessians advanced into the wood and again the Stormtroopers executed brilliantly their response, picking off individuals before the rest of the infantry fled from the wood.

Furious, Cornwallis screamed at his artillery to move up the road. 'Destroy these woods and these rebels, hiding like monkeys within them!'

'Time to go,' said Conze to Hand. Whistling a series of low notes, the fifty Stormtroopers he had placed among the branches, at once eased themselves down from their positions to the ground and set off to retreat to the next position. Hand marvelled at their calm movements. They were agile, fast and quiet.

Within minutes, these Stormtroopers had met up with the Riflemen at a third point, a small ravine, known locally as the Stockton Hollow, which looked down upon the road, no more than half a mile from the centre of Trenton.

They had a longer wait now. Cornwallis had been convinced

that the main body of Washington's army had engaged with them in the trees and spent the best part of thirty minutes grinding the woods into kindling and splinters. But of the American army, there was no sign, which only added to the confusion of the British. It took a further half hour before the general came to accept that the woods were now empty and he had not been fighting the entire Continental Army, before he understood he was a victim of delaying tactics, cursed loudly and had his troops reform. There was not much daylight left and he was still a long way from Trenton. Consequently, he placed some cannon at the front of his columns, prepared to fire at the earliest opportunity and set off down the Post Road once more. This time he would not be stopped.

It was this formation that met the combined Riflemen and Stormtroopers at fifteen minutes past three, the light beginning its descent into wintry darkness.

The Stormtroopers, with their shorter-range weaponry, were placed closer to the enemy, the Riflemen further back, but, on the signal from Hand, both sets let roar with a cascade of shot that pelted the front and middle range of the British columns. Cornwallis's preparation though proved good. Within a few minutes, his guns were firing. The first fusillade from his cannons pierced the top of the ravine. Miraculously, no one was injured, as trees splintered and crashed to the ground above them, but the warning sign was clear to the joint leaders. 'We need to get the hell out of here, Werner. These guns are going to going to do for us.'

From the top of the ravine, Forrest's repositioned artillery replied to the British.

Conze shouted to Hand above the din, 'Take the Riflemen first. We'll keep them off with covering fire while Forrest makes his retreat.'

Hand nodded his assent and passed the message down the line. The Riflemen drew away as Forrest's guns hammered away their reply. Finally, the coal miners picked up the ropes and started to drag the guns back to Trenton, while the Stormtroopers maintained their fire as best they could. In truth, there was not a man among them who did not curse the primitive nature of their weaponry, who yearned for the reliability of a Karabiner 98, or even better the metal regularity of a Maschinengewehr 42. They had only a few months of training in the musket, but it made little difference. The issue was not the men's capability, but the primitive nature of the weapons. The smooth inner barrel of the musket, the lack of sights, the unreliability of flint and the constant frustration of having to rip and pour powder and to deal with the unpredictable flash in the pan, all restricted their ability to seriously harm the enemy. But then the same was true for their foes: not one of Conze's men received anything more than a slight graze throughout the exchange.

The British cannon continued to roar up the ravine, much more dangerous than the flailing rifle shot, throwing up mud and rock. Once Conze felt Forrest and his artillery had enjoyed enough headway, he called the retreat into Trenton, down the main turnpike. They passed Forrest and his artillery, who were finding the Post Road something of a quagmire on the outskirts of Trenton, the miners swearing as they heaved on the heavy ropes. Conze stopped to ask Forrest:

'How long will you need to get to the bridge, do you think?'

'Once we clear this stretch, we should make it through Trenton quickly. The road is cobbled in places there. But this bit, it's like wading through treacle. We're damned if Cornwallis sends any cavalry ahead.'

'I suspect he won't send any advance horses. We've frightened him enough so that he's putting cannon at the head of his column. He'll have the same problem as you, but let me leave fifty men here with you until you reach the cobbled road.'

So Conze stayed with Forrest and the six guns all the way to

Trenton's main thoroughfare. Cornwallis did not send an advance horse party, but he was managing to move his guns quicker than the Colonists, despite the larger size of his cannon. In the darkening light, Conze saw them inching closer on the horizon. But finally, the American artillery hit the hard road and Forrest went off with his men with a cheery 'See you over the bridge' to Conze.

The Pennsylvanian Riflemen and the Stormtroopers now lay in wait for the British, dotted around the homes and buildings of Trenton, covering the main road down to the Assunpink Bridge and the side streets around it. They waited patiently.

Rifle ends poked through window frames. Men crouched around corners. Riflemen poured their powder. Stormtroopers fixed bayonets. Quietness pervaded the air. The tension was palpable.

Among them darted Pat O'Leary. As the expert gunsmith, he issued fresh flints and powder, and cleaned the rifles of the more callow Riflemen. By the time he had finished, not one of the Americans or Germans was not primed and ready for the British and Hessian attack.

Conze and Hand met once more in the timber doorway of a small cottage. 'Your Riflemen should continue to fall back, Ed. My Stormtroopers know how to fight this kind of battle. They have experience that you cannot imagine in house-to-house fighting.'

'I think I'll struggle to persuade my boys to give up the fight just yet. They sense British blood; they're almost too keen for it. No, we're good for this just now. I think there must be an hour before nightfall; we must do our best to hold them back until then. The general was clear on this.'

Conze looked up at the closing sky. 'My instinct tells me we shall be fine.'

A blast from a Brown Bess signalled the start of the fighting in the streets of Trenton. At first, both sides exchanged long-range fire but within seconds men were upon men in hand-to-hand fighting. The Stormtroopers had quickly abandoned their long rifles, throwing them with disdain to the ground, and attacking the British with either short pistols or knives, but always with total ferocity. The speed at which they moved, the courage they showed in directly throwing themselves at British riflemen with fixed bayonets, was a source of awe to all the Colonists, but none more so than Pat O'Leary.

He was as good as any other with a musket in the open field, but reloading and then shooting in the midst of a street fight was difficult for him. His big hands lacked the flexibility and speed for such immediate combat. After discharging a load though, he was crouched in a doorway pouring a fresh purse of powder when a Redcoat surprised him. The Brit used his bayonet to spin the rifle out of O'Leary's hands and prepared to follow up with a charge. O'Leary thought he was done for. He awaited the plunge of the steel, but it didn't come. Instead, he saw the red jacket lifted into the air and then tossed away as if he were a turnip harvested from the field. It was Lothar Kluggman, the huge blond Stormtrooper who had been taking on all-comers in arm-wrestling five days earlier.

Kluggman was a beast, an absolute beast. He followed the flailing trooper into the open street and stuck his knife into his shako and right through the skull. As Redcoats came streaming into the street, he threw himself at them with his knife and an axe, slicing, cutting, chopping, hacking, and carving up the enemy. At one stage, four grenadiers attacked him together, from all sides. Kluggman dropped his weapons and grabbed the first one by the head. Twisting the soldier's neck with a sickening crunch of bone and muscle, so the head suddenly faced backwards, he turned the torso, and the bayonet charge of the next solder went through his comrade's chest. Releasing one of his massive hands, Kluggman cracked his fist down on that fellow's head, sending him senseless to the ground. As the remaining two men leaped on top of him,

Kluggman bit off the ear of one with a snap of his jaw and then smashed a right hook straight into the nose of the fourth man, so splintering cartilage, flesh and blood flew through the air. He then finished the job with an almighty roar that was just as frightening as anything O'Leary had just witnessed.

'Jesus wept, where did you come from?' O'Leary asked.

But Kluggman could speak no English and simply grunted before moving on, with O'Leary running after him.

The fighting made its way down to the bottom of Green Street. In the fading light, Hand could make out the Colonist forces. They stretched for what seemed like a mile along the east side of the creek, from a contingent on the left side of the Delaware and up to the right by the town millpond. Troops were stationed on top of each other, so they appeared to cover the entire slope from top to bottom. Clever, thought Hand, our forces look greater than they are. And close to the bridge and directly in front of the bridge, blocking its path, were Knox's artillery. He could see Washington, just behind the bridge on his horse. And next to him, also on horseback, von Steuben.

They reached the top of the bridge with the Redcoats hacking and prodding them with bayonets, a problem for the Riflemen. A shot of cannon exploded over their heads. And then a human roar: 'Riflemen, Stormtroopers, retreat now across our lines!' Among them, on top of a chestnut mare, was von Steuben, slashing at the British with his sword. 'Fall back at once!' And then in German, directed at Kluggman who appeared to have no desire to stop the fighting, *'Stoppen Sie jetzt, verdammt!'*

Hand, Conze, O'Leary and the others crossed the bridge, ran past the cannonry and fell scrambling on to the embankment, exhausted, panting, their hearts beating fast. The Irishman looked up when he heard a familiar voice: 'Good sport today, gentlemen?' and then George Washington rode off, back to the bridge.

TWENTY-ONE

Three times Cornwallis threw his troops at the bridge across the Assunpink. Three times the Colonists threw them back, with cannon and musket, until the bridge was stained red with blood.

Night fell and further attacks seemed pointless to Cornwallis. He had his troops withdraw to Trenton and made camp for the night, before readying his plans for a fresh and successful assault the next morning. He had the old fox Washington. He would finish him off before lunch the next day. He would bring this war to a swift end, then he could get out of this damn country and return to Britain.

However, in the darkness, Washington was having his men follow the von Steuben plan.

While a small number of men laboured with picks and shovels on the earth banks, to give the impression they were digging in to repel the expected British advance, and the occasional round of cannon kept the enemy from sleeping too soundly, the rest of the army moved out.

They wrapped the artillery in blankets and quietly withdrew from bridge and bank, by regiments, setting out silently on the back roads to Princeton, a squadron of infantrymen leading the way. By two in the morning, all – aside from the five hundred men Washington had ordered to stay to confuse the enemy – were on the road and heading towards Princeton.

Von Steuben, whose bravery on the Assunpink Bridge had been widely commented upon by both commanders and soldiers, travelled with Mercer. He had asked permission from Washington, who had readily agreed. Nor did the general have any issue with Hanna Reitsch joining them. The Stormtroopers had proved themselves alongside the Pennsylvanian Riflemen. Washington appeared keen to embrace whatever innovation the Germans brought with them, and Reitsch seemed to be just another example of the way they thought differently.

Mercer remained sceptical of the baron and this very modern woman, but could not refuse the request. The necessity for quiet restricted their conversation during the route march, but when Washington sent an order for Mercer and a detachment of his men to destroy a bridge at Worth's Mill, it created an opportunity. Close by the bridge, there was an orchard and Mercer suggested von Steuben and Reitsch join him and his second-in-command, John Haslett, for a walk while charges were set and lit.

'You served under that great monarch Frederick, sir?'

'I was privileged to serve as his aide-de-camp until the close of the war in 1763.'

'We have long studied his victories such as Leuthen, Rossbach and Torgau. I would suggest he is the finest military mind in all of Europe.'

'Europe and probably the world – although perhaps we will be forced to reconsider once these events have played themselves out.'

'Ha! We may indeed, sir, although our general would be far too modest to seek out such comparisons. Why did you not stay on his majesty's staff?'

'I would have hoped to have stayed for a further period, even once the wars had ended and peace had arrived. But I fell victim to an implacable enemy in the court. That, General Mercer, is one of the issues around a monarch: those who look to serve and maintain only themselves. It is one of the benefits of a republic, sir. The lack of sycophancy, of plotting.'

Mercer nodded in agreement. 'I am sure there will be vices as well as virtues in any republic we form. That said, I have witnessed first hand the brutal tyranny of monarchs. I was a young surgeon, not yet twenty, in Bonnie Prince Charlie's army at Culloden. I saw the brutality not just on the field, but after. The best of my nation, friends, relatives, hunted down and slaughtered in their beds or in front of their wee ones. I was in hiding and smuggled myself out to this continent. Here we regard your Frederick as the very model of an enlightened monarch. If King George had demonstrated a tiny bit of the common sense of your king, I daresay we would not be fighting his army and there would be no talk of a republic.'

'I would agree with you. Unfortunately, although a monarch may be absolute, he may not be absolute on the details of those around him. As I said: there was an enemy and I suffered as a result.'

'The name, sir, of this enemy?'

Von Steuben had no recollection of a name, as Conze had never provided one in his briefings. He toyed with creating one. He also wanted to avoid coming close to why the real von Steuben had been forced out of Frederick's court: his homosexuality. 'I would rather not divulge it, sir. One is never sure how far the tentacles of a beast reach. Perhaps when our adventures have brought us closer to friendship, then, over a glass or two of brandy, I may allow myself – through a slip of the tongue – a name, to perhaps allow you some security.'

Sensing the unease, Reitsch aimed to deflect the questioning: 'And you, General Mercer, I believe you and General Washington both served together in the British army.'

Mercer turned to face her, a smile across his face. 'Indeed, madame. We served together under Johnny Forbes in the attack on Fort Duquesne, back in fifty-eight. I then retired to Fredericksberg, and took up medicine once more. George and myself were both members of the Masonic Temple, so we retained our close friendship. Indeed, I bought my family home at Ferry Farm from him. So I am as close to General Washington as any man can be. And as loyal.'

Reitsch thought to herself, And you may shortly see the price of that loyalty.

'General, I think we have a problem.' Haslett pointed up to the ridge along which ran the Princeton to Trenton road. Down it marched a column of British troops.

Von Steuben and Reitsch looked at each other, he making a curt nod towards her. Once again Conze's preparation was proving to be excellent.

'Come, let us quickly prepare. Men fall into line! The enemy is upon us!' Mercer yelled, as he mounted his horse and galloped towards his troops.

The 300 men under his control were surprised; it took them some minutes to collect both their weapons and their wits. By which time, the British were off the road, down the hillside and marching towards them, preparing an opening volley as they went. Eighty yards away, they stopped, presented arms and a burst of fire followed. The barrage had no bite, however, and not one colonist was hit. Mercer ordered his troops to return fire. One volley fired and was met almost instantly by a return from the British, to which the Americans replied. Mercer's line was forced to step back, until it was mostly in the orchard.

Men began to fall, as much from shot ricocheting off trees as from the accuracy of the marksmen. A burst of cannon from the British brought down several limbs of an ancient apple tree, more annoying to the Colonists than dangerous. But the battle was soon bloody; casualties began to mount on both sides as they exchanged shots for a good ten minutes. Then the British made a significant change in tactic – a bayonet charge.

The Colonists, with their bayonet-less muskets, were at a definite disadvantage. Mercer had no option. 'Retreat!' he roared and almost at once his boys ran for their lives deeper into the orchard. In the chaos, they gave up the two small cannon that they had brought with them, which were soon turned on them by the British overrunning the line.

Throughout, remaining on horseback, von Steuben and Reitsch had kept their distance from Mercer and Haslett, staying behind the front line. They had a forewarning of how events would play out and now they saw it becoming real.

In the scramble to retreat, Mercer had become detached from the main body of his men to the right. As the Scotsman attempted to restore order to his retreating line, a British rifleman shot his horse from under him. Mercer was thrown to the ground, the horse, thrashing about next to him, threw itself wildly about in agony. Very quickly, Mercer was surrounded by a small group of British soldiers. 'Surrender, you fucking rebel!' one of them shouted.

'Damn you, damn you all!' cried Mercer, advancing a few steps towards them, slashing his sword in the air. There was a stand-off, the British seeming unsure of what to do. They had an American general. That was some prize, but the order of the day was to take no prisoners.

Now Haslett, von Steuben and Reitsch rode towards the group. Mercer, spotting them, cried out, 'Damn you, help is at hand!'

But von Steuben shouted at the Redcoats: 'That is General George Washington, you would do well to leave him!'

Mercer looked puzzled. Why? What? he thought, but the announcement changed the British. Immediately, they lost any reticence.

'Hey up, lads, it's that cunt Washington!'

'You fucking shit, you deserve this,' said another, as he plunged his bayonet into Mercer's chest.

Suddenly there was a frenzy of stabbing, Mercer disappearing under a blanket of red. Von Steuben fired his musket into the body of the men, the shot pelleting three of them in the back and buttocks. Waving his cutlass, the German charged his horse into them and they ran from the scene. Haslett jumped down from his horse, scrambled to Mercer's side and lifted up the wounded general's head. He was alive, terribly wounded, but alive.

Squinting up at von Steuben on his horse, Haslett screamed, 'Why did you say that? Why single him out as General Washington? Why did you not save General Mercer?'

But he would ask no more questions, for Reitsch raised her pistol and deposited a shot clean to Haslett's forehead, fracturing his skull instantly.

Mercer lay on the ground, blood seeping from a number of wounds, and yet he was still conscious. 'Cover me,' von Steuben whispered to Reitsch, who turned her horse so as to hide him from any onlookers as he dismounted.

On the ground, he lifted Mercer's head. 'Help me, Baron. My wounds are great, but I may yet survive.'

'I think not,' replied von Steuben and with a flash of his knife, he pierced the general's heart.

TWENTY-TWO

What might have been a rout was saved by the sudden appearance on the field of two factors.

First, a thousand militia under Cadwalader arrived. They both stopped the flight of Mercer's men, and also held down the British and resisted their advance. However, as the British reorganised themselves into a battle line, the weakness of the Americans became obvious. These men had little combat experience, basic military orders and manoeuvres were beyond them, and once the British line had recomposed itself and started to enjoy success, the American line broke easily again: at first a few and then the majority started to run. At that moment, the second factor altered the course of the day.

Riding into their midst came Washington. Once more he demonstrated the innate bravery that was his greatest strength. Going over to Cadwalader's fleeing men, he calmly, but loudly, said to them: 'Parade with us, my brave fellows! There is but a handful of the enemy and we shall have them directly!'

Now they stopped in their tracks and in a rough and ready way reformed a line. Holding them firm, Washington sent messages to the brigades of the Virginian and New England Continentals that they should go to the right side of the line. Order restored, impervious to the musket shot that fell close to him, Washington, with his hat on his head, rode forward, waving for the Colonists to follow him. Again, in an extraordinarily calm voice, he shouted, 'Wait for my command before you shoot. Let us be ready!'

His disdain for his own safety steeled his men amid musket and cannon shot. Fifty yards from the British line, he turned his horse, faced his men and simply said 'Halt!' Then he cracked as close to a smile as he was capable and said, 'Fire!'

Von Steuben and Reitsch watched from the edge of the orchard, Mercer's dead body lying across the baron's horse. It was theatre, wonderful theatre. And both the Colonists and the British had met Washington's order of 'Fire', so that both the field and orchard were covered in a dusty white cloud, enveloping the screams and madness of a ferocious firefight. The Germans both wondered if that was the last they would see of Washington, but the cloud lifted and there he was, still on his horse, urging his men forward, the British line buckling under the Americans' advance.

Von Steuben turned to Reitsch. 'Conze will be disappointed. I failed to rally the troops. But history was right: George Washington really was something.'

TWENTY-THREE

It was the Continental Army's finest day.

Washington's intervention turned a rout in an orchard into a famous victory. The British fled the field, down the highway, Mawhood looking to join up with Cornwallis who, at the same time, was learning that the full Continental Army was not waiting for him on the other side of the Assunpink Bridge and that his enemy had sprung the greatest of surprises.

The main body of Washington's army now marched on to Princeton where they overwhelmed a small group, whose resistance ended with a white flag being lowered from Nassau Hall and 194 British regulars surrendering.

But the biggest prize of all was the British army's winter supply depot in New Brunswick, a few hours' march from Princeton. And that was the aim of the joint force of Stormtroopers and Pennsylvanian Riflemen who had bypassed the fighting in Princeton and were closing in on their target.

The weather was good for marching: cold, but not too cold, an absence of wind, rain or snow, the turnpike to New Brunswick in good condition. They encountered little on the road, the occasional jig and carriage, but no British forces. They were making such good time, they stopped for half an hour or so of snap and grog. At that stop, Hand reflected on the differences between Conze's Stormtroopers and his own Riflemen.

First, there was the appearance. The Americans were a ragged outfit. The Pennsylvanian Riflemen were the elite force of the Continental Army, insofar there wasn't a man among them not wearing boots or in possession of at least a jacket if not a winter coat. But their clothes looked what they were: whatever had come to hand when they had first left their town houses or farmsteads eight months or more ago, worn out from months of sleeping rough, of marching across the country; patched, frayed, worn out. But the Stormtroopers' grey-green uniforms were smooth and elegant, their belts and boots shone in the winter sun. They appeared to have been freshly laundered and they all looked the same. They looked like an army.

Then there was the physical appearance. Throughout the march, it was obvious after only a few miles that the Riflemen were holding back the Stormtroopers. Now, as they brewed coffee in an open field, the Pennsylvanians lay exhausted on the ground, barely able to move, whereas the Stormtroopers gave the appearance of being as fresh as the moment they had started. Many of the Americans had immediately fallen asleep, few of them had the energy to talk, whereas a group of the Germans had started a ball game while the others were laughing and shouting at each other. Hand could not only see the difference, he felt the difference. He and O'Leary sat on the ground, exhausted, staring at the earth, their bodies aching from five hours of marching, still feeling the effects of the previous day's fighting.

'Edward, Pat, coffee, here.' Conze stood above them, offering tin cups. Tall, his blond hair short-cropped, blue eyes, chiselled cheeks, muscular, the epitome of a Stormtrooper.

O'Leary grunted and took his, Hand made to stand up to receive his.

'Stay, stay seated, you need to rest. Here.' Conze handed him the drink. Hand gulped down the lukewarm, sugared drink. Conze dropped down on to his haunches.

'You are feeling it, no?'

'You could say that,' replied Hand. 'Your Stormtroopers, where do they get their energy? They're like supermen.'

Conze laughed. 'That's because they are. They are highly trained professional soldiers, they are the elite. Your Riflemen are, what, farmhands, clerks, mechanics? They are serving a cause, but this is not their life, is it? When this war is over, they will go back to their families and live again the lives they had before, but the Stormtroopers, well, they will look for another battle. They will return to Europe or perhaps they will expand your frontier. They can easily overcome the savages of the wild lands. But they will not lose their discipline. That is what they have. The discipline to look after their bodies. They regard their bodies as a tool, a tool they need to maintain.'

'When I first saw you parading at Trenton, I commented to Pat that you reminded me of the Spartans at Thermopylae.'

'Oh, that is good, we will take that, Edward Hand!' Conze laughed again. 'A wonderful analogy. It is my belief that a small group of individuals, highly trained and focused, the flower of their generation, could defeat far larger forces. That could certainly be the case here in America.'

'I fear we are holding you back.'

Conze replied bluntly: 'That is the case, yes. Left alone, we would be in New Brunswick by now. But I hope by our exertions and example, we may inspire some of your boys. That there will be among the Riflemen, some who may say, "I would like to develop like these Stormtroopers". That would be as great a victory for us today as seizing the winter supplies of the British. That they may take inspiration and look to learn and adopt our methods.'

Their conversation ended because the six-man scout team Conze had sent on ahead appeared among them.

'Obergruppenführer.' Another impossibly perfect Stormtrooper stood before them. 'New Brunswick is but thirty minutes away.

142

As you predicted, it is poorly defended. There are no guards before the town. By the waterfront there are twenty wagons. There is a redoubt. The treasury may be there. Overall, just under one hundred men. They appear unprepared for any attack.'

'Good work, Oberführer Breitner. So your suggested plan for an assault?'

'We continue along the turnpike. At the town's edge, we divide our forces. The major body continues along the Albany Road to the waterfront, makes a direct attack. A second force approaches from behind. There is a track.'

Conze nodded his head, 'We need to secure the landing. That is our route to Morris Town. There is a bridge?'

'To the west of the depot. Primitive. Wooden, but we can cross.'

'Very well. Speed is of the essence. We have to pick this English pocket and be off to Morris Town before the English general Cornwallis turns up here.'

The Riflemen had secured the wagons and were ready to move out of New Brunswick. The defence of the depot had been close to pathetic. The Stormtroopers had approached from the front, the Riflemen from behind; after a couple of volleys, and no casualties, the British had surrendered. In truth, there were no more than fifty Redcoats, and the depot consisted mostly of unarmed civilians, camp followers and sutlers. There were around forty women, wives of British troops who acted as cooks and nurses for the army, and a few children. The soldiery had been disarmed and the whole group was standing or sitting in a cleared area in front of the redoubt.

There were eighteen wagons, loaded with winter supplies for Cornwallis's army. One wagon was full of tents, something the Continental Army was in dire need of, another held uniforms, winter clothing and even linen. Then there were the dry foodstuffs, barrels of pork and beef, sacks of potatoes, onions, parsnips, carrots, oatmeal and flour, enough to feed an army for the winter. A wagon full of porter was especially welcome, but more useful were the three carriages stocked with fresh shot and rifles. Cornwallis had lost a battle even greater than those of Trenton and Princeton. He had lost the means to keep his army in the field. He would have no option but to return to New York for the winter with the main body of his troops. What forces could be maintained outside of the city would be forced to scavenge off the locals.

However, in the redoubt they found a further, greater prize: a treasure chest of £70,000. The entire war chest for the British army in the Americas, to be used to pay the British soldiers, mercenaries and spies, to acquire further food and armaments. Seventy thousand pounds, an unbelievable amount of money, that would immediately ease the financial worries of Washington and his army.

Now they had to move out quickly before Cornwallis and his troops could reach New Brunswick.

Hand gave the order, the covered wagons made their way across the wooden bridge, over the Raitan River and off towards Morris Town, where the rest of the Continental Army was already headed. It was a thirty-mile journey. If the weather held up, they could be safely camped with the rest of the army the following morning. As the carriages left, so did the remaining Riflemen, and Hand joined Conze, who was standing among the Stormtroopers guarding the captured British. The plan was for the Stormtroopers to stay for an hour or so in New Brunswick, so if Cornwallis was able to send an advance party of cavalry ahead, the Germans could delay them.

'We have started the march to Morris Town. I shall see you further along the road before we reach it, I suppose?'

'Yes, we'll stay here, give you a head start – and still beat you to Morris Town!'

'I'm sure you will. And what will you do with these prisoners?'

'I'm not sure just now what to do with them.'

'General Washington is adamant that we must treat all prisoners, in his words, "with humanity". The British have been brutal towards many of our men; we have no wish to match them.'

'Then what would you have me do with them?'

'I would organise them and have them march with us to Morris Town for now. We could then send them to work on those farms that lack hands because of men serving in the army. We have done that before.'

'They will slow me down though,' replied Conze.

'It would take no more than a dozen men to guard and march them; they don't have to be part of your main body.'

Conze looked away vaguely in the direction of the prisoners. 'I will think about it. Get on with you now, you can't afford to wait any longer.'

There was something in his tone that alarmed Hand. Nevertheless he agreed, shook Conze's hand and moved off with O'Leary.

They had crossed the wooden bridge, walking at a fair pace, when they heard gunfire, considerable gunfire, one volley, followed quickly by another.

'Cornwallis is upon us!' shouted O'Leary.

The two men stopped in their tracks on the high ground. They had a clear view of the waterfront area of New Brunswick. And if they could not see clearly what was happening, they saw enough to realise that Cornwallis was not attacking New Brunswick. Without thinking further, Hand ran back immediately across the bridge, followed by O'Leary.

What they saw shocked them.

There was a mound of bodies where the prisoners had previously stood: men, women and children, soldiers and civilians, bloodied, fallen where they had been hit. Around them a group of Stormtroopers were prodding bodies, stabbing bodies. To the right, a group of a dozen women had been separated and were being dragged away by a group of Germans. There was little doubt about what was going to happen to them.

Breathless, Hand ran up to Conze, who was supervising the executions.

'What the fuck is happening?'

Conze was surprised, taken aback. 'It is war. It happens.'

'What happens? I told you, Washington has been clear. We have to treat them with humanity. What are those men doing over there with those women?'

Conze looked over and dismissed the scene. 'These men have travelled thousands of miles to come here. They won a famous victory yesterday; it is only natural that they look for a way to satisfy their urges, their natural urges. None of those women has gone without agreement. They had a choice.'

'To my eye they appear anything but willing. What choice have you given them? Stand there and be gunned down or go off and be raped? You call that a choice? And is this the behaviour you expect from your professional, disciplined supermen? Or do you condone it?'

Conze moved closer to Hand.

'My friend, this is war, this is what we call "total war". If you wish to win this war, you cannot play at it. You have to be prepared to do what it takes. Our regiment has a simple motto: "Terror must be broken by terror." That is what we are doing.'

'What terror? These people surrendered immediately. They had no weapons, no defence, you have killed them in the most terrible way.'

'It will send a message to anyone who dares oppose us: that all opposition will be stamped into the ground. Whether they are Americans who stay loyal to the king, the British who come here to fight us, the savage Indians or the Negroes on the plantation, whoever they are, wherever they are, they have to learn. Strength and power, only a heart of iron brings victory. Listen to me, my friend, I have no time to play games. I am here to win and I will do all that it takes to achieve victory. The question you have to ask yourselves, Edward Hand and Patrick O'Leary, is: are you prepared to do what it takes to win?'

TWENTY-FOUR

'Hugh Mercer was my finest friend. He and I had seen so much together. It breaks my heart that he will not live into a grand old age, surrounded by grandchildren, entertaining them with stories of his glorious past. His is the first great sacrifice of this war. Gentlemen and Frau Reitsch, I ask you to raise your glasses.'

In the midst of triumph, despair.

From the military command down to the lowest foot soldier, the events of the past week seemed little short of miraculous and a cause for nothing but celebration; for George Washington, the victories were bitter-sweet.

He had lost his best friend, his closest confidant, a man weathered by experience into being the best adviser possible.

Mercer was gone.

Washington felt the loss keenly. Who would now fill that gap for him? He loved Knox, Greene and Hamilton in equal measure, but they were callow youths, blindly loyal, but lacking the experience of age. He could not trust those two-faced bastards Lee and Gates. He found the likes of Sullivan, Ewing and Cadwalader lacking in something: too often their judgement was poor; they lacked the ability to read situations and impose their will on their men and the other generals. There was one man he recognised as having those skills, but could he really put his faith in von

Steuben? A man he had barely met, yet one who had delivered the victories they had been so desperate for.

'To Hugh Mercer, a true patriot.'

'A true patriot!' echoed around the room in Arnold's Tavern, which Washington had taken as his staff headquarters. The glasses chinked in the darkening light, the rum quickly drunk, followed by refills. Knox, Greene, Hamilton, Sullivan, Ewing, Cadwalader, von Steuben and Reitsch were all present, awaiting news of the raid on New Brunswick.

They had swiftly turned Morris Town into an army town. Washington, Hamilton, Knox and Greene had taken rooms in the taverns; the others dispersed among private houses, over which aides were presently negotiating with the owners. Quartermaster General Tom Mifflin had immediately set up a supply depot in the county courthouse. English prisoners were in the town jail. The Baptist and Presbyterian churches were now hospitals, and outside the tavern, on the town green, the army itself lay, literally. Through the windows, if they had cared to, the generals could have made out the flickering fires of an army at rest. Exhausted, the Continental Army had arrived at the green and as one had simply fallen on to the ground, made camp and slept. Those arriving late had made makeshift camps in private gardens, orchards and the highway itself. Already, it was difficult to move through Morris Town. Within a day, the stench itself would be overpowering and the town would be an open sewer.

'George, we must plan. Is this to be our headquarters for the rest of the winter?' asked Sullivan.

'Yes. It's perfectly placed. Two days' march from New York and Pennsylvania. High enough for us to easily discover any movements on the part of Cornwallis or Howe. It's easily defended, the locals are loyal and round about are local trades and industry. I cannot think of anywhere better. I have sent word for Martha to come join me here. I would suggest you send dispatches to your

149

own families. We could do with the joy of women about us. I fancy a few nights of dancing would lift our spirits still further.'

'Hurrah to that,' said Greene.

'Agreed, but what are we do with the men? They are sprawled out all over the town. We have to put some order into the town. I would suggest we draw up some plans immediately,' said Knox, pouring himself another glass of rum.

'My immediate concern is the avoidance of disease,' replied Washington, clenching his jaw, raw with pain as usual. 'We must ensure our army and militias do not continue to suffer from the diseases that are more likely to defeat us than the British army in battle. I am especially concerned about an outbreak of the pox.'

'Organise the men in ranks on the green, with plenty of fresh air between them, that'll do,' said Ewing.

'Frankly, James, that will not do,' replied Washington sternly. 'We should have all troops here in Morris Town, and those supporting them, inoculated against smallpox as soon as possible, by the spring perhaps, and continue this process for all new recruits.'

'The entire army inoculated! Totally impractical,' Sullivan erupted.

'Not to mention the dangers of further contamination,' argued Cadwalader. 'I'm not convinced by this inoculation business. From what I can see, the science is unproven. My understanding is you give healthy people the pox itself and among them a size-able number go on to die of the disease and it spreads. There is a danger that the whole army would go down with the pox. And what is more, it could spread to the civilian populace. It is too much of a risk, George.'

Ewing, emboldened by the support, re-engaged, 'Which is why the Congress issued a proclamation only last June prohibiting surgeons from inoculating the soldiery.'

'John is correct, General,' responded Knox. 'We simply don't have the resources to inoculate everyone. When we were in

Boston last March and the pox broke out, you used a brigade of men formerly contaminated by the disease to help us maintain the city. But we discovered that less than three-quarters of our men were safe. So, we would have to inoculate three-quarters of our men, which would be at least, what, six thousand men here in Morris Town alone.'

'And inoculation will take men from the field. All those inoculated suffer a small form of the disease. They will need time to recuperate,' added Greene. 'I'm in agreement that we should seek to inoculate, but the whole army by February, no, that is simply impractical.'

'And if the British hear of this? Well, they will attack, winter or no winter,' said Cadwalader.

'We can manage this by isolation. That is the proven way. Put those affected in hospitals,' Sullivan said. 'That's what you did at Boston, sir. You isolated men, restricted access to the camp and checked refugees. We had no epidemic. We controlled it.'

The room was against Washington, but as he was about to reply, to attempt to cajole for his generals' support, von Steuben spoke up.

'If I may, gentlemen? I would agree with General Washington. We cannot afford *not* to make this our first priority. Listen, the British and German forces are inoculated. My men are inoculated. This is what happens in Europe. It is only your army and the militia that are not. If it is safe enough for European armies to inoculate themselves, with no side effects, it should be safe itself for this army. There is an epidemic across the colonies now. You witnessed this in Boston and it harmed, no, ended, your advances in Canada. You cannot be blind to it. If we do not act now, we run the very real risk of being overwhelmed by smallpox.'

'The retreat in Canada had more to do with Montgomery's death and that blunderhead Benedict Arnold than smallpox,' interrupted Ewing.

151

'I would beg to differ, sir, and I suggest history will agree with me. But why take such a risk? Make inoculation our priority. Throw everything at it and the issue is settled.'

'I know only too well myself the destructive impact of the pox. I suffered it in Barbados when I was nineteen,' said Washington, and the others saw it in the facial scars that marked his face. 'Terrible, most terrible. There may have been tactical errors in Canada last spring, but the major cause was the loss of men to the pox, as the baron says. That broke our men and forced the retreat to Ticonderoga.'

'Aye,' replied Sullivan. 'That is true. But a total inoculation as you and he are recommending is simply not practical.'

'Then it must become practical. We have to ensure that this disease does not infect the army again. That deplorable situation in Canada must not be repeated. For in truth's sake, we have more to dread from it than the sword of the enemy. An epidemic of the pox would end this war. And not in our favour. The baron is right. And now, when we have victories under our belt, the British are wounded and winter approaches, now is the time to undertake this mass inoculation. Hamilton, send word to Doctor Shippen, the director of the Hudson Hospitals. He, I believe is the best man to organise this process. Have him come immediately, as soon as he can organise the necessary supplies for the inoculation.'

'I would offer my Stormtroopers to assist him. They run no risk of the disease and are well drilled in the organisation necessary to run a mass inoculation.'

'Thank you, Baron. Thank you.'

Sullivan, red in the face, now said: 'Congress will not approve, George. They simply will not have this.'

'Congress be damned, John. Have they not asked me to win this war and presented me with the powers to achieve such an outcome?'

'General Washington, if I may, Frau Reitsch and myself have some other suggestions that are pertinent to our situation.'

'Please, Baron.'

'We have to organise our troops in a way that minimises the threat of disease among them, but also maximises the potential for discipline. We have in this last week achieved tremendous victories, but we have to use the next few months to ensure that when the British come at us again in the spring, we are more than ready for them. And that begins with the layout of the camp. Hanna has found the best place.'

'We cannot camp here in Morris Town,' Reitsch explained. 'The town cannot cope with our army, especially if, as we hope, we add to our numbers. The buildings are not fit for purpose and they reduce the land available. If we cram ourselves into Morris Town, we will inevitably breed disease. We have to look elsewhere. There is an area just to the south-east close to the Lowantica Brook. The brook will provide fresh water. The land has a slight slope, which will give protection from the winter winds and storms. I would suggest we immediately start to build log cabins to house most, if not all, of the men. If we provide good housing, we will be more successful in attracting further men to our cause.'

'There is also room for a parade ground,' added von Steuben. 'This army needs to be drilled, trained to the standard of the British and Germans if we are going to win this war. I think it was you, General Cadwalader, who remarked before Princeton that the Continental Army lacked the discipline of the British. I would respectfully suggest that my senior men could be used to help raise standards across the army and the militias.'

'How do you know of this area then?' asked Sullivan suspiciously.

'When we arrived in the continent, I asked Hanna to scout the colony for prospective camps.'

'And I sent out two prospectors to do that for me.'

'You have spies, spies about the land?' asked Sullivan, suspicion turning to thoughts of conspiracy.

'I wouldn't call them spies,' replied Reitsch. 'Agents, if you like, not spies. They have experience of establishing camps for armies throughout Europe. They understand what is required to keep a modern army in the field. They recommended Lowantica Brook. Our good fortune is that it lies so close to Morris Town that the high command can stay here, while the main army are there.' She met Sullivan's glare of antagonism with a steely response. She was not finished yet.

'It is vitally important that we establish the camp in such a way that we can maintain order and discipline among the men. We are moving into a new period. We have to plan for the winning of the war and for the peace that comes after.'

'The peace that comes after?' Greene was puzzled.

'Yes, sir. Once the British are defeated, you will still require an army.'

There was a murmuring of discontent. Experienced war generals they might all have been, but to a man they did not envisage a new America with a standing army. Local militias, perhaps, but a standing army, no. Von Steuben sensed that Reitsch had gone too far.

'What Frau Reitsch means is that the wild lands to the west will require pacification, and for that you will require an army well organised and ready to achieve that purpose. It will take many long decades, a century perhaps. And you have to be mindful of any threat from the French, or even the British from Canada.'

'The French are our allies, sir,' replied Cadwalader.

'They are for now, but history teaches us that allies can soon become enemies. But we are running ahead of ourselves. The issue we face today is the encampment of our troops.'

'It is my fault, gentlemen.' Reitsch realised she was in danger of losing her audience. 'Please forgive me. This area I am proposing will also give us room to construct sheds for our horses and build a commissary area to feed the men properly.'

'There is a saying in Europe that "an army marches on its stomach." It is a good one, no?' said von Steuben.

Reitsch continued: 'We should establish a central commissary At present, your camps are haphazard. Units lie where they can find a suitable space. Kitchens are set up with no plan; brigades look after themselves with no thought for the wider need. At your last camp, I was horrified to see where animals had been stripped of their meat, the carcasses were left to rot in the ground in the same place. This may well suit the conditions of winter, but in the summer months, it will become a proving ground for infection. We cannot have this. Similarly, the men relieve themselves wherever they care with no thought beyond their own need.

'I propose that we have a simple layout to the camp. Latrines and food rubbish on the eastern edge, on the downhill side. The kitchens and dining areas to the west. No units to be allowed to provide their own food. Any that do so will be disciplined.'

'And the same with the latrines,' said von Steuben. 'Men who relieve themselves, other than in the designated area, will be punished by incarceration.'

'We are to imprison men for pissing in an open field?' asked Sullivan. 'Is this what we are to become?'

'There can be no exceptions, General Sullivan. Discipline is all. Our enlisted men must understand this is not only the price they pay for victory, but the cause of victory itself. In the same way, we have to ensure order in the camp. Order is the cornerstone of any army, as I'm sure you will all agree. The huts and tents for the men should be organised in rows, clearly designated, allowing for easier mobilisation, but also for exchanging information.'

'I agree with that, Baron, but really – imprisoning a man for taking a piss?' asked Knox.

'That's the Boston bookseller talking, Henry, not the artillery general!' joked Cadwalader. 'The baron is right. I agree with you, sir. Discipline. We need more. We have tweaked King George's behind; he'll come at us with more Hessians and the best British fighters, mark my words.'

'Yes, they will come harder than ever at us, that is true,' Washington filled his glass and made his way to an armchair next to the roaring fire. His jaw was aching, his body ached, everything ached, and he yearned for a deep sleep. 'I am taken with this idea. This winter we need to establish a permanent home and bring our men up to the necessary standard. We should take advantage of the experience of the baron and his Stormtroopers to raise the quality of the army. Let us ride out tomorrow to this brook and survey the land. If it is as you describe it, Frau Reitsch, then we shall immediately begin work on building a permanent camp.'

'Thank you, Your Grace.'

'There is one more issue that I must press.'

'Go ahead, Baron,' replied Washington.

'In Europe we discovered that to be effective an army must be a machine that is maintained and monitored; it needs management, especially all its supplies. An army is always surrounded by swindlers, people profiteering from its need for food, drink, clothing. The only way to avoid overpaying, corruption and waste is to have a central team doing that for the entire army.'

'We have such a system in place, Baron,' interjected Cadwalader. 'Thomas Mifflin has been our quartermaster for the army since the summer of seventy-five.'

'And doing a fine job too,' said Sullivan.

'Then why is this army lacking in so many of the necessary supplies? Why are you praying that my men have captured the British supplies if you are so content with Mifflin? Let me ask you this, where is the bookkeeping?'

'The bookkeeping?' Sullivan was puzzled.

'A well-organised army keeps records of all that it buys, from whom it buys and at what price. Ask Mifflin, where are his records? I can tell you, he has none. You have no records of your supplies, your armaments, even a central register of the men serving under you. None. I would suggest that there is enormous waste. You need a procurement team as professional as the army you are building.'

'It is true that Tom Mifflin has little desire to be quartermaster. He is much happier in the heart of the battle than behind, counting sacks of flour,' said Greene. 'Our problem has been to find a character of the right bearing to take on the task.'

'I have just the person.'

'You do?'

'I have. She is right here.'

'Frau Reitsch? What experience does your woman have in running the operations of an army? Any woman, for that matter?' blustered Sullivan.

Calmly, Reitsch replied, 'Who is running your home in your absence, General Sullivan? A woman, I daresay your wife, Lydia I think is her name. And who secures all the necessary supplies and tends for your children in your absence? Or for that matter, when you return home? Why, your wife. Is this not common to all you gentlemen in the room? Your homes, your families, all you need to ensure that you can take to the field, is that not all done successfully by women? Would you not agree that women have a natural ability to run home and hearth? We women are far less corruptible than men when it comes to this. We are used to hard bargaining, otherwise our families would starve.'

'Madame, you cannot compare running an army of this size and complications with a family home in New Hampshire.'

'Why not? It is a question of scale, but the principles are the same. Sound finances. Is your issue with myself or what you regard as the inability of women for such complicated tasks?'

'I fear it is both. There is a reason why we call it husbandry.'

'So you would tell Catherine the Empress of all Russia that her sex makes her unfit to lead her country, would you? Was it not a woman, Elizabeth, who set about establishing the first British colonies in this land, and isn't it a man who by his own stupidity, ignorance and inflexibility stands to lose them?'

'She has you there, John,' laughed Greene. 'Your argument cannot be against her sex.'

'Then I will argue that she has no experience of organising such forces as ours.'

'There I must intervene, sir.' It was von Steuben. 'At the beginning of our adventures, when I was persuading the men under me to make this journey to the Americas under the pretence of serving the British crown, there was one person who I entrusted with our safe delivery here, one person who I knew would deliver us to the Americas in the best possible condition. That was Frau Reitsch. From the state of our men, I would think you could not disagree with that decision. How do we compare with other fighting forces you have come across? General Sullivan, how do we compare?'

'You are in most excellent shape, I would allow that,' he said more meekly.

'Good, I am happy that you would accept that. Then you must agree that Frau Reitsch is the author of our success and has the necessary experience to equip the Continental Army.'

'Well, frankly, she could do no worse,' said Knox. 'I think we would all acknowledge that we are dissatisfied with our present arrangements. I have heard rumours of false dealing.'

'Rumours, Knox, rumours,' interrupted Sullivan.

'There's no smoke without a fire.'

'Aye, I have heard tales of profiteering on both sides, from the suppliers and our own men,' added Ewing.

'Regardless of rumours, I see an army in tatters,' von Steuben raised his voice. 'Yesterday I witnessed men with no boots. In winter! And now they are out and about scavenging for food – which will only alienate them from the locals. This has to be sorted.'

Washington now raised himself from the chair, chewed his jaw and spoke: 'Baron, again you are right. The situation is not as we would like. Given her appetite for this, I am happy to place our quartermastering in the hands of Frau Reitsch. However, I expect to find by spring an army that is fully clothed, fully fed and fully armed. Anything less is unacceptable.'

'To me as well as yourself, Your Grace.'

With that there was a commotion outside in the town, an unruly noise.

'Alexander, go and find out what's causing such a racket. I pray it is not an outburst of fighting among the men again.'

Hamilton exited and a few of the generals made for the windows, but it was difficult to see out through the small panes.

'Baron,' Washington continued. 'You have brought to us good fortune in battle and now you and Frau Reitsch inspire us to think differently. Such innovations as you suggest may prove to be bigger wins than the battles we have fought latterly at Princeton and Trenton.'

'I cannot vouch for that, General, but they will lay the foundations for even greater victories in the future. That I can vouch for.'

Outside the noise was getting louder, whoops and cheering now distinct among the hubbub. Hamilton reentered the room: 'General Washington, generals, madame, you must come at once and witness this glorious scene.'

The men rushed out of the door, von Steuben turned to Reitsch and whispered, 'Conze with the British supplies, I would wager.'

Reitsch smiled, 'I expect so. And now we have control of supplying everything to this army, that and its expenditure. These fools have no idea what they have agreed to. But come, let us see how successful Conze has been.'

Outside the coal-black night was lit by a procession of Storm-troopers carrying burning torches, behind them came the wagons containing the British Army's winter supplies and behind them came the tired, bedraggled Pennsylvanian Riflemen. The Americans were almost an afterthought in this great triumph.

TWENTY-FIVE

They buried Hugh Mercer the following week in Morris Town. It was a celebration of the Continental Army's recent victories as much as the man himself, the first time in which the military and political leaders of the new republic had come together since defeat had turned into victory. Into Morris Town came Congress and with it a carnival of the corrupt: speculators from the northern towns, aristocracy from southern estates, snake-oil salesmen from struggling townships, mothers with children, women looking for fathers for children, beggars, paupers, men on the make, men on the break and a new emerging class, the political class. Even Horatio Gates had returned to the camp. For once, Washington and his ragbag army offered the chance of success and there were plenty who thought in turn it offered them the chance of a lifetime.

That evening the funeral party was an opportunity for the emerging political and military elites to come together, many with their wives attached. For the first time, von Steuben, Conze and Reitsch were to be introduced to the likes of John Adams, Ben Franklin, Thomas Jefferson, John Hancock, Charles Thomson and Thomas Paine. This was a time for new alliances to emerge.

'I am told that we owe much to you, madame. The honour is mine.' Thomas Jefferson, flaxen-haired, tall, elegant, in his own mind, a European intellectual cast into an American wilderness.

'Not at all, it is an honour for me to meet you, sir, the architect of the declaration that set this world on fire.'

'Ah, the fire was already lit. I merely fanned it with my bellows, if you will.' He laughed, heartily, the laughter echoed by the sycophants who surrounded him.

'You have a rare talent, Mister Jefferson. No ordinary man can articulate the thoughts and passions of thousands of people on their behalf. To produce a mirror by which they may see their own – yet to be expressed – thoughts so clearly and distinctly. I have met one other person with such a talent, but yours clearly rivals his.' Her tone was flirtatious, and Jefferson warmed to her, flattered by her. He supposed she spoke of King Frederick, but she had another in mind, from a very different world.

'I am again honoured.'

'"We hold these truths to be sacred and undeniable, that all men are created equal and independent; that from that equal creation they derive in rights inherent and inalienable, among which are the preservation of life, and liberty and the pursuit of happiness" – they were your original words I believe?'

'Madame, you do indeed flatter me. Yes, they were my original draft, but the great men of Congress took out some of the words and added others.'

'Yes, the great men of Congress, all men you say, but what of us women, Mister Jefferson? Are we not to be accorded the same rights, to be allowed the same pursuit of happiness?'

'Yes of course, madame. Indeed, I have within a land bill for my colony of Virginia a clause that every native-born citizen, male or female, should be able to receive seventy-five acres of land on marriage.'

'On marriage?'

'To encourage the settlement of the wilder parts of the colony. However, it is my firm view that property ownership should be the right of both sexes.'

'I am pleased to hear it. But these inalienable rights, do they not extend to the rights of the native Indians? Or to the black slaves that work your lands?'

'They do not, Frau Reitsch. The savage and the Negro, their rights may come later, perhaps when they are educated to a necessary level or hold property themselves.'

'Ah, your republic is based on the ownership of property. That is not a democracy, Mister Jefferson, that is an aristocracy, surely.'

'Pish, not an aristocracy! I abhor the aristocracy—'

'Despite being one of their most prominent members.'

Jefferson began to blush. He had been expecting a convivial conversation, but this woman was something different. He was not offended; he admired her pluck. He needed to sharpen his tools. Jefferson was about to respond when into their circle broke a stout figure

'What's this I hear? My friend Thom Jefferson being spiked by the redoubtable Frau Reitsch? I come here to save you, Tommy.'

'Frau Reitsch, this fellow goes by the name of John Adams. He is a lawyer and consequently believes he has seen all the good and the bad of the world. The problem is, he is prepared to offer advice and guidance to both the devil and the angels and often fails to distinguish between the two.'

Adams good-naturedly swiped his friend's cheek. 'Unfortunately, my friend Jefferson comes from our southern colonies, where they regard education rather like the African elephant. They have heard of it, they know it exists, but they have no idea where to find it.'

'I presume it would be in Africa, John.'

'Ah, you are learning, Thom. There may be hope for Virginia after all.'

'Frau Reitsch was questioning me about the rights of women in the new republic.'

'I am disappointed, sir, that only men appear to be invited to play a role in your politics.'

'Ah, you must meet my wife Abigail. She has assailed me on this issue many times over the last few months. I am not unsympathetic. However, we are in the midst of war, madame, and it would seem that under these circumstances, prudence would dictate that it is not the moment to open so fruitful a source of controversy and altercation.'

'I would disagree. Now is exactly the time to open up this controversy. Otherwise, I suspect once we have won this war, the issue will be settled. And conservatism will win out and your new republic would be based not on equality but inequality.'

'Our new republic will be based on many things, madame. Foremost, I would imagine will be property, and property will be open to both sexes,' Jefferson interrupted.

'Property always sides with established power. And emerging power always looks to property.'

'In your Europe, perhaps, but not here, not in a nation where land is almost limitless. Power always follows property, I would argue. Men in general, in every society, who are wholly destitute of property, are also too little acquainted with public affairs for a right judgement, too dependent upon other men to have a will of their own. They talk and they vote as some man of property, who has attached their minds to his interest, directs them. No, from property comes power.'

'Power comes from the barrel of a gun.'

Jefferson was stunned. 'I am sorry, madame. What was that?'

'Power comes from the barrel of a gun – it is an expression I have heard in Europe. Those who have the military means hold the power. This land will be led by those who have the strength and the weaponry to succeed.'

Jefferson's face had whitened. He was reeling, for there was something terrifying in the nonchalant manner in which Reitsch said this. It was at odds with everything he believed in. She held his eyes with a strong, unflinching gaze. There was no flirting now. He felt her coldness. Calmly, he replied: 'I cannot accept that, madame. There will be separation between the military and the civil in our new republic. We have already established the principle. Our esteemed General Washington is answerable to our Congress.'

'But you raise an interesting point, madame,' said Adams. 'We live in the age of political experiments. I am sure that we are not finished with our experiments as yet – you would agree with that, Thom.'

'I would, but tyranny is one experiment we have had enough of in these lands.'

'Tyranny is one thing,' Reitsch replied, 'but the need for strong leadership, that is another. A nation needs strength in its leadership, it needs direction, otherwise it lacks morality. I have seen too many states in Europe fall because of weak men flailing for compromise.'

'Excellent,' said Adams. 'This is the source of our disagreements, Thom. You would rather the emphasis in our future constitution lies with Congress. I, however, wish the balance of power lies more greatly in an executive, for example.'

On the other side of the room, von Steuben, who also had two men in tow, had cornered Washington and Hamilton.

'Sir, I want to introduce you to one of the finest of the new industrialists of Europe. This is my old friend Alfried Krupp. He has established the most advanced iron and steel manufacturing in Germany. You may have heard of the name Krupp. It is famous throughout Europe.'

Krupp offered his hand to Washington. Stiffly, the general replied, surprised when Krupp held his wrist with his left hand in a double embrace. An unusual and intimate greeting that made Washington uncomfortable. 'General Washington, this is indeed the greatest of honours. I have long admired you and your many triumphs. What you have achieved is most wonderful.'

Washington raised his eyebrow. He was hard pressed to imagine what triumphs these might have been. He had taken a dislike to the man. He reminded Washington of the two-faced, moneyed men of New York, so quick to flatter him when the war had started, so much quicker to disappear when the war appeared to be slipping from his grasp.

'I have personally developed a new process for producing steel from molten pig iron in ways that can produce huge amounts of quality steel.'

'Molten pig iron?' Washington asked quizzically, for he had no idea what the man was talking about.

'Yes. Ah, apologies, you must excuse my excitement. The key problem from steel manufacture in this age – I mean, in the present day – is the impurities oxidation creates in iron. By blowing air through the iron when it is in its molten stage, we can minimise these impurities. In turn, the oxidation raises the temperature of the iron mass, keeping it molten. We can reduce the time of manufacture from over three hours to about thirty minutes, and it uses far less fuel than the traditional processes. So the price falls. And the quality, well. You will have the finest steel ever produced, here or in Europe.'

Washington looked about him, confused. 'This is all very interesting, but what, gentlemen, is the point of this information?'

Von Steuben and Krupp exchanged glances before Krupp replied, a look of surprise across his face.

'Why, weapons, sir. Weapons. We can manufacture you a different kind of rifle.'

'Guns that will give you an advantage over the British forces that they will never be able to compete with,' added von Steuben.

'My family have been gunsmiths since the Thirty Years' War.

166

For over one hundred and fifty years, we have led the way in developing the most advanced weapons and—'

Krupp was interrupted by a loud cough from behind him. Washington looked around the tall German to see a smaller, balding, jowly older man. It was almost as if Krupp was deliberately hiding him.

'Hugo Schmeisser, Your Excellency. I am a gunsmith also. I personally have designed many weapons and I have studied the weaponry at your disposal. I have undertaken a review of the efficiency of your muskets, sir. I had my men establish a target at two hundred and twenty-five yards, and only twenty-five per cent of shots hit the target. At one hundred and fifty, we achieved forty per cent, then sixty per cent at seventy-five yards. And this was with no enemy on the field. These are not good returns. We need better gunnery, more accuracy. And I have the answer.'

Washington looked at the smaller man and said, 'And what is this answer?'

'This.'

He held out a Brown Bess to Washington, the standard issue for the British and the most favoured weapon of his own men. The leader took it and inspected it. 'You have removed the powder pan and cock.'

'I have. You are wondering what the small, perforated nipple is for, no?'

Washington nodded.

'Good. We no longer need those flints that are so tiresome and unpredictable. Instead, a small hammer, with a hollow, which fits on to the nipple when the trigger is released. Now if we place one of these on the nipple—' He raised a small metal cap in his hand. 'And we place it on the nipple, we will have a detonation when the trigger is released.'

'And it fires a ball?'

167

'No, sir. The ball is finished. It is redundant.' He held up a thin brass finger. 'It fires this, a brass cartridge that is attached to the cap. The accuracy is completely different. In my tests, I found at two hundred and twenty-five yards well over fifty per cent accuracy, a doubling of the Brown Bess's previous best. At seventy-five yards, the accuracy is close to ninety per cent.'

'With trained men.'

'No, I used some of Colonel Hand's Pennsylvanians. They were most pleased with the results. After further training, I am sure we will achieve even better results.'

'Marvellous, quite marvellous. But how is the cartridge removed?'

'Ah, very good, sir, very good. You have spotted immediately the weakness. We have an issue with extraction and ejection. The Bess does not allow an easy answer to that, I am afraid, but the accuracy of the cartridge overcomes the cumbersome nature of removing the spent case.'

'Even in the heat of battle?'

'In my view, yes. I would rather a riflemen were able to fire five accurate rounds than ten inaccurate rounds.'

'I agree,' muttered Washington. He liked this chap. There was no nonsense with him.

'But if I may . . .' Krupp interrupted. 'This is only the first stage of our plan. There is only so far we can go with the present technology. Our aim is to create for you a new generation of weapons far superior to anything seen before.'

'Yes, indeed,' said Schmeisser. 'My aim is to present you with an entirely different weapon. First, it will be what I call "automatic". The cartridges will be held in a magazine and a rifleman will be able to fire five or more shots without the need to reload. And because we will be using these brass cartridges, the barrel itself will be properly rifled, which will again improve the accuracy of the weapon. But this will take some time to build.'

'How long?'

Krupp answered before Schmeisser could reply. 'Well, first I have to build a modern steel plant using the technology I spoke of earlier. Schmeisser and myself have been travelling around the colonies and reviewing the existing steel plants. Although far from perfect, the best we have found is at Boone Town, established by Samuel Ogden a few years ago along a river. It has the benefit of charcoal and iron-ore reserves close by, the Boone Town falls will provide the necessary power and the river can be used to transport everything. And it is but an hour on horseback from here. They have been making iron there for thirty years or more, so there are skilled operatives we can call upon. We suggest that we seize the factory and instal the practices I outlined above.'

'Seize the factory?'

'I need total authorisation to produce the quality of steel that we require. This man Ogden may serve as an overseer, but he lacks the necessary understanding. I can, I will, train him, but I have to have the authority. The factory must be expanded and quickly. I believe by the autumn we can be producing the type of steel required. We must act quickly and decisively.'

'In New Jersey, we do not seize other men's property, Mister Krapp.'

'Krupp, sir. My name is Krupp.'

'My apologies, sir. But, Mister Krupp, we do not seize the property of others.'

'May I suggest we buy the business from Ogden?' interrupted von Steuben. 'We have the necessary funds, thanks to the New Brunswick raid. More than enough funds. Let us do the correct thing: buy this man Ogden out.'

'I would be happy to act as the negotiator on any deal,' said Hamilton.

Krupp looked over at von Steuben and stammered, 'That will not be necessary. I will be able to handle the negotiations. I have a close understanding of the value of a steel- and ironworks. With respect, sir, I suspect you do not.'

Washington eyed Krupp, 'No young Alexander does not possess your knowledge of the steel and iron trades, sir. But he is sharp enough to devour any knowledge you will pass on. He will negotiate on behalf of the Continental Army. And, should we be successful in this endeavour, you will report directly to him on the progress of your steel manufacturing. Mister Schmeisser, how soon before we have your new rifles?'

'I have the drawings ready. We can start the manufacture of the cartridges immediately. I am afraid your brass industry is not much advanced, sir. However, I met with two gentlemen from Connecticut, the Pattison brothers.'

'Peddlers, they are,' sneered Krupp.

'Perhaps, but peddlers who I believe can deliver the necessary brass cartridges. I have placed an order for five hundred on my own account, sir. As for the gunpowder, I believe that we have no alternative.'

'The Frankford mill,' said Hamilton.

'Indeed, the only manufacturer of gunpowder on the continent. For now we have no choice. Perhaps, Mister Hamilton, you could also negotiate on our behalf. The mix needs to be different to what they are used to producing.'

'It will be a privilege, Mister Schmeisser.'

'But when will we have the rifles?' asked Washington impatiently.

'Next year,' replied Schmeisser.

'Next year is too late,' mumbled Washington.

'Give me control of the factory and a slave-labour force and I will do my best to have supplies to your army by the end of this year, General,' said Krupp.

'You would use slaves, sir, from the plantations? Their experience is agriculture.'

'I need specialist steel-makers, engineers and designers for the parts, but I would put in place a new way of working I call an assembly line. Unskilled labourers can quickly put the pieces together. It will increase the speed of manufacture and not impact on the quality of the gun. Negroes can easily be trained.'

'But you will not gain acceptance for slavery in mills in Pennsylvania,' interrupted Hamilton. 'As General Washington knows, I find the practice both barbaric and inhumane, as do most people in the northern colonies. We shall not have slavery entering into our colonies. The people will not stand for it.'

'The people need not know,' replied Krupp.

'Tsch, Alfried! Listen to the man. We can just as easily find a paid labour force for your assembly line. Let us not squabble over this.' Von Steuben's eyes implored Krupp to back down.

'Sir, we can begin the process of transforming the existing Brown Besses, so that the majority of the Continental Army has them by the start of the spring campaigns,' interjected Schmeisser.

'We can? Good, very good. Let us move quickly. Indeed, tomorrow, Mister Schmeisser, please, if you may, introduce me to this weapon. I wish to see if I can hit a cow's arse from two hundred yards as they say.'

There was a tap on Werner Conze's shoulder. He looked down upon a man in his forties, his mouth an open gap of decayed teeth, his breath stale. 'Tom Paine. You've heard of me no doubt.'

'I have indeed, sir. Werner Conze.'

'Hate these things. Look about you. The seed of future ruins. Periwigged monsters suckling at the breast. This revolution will be suffocated by these types if we give 'em so much as half a chance.'

'Your pamphlet stirred many of these men.'

'Nah, my pamphlet stirred many a man, but few of these. Chancers, most of 'em, looking out to feather their beds with whoever comes out on top. Said this to George, but he's too cautious. You don't want to have to clear the pigs from the stalls; you have to stop 'em breeding first. Too late once they have smeared their shit everywhere, you never get rid of it. Anyway, we owe you Germans a debt of gratitude. We thought we were down and out and then you turned up.'

'I'm not so sure. I believe your forces would have prevailed.'

'Well, Old George thinks you were the difference. We wouldn't be sitting here now, patting ourselves on the back; he'd be sat on his arse on the other side of the Delaware and the rest of us would be hiding out in Baltimore scared shitless. So I should raise a glass of this not-so-bad wine in your honour. So what's your game, eh?'

'My game? I don't understand. My game?'

'What yer playing at, boy? Why are yer really here?'

'To win this war. To create a new nation. Like you. Like you, I find Europe full of tyranny, exhausted, not ready for the future. Here, here we can create something that will change mankind for ever.'

'Aye to that.' He clinked glasses. 'These may be the times that try men's souls, but they may also be the greatest of times. The word they use to insult us is "utopia". "You want to create a utopia!" Too bloody right I do. A land where every man, every woman, regardless of colour or race is free. We can do that. Here, Mister Conze, we can achieve that.'

Conze paused. 'Do you really think that's practical?'

'Oh yes, oh yes, of course it's practical. It's going to happen. Well, it will if we keep these pigs out of the trough. All men equal!'

'You really think that's true, Mister Paine, that all men are equal?'

'No, they're not, but from birth everyone should have the same rights, the same opportunity to succeed, to be happy. That is what I mean by equality.'

'But why? People are not equal. The sick are not equal to the

172

healthy. The idiot is not equal to the intellectual. The weak is not equal to the strong.'

'Then we do our best to create a society which makes the sick healthy, the idiot clever, the weak stronger. Not discard them on the rubbish heap or exploit them.'

'But is that not human nature? To exploit. To exploit the land, the animals, each other? Exploitation is natural to the human. Look at your friend Washington. He is leading a charge for freedom, yet his estate is farmed by slaves.'

'Slavery is a stain on this nation, I agree. George agrees. This is where his natural caution betrays him. He says he cannot raise the issue now, because the southern colonies will fall away. But I fear, I fear for a nation born with this at its heart. It will leave a residue, for decades, for centuries, if the Negro is not afforded the same rights as the white man. And the same for the native Indians. We must find a way to live in peace with them.'

'But you are wrong.'

'I am?'

'You are. Just as the human is superior to the monkey, so different races are superior to others. The Negro, the Indian, in Europe, the Slav, the Jew, all inferior people to the Anglo-Saxon. Their culture, their industry, their science, they lack all that the civilised Anglo-Saxons have brought. It is not their fault, it is their genetic inheritance, that has left them inferior.'

'Their genetic, what was that?'

Conze stepped back. 'It is some recent scientific work in Germany. A new branch of the natural sciences. Genetics. Characteristics that are passed down from one generation to the next.'

'I've never heard of this and I like to think I know what's happening in the sciences.' Paine pulled out a tattered notebook, a stub of pencil tied to it. He licked the stub. 'How you be spelling that?'

'G-E-N-E-T-I-C-S. Genetics. A new word for a new science.

It has a simple premise that we pass down traits through the generations, traits that are impossible to overcome. So, the Negro is inherently lazy. The Jew untrustworthy.'

'I know very few Jews, but I can't say I've ever found any of 'em untrustworthy.'

'You must hold that the civilisation of the West is superior to that of the east or the southern nations?'

'Well, I suppose I might, never given it much thought. I'm more concerned about the problems we face with Western civilisation. It hardly seems proper we should think ourselves superior when we make such a sow's ear of it, wouldn't you say?'

'No, I would not. Surely our role as intellectuals must be to help the agents of civilisation prosper? This is our chance now to ensure the survival of the fittest, of the best. We have one chance with America. We can populate it with the best, or we can open the sewers of Europe and let all the scum and filth come here. We build this nation only with the best Aryan brains, create a race of superhumans.'

Thomas Paine looked upon the young German and scratched his head. It had been a long day. The road from Baltimore had been difficult. The wine was fogging his mind. The earnestness of this young man was something, but he was quite mad, Paine thought. A race of superhumans? What was this nonsense.

'I am afraid it is time I retired. Will you accept my apologies, Mister Conze?'

'I will, but we shall meet again. I promise you that, and we shall debate this issue again. Many times I believe.'

Paine shook his head and walked away. Mad men. Wherever you moved in this world. Mad men.

Hand had been waiting patiently in the anteroom for close to an hour. He was anxious, playing with his fists as he often did when his mind was distracted.

The door to Washington's room opened and out came Charles Thomson, John Hancock, Thomas Jefferson and John Adams, the most important members of Congress, newly arrived from Baltimore.

Jefferson spotted Hand sitting on a chair and reached out to him.

'Colonel Hand, my congratulations to you and your men. Gentlemen, may I introduce to you one of the finest leaders in the Continental Army, Colonel Edward Hand of the Pennsylvanian Riflemen. It was my pleasure to be introduced to the colonel last summer. And, as General Washington just informed us, Colonel Hand was the architect, along with the Hessians, of the successful seizing of the British winter supplies.'

Thomson, Hancock and Adams introduced themselves, with florid congratulations, much to Hand's embarrassment. He was never comfortable receiving the acclaim of others.

'Thank you, gentlemen. I shall relay the good wishes of our Congressional leaders to my men. It is they who deserve the acclaim, for their efforts not just at New Brunswick, but also at Trenton.'

'The most marvellous times,' said Hancock. 'We have outfoxed Cornwallis. I can almost smell victory in the air. I expect we shall be rid of the king's men before another year is out.'

'I think you are perhaps a little presumptuous there, John,' replied the sober Adams. 'This war has some time to run yet. We shall have victory, but I suspect there will be a few defeats along the way yet.'

'If Congress is behind us and can produce a ready supply of troops, fully clothed and armed, then, yes, we shall achieve that victory,' said Hand.

'Congress will do its best, but it is not a bottomless pit of money. Thankfully, your efforts in New Brunswick have secured a ready source of funding, which may stay a potential bankruptcy.'

Alexander Hamilton appeared at the door, 'Colonel Hand, General Washington is ready for you now.'

'Well, we shall leave you for now, Colonel,' said Jefferson. 'No doubt we shall find cause to meet with you in the future. I sense, sir, the tide has turned. The tide has turned.'

'I hope so, sir. I look forward to our next encounter,' replied Hand, taking his leave and entering Washington's office.

There was a roaring fire in the hearth and Washington stood before it, his hands clasped behind his back and his jaw making the peculiar gurning motion, which betrayed the pain of his gums.

'Colonel Hand, sir,' said Hamilton, closing the door behind him.

Washington turned immediately and threw out his hand to Hand.

'Edward. How much happier the circumstances of this meeting than the occasion of our encounter in Buckingham.'

'That seems to have been many months ago,' replied Hand.

'And yet, it was less than two weeks. I have come to regret the rashness of that moment. If it had not been for the good counsel of my chiefs of staff, I may have proved so reckless as to have lost one of my finest leaders.'

'Sir, please, it does not trouble me. I had behaved badly. Besides which, if you had not sent me out to scout Trenton, well, perhaps we would not have met Baron von Steuben and his men and by now our struggle might have been at an end.'

'Perhaps. Nevertheless, I demonstrated a singular lack of patience and judgement that if it had been another, I would have most viciously attacked him. But the baron, well, he has certainly lifted our hopes. He, that formidable Frau Reitsch and that fellow Conze. These Stormtroopers have formed something of a close alliance with your Riflemen, I see. I was most impressed by their fortitude and spirit on the withdrawal back to the bridge at Trenton.'

'Yes, the Germans do not lack for bravery or cleverness of thinking.'

'That they do not. Although, some of my generals are concerned that I am placing too much confidence in the baron and his men. And yet, whenever I do so, they return my faith many times over. The army, the militia, all seem inspired by them; a new confidence rides among them, according to Hamilton. My instincts, sir, I have no scientific evidence.'

'No, I think your instincts are correct. There appears little wariness on the part of the men. They are much impressed, that much is true. They feel the tide has turned; there is real belief now that we will throw the British out. That did not exist before Christmas.'

'And you too, surely, Hand?'

There was a pause. 'That is why I requested this audience, sir. I am not sure how best to express this.'

'I find the best manner to express oneself is to make a virtue out of honest opinion, forthrightly expressed. The times do not allow us the luxury to shilly-shally. What is it, Colonel, what concerns you?'

'Have you had any correspondence or intelligence concerning the events at New Brunswick?'

'The capture of the supply train?'

'No, after that. From the British side. Any complaints from General Cornwallis?'

Washington looked at Hamilton. 'Alexander, we have had no word from the British, have we?'

'Not to my knowledge. I am not sure they even know we are here in Morris Town.'

'That gives me some comfort, for there was an incident at New Brunswick that may bring shame on us, on all of us.

'The Riflemen left the town with the supply train. We feared an attack from Cornwallis, so the Stormtroopers, under the command of Werner Conze, stayed behind, ready to delay them. We left the surrendered British troops and the women and children from the British baggage train behind with them. There were perhaps a hundred people there, including some children.

'After we left the town, we were just across the river when we heard gunshots. I sent the men ahead, but returned to New Brunswick with Patrick O'Leary. There we saw the most terrible scenes.' Hand paused and looked around him, before saying softly, 'A massacre.'

'Of the troops?'

'Of all of them, the civilians as well as the soldiers. Shot, bayonetted. Several women were being taken off. I fear the worst was to happen to them.'

'At the hands of the Hessians?'

'At the hands of the Hessians, yes.'

'Did you attempt to stop this?'

'The murders had already been committed, we were too late. I made efforts to stop the rape of the women, but Conze would not listen to me. He said they were fighting terror with terror. I was unable to stop him.' He looked down at the floor. He felt ashamed. 'I said that you were always of the opinion that we had to behave with humanity to our enemies. That did not sway him.'

'I see. No, I was unaware of this. It is almost a week, but as yet the British have not made propaganda play of this. They will, I'm sure. We do not want our army to win a reputation for such atrocities. European wars are marked by these kinds of actions. We do not want our German friends to infect our country with them. I will discuss this with the baron and determine a course of action.

'In the meantime, you must not allow yourself to be embarrassed by this event. War is cruel, terrible things happen, but your conscience should remain clear. We will ensure this is not repeated.'

PART 3

MORRIS TOWN, PENNSYLVANIA

4 March 1777

TWENTY-SIX

For three months, the Continental Army had been camped at Lowantica Brook. Von Steuben's plan of a modern camp had come good. The camp had been free of all disease. While the smallpox was causing havoc in the small towns and villages of the northern colonies, there were no reported cases at Lowantica Brook. And as spring started, so the change in season was marked by a change in mood, with a growing optimism within the camp. And, for some, love had started to blossom.

They had begun taking strolls down to the banks of the Stony Brook most afternoons, once Conze had finished his duties. Sarah Hand had never felt so comfortable with a man, never enjoyed the pleasures of such a man, for Conze was a world away from the men she had lived among, the boys who had so often attempted to woo her with their simple lives and simple ideas.

Has anyone such an instinct for knowledge as Werner Conze? she often thought. He knew more than she did of the history of the colonies, of the politics of Britain, of the geography, even the botany of the Americas. As they walked through the woods, he would point out plants she had never noticed. He talked about the forests of America, about deforestation. And he talked mostly of how this was the greatest chance in the history of humankind to build a new kind of society.

In truth, there were times when he did go on just a little bit too long. Times when she found it difficult to stifle a yawn, as Werner embarked on yet another explanation of *Lebensraum*, or the virtues of the Aryan people. She didn't quite understand these issues around Jews. She was pretty certain she had never met a Jew. She knew many different kinds of Christians outside of her Catholic family, had come across some Puritans, there were plenty of those in New Jersey and a right pain in the arse they were, but Jews, no, she wasn't aware of having met any. Apparently, though, if you went to New York or Philadelphia, they would overwhelm you. They lent money to both the Colonists and the British. 'There is only one people who benefit from both sides in a war: the Jews,' Werner had told her. 'They sit at home, count their money and back both sides,' and she saw no reason to disagree. She had been to New York, retreated with the army through Manhattan, remembered those large houses, their candles burning brightly through clear glass windows, well-fed faces staring out at them as they shuffled past, hungry, cold, clothed in no more than blankets, their shoes falling apart on them as they marched out of the city. She supposed those were the Jews he spoke of.

And, of course, it wasn't just his mind she enjoyed. He was beautiful to look at, his body honed by the daily exercise routine he insisted on. The scars he had collected from battles in France and Russia (he had travelled so far, seen so much, she felt so small, so insignificant compared to him), purple and proud on his legs and back, added to his allure. And she had seen them. Seen them that first afternoon on a blanket on the ground, in the meadow where he and she had first enjoyed each other, an event that now occurred almost daily.

In the evenings, Conze would leave her. He had two major occupations then: either what he described as a 'conference' with von Steuben, Reitsch and the other Hessians or his educational sessions with the Colonists.

Sarah had occasion to attend one or two of these meetings, but after a time, she realised she did not need this extra tuition in philosophy and history when she could enjoy her own individual tutorship. If she had had a girlfriend to confide in, she would have admitted to her that they were just a little dull.

Conze's lectures, however, were becoming much talked about at the camp. They began with the Philadelphian Riflemen, but soon he was delivering them to all the northern regiments and began to collect a group of acolytes around him, chief among them being Patrick O'Leary.

The lectures were always voluntary. Conze often said he had no wish to bore anyone who did not wish to expand his mind. Their subject matter was philosophy and history and word began to travel among the enlisted men. In truth, a sitting army is a bored army and since the excitement of Trenton and Princeton, the army had been doing just that, sitting at Lowantica Brook, waiting for spring to break. Numbers were reduced, as some men had returned to their families for the winter, but there were still 7,000 men in camp and of those four hundred had become regular attendees at Conze's lectures. And with each talk, their numbers increased. By the start of March, close to a thousand would be listening to him on the parade ground, with Conze standing on a raised crate, the men standing or sitting in a large semicircle, straining to hear his words.

He was an engaging speaker. He talked for up to an hour, without any notes, often coming down from the crate, walking among them as he spoke. He would stop and directly address an individual. He constructed the lectures so that there was always a simple message that he would touch upon several times before returning to it at the end. The men often left with their heads buzzing with new concepts.

As word spread around the camp, different regiments would send word for Conze to come and address them, which he would

183

do, eagerly. Until finally came the invitation he was looking for, to address the North Carolina regiments who had only joined the main army in February. It was to be a fateful meeting, held in the open air on a warm March afternoon after parade.

Its subject was 'A Land Fit for Heroes', and in it Conze discussed what kind of America they wanted to build after the war had been won. There was no doubt in his mind that the war would be won, so the issue was to win the peace afterwards and to create a nation that would enable the American people to fulfil their potential.

'What kind of people do we want here in the Americas?' he asked. 'Do we want a nation populated by the scum and filth of Europe? Make no mistake, the princes of Europe will be looking to empty their prisons and send their worst criminals here. Do we want a nation built of thieves, murderers, rapists? A land where our children, our women will not feel safe?'

There was only one response to that question and the cry from the 400 men echoed around the parade ground, 'No!'

To which Conze added: 'Or do we want a nation of the pure, the wise and the best?'

Which brought a large cheer of 'Yes!'

Emboldened, Conze moved on to the real meat of his argument: 'So to whom do we open the doors of this great country? If we are not going to accept just anyone, who should we accept? We want only the most noble and the pure to build this nation. It is part of that nature that some races are superior to others, the Anglo-Saxon races, those who have made Western Europe the home of civilisation, are undoubtedly the most advanced, superior to all others. This nation has been established by people from Britain, Germany, Scandinavia; it is they, our forefathers, who have torn down the forests, turned the land into pasture, started great industries and businesses, made this a land fit for civilisation. They are linked not by the false claims of nations, of loyalty to kings and queens, but to a pure bloodline. We Anglo-Saxons, we

Aryans, share a common heritage that has been masked by the false boundaries of nations. Here in America, should we revel in our common blood heritage and work to improve the human race – or should we allow our blood to be polluted by those who have weakened the great Anglo-Saxon countries?

'Our task in America is simple: to improve mankind and create a race of superhumans, to make the most of the new openings that science is about to present to us. Nature has an iron law: each beast mates only with a companion from its own species. Why would human beings be any different? All the ills of old Europe spring from this one betrayal of nature's law, from races breeding with different races. It spreads disease, it creates the feeble-minded, it weakens the human race. In America, we can overcome this weakness. We can insist upon racial purity and in doing so, we will overcome the perils that afflict Europe. We can create a master race, endowed with superior minds, physique, health, the natural, rightful lords of mankind, who will ensure the potential of the human race.'

Conze stabbed his fingers out to his audience to emphasise points, screaming the most important words, creating a hypnotic spell that had the audience, men from the Carolinas, cheering along with him.

'So what does this mean for the new America? It means we have to resist those races that are inferior. We have to stop them coming here and breeding with us Teutonic peoples. Already, in New York and Philadelphia and Boston, in the growing cities, you can see the first signs of these people coming and the havoc they wreak. Especially the Jews. They are the worst of all races, root-less, materialistic, unclean. If you read the history of the Jew, you will know it is a history of betrayal, from Jesus Christ onwards. If the Jews were the only people in the world, they would be wal-lowing in filth and mire, would exploit one another and then exterminate one another in a bitter struggle. There would be no human race. They cannot help themselves. It is their nature. We must ensure they cannot be allowed to do the same here in the Americas: they must be resisted. We need to control the immigration of people into this land. We must have at all our ports, the ability to stop the Jew, the Slav, the Chinaman, the Arab from entering. If we can stop the British bringing their tea into this country, we can stop these people!'

There was a cheer at this stage and a general muttering of agreement. Warming to his theme, Conze now pushed it further, raising a subject he had never dared mention to the northern units, who included among their number many free slaves.

'And what of those inferior races who are already here? The Indians and the Negroes that serve on the plantations of the south? They have been provided by providence, by God, if you will, like the forests, river and wild animals of this continent, as a natural resource for the Anglo-Saxon people. They are simple people and they can fulfil a function. They can work the land for their superiors. We will offer them the paternalism of the superior; we will provide them plantations or ghettos in which they can exist among their own kind, breeding with their own races, in return for their providing the raw power we need to conquer this land. But there can never be any mixed breeding between our people and those races who are closer to the beast in the field than the Anglo-Saxon. Mixed breeding must, if we are to protect the bloodline, be punished by death!'

As he reached this point, there was a loud shout from the midst of the crowd, 'Shame! Shame on you!'

The men turned to one character: a Rifleman from Fort Watson named David Sloman, a twenty-eight-year-old Methodist preacher. He was perhaps the most educated man in the crowd, his family having sent him back to England, to be schooled at Cambridge, where he had fallen in with the Wesleyans. Sloman had become a supporter of the abolitionist cause, playing a role in the court victory of James Somerset, an escaped slave judged to have been unlawfully imprisoned by his owner. Returning to North Carolina and the family plantation, Sloman soon found himself ostracised by his family and he had volunteered for the rebel forces. As he stood up, there was some hissing from the edges of the crowd, but the man was unbowed.

'You are a disgrace, sir! The Negro is not an inferior race. He is our brother. Galatians 3:28: "There is neither Jew nor Greek, there is neither bond nor free, there is neither male nor female: for ye are all one in Christ Jesus."'

'Preacher, you quote the Bible at me, to defend the Jews?'

'I do. Enough of this filth, there is no place for such hatred in these colonies. Away with you.'

'You quote one verse, but what of the rest of the Christian New Testament? Did not Jesus call the Jewish leaders a "brood of vipers"? When he was taken before Pilate, what did all the Jews say? "Let him be crucified." Christ killers. You defend the Christ killers!'

There was some murmuring and then a distinct shout of 'Christ killers!' that quickly became a chant, echoing around the square. Then, from somewhere, something was thrown, a rock perhaps, and it struck Sloman on the side of the head. He fell and for a moment there was quiet. And then suddenly, explosively, three or four men rushed to him and assaulted him as he lay on the ground, giving one terrible shriek.

They kicked him as he lay curled on the ground. Others joined in as well, until there were at least twenty of them. And then, they pulled away, leaving the bloodied corpse of Sloman, still on the ground, a pulpy mass of blood and flesh.

Towards the edge of the group, a number of men, offended and terrified by what had occurred, slunk away, but the greater number stood still and then, perhaps most frightening of all, let loose a loud cheer. Conze had a new and hugely appreciative audience.

Hand pulled off the swastika armband. He had never wanted it to be part of their uniform, to him it was the symbol of a foreign army. It was his men who had overruled him. They wanted to be closer to the Germans. They saw them not as foreign mercenaries, but rather an ideal to aspire to. They were amateurs, they knew that, but the Stormtroopers, they were professionals, and the Riflemen liked that. They wanted to be part of something better; they wanted what these Germans had. So he had agreed that they would wear the red band with the black swastika and embroidered below the word 'Pennsylvania'.

He was sat in his hut that evening, exhausted emotionally, mentally and physically, reflecting on the blistering row he had just had with Pat O'Leary. It was an argument that had been brewing for weeks, but finally it had all come out into the open. As he stared at his boots, he knew he had lost not just Pat but all his boys.

Back in December, when things were beyond unbearable, they were his men, these Riflemen. They had been together for the best part of eighteen months; they had grown together through the pain of defeat and the endless retreat, through hunger, injury and death. But they had never waivered in their belief in him as their leader, they were proud to be called 'Eddie Hand's lads', and they had sung a song with that title.

All that was gradually changing. Slowly, but surely, he could feel his hold over them draining, hour by hour, day by day.

And he understood what was happening. In the eyes of his men – and he heard the same from other field commanders, even from those who came into the camp from the towns and villages of the colonies – the reversal of fortune was down to one thing: the Germans. The victories at Trenton and Princeton, the capture of the baggage trains at New Brunswick, all these were directly caused by the arrival of the Germans. They still loved Old George, but really, had he any victories before the baron and his men arrived?

Then there was the change in the camp.

At first there were complaints about the endless drills, about the barking of the German sergeants in their broken English. The first few weeks had left most of them exhausted, collapsing in their new tents at the end of the day, unable to rise for grog even. A few, quite a few, said they had had enough, took off back to their wives and families, saying they had no stomach for it. But those that stayed behind, by the end of March were transformed.

They were transformed physically. There was regular food now, properly cooked in the kitchens Reitsch had established. No one went hungry. And the drills, the forced marches, the strange outdoor gymnastic routines, had honed their bodies. And suddenly they began to wash on a regular basis, there was even regular changing of clothes. Not only did they look different, they smelled different. The men were taking a pride in themselves and their appearance that was at odds with the bedraggled, miserable men who had crossed the Delaware last Christmas Day.

And all this they attributed to the Germans.

They worshipped von Steuben, 'The Baron', and they adored Hanna Reitsch, the Angel of the Camp, beautiful, always with a joke and a word for any man, no matter how young or inexperienced. And then there was Conze, who encouraged them to think differently about the world, think in a way they never had before. And the regular men, the Stormtroopers, quickly they came to see them as comrades in arms, until for all intents and purposes there were no Riflemen. They were all Stormtroopers now. All were wearing variations of the swastikas, the symbol that was said to strike fear into the hearts of the British.

They still had respect for Edward Hand, he knew that. He was still 'The Boss Man', but there was a weakening of the bond. He saw that with every man under his command and he especially saw that with Pat O'Leary.

Pat had been his protégé for years.

They had first met when Hand served as a surgeon's mate in the British Army's 18th Foot Regiment. The barely teenage O'Leary had travelled with the regiment from Cobh in 1767. He had suffered terrible seasickness on what was a wretched crossing and Hand had taken him under his wing. For seven years, they remained close and when Hand resigned his commission in 1774 to start a medical practice, O'Leary joined him with the aim of setting himself up as a gunsmith. There was ten years' difference in age between them and it was clear to all that Hand served as a proxy father for O'Leary, who had been an orphan from the age of seven, running the narrow streets of Cobh, uneducated, half-naked and starving most of the time.

Hand had taught the lad to read, worn off the roughest of the edges, encouraged him to think differently about his future, to think that he could have a future. And as the colonies moved towards rebellion, so Hand had furthered the boy's education, introduced him to Tom Paine and his *Common Sense*. But now the pupil appeared to have outgrown the master and had found a new tutor; now he had a new man to listen to: Werner Conze.

At first, Hand had enjoyed Conze and his taste for debate. But over time, he had found him tiresome. He was like one of those Methodists you hear about, forever preaching, banging on about how the world should be better, how he alone had the answer. He started to avoid his company, but it was quite difficult as they were joint commanders-in-chief of the Riflemen. And it was even more difficult when his best charge started to parrot some of the German's phrases. Hand had finally broken one day when Pat had started on about 'blood and iron' and the need for 'a people's iron will to be established'.

'What the fuck does that mean, Pat?'

'Wha? What d'yer mean, Ed?'

'What does all this stuff about blood and iron and sacrifice actually mean?'

'Well, it's about sacrifices, the sacrifices we will all have to make for the greater good, for the new Reich we're going to start.'

'New Reich? What's that?'

'Ah, it's a German word, it means, ah, it means, country, for sure. We will build this country on the blood of our enemies, on our own blood, the blood we will spill to see our enemies defeated.'

'That's bollocks, Pat. Absolute bollocks. How bloody stupid are you to fall for this? I thought I had educated you better than this.'

And then the mist descended across O'Leary and in that moment, Hand saw years of resentment that he had not been remotely aware of. It came gushing out in a torrent of abuse. 'That's yer fucking problem, Ed Hand. You think you're better than everyone else, because you went to Trinity and got some fancy education. What you can't bear is me having my own opinions, fella. It's all right if I'm your parrot, but God forbid me showing any thoughts meself. You're jealous you are, jealous of Werner and all the German lads. Well, fuck you, Ed. I'm me own man, not your fucking puppet.'

Hand shook his head at the madness of it all and simply walked away, close to despair.

Now, as he sat in his hut, the door opened and in came his sister. He looked at her and simply said:

'You been off a-whoring again with Werner Conze, Miss Sarah Hand? Or have you been fucking any German that takes your fancy?'

The bluntness was out of character. The colour drained from Sarah's cheeks, she burst into tears and ran out of the hut, leaving him alone, again.

He sat there, a single candle flickering amid the darkness.

*

191

She ran out of her brother's billet. She had never been spoken to by him, or by anyone, like that. Through the camp she ran, stumbling over tent pegs. The night was dark, the camp lit by flaming forces, running back towards the kitchen, she ran into Hanna Reitsch.

The girl was sobbing, Hanna took her in her arms and tried to calm her down. The German's first reaction was that Conze had treated her cruelly, so she took her back to the hut she and von Steuben shared.

The girl was almost hysterical. Reitsch poured her a brandy and insisted she take it. In between sobs, she started to tell the story and Reitsch was relieved to hear Conze was not the villain but her brother, the previously impeccable figure of Edward Hand. He had cast her out as a whore.

'There are two types of men,' Reitsch told her. 'There are the men who look to dominate women. Weak men. What we call insecure men. Powerless men, terrified by the power women naturally hold, who are intimidated and challenged by the natural strength we women have. Then there are the men who cherish women for those strengths, men who see us as different, but equals, superior even. They see the great possibilities of womenkind. There are fewer of them, but by our actions and behaviours, we can help more men see the possibilities of womenkind.

'Your brother is threatened by you, threatened by you starting to emerge from the chrysalis he has entombed you in. You are lucky you have found a man such as Werner who sees all those strengths in you and is not intimidated by you. He is a man of the future. Your brother . . . your brother belongs in the past. He is to be pitied, not damned. Do you understand?'

Sarah looked up at her, her eyes red, and nodded.

'I have been thinking for some time that we should look to do something to give the young girls of the colonies something to aspire to. I would like to set up what I call the League of American Girls.'

Sarah looked back blankly.

'It will be a group to inspire young women throughout the colonies to engage in this fight, to support our menfolk in their physical struggle, but also a group to spread the message.'

'The message?'

'The message that we are a new generation of women. Women who refuse to be chattels of men. We are building a new society here. You have heard Werner talk of creating a breed of super-man, a new kind of man for a new age? Well, we also need to create a different woman for this new age. We need women with strength and fortitude, powerful women who demand to be treated as equals to their brothers, fathers and husbands. This is our chance to change history. So that your sons are not tyrants to their sisters. So that your daughters have the same opportunities as your sons. What do you think?'

Sarah smiled at her, 'I think that is something I would like to see happen.'

'And I want you to lead the League of American Girls.'

'Me?' Sarah replied, astonished.

'Why not you?'

'Well, I, I have no, I—'

'You have everything, dear Sarah. Do not doubt yourself and what you are capable of. You alone will inspire thousands of young women across these lands to think differently. There is no one better to start such a league.'

'I, I don't know what to say, Hanna. I can't believe this. You think I can really do this?'

'I do. With all my heart. You are very dear to me, Hanna, to the baron and, of course, to Werner. I hope you won't mind me saying this, but we see you as family. If your brother has cast aside you, then please, come and join our family. We may be an odd bunch, but look upon us as your closest friends.'

Sarah smiled, a big, grateful smile. 'That means everything to me, Hanna, that you and the baron think so much of me.'

'And Werner of course. He has a special affection for you, that much is quite clear.'

Sarah blushed. 'And me for him. He has my heart.' She whispered, 'I love him Hanna.'

The older woman hugged her close. 'He is the luckiest man alive, Sarah. I have something I would like you to have.'

She pulled away and went to a small box sitting on a table. 'This was given to me by a very dear friend, a very strong woman, someone who had all those qualities we would like to see in our League of American Girls.'

'Where is she now?'

Reitsch thought wistfully for a second. There was no easy way to answer that question.

'She is in Europe. Safe, I hope. She gave this to me as a memento of her affection for me and what we believed in and I am passing this on to you, to wear it proudly as a token of my affection for you and as a symbol of the new world we are going to build.'

And she handed over a beautiful ring, diamonds surrounding a blue sapphire, unlike anything Sarah Hand had ever seen in her life.

TWENTY-SEVEN

The following week the Stormtroopers and Riflemen left Lowantica. The men were getting itchy in camp and Washington wanted a survey of the country and small towns of northern Pennsylvania. Rumours persisted of British units operating in the countryside, and there was a desire to close down any remaining supply lines for the enemy before the spring brought a return to full-scale operations. In practice, however, the survey soon became little more than a goodwill tour. Wherever they went, they were showered with warmth, especially the Stormtroopers, as recent German immigrants had populated many of the towns, villages and farms. On the seventh day, they arrived at Heidlebergtown, and here the warmth of the greeting exceeded any previous encounter.

Their drummers and fifes gave advance warning of the Stormtroopers' and Riflemen's approach to the town. Small children came running out of Heidlebergtown towards them, their voices screeching, in their hands tiny swastika flags. Parading down the main street, it appeared that every citizen, male and female, had come out to cheer them, lining the rough sidewalks, calling from the few first-storey windows there were. The troops halted at the centre, outside the King George Hotel, and even before the call to rest arms had been made, a small, bullish man appeared in front, hysterically shouting English in a heavily accented German voice.

'Gud morning, gud morning! Velcome Stormtroopers to Heidle-bergtown! Ve heard news of your forthcoming and pleased to greet. Here ve are a town of Germans, from Hesse, from Bavaria, from Silesia, from Swabia, all over from Germany. This town was founded by me, Alexander Schaeffer, and ve are proud to velcome our brothers from Motherland here. There is beer, beer for all of you, but furst, ve have a surprise for you. Please, looking towards the porch. Heindrich!'

On the roof of the porch, a teenage boy stood up and rolled out what appeared at first to be a carpet. Down from the roof it unfurled, revealing an enormous flag. Gently flapping in the breezy March afternoon, was a long red banner, in its centre a white circle with the black swastika at its heart.

'For our Stormtroopers!' shouted Schaeffer as the local audience burst into applause and cries of 'Hurra!'

Conze waited no time, embraced Schaeffer warmly and then addressed the town.

'This is most excellent! When I return to Lowantica Brook and the army headquarters, I will at once rush to His Excellency the Baron von Steuben and tell him of the great honour you have presented us with today. This most beautiful banner, this most honourable of banners! I am sure it will be but the first of many that will illuminate this great land of America! So I can say that today, Heidlebergtown is the leader of the Thirteen Colonies. For every Stormtrooper here, this is the most special of days, to find such a welcome from their fellow Germans, that is indeed most wonderful. But I would also ask you share such warmth with our dear colleagues, the Pennsylvanian Riflemen, who are with us this morning. Perhaps a few words from their leader, Colonel Edward Hand.'

Again, there were wild cheers and clapping from the townspeople, and Hand, never comfortable with such moments, found himself propelled alongside Conze.

He cleared his throat. 'This is indeed a great morning, a great morning to be alive in America. We have fought bravely these last two years and I expect we will have to fight for another two years or even longer before our victory is complete, but we will all be sustained by the memories of the day we came to Heidlebergtown and the welcome we received. But I must not go on for any longer. We have marched already many hours since daybreak, and, sir, I heard mention of beer, and knowing my men, they wish for nothing more than for me to be quiet and for the beer to be broken out.'

'Yah, *bier – und weisswurst und schweinshabe und spekkuchen*. Eat and drink!' screamed Schaeffer. The troops broke rank and quickly, a seemingly never-ending river of drink and food was being passed through the windows of the tavern.

Once the excitement had died down, the men relaxing in small groups around the building, smoking pipes, flirting with the local girls or having their weapons examined by young boys, Conze and Hand sat down with Schaeffer.

'A beautiful town you have here, sir,' said Hand, small talk never his greatest strength.

'Yah, very beautiful. You know, ve have the furst waterworks in America. Only here. Ungerground pipings, water here to this square. I did this. No other town in Americas has this. Water piped from spring to here. My wife and I, ve have gifted these to the town.'

'This is your town, sir, you founded it?' asked Conze.

Schaeffer shifted a little uneasily. 'Vell, I named it and build the tavern – vhich now we vill call the Baron von Steuben, yah!' He raised a tankard, which Conze clinked. Hand was drinking a pitcher of water.

'So you didn't start the town?'

'Nein. There were were others here before. From Germany. Juden.'

'Jews. Ah,' said Conze with a knowing tone.

'Yah. I was firsting in South Mountain, but not so good. So moved here, land better. Here was a small village, some craftsmen, traders, trading with Indians. People not so mix. I see future, a town laid out like in Germany, no? So, so . . .' He moved his hands about him as if trying to pin something down. 'So, I bought the Jews out. They move, up the road, just a mile. They still there. They have trading, they call it the Lebanon Trading Post.'

He moved closer to Conze, conspiratorially whispering, 'They not make banner to welcome, no. They trade vith British. Cornvallis. They sell. Indians. They sell. Sometimes, ve need things and they don't have them. But Britishers, oh, they have for them. Anyone with this,' he rubbed his fingers together. 'Heidlebergtown need no Juden. Keep them out of town. Best.'

'Supplying the British, are they?'

'Oh yes, sir. Britishers there all the time. Special reserves for Britishers.'

'Well, very interesting,' Conze replied. 'We are on what we call a scouting mission, to find where the British might find some friends. In the morning we shall pay a visit to the Lebanon Trading Post for ourselves, but for tonight, we'll share more of the glorious hospitality of Heidlebergtown, if that is all right with you, Herr Schaeffer?'

'Uh? All right? It will be our pleasure. Bier!'

The following morning, the sun slowly dragged itself up to reveal the surprise of a frosted morning; spring appeared to have retreated. The men's boots crunched over the crusted, rutted road, the Stormtroopers leading with a pace that the Riflemen found difficult to keep to. Where the Germans had risen early, briskly, and fell uncomplaining into line before setting off, the Pennsylvanians wore too obviously the effects of Schaeffer's beer. They woke grudgingly, complaining, falling into a shabby, farting, uneven line, their moans and groans contrasting with the quiet professionalism of the Stormtroopers. Even now, despite their new bright blue coats, white trousers and stout brown boots, they appeared bedraggled next to the aesthetic Stormtroopers, in their grey-green belted suits. Looking back at the shambling line, Conze reflected there was still a long way to go before these troops had reached the necessary standard.

Within twenty minutes they spotted the Lebanon Trading Post ahead. A collection of five buildings tucked away from the road, nestling among the near naked trees, a staging post, general stores and two or three houses – rough, timbered pioneer houses. Conze halted the line and called Hand to him.

'Have the Riflemen secure both sides of the road, Ed. I'll take the Stormtroopers and have these buildings inspected. Who knows, there may be British troops staying here. Let's not let any of them escape, eh?' Behind Hand's back, a Rifleman was retching. 'I see your boys are ready for the day as usual.'

Hand turned to see the trooper. He could smell his men from ten yards away. They embarrassed him this morning. Over the past ten weeks, they had taken to the drills and discipline of the Germans; they wanted to be like the Stormtroopers. They had seemed close, but now they had reverted to type. They had taken to the drink with gusto and were paying the price. In the cold of the morning, they looked like the old Riflemen, not the Stormtroopers they aspired to be. 'That Rifleman, fall out. Sergeant, discipline him!' he shouted at O'Leary.

Turning to Conze, 'We'll secure the exits. No one will escape. If there are British here, that is.'

Conze made off down the still hard, rutted highway with his Stormtroopers. From the first house came a thin, flickering candlelight. With a swift hand movement, he ordered his men to take up position around the house before marching up and hammering on the wooden door. From inside came the sounds of surprise, indecipherable mumblings, the scuffling of furniture, before the door opened, cautiously. A bearded man in his mid-twenties, wearing a nightshirt, stood before Conze.

'Good morning!' shouted Conze at the still foggy man. 'This is the Lebanon Trading Post, no?'

'It is,' replied the man, looking nervously at both Conze and the Stormtroopers who stood in a semicircle, their weapons pointing directly at the house. 'Are you after supplies?'

'No, we are after the British. We are the Stormtroopers of the Continental Army and we are hunting down British units – and those supplying them. And we are here this fine morning, at the Lebanon Trading Post, because we have reports of British troops in this area. And we are wondering, why would they be coming to the Lebanon Trading Post? Have they found friends at the Lebanon Trading Post?'

'We are no friends of the British here. We keep ourselves to ourselves. Our only friends are those who wish to buy our goods or use our staging post.'

'Would that not include the British then?'

'We have seen no British here since last year. General Washington saw to that, when he beat the British at Princeton. They are affeared of coming down these roads now.' He indicated the Stormtroopers. 'And I can see why. Would your men like breakfast, coffee?'

'They would. They would like coffee. And eggs. And bacon.'

'We can make coffee and eggs.'

'But no bacon.'

'No bacon, no.'

'How unusual. Juden?'

The man shifted uneasily. He understood the sly vehemence behind that question. It had driven his family from the town twenty years earlier. It was why the skilled craftsmen and artisans who had founded Heidlebergtown had moved on, to blend into the larger towns of the colonies. It was often there among those who stopped at the trading post: the freshly arrived pioneers making their way down from New York to find new lives in western Virginia; the gnarled, bearded loggers returning from Philadelphia to the forests of the north for the season; and the merchants peddling their wares from town to town, village to village. A constant drift of people coming out to populate the new continent, all of them bringing with them the the vices and prejudices of the old continent.

'Yes, we are a Jewish settlement. We have been here for many years. Before others came, we were here.'

'Before the Indians? No, I don't think so. What is your name?'

'Solomon Mandabach.'

'Dutch?'

'Our families came from Eindhoven, fifty years or so ago.'

'So, Solomon Mandabach, before we have coffee, before we lay down our weapons, you'll understand I have to secure the safety of my men. So, please, I would ask you to have all your families out here, so we can rest assure that there are no British here, waiting to trap us.'

'There are no British here.'

'Well, then, you have nothing to hide. I'm sure you would rather ask your people to come and meet me, rather than have my men wake them from their beds? Chop, chop, let us get this day started.'

Mandabach gave something of a nod and returned to the house. Conze walked away from the porch towards his men. From the outskirts of the village, he could see Hand watching him. He gave a cheerful, if disdainful, wave.

Within a few minutes, Mandabach reappeared, dressed now, along with a woman and three small girls. They huddled on the porch of the house. Conze shouted, 'Mrs Mandabach, please come and join me. Your husband is going to wake the rest of the village.'

The woman looked anxiously to her husband, who nodded his assent and then, obediently, she led the girls towards Conze, who walked a little towards them.

'What is your name?' he asked the mother.

'Caryn, Caryn Mandabach.'

Conze nodded in turn, before crouching down on his haunches to address the girls, a warm smile across his face. 'And who are you, such beautiful young ladies?'

'Sarah,' the oldest, perhaps seven, replied.

'And these are your sisters?'

'Yes. This is Rachel and Rebecca.'

He looked at the two sisters. The older around five; the younger one, Rebecca, no more than three, held a battered doll. Their clothes were old, ragged, passed down through too many generations. It was obvious that the Lebanon Trading Post was not thriving. Conze could hear their mother's shallow breathing, almost feel her heart beating.

'And what is this young lady called?' Conze asked of the doll.

'She is Martha,' Rebecca replied.

'The girls have named her after General Washington's wife,' the mother spoke up nervously.

Conze did not look at her; instead he continued to crouch down and smile at the girls. 'Ladies, are there any British soldiers here?'

The girls looked up at their mother, nervously.

'Tell the gentleman, girls,' she said.

Sarah replied, 'No, there are no soldiers here. Only our family.'

'Very good,' said Conze, raising himself from his haunches. Standing, he then reached down and lifted up Rebecca, putting her on his shoulders. 'Here, young lady, you and Martha can have the best view of the morning.' The mother was gulping air, frightened for her child, not knowing whether to protest or not.

The families were making their way out of the houses and the inn now, dazed, half-dressed in some cases. There were a dozen

202

in total, ranging from two small boys to an elderly man who was having trouble walking, leaning heavily on a stick.

'Here!' barked Conze.

The group, led by Mandabach, made their way towards Conze.

At his location near the trading post, Hand looked on. He was anxious. He had seen something similar before. Images from New Brunswick crossed his mind. He called to O'Leary, 'Pat, I'm going over. I've a bad feeling about this.'

'Werner knows what he's doing, leave him be, fella.'

Hand looked at his friend. There was a coldness in Pat's eyes. They had witnessed the massacre at New Brunswick. Had O'Leary forgotten that, or, even worse, did he no longer care? The distance was great between them now. Without replying, he walked away and towards Conze.

'Where are the English soldiers?' asked Conze of the group of families.

'I already told you, there are no British soldiers here,' answered Mandabach.

'Mister, I was not asking you. You,' he pointed at one younger but bearded adult. 'Where are the English hiding?'

The man looked puzzled. 'My brother told you. There are no English here.'

'We know that you trade here with the English, you support the English?'

'We support no one, we take no sides in this war,' Mandabach replied.

'You take no side?'

'We keep ourselves free of politics, of the world as others wish it to be. We are content to live our lives separate from others here. This is our colony within a colony.'

Conze looked at Mandabach with distaste. 'That is a problem. By taking no side, you choose a side. You are either for America or for King George.'

'We support neither side. These are not issues that concern us,' the younger brother answered.

'That is impossible. By not supporting one side, you reveal yourselves to be agents of the British. You are for us or against us. Let us see what you are hiding in this shitty village of yours. Is everyone out of their huts?'

The younger man replied. 'The houses, you mean? Our homes?' There was defiance in him; Conze recognised it. 'Yes, but there is our elderly grandma, she is unable to leave her bed.'

'How convenient,' replied Conze and he flicked his hand in the air, narrowly missing the girl still sitting on his shoulders, and shouted, 'Search these filthy huts.'

The Stormtroopers ran into the houses, followed immediately by the sound of furniture being overturned, the smash of pottery breaking, the dull thud of pots and pans thrown around. The women, bewildered, began to shriek in despair.

'What are you looking for?' asked the younger brother. 'We have told you, there are no English here. There is no one but us.'

'We will see. See what weapons you are hiding, what supplies you are keeping for Cornwallis. Tell your whores to be quiet.'

'You are welcome to what food we have, but we have little,' said the older brother, fear in his voice. 'This winter has been hard for us. And we have no weapons.'

Hand appeared by Conze's side. 'What is the concern here, Werner?'

The German didn't deign to answer.

One of the Stormtroopers dragged an elderly, confused woman in a nightgown out of one of the houses. 'Mama,' screamed Caryn Mandabach, running towards her as a soldier pushed the old woman to the ground – the children following their mother to their great-grandmother.

'What is this?' shouted the younger brother at Conze. 'What

harm was she doing? What harm are any of us doing? Have your men no respect?'

Conze gave him a cruel, withering look. 'Respect? You Jews expect "respect"? "What harm are we doing?" The cry of the Jew down the ages! What harm do you do? What harm do you not do? Filthy, stinking subhumans. Look around you, look how you live, in shit. And you'd have us all live like you.' The abuse poured out of him, shocking in its vehemence.

Hand stood next to him. He felt slightly nauseous, sweating despite the chill air, unsure what to do.

'Obergruppenführer, weapons.'

One of the younger Stormtroopers came out of the grandmother's house, an old blunderbuss in his hands. It was rusted and clearly had not been used for many years.

'What is this?' screamed Conze. 'You said you had no weapons and we find this?'

Mandabach was surprised, 'I had no idea. I, I, that, that was in our grandparents' house.' He pointed towards the old man now leaning on another. 'He, he, his mind has gone. He has no idea where he is or what is happening.'

Conze walked over to the crowd, staring intently at the old man. His eyes gave nothing back to him, just the blankness of senility. The ancient man muttered something in Yiddish.

'What's he saying? What is this gibberish?' asked Conze of Mandabach.

'I, I don't know, nothing, nonsense. He has the mind of a child. It means nothing. Nothing.'

Conze looked at the group. Seventeen of them, huddling together, shivering in the coldness of the morning. They were a pathetic and sad-looking group. Hand touched him on the elbow.

'Werner, there are no British here. This is just a poor trading post. They can barely keep themselves alive, let alone supply the British army. The men are hungry. Let's return to Heidlebergtown and have a good breakfast. We have more important things to attend to.' He was tense, sweat prickling his neck despite the cold.

Conze was still holding the youngest girl on his shoulders. He looked up at her. 'What do you say, Rebecca? Shall we leave you all?'

'You're scaring me.'

'There's no need to be scared. I'm a good man. I'm here to protect the good people. You're a good girl, aren't you?'

'Yes,' she replied.

'Then you have no reason to be scared, no reason at all.' He looked around him. 'Very well. I can see there are no British here. But take this as a warning. If I ever hear of you trading with the British again, we will return and we will destroy this post.'

'We will not, thank you,' said Mandabach, relief in his voice.

'Men, fall back in line. We will follow Colonel Hand's suggestion and return to Heidlebergtown for a good breakfast. Onwards.'

Hand relaxed, threw an apologetic smile towards Mandabach and turned back towards his men.

Conze strode off, with Rebecca still on his shoulders.

Now there was new consternation, the mother shrieking, the sisters crying, the father screaming: 'My daughter! Give me back my daughter.'

Hand turned round to see Conze bounding towards him, the girl crying as she sat on his shoulders. 'Werner, what are you doing? The child, give them back the child.'

Conze increased his pace and walked past Hand. 'No, the child comes with us.'

'What? Why? Why on earth are you bringing the child?'

'As an act of good faith. It's the only way I can be sure these Jews will do as I say. Otherwise, they will be laughing behind our backs and reporting back to Cornwallis. That is their nature. They cannot help themselves.'

'Give back the child!'

Behind them the screaming was louder, the whole group was convulsed, the younger brother started scuffling with a pair of Stormtroopers.

'I want my mama!' Rebecca was crying.

'For pity's sake, Conze, return the child to her mother!' demanded Hand.

The child's screams grew louder, her mother ran towards her, but a trooper caught her around the waist and threw her to the ground. 'Mama!' screamed Rebecca.

Hand scrambled to stand in front of Conze, stopping his march. 'Conze, I am telling you to give the child back to her family.'

Conze stopped and stared at Hand. 'You are weak. You have no backbone. You like always to take the easy road. I prefer the harder road, cruel it may be, but necessary.' He looked up at Rebecca. 'You want to return to your mother? Go.'

And he lifted her up with both hands and threw the three-year-old towards her mother, with such hatred and force, that she landed not in the arms of her mama, but head first on the cold, firm rocky path that served as a road, her head cracking open on a small boulder that lay at the edge.

There was silence. Then the most terrible, heart-wrenching screams, as the families saw the blood streaming from the head of the dead child.

Hand ran to the child. Her head was shattered, scarlet blood and grey brains smearing the ground. He was shocked to his core by the brutality of what he had witnessed, incapable of comprehending what had just happened. Something snapped in him. He left the child and ran towards Conze, who was marching off as though nothing had happened.

Catching up with the German, he pulled at his jacket, stopping him again. 'You've killed that little girl, an innocent child. You're nothing but a brute.'

'She was a Jew. She wasn't innocent. They are never innocent from the moment they are born. They are a threat. And you have to understand that.'

'No, you're the threat,' and, without thinking, Hand threw a punch that floored the German.

Now there was chaos. The Mandabach brothers made to charge up the road towards Conze, but a group of Stormtroopers held them back amid punches and kicks. Hand attempted to fly at Conze again, but two Stormtroopers moved in on him, pulling him away and pinning back his arms. The sounds of wailing around the dead child were terrible, and from nowhere a wind suddenly whipped up and the sky became a grey, miserable blanket.

'You seem to make a habit of striking fellow officers, Colonel Hand,' said Conze, wiping his mouth as he raised himself to his feet.

'Only with good cause. You disfigure our cause by your actions, you animal,' spat Hand.

'Do I? Do I really? Or do I make it a greater cause than you can imagine?'

'You're insane, truly you are.'

'Take him away for now,' Conze said to the Stormtroopers holding Hand back. 'Let us resolve this.'

He strode towards the Mandabach brothers, struggling still against a small group of Stormtroopers, until he was face to face with the Mandabachs. 'An accident,' he said calmly. 'War is full of them. Now you must ensure no more accidents befall your family. So, no more trading with the British.'

The older brother was weeping, but the younger one was full of rage and spat at Conze, throwing insults in Yiddish at him.

'You make this so difficult for yourself. Would you like another lesson, mister?'

The younger Mandabach, bruised and bloodied, made again to break free, to attack Conze, but had no chance against the Stormtroopers.

'Tiresome,' said Conze. 'You people will never learn.' And he pulled out a dagger from his belt and slit the young brother's throat. As the blood poured out, Conze looked at his men and said calmly, 'Burn the village, burn it all. And these Jews with it.'

TWENTY-EIGHT

Hand stumbled back to his men, dazed by the events, and humiliated. All O'Leary said to him was, 'I told you not to mess with him, Ed.' And with that he walked away, leaving Hand standing alone.

Hand watched his friend go back to the Pennsylvanians, and cried out in a weak voice, 'Riflemen, fall in line.'

From their position, they had not had a clear view of the events. Some of the older fellows asked him, 'What's happening, Ed?' He did not acknowledge their questions, just walked past and barked to start the return to Heidlebergtown. As they moved off, the screams from the women grew louder. 'Eyes straight ahead,' he said to the men. 'We're returning to Heidlebergtown. There'll be breakfast for you all.' And then he heard the crackle of fire and he knew the Lebanon Trading Post was going up in flames.

They breakfasted with Schaeffer fussing over them, on cornbread, porridge, cold meats, beer and coffee. Hand sat alone, caught up in his own thoughts, unaware of the whisperings of the men around him. Half an hour into the feast, the Stormtroopers arrived. They smelled of smoke and fire. They were animated, excited, eager to celebrate. They had friends among the Riflemen and told them what had occurred: the villagers were British sympathisers, they had turned on them, the Stormtroopers had been attacked, they had no option. After that no one talked to Hand. Then or the next day.

Those days were miserable for Colonel Hand. He was isolated and shunned by his own men as they marched from Heidlebergtown and on to Hummelstown. On the second day, the temperatures dropped again, the frosted ground became icy, and five miles outside of Hummelstown, snow began to fall, heavily and fast, so that the trek became even more difficult and hazardous. The abrupt return of winter was all too symbolic to Hand.

He went about his boys, cajoling, encouraging. He had done this many times before, often in worse conditions, and he was used to the grumbling and moaning, but it was different now. There was no love any more, respect had gone, the grumbling replaced by indifference or even outright hostility towards him. As they trudged past him in the swirling maelstrom, he thought he heard one of them hiss 'Jew Lover'. He could not be sure, the words were lost in the seething white wind, but he saw only too well the burning hatred in the coal-dark eyes of the icy white figures that passed him. But when Werner Conze walked down the line and made similar noises of encouragement, he received cheers and shouts of approval. The Riflemen were no longer Hand's.

They lodged overnight in Hummelstown, another town established by German immigrants, husband and wife, Frederick and Rosina Hummel, just over a decade ago, and the welcome was as warm as Heidlebergtown. The men patted down the snow and laid their tents out on the town's green, and then most of them accepted another evening of beer, sauerkraut and sausages.

Normally, Hand would have tented with Pat O'Leary, but the Irishman had made an excuse the previous night and showed no intention of returning this evening. Hand went looking for him. The sergeant was cleaning muskets with a group of Riflemen. 'Pat, we have to talk.'

'What about, fella? You wanna lecture me again? You wanna

warn me off the Stormtroopers again? Going to talk to me like you did with Sarah? That went well, didn't it?'

'What's happened to us? We've been like brothers for years.'

'What's happened is that I've woken up. Yes, we were close, like brothers as you say, but you were always the big brother and me the kid and that was all right, mostly. But I don't wanna be the kid any more, Ed. I looked up to you. Perhaps you weren't like a brother, perhaps you were like a father. And I believed in what you told me, but now I see things differently.'

'Because of Werner Conze?'

O'Leary continued to strip the musket. The other men sat silent, cleaning their muskets, exchanging silent glances with each other. None of them wanted to be there at this moment.

'Not just Werner, all the German lads, they're a great bunch. We were just a bunch of pissheads playing at it like, these lads have taught us how to do it properly. And the crack is great wi' 'em. Ain't it, lads?' There was a mumble of agreement from the Riflemen. 'Like I said before, you don't like it because you were the top dog and now Werner is.'

'We're joint commanders of the unit.'

'Ach, no one believes that, fella. Werner's in charge, he's the one everyone listens to. No disrespect an' all that, but nobody's listening to you any more, Ed.'

'Why not?'

'Why not? You gotta ask me why not? Christ alive. Ain't it obvious?'

'No, it isn't.'

'After New Brunswick you went around telling anyone who would listen what the Stormtroopers did to those British.'

'And that was wrong, was it?'

'Hell, yes, it was. You never heard of loyalty to your own boys?'

'What they did wasn't acceptable. You saw that. You stood there with me, watching it. They shot them all, they were unarmed, those women were raped.'

'Those women weren't raped. You didn't see it.'

'What, they went off with them because they wanted to?'

'They were taking them away to protect them after they shot the soldiers.'

'What about the children?'

'What children?'

'There were children killed in New Brunswick.'

'I didn't see any children.'

Hand was incredulous. 'You didn't see those little kids lying there, in their own blood? You were standing right by me.'

'No, you imagined that. There were only soldiers killed. Talk to the lads who did it, they'll tell you. What were they supposed to do? Free those British soldiers so they could join up with Cornwallis an' his gang and come back after us? This is war, Ed, for sure it is. It's them or us and I'm happy in my heart we're wi' the Stormtroopers. Happy in my heart, we're going to win and not have the British rubbing our faces in it. You think the British would have done any differently if they'd caught us?'

'I don't care what the British would do. I only care what we do. What we stand for.'

'What we stand for? That's the point, we stand for something now. When we started it was all a lot of hot air about freedom and liberty an' all that, but did anyone believe all that? Those posh, rich, fancy people, those people you look up to in the Congress or whatever, I don't see many of them freezing their bollocks out here or getting shot at in Trenton. Where are they? Some nice warm house in Philly or Boston or New York. Those people like John Adams and Thomas Jefferson, with their powdered wigs and perfumes and tights and what have you, they're no better for the likes of people like me and these lads than King George and all his nobs. They don't give a fuck about us li'l people. Whoever wins, those people will be all right, but not now.'

'Well said, Pat,' said one of the Riflemen, giving the others confidence to grumble their agreement.

Ignoring the others, Hand replied, 'Not now?'

'No, not now, because we're finally for something now, we're fighting for National Socialism, that's what we're going to create here.' He looked at his former mentor. His face was puzzled. 'You really don't know what I'm talking about do you?'

Hand did not.

'If you had come to more of Werner's meetings and listened and debated, you'd know. You'd understand then, but you're too busy feeling sorry for yourself because you're not the main man any more, fella. Werner, Hanna, the baron, all of them, they've brought us these ideas and educated us into more than we were before. Look around you, every single member of the Riflemen, look how proud they are now to be wearing that swastika on their arm. They asked us, you know that? The Stormtroopers, they asked us. They wanted to know if we would do them the honour of wearing their swastika. They asked us! The honour was all ours, believe me. I've never been so proud.'

Again, echoes of agreement from the other men.

'Like you were when they burned that Jewish village.'

'There you go again. Those Jews were supplying the Brits. They were keeping food an' supplies an' all back for the Brits. And they attacked some of the lads.'

'No, they didn't.'

'They bloody did. Franzy Mueller is covering in bruises and cuts, they had a right go at him.'

'Well, they did, but only after Conze had killed one of their children.'

'Thought you said they didn't attack our boys? Turns out they

214

did, eh? Look, Ed, it's simple: you're either wi' us or agin us. And the boys all think you're agin us.'

'And what do you think, Sergeant?' Hand looked at the faces of his men. They had stopped cleaning the muskets. They were all staring at him. There was aggression in their eyes.

'Well . . . well, I think this war might not be for you any more, Ed. You should go back to Trenton or wherever and take up your doctor's bag and start practising medicine agin, fella. You'd do more good for ev'ryone there, cause if you stay here . . . well, I worry that we won't be friends for much longer.'

TWENTY-NINE

The following morning they moved out from Hummelstown, down to the Susquehanna River and then up towards Queen Esther's Town.

This was the village of the so-called Queen Esther, an Iroquois woman who had married the leader of the Munsees, one of the Delaware tribes, and assumed leadership on his death. The scouting report was clear: she remained sympathetic to the British and there was the possibility of British troops hiding in the settlement and a weapons cache.

They approached by the icy river road, two abreast. There were in total 400 of them in the joint unit, Conze at the head, the Stormtroopers followed by the Riflemen.

It was one of the rear Riflemen, Simon Haigh, who saw the Iroquois first. Or perhaps he saw nothing of the kind, still innocent as the tomahawk flew through the air, splitting his skull open. He staggered backwards, the blade wedged deep in his head. As he stumbled into the line, there were shouts from the back and Hand raced around. Haigh had collapsed, crimson brine staining the ice-cold ground. The line was still moving ahead, with the exception of Hand and the seven or eight Riflemen around the fallen body.

'Better look sharp, boys,' Hand said. 'Simon's gone. Let's get back to the line and look lively. Send word up front.'

He hardly needed to do so, for out of the woods ahead of them came charging four or five Iroquois, heads shaved, their tattooed torsos seemingly impervious to the bitter cold. They charged, tomahawks raised, into the main body of the Stormtroopers, cutting and hacking, not stopping as they ran through the lines down to the river. Then from the bushes came the first gunfire, spraying the line, more accurate than expected, Hessians and Americans falling wounded or dead.

Both Conze and Hand screamed orders at their men to form three lines facing in the direction of the wooded area. The professionalism of the Stormtroopers and the new-found confidence of the Riflemen became apparent. Oblivious to the shots pelting around them, the Pennsylvanians steadied themselves, the line prepared their muskets and within a minute were returning fire. Shot peppered the wood, one volley followed quickly by another, to the sound of branches and skin being ripped apart.

But then from the rear returned the braves who had cut through the ranks, their numbers increased to twenty or more. Conze screamed: '*Hintere Linie, um die Kurve!*' and the Stormtroopers' rear ranks turned at once. They fired off a round, largely without effect as they had little time to line up their targets before the Iroquois were on them, hacking away at them with tomahawks. In return, the Hessians fought with their own knives and axes. It was brutal. It was senseless. Men from both sides simply hacking at anything in a mad desperation.

Above the fray, Conze shouted, 'Colonel Hand, have your men march towards the woods and get them out of there!'

Hand followed the orders, the Riflemen set off towards the woods, firing as they did so. Now the Iroquois came out of the woods, running at speed, tomahawks flailing in the air. The two sides clashed and there were now two separate hand-to-hand fights along the road, each as bloody as the other.

For more than fifteen minutes, the fighting continued. Then

the Stormtroopers finished off the last of their Iroquois, inevitably the final axe blow coming from Lothar Kluggman. Their position secure, they ran towards the Riflemen. Seeing them come, the Iroquois, still fighting, withdrew into the woods. The Americans and Germans chased them into the thickets, but stopped before the trees became too dense. They had victory. If they moved deep into the woods, they feared the savages would yet win the day.

The Stormtroopers and Riflemen trooped back towards the road. The sight before them was pitiful.

The river road was littered with bodies, the icy pathways melting from the hot red blood, turning to a hot pink slush underfoot. Men lay moaning on the ground from their wounds. There was no mercy: any Iroquois still alive had their throats cut where they lay. They counted them up: twenty-three dead Indians. Of their own forces, four Riflemen and three Stormtroopers were dead, but there were many injuries. There was hardly a man who did not have a sizeable wound, but some had hacked arms, thighs sliced open, fingers missing. Tourniquets were applied, but several other men were unlikely to see the next morning.

The men were exhausted, but at the same time, that strange sense of elation that follows those victorious in battle came over the group. There was much hugging, and laughter now, Stormtroopers and Riflemen together; they had survived, they were alive, that was enough.

Hand put his training to good measure, tending to the men. Conze wandered over, saying formally, 'What needs to be done for these wounded men, Colonel? Can any be saved?'

'There are four or five who are unlikely to make it through the night. We should perform amputations on another two, one below the knee, the other more difficult. The rest we can bandage up. As long as we get back to Hummelstown within an hour or so.'

'We are not doing that.'

'What do you mean?'

'We are close to this Queen Esther's village. That was her welcoming party. We will destroy that village and her savages with it. You can stay here with the wounded if you have no stomach for it, but these men want revenge for their fallen comrades. We go now. We'll collect the wounded when we return.' And then coldly, 'We won't be long.'

'If we don't get these wounded to Hummelstown for proper treatment, they will die.'

Dispassionately, Conze replied: 'Then they die. They will be of little use anyway. We will not allow this Queen Esther to roam the land slaughtering others.'

'You don't know if this was her party. It bears the hallmarks of an Iroquois raiding party. They're as much a threat to an Indian village as they are to us, they—'

'What a surprise. Now you are on the side of the savage, Hand.'

'I'm not on their side, I'm saying you need to know the facts before—'

'Facts! I have no need for facts! I have my eyes. My instinct. Queen Esther will pay for this, her and every one of her filthy swine.' Walking away, he ordered: 'Men, form up, let's go and treat that bitch Queen Esther to a lesson.'

The village consisted of around seventy log cabins, of various sizes. In the centre was one larger than the rest, with a chimney and porch, presumably the home of Queen Esther. The settlement was eerily quiet, no one was outside, but the smoke of fires from some of the cabins suggested there were people at home.

Conze stood on the edge of the clearing and looked around him. 'Set every fucking building alight and have all the savages that don't burn rounded up down by the river.'

Immediately, the men went to work. They used their flints to start fires and within minutes the thatched roofs of the buildings were ablaze.

Now there was noise, terrible screeching, ear-splitting shrieks, and from the buildings, men, women and children came running out in a crazed frenzy. They were fleeing everywhere, and the soldiers did their best to stop them, at first trying to hold them back, but soon there was more violence, as the soldiers struck anyone they came in contact with. The Indian men tried to fight back, but they were outnumbered and weaponless. From the big house came Queen Esther. A large, round woman, neatly dressed in buckskin, with her two teenage sons, young braves.

'Monstrous villains!' she bellowed in English. 'What crime is this? You devils!'

'Queen Esther?' asked Conze, walking towards her, surrounded by five Stormtroopers, rifles at the ready. 'You sent some braves out to meet us. We are merely returning your hospitality.' Turning to his men, he said, 'Kill the boys, but keep this old hag alive for now,' and he walked away as the Stormtroopers slaughtered the sons and tied up Queen Esther.

The village was an inferno. Every building on fire, already bodies scattered around it, those still alive herded down towards the water, where they stood, shaking from both the cold and fear.

There were about seventy women and children, of all ages, and a few men. Most of the males had been slaughtered in the mayhem, and those that remained were pitiful, bloodied and beaten. The troops formed a semicircle, Conze stood at their centre and Queen Esther was dragged along the ground and then thrown at his feet.

'See what you have done, Queen Esther. See what you have achieved by attacking us?'

'You devil, you are as stupid as you are evil. We are not warriors. We plant corn, we have pigs, hens, we trade. Most likely you were attacked by a Lenape raiding party. There is one around this place.'

'Of course, of course. How silly of me. We come to your village, known for siding with the British, we are attacked and it has nothing to do with you. Of course not. Well, we have no time to debate this. The issue is clear. You will watch your tribe perish and then I will kill you and that will be that. Men, arm yourselves.'

The soldiers primed their weapons and raised them towards the shivering group, but then there was a shout of 'No!'

It was Hand, running towards the group, putting himself in front of the Indians.

'No. I will not let this happen again. These are women and children and a few wounded men. This is not what we are. We end this here, now. We have destroyed their village, their animals, their crops. That is more than enough, even if they are guilty. We walk away with our wounded and end this now.'

Conze shook his head. 'I don't believe this. Will no one rid me of this man, this friend of no one but our enemies? Move, Hand, or you will suffer the same fate as these savages.'

'I will not move.'

Unflinching, Conze replied, 'Then you will die. Fire!'

Without hesitation, the joint force of Stormtroopers and Riflemen let fire at the group and, with it, Hand. The combined fire was so ferocious that it threw many bodies into the icy water of the Susquehanna.

'Reload and fire at will,' shouted Conze, and soon another round was fired into the remaining bodies, until all were down on the shoreline, or in the water.

'You devil,' spat Queen Esther. 'Deliver my people from the water to me so I may bury them as is our tradition.'

'Bury them? You're not going to bury anyone, old lady. String her up from that tree and leave her there for the crows. And throw all those bodies in the lake or leave them for the crows, whatever you like, it means nothing to me. Then let's get out of this shithole.'

Three Stormtroopers dragged the screeching woman away, other men walked to the water's edge and started throwing the bodies into the river, the current dragging them slowly out. Lothar Kluggman strode among them, looking for one body in particular. He was not disappointed. Edward Hand, in his blue Pennsylvanian coat, lay across some teenage girls, blood seeped from a wound in his shoulder, his face red from his blood mixed with others. Kluggman did not care to see whether the colonel was still alive or not, simply picked the body up in his giant paws and threw it into the fast-running waters of the Susquehanna.

At the water's edge, Pat O'Leary had watched it all unfurl. 'I warned you, Ed. I told you,' and he spat on the ground and turned on his heel.

THIRTY

'It is driving me insane!' Reitsch exploded. 'This primitive land, where nothing is as it could be, where everything is so, so, so damn primitive!'

Von Steuben laughed out loud. His lover's penchant for drama was a source of amusement to him: Hanna's constant anger at the ineptitude of the Colonists, the lack of any modern technology, the poor food and drink, the itchy, cumbersome nature of the clothes. Best of all was her dislike of the smells of the eighteenth century.

'Don't laugh. Travel around these colonies and what do you meet? Small-minded men with no imagination. I tell them I want forty thousand blankets. What do they tell me? I can get you five hundred. What good is that? And these people, they are after dollars for themselves. Every single price negotiated. And the worst? The worst are the Jews, of course. They tell me there are no Jews in America. Well there are and they are doing one thing: trading. Trading with us, with the British, even with the Indians. They don't care, they sell to whoever offers the most money.'

'You are witnessing the birth of capitalism, my dear. When everything went to shit in the nineteen twenties, you could have drawn a line right back to this time, where the seeds were first planted, and are germinating already. The cult of the individual, the obsession with personal freedom, the pandering to large business at the expense of the state, market instability, a lack of overall planning.'

'And these towns. Such shitholes. Even Berlin bombed to the edge of death is better than Philadelphia or Boston. There are no buildings to speak of, everything temporary, barely any paved streets, mud and shit everywhere. No sense of art, even decadent art would be welcome here. Anything to escape the monotony of the lives of these people. What I would do for one proper cup of coffee! One cup of coffee from Café Bauer, instead of this ground dirt! A coffee and schnapps from Café Bauer, that's what I want!'

'When we've won this damn war, we'll build you your own Café Bauer on your own Unter den Linden in whichever town we decide to make the capital of the Reich, my darling. But for now, remember where we are. This is the eighteenth century. These people are surviving on the edge of the world, Hanna. You expect art, opera, theatre, fine dining and wines. They expect an Indian to come through the doors and scalp their families.'

'In Boston? I hardly think so. You see plenty of Indians there. They aren't about to start a revolt, they're lying down in the mud, drunk. They have given up. You'll find nothing of the noble savage there, believe me, Friedrich. The stench of those places. Urgh, terrible. You want to retch every metre. Even this camp smells better than the towns.'

'So I take it my dear, your colognes and perfumes have not arrived from Paris?'

'You, you dog!' she screamed, laughing at herself and hitting him with a pillow around the head.

They fell into an embrace, hot, damp, passionate kissing. She had been away for two weeks, meeting the suppliers, negotiating better deals, putting into place a modern supply chain. She had loved that, but she had missed him. And he had missed her too.

She enjoyed his strong, masculine presence, his quiet force. She had rarely, if ever, seen him lose his temper, yet all who served under him knew there was a beast under that sophisticated veneer that would come out raging if necessary. It had seen him from the beer halls of Munich through the Luftwaffe years. In Germany, people did not look to cross Robert von Greim and here in America they were not looking to cross Baron Friedrich von Steuben.

And he enjoyed her company as much as the physical thrill of her body. He had not shared his fellow Nazis' conservatism on the role of women. Rather, he actively sought out strong, fierce women. He enjoyed Hanna's combative nature, her searing intelligence and refusal to accept second best in anything. She was driven by righteous desire, whereas he at fifty-four had calmed down. He trusted her judgement in every matter. She had never once been wrong about anything. And he loved her, deeply.

Their lovemaking was always fast and passionate. Occasionally, he would slap her across the face and she would return the same, harder, and again. He enjoyed it. He enjoyed her dominating him in this way and she enjoyed dominating him. Sometimes she would tie him up, sometimes he her, and there were bruises when the play became too rigorous. But not tonight. This evening, there was tenderness brought by two weeks of separation. There was kissing and then slow penetration. Astride him, Hanna held him deep inside her, their eyes holding each other, a deep well of desire. And a tear slipped from her.

'I love you, Rob – damn – Friedrich! With all my heart.' She laughed.

He took in her wide, happy smile and replied gently, 'And you are the great love of my life, Hanna. I could not be here, living here, in this place, among all this shit, if I didn't have you alongside me. My love.'

Rolling over, he gently put her down on the bed, held her arms above her, stretched her out, pushed his hips flat to hers and thrusted himself deep into her. Soon she released herself, her orgasm exciting von Steuben, until he too climaxed, the moans of ecstasy so loud that a few tents away a group of Stormtroopers playing cards and drinking brandy started laughing. 'Hanna is giving the boss another good seeing to!'

Exhausted, they lay in each other's arms, real affection from both to each other, the coarseness of the bedclothes, the softness of the mattress, unfelt among the warmth of their love.

'I have some news about your protégée, Sarah Hand,' he said.

'Let me guess, she is pregnant by Conze.'

'Not yet, no, but they are to be married.'

'He's so bourgeois that one. Despite everything, all he wants to do is settle down with a lady and raise his dynasty of Conzes. Honestly, he has no imagination.'

'We need some little Conzes, we need lots of little Conzes if we are to secure the future. That's why we're here, isn't it? To win the future for our children.'

'Those of us who can bear children,' she said.

He regretted instantly his choice of words. 'They will all be our children when we are finished, Hanna. Future generations will cherish you and me more greatly than any blood relative. They will forget the names of their great-grandmothers, but they will not forget the name of Hanna Reitsch.' He stroked her hair, kissed her cheek.

'What of her brother?'

'Ah, I'm afraid he is no longer with us. Conze's patience with him ended on their scouting trip. First, there was some unpleasantness with a Jewish village.'

'A Jewish village? I thought there were no Jewish settlements here.'

'None that we would recognise, but there are a few scattered settlements here and there, the first pustules of a greater contagion. Conze came upon this village by chance and did what we would expect of him. Colonel Hand attempted to stop that and

226

then later attempted to save an Indian village that had sent out a war party against our men. Apparently he stood in front of them to protect the women and children and in doing so was shot with them all.'

'By Werner?'

'Actually, by a firing squad Conze had lined up, of both Stormtroopers and Pennsylvanian Riflemen. Colonel Hand rather overestimated the loyalty of his men to him. None of them batted an eyelid, including his former friend O'Leary.'

'You have to hand it to Werner, he has done a splendid job on those men.'

'He has indeed. They are quite the junior Stormtroopers now. The sister is being informed this afternoon that her brave brother was killed by wild savages.'

'Her loyalty passed from brother to lover a while back, I think. She is doing the most marvellous job with the League of American Girls. I am very pleased with her. There may be hope for these people yet.'

PART 4

PHILADELPHIA, PENNSYLVANIA

5 August 1777

THIRTY-ONE

Congress had wanted Washington and his senior generals to come to Philadelphia for a briefing on the conduct of the war. The spring had given way to summer, but aside from minor skirmishes, the expected showdown with the British had not happened. The politicians and bureaucrats in Philadelphia were irritated at the cost of inactive armies, not just Washington's main army at Lowantica, but also the Northern Army under Schuyler. They wanted – simply put – to see something for their money.

The commander-in-chief had delayed responding to their request for some time, but now there was a pressing issue.

On 24 July, Washington had learned that Howe, along with Cornwallis and most of his key forces, had left New York in a flotilla of almost three hundred ships. The estimates for the numbers of troops aboard ranged from 11,000 to 18,000 men. Washington's instinct had been that Howe was going to sail up the Hudson River and join forces with Burgoyne to launch an attack on the Colonists' Northern Army. Von Steuben argued that this would not be the case. In his words, Howe would be looking to, 'Fix upon those objects that will appear the most splendid. He will make for Philadelphia.'

In this, the baron was in a minority and Washington agreed with the rest of his generals that they should bolster Schuyler. Consequently, Washington's army left camp and marched to

Ramapo in New York. While making camp there, he received news on 30 July that the fleet had been sighted off the Delaware Capes, which led to an about-turn south. It was possible, after all, that Howe was planning to attack the capital of the rebellion. Accepting the inevitable, Washington rode off ahead of his army to meet with Congress.

He invited von Steuben and Reitsch to escort him, along with Nathanael Greene and Alexander Hamilton. It was not entirely Washington's idea. John Adams had suggested as much in a letter to him; Congress was much fascinated about von Steuben and the remarkable woman who had become the quartermaster for the Continental Army. It would please Congress for them to attend. Washington, for once undiplomatic, told the pair not to expect too much: 'Chimney corner patriots abound: venality, corruption, prostitution of office for selfish ends, abuse of trust, perversions of funds from a national to a private use, and speculations upon the necessities of the times, pervade all interests. That, I am afraid, is Congress.'

Von Steuben and Reitsch soon found Washington's assessment to be correct. The members of Congress were a dreary collection of bookkeepers, small businessmen and nosy ideologues. Von Steuben had met their type before. They had come flooding into the Nazi party when there was the smallest whiff of possible power. The same kind of men, he reflected, happy to sit in on judgement of those who were physically and morally braver than themselves, happy to carp from the sidelines when things went badly, happy to swivel their faces the other way when success came.

Both Reitsch and the baron were pleasantly surprised that none of the members of Congress was openly opposed to the idea that a woman, and a foreign woman at that, should be in charge of the army's supply strategy. True, from their patronising tone, it was evident that Congress regarded Reitsch as something of a freak of nature, but there was no outright hostility. However, the questions put to both them and Washington on the conduct of the war and organisation of the Continental Army were banal, and betrayed Congress's lack of real understanding.

There were two outstanding men, however, who stood shoulders above the rest in their general comportment as much as intelligence: John Adams and Thomas Jefferson. And it was noticeable how they both allowed the other members to fill most of the formal hours, while they reserved the appropriate questions for the moments when they were alone with Washington or, more frequently in the case of Adams, with von Steuben and Reitsch.

That the Germans were the toast of Philadelphia was clear from the rounds of soirées and dinners they found themselves invited to. For a city full of Quakers ambivalent about war, there were a lot of parties to celebrate the warriors.

The central object of fascination, however, was Reitsch. No one in Philadelphia had come across a character like her before: a woman who clearly saw herself as the equal of any man, one determined to set her own path. Whenever she left the State House or their lodgings at the City Tavern, Reitsch would be immediately surrounded, especially by young women, many of whom had taken to dressing in what was described as the 'Reitsch mode' – the grey jacket with jodhpurs she wore. Tailors had taken to copying the design throughout the colonies and teenage girls, often to the disquiet of their parents, had taken to wearing them. In Philly, most well-to-do girls had cast off their formal dresses to don the Reitsch style. As one young girl told her: 'You inspire us all, madame, to see a future for ourselves where we can be judged not as females, but as people equal to the men who surround us. You have freed us from bondage!' In return, Hanna promised she would send Sarah Hand to the city to establish a branch of the League of American Girls.

It was the last day of the visit. The next morning they would return to Morris Town and Lowantica Brook, but there was one final formal dinner to sit through, this one hosted by the Sons of Liberty. As they sat down to dinner, there was a notable new addition to what had become a familiar group. Sat to Reitsch's right, across the table from Washington, was a handsome nineteen-year-old man who spoke English with a heavy French accent.

Rather stiffly, he introduced himself to Reitsch, 'Gilbert du Motier, Marquis de Lafayette. I have come travelling to ze Americas to give support to zis most juste de causes.'

So this is him, she thought to herself. You grow to become one of the most celebrated men of the age. This spotty young man becomes a confidant of all the great Americans of the age, Washington, Jefferson, Adams; is wounded at the battle of Brandywine; and grows to be one of the great heroes of the American Revolution. He will be the chief cause of the alliance between France and the colonies that turns the conflict into a global war and wins independence for the Americas. He will then become one of the key players of the French Revolution, stand up to Napoleon and help create a further revolution in 1830, and turn down the offer to become dictator of France. How astonishing to think of all this happening to this thin, acne-faced young man.

Or rather, she mused, how history may change now. How whether the name Lafayette comes to mean anything at all in the future depends on what she and her lover determine. A lover betraying just the smallest amount of jealousy, she thought, as she talked to the young Frenchman.

The dinner was interrupted by a message brought to Alexander Hamilton by an exhausted, dust-covered rider.

'What is it, Hamilton?' asked Adams. 'The news cannot be good, your face alone tells all the room this.'

'Sir, ah, it is news of General Howe. It is not that the news is necessarily bad, it is that the news is perplexing. He appears to have left the Delaware Capes and headed south.'

'Charleston,' uttered Washington. 'He is going to attack Charleston. This was but a feint.'

'Then we must head south, to defend the city,' said Lafayette.

'No, there is no point,' replied Hamilton. 'The defences of the city are such that it cannot easily be defended. And our supply lines and forces would be intolerably stretched. Take our forces to the south and we would seriously weaken the entire north and east. We have long agreed in our war councils that should such a event occur, we would have to leave Charleston.'

'Then we must turn about our forces and take advantage of the situation,' said Jefferson. 'New York lies open to us. Let us take her.'

'Or we should consider breaking his Northern Army under Burgoyne. With Howe and Cornwallis south, that army sits alone. I would counter we destroy the British army in the north for good,' argued Adams.

There was a further to and fro of debate before tacit agreement that Washington would take his forces and march north. There was a hubbub of cheering and then one dissenting voice raised itself above the din. The voice of Baron von Steuben.

'Gentlemen, I have listened to your debate in the spirit of one who has not been among you for long. With a heavy heart, I must tell you, you are wrong. There will be no attack on Charleston. This, my Lord Washington, is the feint. This is the tactic of a general. As soon as you have started the march north, mark my words, Howe will turn north again and head up Chesapeake Bay. He has eyes for only one city, and that city is Philadelphia.'

'My dear baron, what is your evidence for this?'

'My evidence is a lifetime's experience of studying warfare, preparing for warfare, of studying men and their ambitions. Charleston makes little sense. Frankly, attacking Philadelphia makes little sense in the grander strategy of a war to win back the colonies, but it makes a lot of sense if you are Sir William Howe. He wants a notable scalp to boast about in London. You're fighting a war for your freedom. He is fighting a war to enrich himself and his brother, to grow his reputation at the court of King George. If he can take Philadelphia, if he can rout the rebels in the heart of their country, well, imagine how that will be heard at court. Those are my reasons.'

'Baron, while I appreciate your understanding of the human condition, I prefer to concentrate – as I'm sure George does – on the hard evidence. And the evidence is that Howe is moving south,' Jefferson replied.

'Charleston makes little military sense, Mister Jefferson. I do not believe for one moment that General Howe is the kind of dummkopf who would go there.'

'But a dumpkoft who would attack Philadelphia?' the young Frenchman Lafayette had found his voice. 'Zere es no reason fer Howe to attack Philadelphia. Zere ez no strategic reason, but zere ez with Charleston, ez zere not? Charleston ez the key to the south, ez et not?'

'Charleston is no Philadelphia. It will carry little weight back in London. Howe is playing to the gallery in London, he is not thinking about how the war will end here in America. This I know from my experience of warfare and the men who wage it. One could not expect you, young man, to have such an understanding.'

'You must excuse my English, ez poor,' replied Lafayette. 'It ez true. I am much younger than you, Baron. Much younger and I may not carry ze experience nor prejudices of age, but I have experience from my family. Ze Lafayettes are one of ze oldest, most chivalrous and courageous families in France. My ancestor Gilbert de Lafayette served under Joan of Arc, we served on the crusades, the British at the battle of Minden killed my father. At the age of thirteen, I was commissioned as a musketeer in the service of King Louis, at fifteen a lieutenant in the Noailles Dragoons. I have enjoyed ze finest tutelage at ze Académie de Versailles. So warfare runs through my blood and my education. I have a distinct understanding. And I say, with ze greatest respect, Baron von Steuben, what you say ez nonsense.'

There was something of a general intake of breath at this. It was rare among Washington's staff to have officers directly attacking the views of the others. And what made this rarer was the arrogance of Lafayette, the young Frenchman, who had only just joined the camp with a letter of recommendation from Ben Franklin, in attacking the hero of the hour.

Von Steuben held himself back. He was looking to give the young man just enough rope to hang himself.

'Your confidence, from one so young, is admirable. Your arrogance, ah, the young are always arrogant. Which of us around this room has not felt the power of such youthful arrogance? And then only to look back later at our rashness with regret. As you will. I'll wager you, young man, wager you a thousand dollars, that Howe makes landfall along the Elk River and attacks Philadelphia.'

'The Elk? Why would he run a course up that river, when the Delaware is much deeper and gives instant access to Philadelphia?' asked Adams.

'I am sure he would prefer to carry up the Delaware, but he will find that impossible. Once he scouts the river, he will find not only Fort Mercer with its excellent artillery, but that we have sunk ranges of iron spikes in the bed of the river which make the upper channel difficult if not impossible to pass. Thus he will look to the Elk.'

'I will gladly take your wager,' said the cocksure Lafayette.

'Gentlemen, as much as we are enjoying your jesting, there are serious matters to hand,' said Washington. 'Baron, I have enjoyed your contribution, but I am afraid I must disagree. We will prepare the army to march north. Our aim will be to squeeze Burgoyne's forces and secure the north-east, retake New York. If Howe wants to parade around Charleston, let him. This will enable us to secure the north. Monsieur Lafayette, I would have you join me.'

'I am obliged, sir.'

'General Washington, may I plead with you?' asked von Steuben.

'Baron.'

'Although you disagree with my analysis, you would surely agree that Philadelphia is a city without any defence. If you are right and Howe intends to sail to Charleston, there will come a time when he will set towards the north. There may then be a decisive battle that will determine the outcome of the war. Regardless, we need to give the people of Philadelphia comfort that this city is well defended. May I request that you allow my Stormtroopers and the Pennsylvanian Riflemen to make camp hereabouts and oversee the construction of such defences?'

'It would be a reduction of the capabilities of our forces to not have you and your troops with us in the north,' Washington responded.

'I thank you for the compliment. However, you will be travelling with over ten thousand men. Schuyler has five thousand or so, while Burgoyne has no more than, what, eight thousand. And you can call on the New York colony militia, twenty thousand men, not to mention the New England militia, which I believe is up to thirty thousand armed. You will have numerical superiority without us.'

Washington reflected. He wanted von Steuben with him, he understood how the rest of his army responded to having the Stormtroopers in their midst. He was about to refuse the request when John Adams interjected.

'George, it would go some way to alleviating the fears of both Congress and the people of Philly if the baron and his men were able to undertake this task. As he has stated, you have such superiority of forces that success should be within your grasp. I would request you agree to this suggestion.'

Washington bowed his head. 'I only seek to serve Congress and through it the people. The baron and his troops shall be stationed in Philadelphia for this period.'

The dinner broke up, and as they prepared to leave, Adams sought out von Steuben.

'Baron, how firm is your mind on this issue?'

The German looked closely at the Congress leader, bent down to him and whispered in his ear: 'I have never been more sure of anything. Howe will enter through Chesapeake and up the Elk. But I shall stop him before he comes close to Philadelphia. The capital will not fall.'

He stepped back.

'Thank you. We must maintain a closer relationship.'

'We shall, Mister Adams, we shall.'

THIRTY-TWO

In the darkness, they lay along the banks of the Elk, watching and waiting.

Howe's flotilla had slowly made its way through Chesapeake Bay and up the Elk river. The river itself was shallow and muddy, far from ideal for the seagoing frigates and ships-of-the-line that carried his men, horses and supplies. Several had already become stuck in mudbanks, creating a logjam along the relatively narrow river, a logjam that was several miles long and contained 254 boats of various sizes.

General Howe was in the fleet's flagship the *Eagle*. Further along the river, on the frigate HMS *Roebuck*, his brother, Vice-Admiral Richard Howe, oversaw the movement of the forward ships and the landing of the troops. Landing though was slow. The ground was rocky, with no obvious moorings. However, the real issue was the state of the men.

They had been at sea for five weeks all told. The Howe brothers had envisaged a much shorter voyage, but prevailing winds had extended the journey. Conditions on board all of the ships were terrible. Supplies had run low, so that the men were on short rations and the water was putrid. Over three hundred horses had died, which would severely weaken General Howe's cavalry and ability to move artillery quickly. And as the men left the boats for firm ground, the effects of the weeks of seafaring were all too clear, as they staggered around.

Patiently, the Stormtroopers and Riflemen watched all this unfold. Von Steuben's plan was simple: allow only enough of the men to be unloaded that he could be certain his forces could take. And when that number was close, unveil his direct attack on the rest of the fleet, before a direct assault on those on the riverbanks.

And that moment had come.

Out among the bull reeds and mudbanks of the Elk, a keen observer might have witnessed some slow movements in the darkness as the tide started to come in. Small barges and rafts were easing themselves out of cover along the far bank. At first a pilot guided each, but then they slipped away and into the river, confident that the tide would carry the raft or barge to its intended target. These were fire rafts. Full of dry timber, doused in oil. Before slipping off, each pilot lit the fuse on their vessel, so that suddenly in the darkness hundreds of small lights suddenly appeared, like fireflies on a summer's evening.

But those tiny sparks quickly became larger and larger fires. Now there was consternation aboard the fleet. They were under attack from these unmanned craft.

In the shallow water of the Elk, the sheer numbers made it difficult for any boats to evade the fire rafts as they drifted towards them. Frigates bumped into the ships-of-the-line, sloops into rowing galleys, and then as one of the rafts slowly ran into the hull of a frigate, the full potential of the damage to the fleet became clear. Flames immediately encased the frigate, running like a fiery sprite up the hull, over the deck, up the mast, with smoke and flames entwining to create a catastrophic red mist. On board, men urgently sought to dampen the fire, hauling water up from the muddy Elk to disperse the flames. Then from the top of the frigate's mast, sparks leaped over and across to an eight-gun sloop. Within moments, that too had sparked into life. Now, further down the line, a schooner was alight.

Satisfied that the fire rafts were doing their work, von Steuben gave the command for the start of the land assault.

At the landing stage, the battalions of Jaegers, light infantry and grenadiers who had been put on shore, watched in astonishment, as the fleet appeared to be going up in flames. They had set up a temporary perimeter to secure the area, but had been confident that there was little resistance on the ground. That changed when the first fusillade of round shot appeared from the cannon on the Elk's banks.

Von Steuben had brought two pieces of artillery from Philadelphia which he placed on higher ground and these now signalled the attack on the ground forces. While the round shot peppered the unprepared British and German troops, from the surrounding creeks and marshes the Stormtroopers and Riflemen arose and started their assault.

In three lines of attack, they moved in on the perimeter, which was quickly overwhelmed. There was some minor skirmishing, before bayonets affixed, the Stormtroopers, led by Conze, moved in for the kill. The British light infantry had quickly formed two lines and prepared to fire, but Conze stopped his men and got off the first round. And so the advantage of Schmeisser's modified Brown Besses became clear. The joint brigade of Stormtroopers and Riflemen were firing rounds more than twice as quickly than the British. For ten minutes, a fierce firefight ensued. The burning fleet providing a backdrop of demonic lighting, the red and yellow haze allowing both sides to find their targets. Casualties fell on both sides, but mostly on the British.

From the rear, a second group of Stormtroopers, led by Kluggman, had got in among the Jaegers. There was no gunshot here. Just knife, sword and axe work, brutish, nasty, bloody, the screams of men falling as loud as the crackling tinder of the fleet.

The artillery changed their range, firing upon the boats at the head of the flotilla, stopping any possible reinforcement on the land. Aboard HMS *Roebuck*, with its forty-four guns, the younger Howe grasped the severity of their position. On land, his men were under direct assault. To the rear, the fire rafts were doing terrible damage to his fleet. The troop landing had been slow and painful due to the unstable land. Under artillery fire it was almost impossible without great casualties. He had the *Roebuck* train its guns on the Colonists' artillery.

Within minutes, after the *Roebuck*'s right side opened fire, the hillside above the banks was scorched by its shot. The American artillery fell quiet. A further fusillade from the *Roebuck* pounded the higher ground. A terrible explosion tore the air as one of the cannons received a direct hit, and exploded, sending hot metal and burnt flesh high into the air.

On the ground, the fight was almost over. The Stormtroopers had the combined British battalions encircled and Conze had his men hold their fire. Shouting out, he offered a simple choice to the British and Germans penned in between the Elk and his men: 'The day is done. Throw down your weapons! We offer you safe passage. Surrender yourselves now.'

In the stuttering early morning dawn, the sound came of 3,000 men throwing down their muskets.

Aboard the *Roebuck*, Howe spied the scene through his eyeglass and turned to his aide-de-camp: 'The game is up here. Signal to the *Eagle* and the General. We turn back down this damned river.'

THIRTY-THREE

The bells of Philadelphia had been ringing for hours.

Once Howe and his armada had retreated, von Steuben sent riders ahead to the city with two messages. The first was for John Hancock and Congress, stating: 'Howe's navy defeated. British have turned back. Three thousand men under captivity. Von Steuben.' The second was for Hanna Reitsch and read: 'Howe defeated. We return immediately. Prepare for victory parade. We will enter at noon on 28 August.'

Now it was noon on 28 August 1777 and down Philadelphia's Chestnut Street came the Stormtroopers and Riflemen. At their head rode von Steuben, on a splendid white charger, which had been landed by the British, and was presumed to be the mount intended for Howe to enter the captured city. Behind him, the bedraggled British and German prisoners, followed by the smart, victorious Stormtroopers and Riflemen. The streets were full, many in the crowd holding paper swastika flags given to them by the League of American Girls, victors cheering them as they made their way to the State House.

Arriving there, von Steuben halted his mare, looked up and said to himself, 'Good, very good, Hanna.'

Before him, stood the imposing red-brick building, perhaps the finest building yet built in the colonies. In front of it, a platform of dignitaries, the Congress leaders, and above them, from the bell tower hung a huge banner, red, the black swastika in a white circle at the centre. A group of trumpeters to the left of the platform let forth a triumphal din.

He dismounted from his horse, walked to the leader of the prisoners and theatrically took from him a folded British flag. He held it aloft to cheers from the crowd and then slowly walked up to the platform, bowing before John Hancock and presenting it to him. Von Steuben then stood upright, turned to the crowd and bellowed:

'I present to the Congress of the Thirteen Colonies this symbol of the defeat of the British forces under General Howe. Three days past, our Stormtroopers and Riflemen surprised the British forces who believed they were close to capturing the capital of this our rebellion. If we had failed, then the war may have been lost. But by our own energies, we have defeated Howe. It is but one step on the road to victory, but by each day, by each action we take, that victory becomes yet more certain. The events at the Elk will reverberate past Philadelphia, past New York, across the Atlantic and on to London, where they will assail the ears of King George! This is a victory that will echo down through the decades, through the generations, one that will echo through all eternity!'

A large roar went up from the crowd gathered before him.

He looked around, savouring every moment. He sensed this was an opportunity for something bigger. And he knew what he wanted to say.

'Friends, Colonists, Americans. This war is far from over. This is not the end. It is not even the beginning of the end. But it may be the end of the beginning. I and my men, the Stormtroopers, have been here in America for less than a year. But in that time, we have been overwhelmed by the way you have taken us to your bosom. It is true that I can say, with modesty I hope, we have helped overturn the defeats of the past and bring you victories. Great victories.'

Von Steuben was drowned out at that point, cheers of 'Hurrah!' and then 'Von Steuben!' for the first time. The baron started to talk again, but the noise was gaining, the cheers now becoming a chant of 'Von Steuben! Von Steuben!' echoing around the square, from man to woman and from adult to child. He rode the wave for a while and then raised both hands, quieting down the crowd until there was near silence.

'Friends, I came here to be your servant and I wish to remain your servant. I have nothing to offer but blood, toil, tears and sweat. We have before us an ordeal of the most grievous kind. We have before us many, many long months of struggle and suffering. You may ask me: what is your policy, what are your aims?

'I will say it is this: to wage war on the foreign tyranny by sea and land with all our might and with all the strength that God can give us; to wage war against a monstrous tyranny, never surpassed in the dark and lamentable catalogue of human crime. This is our policy. You may ask, what is your aim? I can answer in one word: victory. Victory at all costs. Victory in spite of all terror. Victory, however long and hard the road may be, for without victory there is no survival.

'So I ask this of you. Are you with us or against us? Will you join me and my Stormtroopers and accept this challenge? Will you be with us until we have won victory and created a new America?'

At which point the entire crowd, which was perhaps the whole population of Philadelphia crammed into the green before the State House and the narrow streets around, let forth an almighty cry that one could imagine might have been heard as far away as the court of King George, awaking the monarch as he slept in his bed at Windsor: 'Victory! Victory!'

THIRTY-FOUR

One man felt uneasy, queasy even, as he watched the victory parade unfurl and with it all the antics of the crowd.

He walked on his own, his clothes shabby and torn, his body thin, face gaunt and with barely healed cuts, his hair closely cropped. If a fellow spectator had looked carefully, they would have seen that his right shoulder drooped a little. He appeared to be one of those phantoms who have inhabited every city on the earth since cities were first founded, those who appear to have given up the ghost of life itself, hoping that they will eventually disappear into the ether, leaving no trace of a life behind. They might have heard of him, because once in this city he had been celebrated, but those who knew him now would see his name as that of a traitor who had put others before his own people. His name was Edward Hand.

At Queen Esther's Town, Hand had taken a shot clean through his right shoulder, throwing him back into the crowd of women and children. As he fell, he cracked his head on the rocky shore, and was unconscious, as other victims of the firing squad collapsed around him. When Kluggman came to him, he mistook Hand's lifeless, bloodied body for a dead man and threw him into the river with the others.

The river was icy, but fast-flowing, shallow and full of bracken and branches. Hand's body was not the only one to be caught up in timber moving down the river, not the only one to come to a stop on top of a rocky outcrop but a few lengths downstream. Not all the villagers had perished in the onslaught: some women, who had been out foraging for firewood, had witnessed the events from hideouts in the woods, had seen with their own eyes the murder of their families and the American who had tried to protect them and apparently paid for it with his life.

They found him that afternoon on his back on the rocks, his face lacerated by the sharp rocks of eddies he had slalomed down. He was barely alive, but they took him away, cleaned the shot out and dressed his wounds with poultices of spikenard bark and roots, gave him daily emetics of boiled spring-blown branches and when they moved off, to the protection of the Iroquois further north, they took Hand with them.

He found friendship with these people. He learnt their ways, their desire to live in harmony with the earth. He stayed, his body slowly recovering, but for all their kindness, he knew he was an outsider. Three months after Queen Esther's Town, a French fur-trapper came into the camp, with his Iroquois wife and four children. David Fortier lived between the two worlds of the natives and the colonists. He was taking racoon, beaver and doe skins down to Philadelphia, leaving his wife with her family. He offered to take Hand with him, he knew the tracks through the wilderness and he would welcome the company. That was how Hand had come to be in Philadelphia.

He had been there for three weeks, living among the under-class, among the illiterate criminals and strays that had washed up at the far reaches of the British Empire. For food and drink, he offered his services as a doctor to anyone who needed it: the victims of knife fights, the whores who had got unlucky, the rotten-toothed drunks who needed quick relief. He could survive for now like this. The nights were long and warm, he could huddle deep in the recesses of the shanty buildings, the waters of the Delaware never too far from him.

But he was also watching, learning, biding his time, planning. Planning what he wasn't sure of, until the victory at the Elk River and the days in which Philadelphia embraced the Stormtroopers.

When news came into the city of Howe's fleet landing at the Elk, the city was thrown into panic. Members of Congress, rich merchants, society ladies, propertied men, all suddenly had reason to leave for Boston in the north, or to go south to Baltimore. For a day, the streets were churned up by the wheels of their carriages, heavy with their chattels and treasures; fear had a sound and it was the rumbling of wheels, the shouts of drivers and the neighing of the horses. But that was the rich elite. The rest of the city shrugged its shoulders and prepared for the worst. When the Stormtroopers and Riflemen marched out of the city on 25 August, they stood in line to cheer them off, but there were few who believed they would see them again.

So when word arrived of the victory, the city went mad.

The Riflemen and their German allies had saved them and they were going to give them the greatest homecoming since the Roman emperors had celebrated their triumphs. When the League of American Girls went around asking for help to decorate the city, they found a new army of willing volunteers. Among the destitute in the filth and grime of the port, the enthusiasm was as great as in the market streets and the grand houses uptown, great houses that were once again opening their shutters to the August heat and their doors to those suddenly returning.

So on this day, there was no one who did not want to venture the few blocks up town and see at first hand the victors of Elk River. And as the bars and workshops, the pier buildings and the dock offices, emptied, so Hand went along, finding anonymity in the crowds who pressed and screamed their allegiance to von Steuben.

Von Steuben's speech had been followed by a parade of the victorious Stormtroopers and Riflemen, but it was difficult to tell the two apart now, so closely aligned were they, so closely had the Riflemen adopted the clothing of the Germans. Hand looked at familiar faces, faces he had looked after, faces he had nurtured, faces he had suffered with, but those faces were different now. Harder perhaps, even in the midst of victory. And chief among them, clad in a black jacket and matching trousers, was his former friend Pat O'Leary.

The crowd was as frenzied with the parade of the victors as they had been throughout von Steuben's speech.

After the parade, the crowd started to disperse, Hand with them. Making his way slowly back towards the river, he fell in with two men. One was slow to move on account of a wooden leg. Both had the grizzled appearance of war veterans.

'Hey, Tommo, what'd yer give to be young and part of this fella's army, eh?'

'Wouldn't be wearing ol' Dick here if this baron had been leading me. You know Fritz over there?' He pointed in the direction of an even older, grey-haired man, limping away in a group of three men. 'He did serve wi' him. Hey, Fritz, that's true, ain't it? You were serving with him in Prussia?'

The grey hair looked up: 'The Baron?'

'Yup.'

'Well, va real Baron von Steuben. Vat's not Baron von Steuben I knew.'

Hand's ears pricked up at this.

'What's that?' asked the first veteran.

Fritz limped over towards them; a small group of beer-stinking veterans formed a close group, Hand on their edge.

'I voz wit va baron ein Kunersdorf, va most terrible day. Fifty-Nine. King Frederick's army, butchered. The baron, he vasn't baron then, just Fred Steuben, vurst lieutenant. He was a Miss Molly un.'

'Uh?'

'You mean he liked to visit the Winward Passage, Fritz?' said the first veteran, laughing.

'A buggerer. This one don't strike me as a buggerer.'

'Say he ain't. And he's older, five years or more. And taller. Fred Steuben shorter van vat. And his nose. All his face. Everyvin' bout him, wrong. I tell yer that ain't Fred Steuben.'

Hand pushed through and confronted Fritz.

'You're saying that this Baron von Steuben is not the man you knew in Prussia?'

'Saying exactly. Some other fella, I'd wager my last glass of porter on it. He might be a fine general an' all vat, but he ain't the man I stood alongside at Kunersdorf.'

THIRTY-FIVE

Adams poured a glass of brandy, passed it to von Steuben before sitting down in the armchair to face him. They had dismissed all their retainers. It was just the two of them now. Two men who held no formal title, but were close to having control over the military and civil establishment of the emerging republic. Von Steuben, the garlanded war hero; Adams the acknowledged 'first man in the House', the most powerful voice in Congress, the man who could carry the day. The President of Congress may have been John Hancock, but the leader was John Adams.

'So, Baron, the question we face now is how we proceed to end this war and establish a new system of government for these colonies. And I daresay your role in that settlement.'

Von Steuben rolled the glass, took a sip and said nothing. He had long learned the value of silence at such moments.

'There can be no denial. Our fortunes have changed considerably since your arrival on our shores. Where we previously faced defeat, humiliation even, now we can proceed with the comfort of certain victory. We may not achieve our aims immediately, but we will achieve them. That is, if you continue to inspire our forces and people.'

Adams peered deeply at the baron. There was no response.

'Do I detect a reservation on your part, Baron?'

Von Steuben placed the glass on the table, ran his hands down the fabric of his trousers and then leaned towards Adams.

'Let us trust in each other, Mister Adams. It is not so much a question of my place in the new America as *our* place. How do we ensure the talents of both of us are employed in their most effective way to finish the war and establish the country we dream of? We do not want to win the war and lose the peace. We both want, I believe, a model society that will be a beacon for the rest of the world to emulate. For that, we need strong leadership, both civil and military. I believe you must provide the former and myself the latter.'

Now Adams paused for reflection, then, 'Pray, continue, Baron. Your assumptions are correct.'

'I can achieve victory here. But I cannot do so if my hands are tied behind my back.'

'How can I untie your hands?'

'I must have complete control of the army. I cannot serve under your General Washington any longer. You saw at the conference here in Philadelphia what he lacks. His form of leadership is conciliation; he follows the course the majority of his generals prefer. That is not leadership. That is an abdication of leadership. Where is he now? Wherever he is, it does not matter. He has made himself inconsequential.'

Adams paused for a beat before deciding there was no point in prevaricating: 'Indeed. Indeed he has. And his generals, are they too inconsequential?'

'They are in many ways fine men, but they are not experienced men of war. He prefers Greene, Hamilton, Knox, even that preening French peacock Lafayette, and pushes experienced men such as Gates, Arnold and Lee to the margins. If you want victory, you need to seize the opportunity we created on the banks of the Elk. This must not be squandered.' He sat back in the chair.

'It will not, Baron. You have my word.'

'My men and I are no longer prepared to suffer such ill leadership. There are those among them who have suggested we should seek an alternative arena rather than suffer further.'

'An alternative?'

'Perhaps Canada. Establish a new colony of our making there. Throw ourselves in with the French even, in Louisiana, perhaps. They would welcome us I believe.' In the glint of shock that passed like an electrical spark across Adams's eyes, he saw it had the desired effect.

'We would be most unhappy if that was to occur. I am certain that we can provide you with the necessary assurances. Congress will follow my lead on this matter.'

'Total command. The ability to wage war as we see fit. That is what I require.'

John Adams paused. He stood up, his hands behind his back, and contemplated for a brief moment. 'The primacy of Congress must be maintained. That is clear. Any war leader must be accountable to Congress. We are to be a civil society. Not a military one.'

Von Steuben nodded his head, a little curt nod, one that was entirely full of deceit. He knew where power resided, both in the present and in the future. There would come a time when he would deal with Adams and the lackeys of Congress. 'Of course. We understand, respect and share your belief in a civil society. The war leader must be accountable to Congress. I would honour that. As long . . .' he smiled now, 'as long as you do not expect me to have to attend to lectures by Thomas Paine every month?'

'Ah, no. I think the corset-maker may be reaching the end of his use for us all. Time we sent him back to England. Tell me, what would your stratagem be for ending this war?'

Confident now, von Steuben stretched out his legs, folded his arms and began his lecture. 'Howe is returning to New York, bloodied, but not broken. I sense that he will return to London with his tail very much between his legs. The leadership will then be passed to Cornwallis. In London though, they will be confused. King George will have great difficulty in persuading his parliament to approve further expenditure on the Americas, especially as the French, with the prompting of your Ben Franklin at the court of King Louis and smelling the opportunity to bloody the British themselves, will begin to attack British colonies in the Caribbean.

'Our aim over the autumn will be twofold. To squeeze the last drops out of the British forces in New Jersey and Pennsylvania by the use of the local militias. And to march the main body of the army north and defeat Burgoyne in battle. So by the end of the year, the British will have no troops outside of New York. They will be encircled. By the spring, they will either have to break out and attempt to defeat us in battle or they will sue for peace.'

'And how certain can you be that you will defeat them in battle? We have yet to win any engagement in which there has been a traditional land battle.'

'That, sir, was in the past, where your armies suffered from poor organisation, discipline and leadership. By the spring of next year, this will be the finest army in the world. However, we will also have a great advantage over the British. By the spring of next year, we will have the new weaponry that our gunsmith Schmeisser is working on. The British muskets will fail against them. And we have another weapon, one that we are manufacturing right here in Philadelphia under our man Krupp. We call it an iron horse.'

'Really? What is this?'

'Ah, you will see it soon enough. We should be ready to unveil it in a matter of days. It will help us bring this struggle to a quick end. Victory is within our grasp, Mister Adams. We cannot let it slip away.'

'I would agree, but what would lead you to think we would let this opportunity slip away?'

'You cannot run a war as a university debating society.'

'A university debating society?'

'Listening to conflicting and contradictory opinions, looking for consensus. In war, strong, firm leadership is required. General Washington has many qualities; he is a man of moral force, but he is a vacillator. Once he arrives in Philadelphia, he will thank us for this great victory, but we will then return to his policy of muddle and dithering. There will be those in his entourage who will disagree with the strategy I have outlined and—'

'And they will have the ear of Washington,' Adams interrupted.

'I fear so.'

Adams paused, put his glass down and stood up.

'Baron, this struggle is greater than any one individual. We must all do what is necessary for the victory we desire, regardless of our own personal ambitions.' He started to pace around the room. 'This is a most difficult issue. A most difficult issue.'

He stopped and faced von Steuben.

'I will discuss the matter with Congress, and ensure we have an outcome that will deliver us victory.'

THIRTY-SIX

Hand had been watching the City Tavern for a few hours.

It had been von Steuben's and the Stormtroopers' headquarters since their arrival in the city and they had returned to it following the defeat of Howe. A steady flow of well-wishers and those seeking advancement had made its way to the tavern, filling the downstairs rooms, spilling out into the streets. The merchants, tradesmen and ruling elite of the city were keen to come and ingratiate themselves and establish relationships with this other elite. Consequently, the tavern was awash with free drinks, loud good wishes and, on the edges, Stormtroopers disappearing with women.

Finally, Hand saw what he had been waiting for.

His sister Sarah.

Although at first he failed to recognise her.

A group of half a dozen young women were walking down Chestnut Street in the afternoon sunshine, joking and laughing. All six seemed close to identical; blonde hair pulled back in ponytails, they wore long jackets, in the grey-green of the Stormtroopers, with matching long skirts. On their heads, a jaunty black beret, with an eagle sat atop a swastika. That these young women, looking like no young ladies he had ever seen before, created little or no comment on the streets of Philadelphia was in itself cause for comment, he thought.

It was then that Hand realised the leader of the group was Sarah.

She had a new-found confidence about her that surprised him. This was not the callow girl he had so long taken her for. At that moment, he understood that he had always underestimated her, that he had never regarded her as having any potential. Whatever the issue he had with these Germans, they had given his sister a new sense of purpose, perhaps real meaning for the first time in her life.

She bade goodbye to the other women and turned into the tavern. Hand quickly followed her.

His unkempt state would normally have seen him rejected from the City Tavern whose proprietor, Little Smith, was determined that his inn was to be the most upscale establishment in the emerging capital. However, the press of people was so great that he was able to slip in, keeping an eye on Sarah as she too squeezed in among the throng.

He saw her break free from the crowd and make her way up the stairs to the lodging rooms, and he followed her. Reaching the landing, he saw her disappear into a room. Outside, his heart racing, he waited a beat before knocking on the door and without waiting for a reply, opened it and stepped inside.

Sarah turned around in surprise and then greater surprise when she saw her brother.

'Ed! I, I thought, I thought, you were . . .'

'Dead?' he finished for her. 'I feel I have been dead these past six months.'

He rushed to her and they embraced.

'What happened?'

'I survived.'

'But how? Werner told me, those Indians, they cut you into pieces.' She held his face, her hands feeling his scars.

'No Indians cut me. It was Conze who ordered me shot by my own men.'

'What? How, why would Werner do that?'

'Because he is an animal, more savage than the Indians.' She pulled away from him. He knew he did not have much time, every word had to make its mark. 'Sarah, these people are not what you think they are. They are capable of great cruelties. I have seen that. I have suffered for it.'

'No, no, you are wrong. Werner told me you were attacked outside a village. Pat told me the same. Why would they make up such stories?' Suddenly some form of truth dawned on her. 'You're not . . . you're not a traitor? You're not in the pay of the British, are you? We are surrounded by spies, there are traitors all about us. Not you, not my brother!'

'No, I am not a spy. I tried to stop Werner massacring the village, like he had done to a Jewish village. He had me shot.'

'A Jewish village? What do you mean he had you shot? If he had you shot, how have you ended up here alive?'

'I was lucky, very lucky. Indians saved me. They nursed me back to health.'

Now she scoffed at him. 'Indians nursed you? Your own men shot you and Indians nursed you back to health? You expect me to believe this?' There was a bluntness to her he had never seen before. It threw him.

'And von Steuben, I don't know who he is, but he is not Baron von Steuben.'

'Oh, what is this now, what do you mean, brother?'

'This von Steuben is an imposter.'

'Oh, away with you, such madness. What do I care if he is an imposter or not? All I know is that he has brought us victory and given me and hundreds of others hope. What were we before, what hope did we have? What hope did I have for my life? What hope did you have for me?'

Her words cut him. He knew what she was going to say; he could see the words shape and rush towards him. He saw the ring then, the light dancing around the diamond. He had never seen anything like it.

'What's that?' he asked.

'A gift. A gift from someone who believes in me,' she almost spat the words at him.

'I believe in you, Sarah. I've always believed in you.'

'You believed in me? What did you ever see me as? A pathetic girl, there to do your bidding, following you, tending to you until I found another man I could tend. This is all you thought me good for. Or worse. Do you not remember the last words you said to me? When you called me a whore. My own brother.'

Hand blushed with shame.

'These imposters, as you call them, they do not box me in, they do not see me fit for so little, see me as a whore! I am a leader of people now, Edward. People listen to me. The League of American Girls, that is my group. You see these flags that decorate all of Philadelphia? My girls made them. My girls. Under my direction. Two hundred young women who rely on me for leadership. Two hundred. And more and more join us every day. We are a movement, do you even know what that means? Do you have any idea what that means to me?'

He did not. He could have no idea, she was right about that. He closed his eyes and said very softly, 'These people are criminals, Sarah.'

She looked back at him, fire in her eyes. She was no longer a girl. He saw that. He had underestimated her, she was right. 'Not to me they're not. They have given me meaning. You, you despise them not for that reason, but because you no longer control me or Pat or anyone else. That is the source of your desperation, brother. The fault is with you, not them. And you come here with this tall story of being shot by your own men!'

260

'It's true! They are not what you take them for, none of them, von Steuben, Hanna, even your Werner. They will corrupt this country.' He gripped her wrists and pulled her towards him. 'Sarah, you have to believe me. Follow them and devastation will follow. You have to believe me.'

'Let go of me, let go of me, brother!' she screamed at him. 'I want nothing more to do with you!'

'You have to believe me!'

'Go! You're dead to me, to all of us. Go!'

As she spat out these words, the door to the chamber opened and Conze walked in. He stopped, silent at first, unable to believe what he saw, a dead man alive. 'What the hell? You, alive? Where have you come from?' he said as he lurched towards Hand.

Dropping his sister's wrists, Hand went to defend himself and the two men started to wrestle to the floor, before the German pulled free. Standing up, panting at each other, they faced off, Sarah screaming at Hand to leave.

'You're no longer wanted, Hand,' Conze said coldly. 'Has Sarah told you? We are to be married, but even more, see that?' He pointed at Sarah's belly. 'In there is our child. The firstborn of a new world, a world of Aryan perfection. A world with no place for traitors to our race. Traitors like you.'

Furious, Hand screamed, 'No!' and threw a punch at Conze, which the German easily ducked, before planting a firm blow of his own to the Irishman's stomach. Winded, Hand bent over and Conze delivered a succession of punches around the head and chest. On the floor now, scrambling away to safety, Hand was only saved by Sarah stopping her lover from delivering a ferocious kick to the chest. 'Leave him! Let him go, Werner.'

Out of breath, dazed and bloodied, Hand used a chair to pull himself up from the floor. Standing less than firmly, he took a shallow breath and with as much disdain as he could muster, he said, 'I won't go away. I won't let you Germans ruin this country. I will stop you. Not today perhaps, but I will.'

Infuriated, Conze pulled away from Sarah and made for Hand, but this time the Irishman got in a punch that hit its target and the German wheeled away, stunned, before charging back towards his man. Hand made for the door, then for the stairway and the ground floor of the tavern.

The place was, if anything, fuller and more raucous than before, drink releasing any inhibitions the victors of the Elk River might have had. Where he had entered unseen, now as he tried to squeeze past people, tried to make his way to the open space beyond the tavern door, his bloodied face and dishevelled appearance made people look twice. That and the shrieking of Conze as he came after him down the stairs and into the throng below, screaming, 'Stop the traitor!'

In the small, tightly packed tavern, someone in response shouted, 'Assassin! Stop the assassin!', and within seconds the place was transformed into a writhing mass of shouting, screaming people, confused, not sure what was happening, looking to their neighbours for the unknown assassin, the drink colouring any judgement. Any face not recognised was under suspicion and more than one man was prodded and punched. 'Over there! Him!' screamed Conze, but the noise was too great now, he was drowned out by other screams and shouts of 'Murderer!' and 'Assassin!'

Hand was collared by a ruddy-faced German, but the man's grip was weakened by alcohol, and Hand slipped away, and then down to the floor, crawling through the legs of others. It was not dignified, but for the time being it was effective, despite the kicks he received about him.

He saw the door. He stood up and, foolishly, looked back at the confusion and madness of the howling throng. Conze spotted him and let out a hellish screech that flew above the tumult and focused every beer-soaked head: 'BY THE DOOR! HE'S ESCAP-ING! STOP HIM!'

Hand rushed out of the door, knocking over a couple who were trying to enter. Losing his balance, he scrambled back to his feet and made for the wide expanse of Chestnut Street, heading down towards the port. Behind him a crowd of drunken Stormtroopers came piling out of the City Tavern, hurtling after him, yelling insults as they pounded down the dusty street.

The Irishman dashed to the left. He did not know Philadelphia well, but he knew he would be a dead man out in the wide expanse of Chestnut Street. He only stood a chance in the maze of warrens that had been thrown up in the last few years as the city had grown, in the workshops, smallholdings and shanty buildings of the city's poor.

Behind him, the Stormtroopers were charging about, colliding with people, banging into the walls of flimsy buildings, knocking over the fences and stakes of pig pens and chicken coops that sat alongside the homes of the poor. Hand had a lead through the maze of buildings, but he was unclear where he was running. He was just hurtling down any alleyway or side street, no idea where it would go. And then, horror.

Without realising, he had gone in a circle and he now found himself running down a cinder path and straight into a group of the Stormtroopers. He threw himself to the right, over a picket fence and into the middle of a stinking, gurning family of pigs. The adults stabbed at him with their snouts, the piglets screeching. But he pulled himself up and over the picket on the other side, just before the Germans followed him through, dismantling the entire fence, falling over the pigs and each other amid animal shrieks and human expressions of disgust.

Momentarily free of the carnage behind him, Hand turned left down another channel and then right, before a further right turn and into a more open space, where a black man was shoeing a dark brown plough horse. Their eyes met. Without saying any-thing, the blacksmith dropped the horse's hoof, stood up, grabbed Hand by the collar and dragged him into the back of the smithy, throwing him up and over a pile of logs, before walking back out outside and picking up the hoof again, all in a matter of seconds.

The crowd of Germans came rushing into the open area. A few continued to chase off down the side paths, but a greater number stopped.

'*Neger!*' shouted one, his face flushed with the excitement of the chase and an afternoon of drinking, 'Where'd he go?'

'Who?' asked the blacksmith.

'The man who came running through here but a minute past.'

'White man?' asked the blacksmith.

'White man,' replied the German.

The blacksmith pointed his thumb. 'That way. This horse went to give him a good kick and he went off down that way, where those men went,' and he turned back to the hoof, nail placed ready for a hammering.

The German eyed him suspiciously. 'You better be telling the truth.'

The smith looked up at him. 'And you'll be missing him if you don't get a head on,' before turning his head back down to his work and hammering the nail firmly into the hoof. He looked up to see the German still agitated, 'I ain't got time to play your white man's game, search my smithy if you care, but I got a horse that has to be shod, so I'm a-getting on with that.' He picked up a fur-ther nail, placed it and struck it squarely. The German looked at the men with him, unsure. At that moment a further burst of shouting from somewhere else settled his mind, 'Come, follow me!' he ordered and they ran off in the direction the blacksmith had sent them.

The blacksmith continued to do his work, methodically finish-ing the hoof until he was satisfied. He gently placed it on the ground and stood up, stroking the plough horse's weatherbeaten neck and head. 'Good girl, all done, all ready for harvest.' And then, wiping his hands on his leather apron, Oliver Cromwell walked into his smithy to see whether he had broken any of his friend Eddie Hand's bones when he threw him behind his woodpile.

THIRTY-SEVEN

'I came here straight away from that night at Buckingham. I was affeared of my life. Ain't too much of a coward to say that, Ed. I know how these things go. Niggers get the blame. Your boys got me out, but I knew I had to go. Came here. Found this smithy, empty, needed someone to raise it up again. So, that's what I did. Ne'er got a chance to thank you.'

'You don't need to do that now. You saved me. Mind you, could have done it breaking a few less bones.'

The two men smiled at each other. They were in the room above the smithy. The summer's day had turned to dusk. The shouts and screams of the day had given way to the usual night noises of any growing city.

The day's events were already becoming legend, but the truth of the day was grim. A young New Jersey boy, visiting an aged aunt, had been mistaken for Hand and was kicked and punched to death by a group of Stormtroopers. A clerk from the customs office had almost gone the same way before his employer had intervened. Someone else appeared to have used the day's dramatics to take revenge on a rival, and threw him off the wharf where he drowned. Satisfied in their blood lust, the Germans had returned to their camp.

Conze had inspected the body of the New Jersey boy and cursed the air. Hand was a small issue. Put in the historical framework of what was unfolding, he was a speck of dust against the curtain of the night. But so long as he was out there somewhere, lurking, he remained an unknown, unquantifiable source of potential problems. Von Steuben had asked him what had been the cause of the day's kerfuffle – there were many well-to-do Philadelphians alarmed by the Stormtroopers charging about the city – and Conze felt embarrassed to have to admit it was Edward Hand, back from the dead. Von Steuben, he could tell, rather admired the man – that, or he was a convenient tool with which to needle his comrade. 'Quite a thorn in your side, this man Hand. Werner, who will rid you of that troublesome Rifleman, eh?' he said, his voice dripping with sarcasm.

At the same moment, on the Smithy's top floor, Hand was telling Cromwell of his time with the Iroquois.

'They patched me up well, better than I could have done as a trained doctor, I daresay, and let me stay with them for months. We travelled north until we came across the Oneida.'

'They're the Indians who sided with the Colonists, aren't they?'

'They are. Split the Iroquois alliance. I was handed over to Akiatonharónkwen, who had heard of the massacre at Queen Esther's Village. It seems it's not the only attack on Indian villages the Hessians have made. There have been at least three.'

'It ain't good what's happening, Ed, wi' these Stormtroopers or whatever they call themselves. You know what happened at Lowantica with all the black troops? All marched out. All gone. They went back on Washington's words to us. Worst of all, no one knows where they are.'

'What do you mean?'

'They rounded them all up, from every unit and marched 'em all out. All out of the camp, and no one knows where. There must've been, what, five, six hundred Negro soldiers. There ain't any now. Nor any special brigades either.'

'That doesn't give me a good feeling.'

'No, nor me. Where d'you think they've taken them, Ed? I've been thinking on it and I just can't fathom it.'

'I fear for those boys, Oliver, I wish I could say different, but I fear for them. These aren't reasonable men.' Hand rubbed his face with his hand, wondering for a moment what to tell his old friend. He had fought with Cromwell, and trusted him, and he knew that he needed to tell him what he knew. 'It wasn't just an Indian village. I saw the same happen with a Jewish village.'

'A Jewish village? I didn't know there were Israelites in the Americas.'

'Apparently there are. And the Stormtroopers . . . you know what they called them? These men and women – mothers, fathers, children – just trying to make a living and hurting no one? They called them vermin. To these Germans, these poor settlers were just vermin, can you believe it? I saw them torch the buildings and then slaughter everyone, little babies and all. And that's not the last of it. They slaughtered unarmed British prisoners at New Brunswick, raped their women—'

'Dear Lord! Does Old George know what's going on?'

Hand paused. 'That's something I don't know. I never had a chance to talk to him about it.'

'But you know the Old Fella, you know what he stands for, he wouldn't stand for this, would he?'

'I would say no, from what I have seen of him. They say he owns slaves in Virginia, but I never saw him show any disrespect to anyone on account of the colour of their skin or their religion. There is one man I know who would have no truck with this. Thomas Jefferson. Or I would hope he would not, but these are strange times.'

'Strange times they are. Sweet Jesus. And where is our friend Pat O'Leary in this?'

Again Hand paused. 'Pat is with them. He has become one of their keenest followers, I'm sorry to say. Pat wears their armband.

and marches with them. I saw him today. He wears the black uniform of their officers. Pat and I have gone our separate ways and I can't see us ever coming together again.'

'You were like brothers. And Sarah. The three of you were a family; you've been through so much together.'

Now Hand broke down, tears flowing. 'I went looking for Sarah. That's how I landed up in this scrape. It's no good.' He started to sob. 'She's gone over to them. She's in love with Werner Conze.'

'Who?' Cromwell felt embarrassed by his friend's weeping. He didn't know what to do with such an outpouring.

'He's the one who ordered the execution of the Jews, the Indians, the innocents at New Brunswick, even myself. I tried to tell her. But she wouldn't believe me. And then, well, it's too late.'

'Too late?'

He looked up, his eyes full of sadness. 'She is carrying his child. They are to marry.'

'Ah,' replied Cromwell.

'It may be my fault. Perhaps I was more father than brother to her and more father than friend to Pat. Maybe I never saw them for what they were, what they could be, and these Hessians have done that, given them roles that I had never seen them capable of.'

'If they're such capable minds, why have they fallen for all this nonsense then?'

Hand composed himself. 'They can be very persuasive, these Hessians. And look at what has happened since they arrived. Victory, where before we were wandering around with little hope or belief. That's all changed now. Now it's the British who are on the run.'

The two men fell silent. Two men from very different backgrounds who had fought against the British together, finding a shared kinship in the fight against the tyrannical British rule. The thought of the child Rebecca, her poor head smashed against a rock, came unbidden into Hand's mind. What good was the fight against one tyranny when it would be replaced with another, greater tyranny? What sort of victory was it that was earned through the slaughter of innocent men, women and children?

Hand lifted his head and looked over at his friend. Something had just occurred to him. 'Any idea what they're up to down at the port?'

'At the port?'

'In that big warehouse they built. You must have seen it – or rather heard it? They call it a factory. From the outside, it's all noise, inside it's one great furnace I hear.'

'Oh, the workshop you mean? That's how I got this place. They had all the blacksmiths of Philly come to them and they placed them down at their factory. They're building something. It's all a big secret. I mean no one is going to tell a dumb nigger anything, but they keep it to themselves. Something is going on. You curious?'

'I think we should let our curiosity get the better of us. But first, there is a letter I must send to Thomas Jefferson. He is a man who will yet stand firm to his principles, I am sure.'

THIRTY-EIGHT

Congress had called for Washington and his general staff to return to Philadelphia for an immediate war conference. The defeat of Howe along the Elk River had changed everything. The British had returned to New York, 'Their arses well kicked', according to Sam Adams. Now was the time to seize the advantage.

Washington rode into the city with Hamilton, Greene, Cadwalader, Sullivan and Ewing alongside him, as well as Lafayette, who had become a close confidant in a matter of weeks. Knox had been sent off with his artillery units to join Schuyler and the Northern Army, to hold back Burgoyne from breaking out and possibly joining up with Howe and his now depleted, demoralised forces in New York.

Entering Philadelphia, the first thing they noticed were the abundance of swastika flags flying in the city, from the windows of private homes to the wharves along the port and, most impressively of all, from the State House. There was now not one long banner, but three huge red banners, reaching from roof to ground, each with the swastika in its centre.

'What ho, look at this, a festival for the Stormtroopers?' queried Hamilton.

'These Germans seem to think they and they alone are winning this war,' grumbled Sullivan. 'I told you, George, it's dangerous to place too much trust in these Hessian mercenaries. This demonstration of impropriety suggests to my mind that we should be careful we do not exchange one form of tyranny for another.'

'It is, I agree, an unnecessarily ostentatious display, John. The enthusiasm of the people of Philly appears to have run away with them.' Washington chewed at his jaw.

'The enthusiasm of the Hessians has run away with themselves more likely,' Sullivan snorted.

'I must say, I would have expected more of a hullabaloo for General Washington returning to the city,' said Hamilton. 'There is a distinct lack of a welcoming party.'

'Exactly my thoughts,' said Greene, his portly frame uncomfortable in the saddle, despite his experience of many months on horseback.

And mine, too, thought Washington to himself. We almost appear strangers in our own capital.

They left their horses to be fed, watered and groomed at the City Tavern's stables and made their way on foot to the State House.

At last, there, in the open hallway, was a welcoming party of Congress delegates, led by John Hancock, the President of Congress and one of the wealthiest men of the colonies, a man prone to extravagant acts of vanity and theatre.

'Our dear, General Washington, how contented we are that you have arrived in such good spirits. Congress and the people of Philadelphia welcome you here as our commander-in-chief. I say, three cheers for the general, gentlemen, three cheers!'

And the fifty delegates squeezed into the open entrance hall let out three cheers and several 'Hurrahs!', which went some way to placating both Sullivan and Hamilton.

Once the din had died down again, Hancock, with an extravagant bow to the delegates, said: 'Gentlemen, wonderfully done, so wonderfully done. But our war generals are no doubt famished after their trek from the north. So please, we have prepared a

272

buffet of the necessary victuals and I believe there may be some wines and brandies to extinguish their thirst. We have a room prepared for you, sirs, and my secretary here will escort you, but, General Washington, may I ask you for some time with myself first, in my chambers as President of the Congress.'

'Of course, John, but of course.'

'I shall come with you, in case you require any assistance, General Washington,' said Hamilton.

'No, that will not be necessary, not be necessary at all, young man,' said Hancock, who with a brush of his arm led Washington up a staircase and towards his office.

They made their way into Hancock's office, a room that illustrated the wealth of the man: a Wedgewood Blue Jasper vase sat proudly on a stand, Chinese porcelain in a glass cabinet, several classical busts and two large landscape paintings on facing walls. And waiting inside for them were John and Samuel Adams, the Boston cousins, and the most powerful men in the Congress.

'Ah, either we have disturbed you, gentlemen, or I suspect something of a trap?' Washington's forthright response to seeing the Adamses threw Hancock off guard.

'Not at all, dear fellow, not at all, we just thought we should—'

'No point messing about, John, let's get to the point,' Sam Adams, the older cousin said. 'George, take a seat. Want a brandy? John's having one and I daresay Hancock will as well. I myself stick to water. The Puritan in me, as they say.'

Hancock fussed in the background as Washington sat down. He had little idea what was to come, but over the two years he had been commander-in-chief, he had become accustomed to these 'fireside chats', as Hancock called them. The younger Adams passed over a brandy.

John Adams took up the conversation. 'Congratulations on such a magnificent victory, George. It is beyond our wildest dreams.'

'Thank you, John. I cannot claim any credit for the victory, and you are more than aware of that. The credit lies entirely with the baron. As you will recall, I was not of the view that Howe would be aiming to attack Philadelphia. I am as much in gratitude to the baron for his foresight as anyone else.'

'That is extremely magnanimous of you, George,' Adams replied, his cousin harrumphing in agreement and Hancock saying, 'Indeed.'

'It is the truth, that is all,' he replied.

'The baron and his troops have certainly made a difference to our fortunes since they arrived,' John Adams continued.

'Indeed, they have.'

'That is something that has not gone unnoticed by the general populace.'

'So I see from the banners and flags that are flying about the town.'

'Indeed, they have been much taken to their hearts. It was a spontaneous outpouring of affection and joy.'

Washington could not resist the bite. 'Those flags did not seem to have much of the spontaneous about them. They would have required much planning, and industry indeed.'

'The people have chosen,' growled Sam Adams. 'The people. No one asked them to put 'em up.'

'Has Congress decided that this swastika is to be its emblem then, for it flies from the seat of government, I see.'

'Loyal patriots came and attached those banners to welcome the Stormtroopers back from Elk River,' replied Hancock. 'Congress took no decision, except to agree to them staying affixed while the city celebrates a famous victory. In time they will come down, but these Stormtroopers have created quite a reputation for themselves, and are much cherished by the people.'

'And were not the Pennsylvanian Riflemen part of the defeat of Howe? I left two squadrons behind – the Riflemen and the Stormtroopers – were they not both to be cherished by the people?'

'You'll find yer beloved Riflemen are wearing the swastikas these days, Washington,' snarled Sam Adams. 'They seem to know which way their bread is buttered. There's no division between 'em, Stormtroopers and Riflemen. They've formed a single battalion. I'm surprised the commander-in-chief of the army isn't aware of such things. Quite queer that, but I suppose you haven't been around here much, given as you were expecting Howe to be sailing down to Charleston an' all.'

The younger Adams looked to settle things.

'George, you'll remember that it was I who proposed you as commander-in-chief but two years ago in this very building. I have been the most loyal and staunchest of your friends through-out—'

'As I have!' chorused Hancock unnecessarily.

'—throughout much failure, many trying times.'

'I thanked you at the time for that, John, and I thank you now. But now, we have victories.'

'Indeed, we have victories,' repeated Hancock.

'But not your victories, sir!' Sam Adams slammed his glass of water down on to a newly purchased rosewood side table, which much disturbed Hancock. 'Not your victories and that's the point, sir!'

'Trenton, Princeton, they were my victories, Sam!'

'They were no more your victories than mine or our John's or Hancock's, for that matter. They were this Baron von Steuben's victories. You were flailing around in a fog before he arrived. If he hadn't held the Hessians back at Trenton . . . well, you'd have lost that one like you lost Long Island, Fort Washington and New York. If it hadn't been for this baron, Philadelphia would have been undefended and Howe'd be sitting here and King George'd be licking his lips at the beating he'd given us.'

Hancock visibly flinched, but Washington took it in his stride. Sam Adams's temper was legendary, it was how he got his way in

Congress, the Puritan with the brimstone.

'Yes, I was wrong about Charleston, we were all wrong about Charleston. The only one who got it right was the baron. But that's what leadership is about. I listened to everyone and then made a decision that benefitted us all, that's—'

'That's not leadership, George. That's weakness. You are but a cushion, bearing the imprint of the last man who sat upon you. Luckily for us, that last man was Baron von Steuben,' replied Sam Adams.

His cousin signalled for him to be quiet and then said sternly, 'George, whatever the circumstances, it is time for a change. A time for us to bring some fresh ideas into play. I have kept Congress off your back for so long, but now the tide has turned. I, we, would ask you to do one more great thing for the colonies and for our new country: stand down as commander-in-chief.'

THIRTY-NINE

A summer thunderstorm had broken out, rain pelting down on the tents of the Northern Army. Knox was on his daily round of artillery positions. He did not believe that Burgoyne was going to attempt to break out and join with Howe any time soon, but he could not take the chance. Keeping his gunnery crews focused was the most difficult matter he had at the present time.

There had been disquiet among his men when news came through of the events at the Elk. Despite the ever-present danger battle presented, his boys were always up for a scrap. They had songs about the victory at Trenton and the successful holding of the Assunpink Bridge, times when they showed they were more than capable of holding off the British. How they would have loved to be singing songs about Howe's defeat at the head of the Elk. On more than one occasion, he heard men at their fires bemoaning Old George's decision to come north, how the German von Steuben had changed things for the good, how they would love to follow him into battle, how they admired the Stormtroopers, their discipline, their success.

It was difficult to argue against such sentiments.

He was inspecting Neil Rodger's second gun placement, four ten-inch howitzers and a single twelve-inch mortar, when a messenger came riding up to him.

'Sir, General Schuyler asks for you to return immediately to camp. We have visitors from the south and urgently need a conference.'

Shrugging, he mounted his horse, pulled his cloak over himself, and drove his mount down the increasingly muddy track back to Schuyler's staff quarters.

Jefferson had come to Philadelphia for the Conference, but had immediately taken to his bed with a terrible summer cold. Wheezing, coughing, his body racked with tremors, he had been unable to play any role in Congress's deliberations since his arrival. Indeed, he had Sally, his maid, turn away any visitors, delegates or otherwise. It was very out of character.

He had dragged himself out of bed and was pissing in his pot when a commotion broke out outside his chamber. His head still spinning, he dropped down his nightgown and went to return to his bed when the door flew open and Edward Hand appeared, with Sally hitting him around the body and screaming. In the background he saw an agitated Negro whose name he would later learn was Oliver Cromwell.

Slumping to his bed, Jefferson said, 'Good God, Hand, you look worse than I feel.'

Thomas Paine was far from pleased. He had been in Bordentown for several weeks, putting the final touches to the latest pamphlet in the American Crisis series, and now he learned that there was an extraordinary meeting of Congress in Philadelphia, a war council, no less, that he was missing. The defeat of Howe at the Elk had changed everything. While all the leading men of the cause would be debating the plans for the final defeat of the British, he would be stuck a day's travel north reading printer's copy. His fear was not the strategy for the continuation of the war – he never claimed to be a master of the strategies of war – but that important decisions would be made on the future shape of the polity without him being present, and he regarded himself as a key architect of those plans. Furthermore, he was concerned about the pernicious influence the merchants, moneylenders, industrialists and landowners would hold over Congress. He saw how defeat could yet be snatched from the jaws of victory.

Jefferson, the Adams cousins, Hancock, all good men, all had made the most splendid of starts, but Paine was determined that he should be there to provide a solid backbone to their deliberations. There were questions, crucial questions, which could not be evaded at this juncture. Now was the time to settle the issue of slavery, for example. A republic formed on the basis of a slave society could never succeed; aside from the moral issue, it was primitive economics. England was being transformed by great industrial innovations. For all his criticisms of the British polity, even he could recognise that such innovation could not develop in a society in which so many were the chattels of others. If America were to succeed, it would need a free labour supply that could adapt to technology. Slave plantations were a throwback, a pre-feudal throwback that had no place in the modern world.

Now that the British were on the verge of defeat, there was no longer the compunction on the part of either Congress or Washington to ameliorate the south by refusing to tackle the slavery issue. It had to be tackled and now. But when even the angels in the debate, men such as Jefferson, Washington and Hancock, were slave owners, how could Congress understand the importance of the issue without a fierce advocate of freedom? Ben Franklin was in France and he, Thomas Paine, was in Bordentown. Damn it, he would have to forget these proofs (such a tiresome business anyway) and travel to Philly immediately.

They had been waiting for the best part of two hours in the assembly room. The heat of the August day had turned the room overly warm and the food was long finished. Cadwalader was asleep in the corner, Greene was reading Voltaire, in French, Lafayette, Sullivan and Hamilton were playing cards and Ewing was writing letters. As military men they had become accustomed to spending long hours waiting for something to happen. Usually, nothing happened. Not this day though.

The twin doors were opened wide and in came von Steuben, Hanna Reitsch, Werner Conze and Lothar Kluggman.

'Good afternoon, gentlemen,' opened von Steuben.

'Ah, the victor of the Elk River – and all our glories past and present – has arrived,' said Sullivan, throwing his cards to the table.

'Thank you for your kind regards,' said von Steuben, deliberately overlooking the sarcasm in Sullivan's greeting. The others stood up and exchanged pleasantries with Conze and Reitsch. 'And let me introduce you to our comrade Lothar Kluggman, who was much complimented for his efforts in the defence of Trenton and thereafter.'

The German giant towered over all the others.

'Ah, young Lafayette, I see you have made yourself useful to General Washington. We have a wager, young man. I am expecting you to make full payment.'

Lafayette blushed, 'And I will of course honour ze debt. You were proved correct in zat analysis. We are in your debt. As soon as my funds come through from France, I will settle ze debt.'

Von Steuben eyed him suspiciously, 'Of course you will. You are a man of your word. I have no doubt of that. Gentlemen, shall we?' He pointed to the long table in the centre of the room.

'Shall we what?' asked Sullivan.

'Shall we begin our war conference,' replied von Steuben, taking his place at one end of the table.

Drenched from the rain, Knox entered Schuyler's tent to find an unexpected pair of guests, Horatio Gates and Benedict Arnold, both dressed in the grey-green Hessian uniform, swastikas on their right arm.

'Gates, Arnold, a pleasant surprise. What brings you both here?'

'We have new orders. Ones that we were happy to take, from an experienced military man.'

'Ah,' nodded Knox, 'That would explain the uniform. You have become part of Baron von Steuben's retinue, have you?'

'Finally, we have a leader among us, Knox. One who prefers action to prevarication, and look what success it has brought us.'

'The last time I saw you, General, you were certainly not prevaricating – as you sped away from Trenton. Making off to Baltimore and Congress, wasn't it? Certain as you were of our defeat.'

'Which would undoubtedly have occurred had it not been for the baron,' replied Gates stiffly.

'Given that you were not among us, but rather had gone to feather your bed with Congress, I am unsure how you would know how that day or indeed our further victory at Princeton was achieved, and who or who did not play a role.'

'Sir, your judgement is even poorer than I imagined if you do not accept that before the baron arrived we had nothing but failure, abject failure, but now we have nothing but success. Had we enjoyed more assured leadership previously, then we may not have needed the baron's involvement?'

Knox was furious. 'It is easy to play the weasel for you, isn't it, Gates? Seems to come naturally. Perhaps it's because you're an Englishman by birth. Must be difficult to overcome it, the natural arrogance. General Washington has proved himself to be the finest among us. No other could have held the army, the militias together, in the face of such great difficulties.'

'Difficulties entirely of his own design, sir.'

'Please, let us end this debate,' interjected Arnold. 'We have come here to pass on Congress's plans for the future conduct of the northern campaign.'

'Congress's plans?' asked Schuyler. 'Congress is now determining our strategy for war?'

'No, it is not,' Gates replied. 'But it has decided that now is the time for a change of leadership.' He thrust out a parchment. 'Read this. General Schuyler, you are dismissed. I am taking control of the Northern Army.'

Jefferson's head was reeling, both from the tempest inside it and from Hand's and Cromwell's revelations.

The slaughter of the defenders and civilians of New Brunswick, the murder of the families and devastation of the trading post, the destruction of Queen Esther's Town. All this was news to him. That and that von Steuben might be an imposter.

'This last charge, Hand, how can it be proved? You have the word of a veteran, who, by the sound of it, is some old drunk who can easily be dismissed as a peddler of lies.'

'We should write to Ben Franklin.'

'We can, indeed we will, but that will take months. By which time . . .'

'By which time, I fear our revolution will be distorted. We will have won the war for independence, but lost the soul of our revolution.'

'They have rounded up so many of my fellow Negroes and taken them to Lord knows where, sir. All those fine fellows who fought for freedom, gone. They will come for others now – and soon,' added Cromwell.

Jefferson nodded his head. 'Here's the thing. I will have you dictate to my secretary the details of the events—'

'There is no need. We thought it prudent that we should write this all in a letter to you, sir.' Hand handed over a few loose pages of text. 'It embraces my experiences at New Brunswick, Heidlebergtown and Queen Esther's Town and Cromwell's story of the removal of all the Negro troops. I have also included the revelation about von Steuben, although, as you say, it is little more than barrack room gossip.'

'Well, it shouldn't be difficult for the baron to deny it then. I will take this with me today to Congress; it sits again today. And we shall have the debate there and then. What of you?'

'Of me?'

'Yes. Aren't these German thugs still on the lookout for you? Won't they tear you apart if they see you?'

'Don't worry, Mister Jefferson, I'll be keeping an eye on him. We'll be at my smithy along Carter's Alley. You should send for us when you think the danger is over,' answered Cromwell.

'Carter's Alley, you say?'

'Yes. But first Oliver and I want to see what these Hessians are up to down at the port. There is much of a hurly-burly down there, some industry whose purpose seems furtive to us.'

Paine had packed his bags. His mind was settled. He had to be in Philly and a coach was leaving in an hour.

At that moment, there was a tremendous knocking on the front door of the small townhouse he had been lent by Vivienne Clore, the wealthy society widow who had taken Paine under her wing over the previous few months. He assumed it was one of her servants come to summon him to afternoon tea with his benefactress, a regular request that was losing much of its charm. Opening the door, he was surprised to find two Stormtroopers outside.

'Herr Thomas Paine?' asked the first, a tall, blond lad, no more than twenty-two.

'Indeed,' he replied, puzzled by the appearance of these uniformed men.

'Please come with us.'

'Come with you? Where? I am about to depart to Philadelphia.'

'No, come with us, please.'

'Why and where, where would I be going with you?'

'Just come with us, please.'

'I will not, unless I have an understanding of where we are going.'

'Please, come quietly with us.'

'Come quietly with you? What is this? I will not come quietly, I will—'

The other German, older, shorter, simply moved in front of the younger man, and pushed Paine back into his townhouse.

'What the . . . ! Tyranny! What is this tyranny? Help!'

But Thomas Paine's words were lost to the world, as the two Stormtroopers closed the door of his house behind them and silenced the author of *The Rights of Man*.

'Sit down, gentlemen, let us begin our Conference,' said von Steuben, settling into his chair. Reitsch and Conze sat along the left side of the table. Kluggman hovered, menacingly, at the back.

'Where is Washington?' asked Sullivan. 'We cannot have a war conference without the commander-in-chief.'

'Sit down, Sullivan, you old windbag,' sneered Reitsch.

'Why is General Washington not with us?' asked Hamilton.

'He haz been overthrown by zese people, I suspect,' said Lafayette, languidly throwing himself down into a chair.

'Is that true, sir?' asked Hamilton.

'Let us sit down and discuss the matter at hand,' said von Steuben patiently.

'I will not sit down until—' Sullivan was bundled by Kluggman into a chair which was then pushed tight up against the table. 'Have your ape take his hands off me. I will not be treated in this way!'

The ape simply moved on, towards Ewing, who took a seat, as did Hamilton, Greene and Cadwalader. Kluggman did not take a seat, but continued to stand menacingly behind the generals.

'Now we are all seated, we can begin,' said von Steuben. 'There has been a change of leadership. I have been asked by Congress to take on the office of commander-in-chief of the Continental Army and militias—'

There was instant uproar, shouting of 'Shame!' from Cadwalader, 'What, Congress?' from Sullivan and *'Coup d'état!'* from Lafayette. Hamilton and Greene appeared numb from the shock of the moment.

'Gentlemen, please. I understand you all have varying degrees of affection for General Washington, as I myself do' – which caused further yells of outrage – 'but I, like yourselves, am only here to serve the will of Congress and the people of the colonies. This is a great and arduous responsibility, but one that I am prepared to take up if it is the will of Congress—'

Sullivan pushed back his chair, stood up and bellowed: 'I am not going to stand here and be lectured by a German mercenary,' before Kluggman stepped forward and pushed him back into his chair and up against the table again.

'Get your hands off John Sullivan!' shouted Cadwalader, springing out of his seat and making for Kluggman. The German turned around and punched Cadwalader flush in the face, and the general crumbled instantly to the ground.

Sullivan yelled, 'You dare lay hands on our General Cadwalader!', but backed down into his seat as the silent Kluggman made towards him once again. Hamilton moved out of his chair, crouching down to tend to the stricken general. 'You have knocked him out cold, you brute.'

'Get back in your seat, Hamilton,' said Conze.

'This is insurrection! Plain and simple insurrection,' cried Ewing.

'It is no such thing,' said von Steuben, who was maintaining remarkable coolness amid the clamour. 'Congress has looked upon the events of the past few weeks and come to the conclusion that "a change of leadership is necessary to achieve a swift cessation of the present conflict." I believe that is the statement they will make, Werner, is it not.'

'It is, sir, yes.'

'Statement, what statement?'

'More a proclamation, actually,' said Conze, effortlessly smooth and patronising in this moment of triumph. 'It has been sent to all the army units and militias. Most will have received it by the end of today.'

'The end of today!' exclaimed Ewing. 'So this rebellion has been planned for some time.'

'I cannot believe this is happening, and here, in this very room where the Declaration of our Independence was made and signed,' said Hamilton. 'A terrible thing has been done here today.'

'Ah, stop with the drama. Nothing of the kind has happened,' Conze stated.

'Indeed,' agreed von Steuben. 'This alters nothing aside from the direction of the war and its leadership. What you are fighting for remains the same.'

'The army will not stand for this. Mark my words,' said Sullivan. 'They love Old George.'

'They may well do so, but they are more in love with winning this war. They will understand. Besides which Lord Stirling is with the main body of the army now and informing them. With a group of Stormtroopers, of course. A loyal group of American Stormtroopers I should add.'

'Stirling? That turncoat!' screamed Sullivan.

'The Northern Army, under Schuyler, the artillery group under Knox, they will remain loyal to Washington. This will lead to civil war. We will be fighting among ourselves. Howe will not believe his luck,' Ewing joined in.

'I do not believe that will be the case, General,' observed von Steuben. 'Quite the contrary, actually.'

The summer thunderstorm had given way. Outside the canvas tents, the sun had broken through and with it a bright rainbow rose above the Northern Army. Men stood outside admiring its beauty, while inside Knox and Schuyler wrestled with their own impotence.

'I would be most honoured – as would Congress – if you will both continue to serve the Colonial Army under the new leadership of Baron von Steuben,' said Gates. 'The baron himself has asked me to expressly pass on his esteemed regards and hopes that you will continue to serve the interests of the colonies. However, should you wish to resign your commands, we will promise you safe passage to Albany, Pip, and for you, Knox, to your bookshop in Boston.'

'Safe passage? Why would we require safe passage?' asked Schuyler.

'Well, these are desperate days, are they not?' replied Gates. 'We wouldn't want you falling into the hands of the enemy, would we? For your personal safety of course – although, we cannot ignore the possibility that you might seek solace in their camp.'

'With the British!' exploded Knox. 'What kind of men do you take us for? Our loyalty to the cause is not in question.'

'Of course not,' Arnold attempted to mollify both men. 'But you must understand why we have to be certain of your intentions. Such are the times.'

'Are you with us or are you not?' barked Gates. 'It's a simple question. Stay or go, I care not.'

Schuyler and Knox stared at each other. Then Schuyler replied: 'I will stay and serve under you at your discretion, General Gates. This does not alter the cause we fight for.'

'Where does General Washington stand on this?' asked Knox.

'I have no idea. If the past is a stick by which to measure him, he is probably prevaricating somewhere, probably the wrong place, ha!' snorted Gates.

'We have had no communication with General Washington,' Arnold replied. 'Knowing him as we all do, I am sure he would desire you both continue to fight the British.'

'Indeed,' said Knox. 'Then I will continue to serve the Continental Army until I have reason to believe that my services are no longer required.'

'Good,' Gates declared. 'We start preparing immediately for an assault on Burgoyne.'

Von Steuben's patience was wearing thin.

'We have debated this for far too long. I was prepared to allow you some time to comprehend the change of command, but that time is up. It is simple. Will you serve under myself as commander-in-chief? Yes or no?'

'Under you and whose flag?' demanded Sullivan. 'Are we now to serve under that damnable swastika that so blights this city?'

'What offends you so about the swastika?' asked Reitsch.

'Finally found your voice, have you, girl? Thought you were quiet for too long.'

'General Sullivan, your continuous hostility towards me solely on the grounds of my sex never fails to baffle me. What is it that so terrifies you about women?'

'Terrifies me, ha! Don't be so foolish. War is no place for a woman, outside of the kitchen and the hospital. It insults us all to have you around this table.'

'I will have you spend some time with the League of American Girls, they will give you something of an education.'

'The League of . . . ? Oh, please spare me, madame. No, Baron, in answer to your question. I will not serve under you, that banner and your monstrous regiments. I wish you good day and good fortune. I shall take myself back to New Hampshire and respond publicly there. Gentlemen, I urge you to join me. This is a cause I can no longer believe in.'

Sullivan stood up primly and made his way to the door. Von Steuben signalled to Kluggman. The Hessian followed the general to the door. Sullivan turned to him, 'What, are you to escort me off the premises, ape?'

Kluggman raised a knife and calmly drew it across Sullivan's throat.

The general raised his hands, blood poured over his knuckles, his face grimaced in shock and pain. Trying desperately to stem the flow, Sullivan collapsed to the floor.

Immediately, Ewing pulled out his sword and made towards Kluggman. The German avoided Ewing's sword thrust with ease, and caught his right arm. The strength of Kluggman was immense. He wrenched the arm with such force that it almost came out of the shoulder socket. Ewing screamed in pain, the sword clattered to the floor and Kluggman wiped the bloodied blade of his knife along the thin neck of the American. He dropped Ewing to the floor, on top of Sullivan, their bodies twitching in their last throes together, their blood mixing in a scarlet pool on the oak floor.

Greene and Hamilton looked on in shock, terror and awe. Lafayette, younger but educated in Versailles on the realities of power, merely laconically said: '*Il vaut mieux être craint que d'être aimé.*'

Hamilton, shaking, turned to him: 'Machiavelli: "It is better to be feared than loved."'

Conze stood up. 'A student of Machiavelli, eh?'

The French youth shrugged his shoulders. 'I have studied politics at ze court of King Louis. Nothing here today surprises me. This ez politics. It ez as it ez.'

'Let me give you another little piece of Machiavelli,' Conze said, walking around the table. '"If an injury has to be done to a man, it should be so severe that his vengeance need not to be feared."'

'"*Si une blessure doit être faite à un homme, elle doit être si sévère que sa vengeance ne doit pas être crainte,*" I know it well. Vengeance ez a fine art. Of course vengeance may not come from those you directly offend, but from those who seek vengeance on their behalf. Did the prince not also say that ze best way to estimate ze intelligence of a ruler ez to look at ze men he surrounds himself with?' Lafayette splayed his arms wide and smiled contemptuously.

'Ah, the splendid arrogance of youth. You know, Marquis de Lafayette, there is a future in which you will be much celebrated in this country for all you do to win this war and secure an independent republic. And in your own country, do you know what they will think of you?'

'Zey will despise me?' he said arrogantly.

'No, they will not. They will love you, because you will aid the greatest revolution of all time, one that will overthrow King Louis and the *Ancien Régime*. And later, when a dictator called Bonaparte is overthrown, the people will come to you and ask you to take the crown. And you, because of the principles you forged here in America, will say no and save your country, for a second time. There will be statues of you all over the world, cities, towns, roads, schools, parks, all named Lafayette. You will go down in history as a very great man. All this will happen in the future.'

Lafayette eyed Conze in bewilderment. 'What are you, some kind of prophet? Some soothsayer?'

'No, I am from beyond that future, and I come to make a different kind of future. A future that will belong to me. I will be the one they will raise statues to, the one who has cities, towns, roads, schools and parks named after him. And you, you shitty little French cunt, you will be entirely forgotten.'

And he plunged his sword straight into Lafayette's heart, twisting and turning the blade, until the last throb of consciousness left him.

Von Steuben surveyed the room, the squirming Greene and sobbing Hamilton, the still unconscious Cadwalader on the floor. 'So, anyone else have any questions?' he asked.

FORTY

Just a few minutes earlier, a wheezing Thomas Jefferson had entered the State House and gone straight to John Hancock's room, where he discovered Hancock and the Adams cousins in discussion.

'Thom, we called for you yesterday, but we were told you were otherwise engaged on account of the flu.'

'And I am still with it, John, my head is rotten and I need, ah, yes, good man, pour me a brandy, will you. It may revitalise me and grant me the strength I need to impart the most serious of accusations against those we thought were our brothers.'

'Well, we've news for you, Jefferson, something you may be understanding of – or you may regard as a transgression.'

'A transgression. Good Lord, it must be bad if you are going to start using three-syllable words, Sam, quite out of character. And no water in the brandy, John Hancock, I'll take it as it was intended.'

'You unfortunately were not present for the meeting of Congress yesterday, Thom,' John Adams said, seizing the moment. 'That was most unfortunate, for the delegates much needed your wisdom and clarity of thought. It was a most challenging Congress.'

'Indeed, it was,' said Hancock passing the brandy over to Jefferson and pausing to pour himself another.

'However, we could not wait for you to recover,' continued John Adams.

'You could have sent word to me at my chambers. My secretary would have responded on my behalf.'

'No, we could not do that, as well you know, under the Resolution of Secrecy we all took. We could not possibly divulge the debate of Congress while no outcome had been determined.'

'Tosh, that's for the others, this is me we're talking about, John!'

Adams responded quietly, 'Even for you, Thom, even for you. Your absence was highly regrettable, not the least among us three.'

'We had no option, you see,' said Hancock, 'no option at all. There was quite a mood among the delegates. They were unanimous.'

'And we were wi' 'em, frankly,' snarled Sam Adams.

'Put me out of suspense if you will, my body is weak and I may not last these puzzles much longer. Get to the point.'

'We've discharged General Washington of his duties,' said John Adams.

'And not before time, I should say,' said Sam Adams. 'What was it you said of 'im, cousin? He was only commander-in-chief because he was "always the tallest man in the room". We weren't exactly spoilt for choice.'

'What? After we have finally turned the tide? Why now? This makes little sense. Is this the work of that pocket-sized Machiavelli, Horatio Gates? Tell me that Congress did not fall for that embittered man.'

'Nowt to do with Gates. Fella wasn't there. It's the German, von Steuben.'

'You've put von Steuben in charge!' Jefferson yelped.

'Aye, the fella who keeps giving us victories. Damn stupid idea, eh!' roared Sam Adams.

'Sam, this may be a most terrible decision. Von Steuben is the reason I have come from my sickbed this afternoon. I have with me a letter which outlines several atrocities committed by his forces. Some of them are quite, quite terrible.'

'What atrocities?' asked John Adams.

'At New Brunswick, there was a group of civilians, forty or more, chiefly women and children, raped and murdered by Werner Conze and his Stormtroopers. A Jewish trading post outside of Heidlebergtown, several families murdered in their homes by the Stormtroopers, the village burnt. Similarly, an Indian village razed to the ground at Susquehanna River, women and children slaughtered.'

'And where do these stories come from?' asked John Adams.

'A very fine source, Edward Hands, Colonel of the Pennsylvanian Riflemen, a man well known to me and much admired by all of the Continental Army.'

'The former Colonel Edward Hand,' John Adams corrected him. 'I thought he was dead. Wasn't he murdered by those Indians at Susquehanna?'

'A fabrication,' Jefferson replied. 'The Indians did not attack our men. Well, not those Indians. Hand was shot and left for dead by Conze and his men.'

'Well, that runs counter to the testimony of everyone else there, including Hand's own men in the Pennsylvanian Riflemen. Come on, Thom, do you really believe all that? Sounds to me much more likely that he manufactured these claims as an act of retribution. You are aware that his sister is betrothed to Werner Conze, are you not? I believe Colonel Hand is much opposed to the marriage. That may explain these stories.'

'The British have made no complaint to Congress over the mistreatment of prisoners at New Brunswick,' interjected Hancock. 'They rarely miss an opportunity to complain about our conduct.

I am sure they would have made merry with this if they had such an occasion as this.'

Jefferson continued undaunted. 'Who, if anyone, has examined Baron von Steuben's credentials?'

'His credentials?' asked John Adams, 'I would have thought his actions signify the strength of his credentials.'

'He may not be who he says he is.'

'Good Lord, Thom Jefferson, I am aware you have the most splendid of imaginations, but really . . . who is he then? George the Third in disguise?'

'I have it on authority the real Baron von Steuben is in his mid-forties, a much shorter man and a buggerer.'

'A buggerer!' Sam Adams started to laugh.

'Well, on that account you cannot be right. This von Steuben is certainly no buggerer given his closeness with Frau Reitsch,' Hancock joined in with the laughter.

'A buggerer? You been drinking, Jefferson?' asked Sam Adams.

'No, Sam, but that was the reason the real Baron von Steuben left the court of King Frederick: he was caught in flagrante with junior officers.'

'In that case, lad, we should be thankful, we've got the other Baron von Steuben then. I have no time for this; I'm off to my bed. The day is long and I'm not getting any younger. I'll be putting this down to the fever, Thom Jefferson, there can't be any other cause of this madness.' John Adams stood up and wiped his hand along Jefferson's forehead. 'The boy's a fever. Burning up. Best get yer back to yer bed, Thom. Wake up and this'll all be a dream. Good evening, gentlemen. A good day's work on our part. Fare ye well.'

FORTY-ONE

The port was full of life even though it was early evening and the working day was coming to a close. The war and the continual threat of a British blockade had made little difference to Philadelphia's port. As on most days, hundreds of people busied themselves around the wharves, quays and jetties. Molasses from Martinique, barrels of cod from the Newfoundland banks, timber from Canadian forests all coming in; fruit and vegetables making the trip north to feed New York. A Babel of voices: Polish, German, Irish, English, Swedish; a kaleidoscope of faces, white, black, brown, red. Groups of new immigrants huddled together, clinging hard to their paltry possessions, eyed expectantly by groups of dishevelled youths looking for new flesh to exploit. Peddlers, hawkers, merchants, pushers and dealers of this, that and everything. All of the New World was here and going about the business of America, the business of commerce.

At the edge of the wharf, Hand and Cromwell bided their time, watching the world unfurl, keeping an eye on the comings and goings at the far end of the yard.

At that end a rough wooden stockade was in place, guarded by grey-green-suited soldiers. Even from a distance, Hand recognised the sentries at the entrance, Paul and Tommy Parsons, brothers from Trenton, Pennsylvanian Riflemen now wearing the uniforms of the Stormtroopers. From their place on the wharf wall, he and

296

Cromwell surveyed the outlines of the stockade, planning the best way of entry.

From the other side came much shouting and cheering. Through the port marched a small group led by two people Hand knew only too well: Hanna Reitsch and Werner Conze. The river of people in the port parted to allow them to pass, onlookers staring, cheering and wishing them well. Like royalty, Hand thought. They are becoming our royalty. He turned away, his gaze far out to sea, turning back only when Reitsch and Conze had entered the stockade, the gate closed firmly behind them.

Later, as the sun set, Hand and Cromwell eased themselves away from their vantage point and made towards the fish-gutting tables against which the enclosure had been thrown up. Clear now of fish and men, the morning's catch long gone, still the tables and canvas awnings gave off the stench of fish guts, the floor slippery underfoot. Working past these tables, climbing over empty barrels and boxes, they came to a discreet area where the fence of the compound was more rickety, a result of the speed with which it had been thrown up.

Together they pulled at the wooden slats until a gap appeared. There was no need for them to be quiet, because the noise of whatever was happening inside the stockade was overpowering. They slipped through the gap and their faces were immediately illuminated by a luminous golden-orange haze. They had never seen anything like this before.

In front of them, in an open area, a huge furnace fifty-feet high was throwing up yellow flames that licked the night sky. The hungry mouth was fed by coal and coke, white-hot iron running from it, collected in little iron wagons that climbed away to be cooled in hissing vats of water. Their ears were assaulted by the dull thud of forge hammers and the rumbling and clanking of iron chains and wheels. Smut-covered workmen with fierce white eyes moved delicately among the glowing iron, handkerchiefs around their mouths to keep out the sulphurous acid, sweat mingling with the dirt about their naked torsos. Flames, smoke, iron and steel, a pandemonium of the senses. Something new, something thrilling, something terrible.

Hand and Cromwell could not bring themselves to stop watching this show from hell. They had never seen anything like it. Nor did they understand it.

The splashing molten carriages disappeared into a large shed, from which sparks flew and thunderous hammers and drills could be heard, but from their vantage point neither could see inside.

'We need to get into that shed,' Cromwell murmured to Hand.

'There's no way we can see inside without breaking our cover. They must stop at some stage. We must come back when the work has ceased.'

But at that moment the work did cease. A whistle was blown and all the workers downed their tools. For five minutes the hands cleared the yard of all debris and closed down the furnace. Their work completed, they lined up in a single line at the wall by the entrance.

Then there was a rumbling, a clanking and a hissing, the likes of which neither Cromwell or Hand had ever heard, leading to a monstrous noise, and then, from the shed, it came out.

They could not believe their eyes.

It was some kind of machine. On a platform sat a long barrel, at its end a chimney, smoke rising from it, the platform propelled by a collection of wheels, iron wheels with pistons moving like little arms. A man was stoking the chimney, and another was directing the machine by a ship's wheel. Behind them, another barrel and then behind that, incredibly, on a second platform, two men stood alongside a cannon.

Scampering behind the machine came four people, Hanna Reitsch, Werner Conze and two others, who made for an odd pair, one short and squat, the other tall and thin.

The machine was moving fast, and then it came to a dramatic halt. There was a shout from one of the men with Reitsch and Conze – they could not hear it over the noise of the steam. But one of the men spun another wheel around so that the cannon now faced not the rear of the engine, but out to Philadelphia bay. He then spun a third wheel and the snout moved up in the air. The man put what appeared to be spectacles to his eyes and shouted at the other man on the cannon.

This man picked up a brass cartridge from the floor of the plat-form, stuffed it into the cannon and then walked to the rear. Everyone in the yard put their hands to their ears and the man then did something– his body obscuring the view from both Cromwell and Hand – and then leapt clear before – good God! – a most hideous noise, worse than any cannon Hand had ever heard in battle. The cartridge flew out of the mouth of the cannon, high into the air and towards the bay where it landed, destroying a small fishing boat that had been clearly left there for that purpose.

The entire yard screamed in triumph. The smaller of the men threw his arms around Reitsch, while the taller man simply nodded aristocratically before shaking Conze's hand.

Cromwell and Hand turned to each other. They were lost for words.

FORTY-TWO

'I'm not sure it was entirely necessary to see off Lafayette.'

'That preening French cock, I couldn't bear him any longer. Quoting Machiavelli in French. If he was half the intellectual he thought he was, he could have at least used the original Italian.' Conze burst into laughter and von Steuben joined in. Conze and Reitsch had returned from the port in high spirits, to join von Steuben in his room at the City Tavern.

'Now to explain these murders,' Reitsch said. 'They were necessary to our cause, but we need an explanation that is credible. And I think I have one.'

'You do? Let's hear it,' said von Steuben.

'We discovered a plot, a heinous plot, the work of this Frenchman. Lafayette had come to the Americas as an agent of the British. He was seeking revenge against the French court that had banished him – the details can be oblique, it matters little, no one understands the Byzantine workings of royal courts, that will suffice. We uncovered the plot; he did not deny it, or the Americans who were part of it. They attacked us, we fought back, they died.'

'A good explanation, but with a certain flaw,' said Conze. 'We have witnesses who would deny it: Hamilton, Greene and Cadwalader, assuming he recovers from Kluggman's punch. There may be brain damage by the way. Our friend is quite remarkable. That was some punch.'

'Even better,' replied Reitsch. 'Those three are part of it. We put them on trial. Not before we torture them into making a suitable confession. They will not be able to sustain themselves for any length of time; you saw how they shivered with fear in the room. A confession from them is all that we require. And let us be generous. Ewing was not part of it – Sullivan killed him. And if Cadwalader is disabled, let him too be a hero. We need some martyrs for our cause, better for them to supply them than us.'

'Hanna, perfect. And let us take it one stage further,' responded Conze. 'Let us use this to be rid of Washington. He should be part of the conspiracy and in the pay of Howe. That is why he was prepared to leave Philadelphia open. He despaired of winning the war and was prepared to surrender on British terms.'

'I am not convinced that anyone will think that believable of Washington, Werner,' countered von Steuben. 'It is clear he is a man of sturdy virtue. I've grown rather fond of him, halitosis and all. He may be stiff, but he has many virtues. History has treated him correctly. Given the quality of the men he had around him, his was quite a remarkable achievement.'

'Baron, sentimentality is not an easily recognised virtue of yours!' Conze remarked.

'Don't be too surprised, Werner, you should see him with puppies,' chuckled Reitsch.

'Washington is a problem for us. We have disposed of him easily enough, but as long as he remains free, he will be a convenient standard bearer for any opposition. So far everything we have achieved has been easy and predictable, the difficult parts are to follow. To instil National Socialism in this feudal nation may prove to be more difficult than the Führer's struggle to win over industrial Germany and Austria. We have Congress in our pocket for now, but soon there will be those who disagree with our economic and social policies and they will look for leadership. By his obvious moral virtue, Washington would be an obvious candidate.

He may not wish to become an opposition leader, but why gamble?'

'He's right, Frederich. Let's clean this all up.'

Von Steuben sighed. 'Poor old George, destined not to be remembered as the father of his nation, but as a traitor to it. Werner, have the interrogation experts start their work on Hamilton and Greene. If needs be, Kluggman can give Cadwalader another thump. As you say, a cause needs its martyrs.'

'Very good. Hanna, an impressive piece of thinking.'

'Werner, you said that almost without sounding patronising. You're learning.'

'I'm learning not to underestimate women, Hanna.'

'Ah, love and impending fatherhood can work its wonders on even the most jaded misogynist.'

Von Steuben cleared his throat. It was not the time for Hanna and Conze's tiresome bickering. 'Now, John Adams tells me that Congress will formally announce my selection as commander-in-chief tomorrow. They will aim for a formal inauguration in the chamber, but I think we need another one of those rallies. The last one was rather successful.'

'I am slightly concerned, Frederich my darling, that you are enjoying the adulation of the crowds too much. Perhaps I should stand behind you whispering "you are only human".'

'You do that very successfully away from the podium, my dear, my feet are in no danger of getting carried away with themselves. I would like to unveil the conspiracy to Congress in the morning and then immediately afterwards to the public at a gathering in front of the State House.'

'More Churchill? That was quite shameful last time by the way,' said Conze, admiring himself in the mirror, flattening his hair.

'You didn't like that little flourish, Werner? I thought it was rather clever, using our enemy's words for our own cause. I might use Stalin this time, though I'm not sure he has ever said anything memorable.'

'I'm all for oratory, I'm all for this unexpected use of, what? Irony, I suppose, but you need to consider your audience. This is not Plato's academy you are addressing. Nor is it a twentieth-century audience, grown up with mass media. They are simple, uneducated people, illiterate most of them. Keep your words simple. A few phrases they can repeat, chant even, remember always. And give them fear; always give them enemies, real or imagined. Enemies that we alone can protect them from: Indians, free slaves, the British, the French, Jews, Slavs, anyone different.'

Von Steuben paused to reflect.

'Wise words, Werner. I'll keep it simple. Now, can we be sure of the confessions by the morning? I would like to bring them before Congress.'

'Our boys have been breaking hardened Bolsheviks for years, those two will crumble within hours. You will have your con-spiracy all neatly wrapped and ready as a gift by the morning,' answered Conze.

'Very good. And what of our surprises, Hanna. How goes the work with Krupp and Schmeisser?'

'Schmeisser says he is ahead of schedule. The prototype for the new rifle has worked well in its firing tests. Krupp says that the factory at Boone Town will be ready to start manufacturing in October. By late autumn, the Stormtroopers will be armed with automatic rifles and then we will roll them out to loyal units after-wards. The Frankford Mill has proved itself with the necessary gunpowder and the Pattison Brothers are keeping to their sched-ule for the delivery of the brass cartridges. We have been impressed by their industry. There is hope for this country after all.'

'The modified Brown Besses have worked well so far. I must say little Schmeisser is something of a genius,' said Conze.

'They'll deliver Lee an easy victory over Burgoyne at Saratoga.

We have played our cards well with that one, I think. Once that victory is achieved, we will take the main army to New York and defeat Howe, and have this war won by spring if not by the end of the year even. Six years earlier than the first time. And what about your little surprise they are working on down at the docks? When will that be finished?'

'Soon. Werner and I have just come from a demonstration. It is looking good. Perhaps we'll take you down there the day after tomorrow. It may be ready by then, but I do have something that will certainly be ready tomorrow.' Reitsch moved over to the corner of the room and brought back what appeared to be a blanket. 'The same factory that made the banners for your return from Elk, one of our League of American Girls' factories actually, will have something special for you to unveil tomorrow. This is the sample pattern we worked to.'

On the table she unwrapped the blanket. There were thirteen red and white stripes and in the left-hand corner, a red square and in its centre a black swastika. 'This will be the flag of the United States of America, the Swastika and Stripes.'

FORTY-THREE

The following morning Jefferson awoke fresh and early. He had seen off the infection and his spirits were buoyed; he was ready to take his place at the heart of things again. He may not have agreed with the decision to remove Washington, but he could see its logic, cold and heartless as it was. But he was determined that von Steuben answer the charges. The fight for independence was nothing if it was not a moral crusade. He was determined to address Congress that morning, but first he would do the right thing and call on Washington.

The Congressman walked towards the City Tavern where he knew rooms had been booked for Washington.

It was not yet nine in the morning and already the tavern was bustling. He was used to this. Throughout the course of the war, whenever and wherever he had come to call on Washington, he would find his lodgings surrounded by well-wishers, petitioners, business people, salesmen, worried mothers, all looking to grab a moment with the general to press whatever claim they had on him. Yet, there was something different about this crowd.

It was larger than usual, but oddly without the confusion and chaos that would normally surround it. And he soon realised why: a group of grey-green Stormtroopers were keeping the people orderly, in line. He walked through the crowd, a few recognised him, by his height alone, the bony frame already famous, and he placed himself at the head of the queue.

'*Guten morgan, Jungen*!' he said.

The two Stormtroopers, young men, peach-fuzz chins and acned skin, looked at him, confused.

'What?' asked one.

'Ah, I said good morning. I thought by way of the uniform you would be Hessians.'

'Nah, we're Philly boys an' proud of it, part of the new unit the SS Philadelphia.'

'Really, oh, I had no idea. Would you let me through, boys, I have come to see General Washington.'

'General Washington ain't here, sir, you won't find him in the tavern.'

'Why all these people then? Are they not here to see the general?'

'No, they're 'ere to see the baron,' said the other lad. 'He's staying here.'

'Of course,' thought Jefferson out loud, 'of course he is. Well, do you know where General Washington might be?'

'No idea. He ain't here, that's fer sure. Try the State House, might be someone there can help yer.'

Jefferson withdrew gracefully. Sucked back into the press of the crowd, he eased himself back down Second Street and towards Chestnut. It should have been a walk of a minute or so, but the numbers of people heading towards the tavern made it difficult. Those and the occasional well-wisher, happy to shake one of the signatories of the Declaration of Independence by the hand and wish him a fine morning.

Even the broad avenue of Chestnut was full of people. The whole of Philadelphia and its surrounds seemed to be making its way to the City Tavern. Outside the State House, the large swastika banners still floating dreamily in front of the brick walls, there

306

was some building work going on. A stage was being erected and what appeared to be scaffolding. At the front doors, two Stormtroopers stood on guard.

'Good morning, lads!' he called out to them.

They appeared confused and one said in German, '*Kein Einlass. Nur Kongressabgeordnete.*'

This is confusing, he thought, these are Germans it would appear, and he marvelled how chiselled, how much more athletic they were than the Philly boys he had just come from.

'I am a delegate. Ah, *Ich ein Delegater. Ich. Delegater.* Thomas Jefferson, *mich.*' He pointed at his chest, but the boys were not for moving. Luckily at that moment, from inside, John Hancock walked by, spotted Jefferson struggling and came over.

'*Soldaten, erlauben sie diesem mann in. Er ist* Thomas Jefferson, *ein wichtiger Delegierter.*'

The two soldiers immediately gave a strange right-armed salute, clicking their heels at the same time, and allowed Jefferson to pass through and into the hall.

'I thought you were a master of languages, Thom,' laughed Hancock.

'French, Spanish, Italian, Greek and Latin, yes, but I have never felt the need to learn German, John.'

'Well, you best learn quick, Thom. It's going to be a very important language in the future.'

'Is it?'

Hancock smiled at him. 'Oh, I expect so. No harm in learning a few words of it, what, eh? How are you today? You appear much better – you were in something of a terrible state yesterday.'

'Your brandy appears to have had the desired effect, John, although I'm not sure our conversation did much to lift my spirits.'

'Come, come, Thom, we are on the verge of great things. You were more than aware of George's failings. This is much the best outcome for us all, no matter how painful we might find it initially. Much better.'

'Where is George? I went looking for him at the City Tavern and was told he's not staying there. I would like to see him.'

'Indeed, well, ah, I don't know where he is at this moment.'

'Has he taken off already to Virginia, to Mount Vernon?'

'Do you know, I, I don't know if he has.' Hancock shifted uneasily. 'I haven't actually seen him. Ah, John Adams might know. Look, the session is to start at ten, and I have something to prepare before that, so if I may take my leave of you. Let us enjoy a further brandy at the end of the day's events, dear friend. Farewell for now.'

Hancock scuttled off to his presidential office. Jefferson stood rooted to the spot and looked around him, at the comings and goings of delegates and officers of Congress. It could wait. He would catch up with George later. He too had something to prepare for the next sitting of Congress.

FORTY-FOUR

Hancock walked in, taking his seat with a theatrical swoop that had some of the delegates groaning in despair. Of the fifty-six appointed delegates to the Second Continental Congress, more than forty were present in the assembly room for what was a closed meeting, no members of the press nor public were in attendance, Charles Thomson was taking the minutes.

Quiet descended and Hancock, clearing his throat forcefully as if a large marble was inside, shouted: 'I call this meeting of the Second Continental Congress to order. There is this morning one agenda issue alone and that is the furtherance of the discussion of yesterday regarding the leadership of the war council of this Congress and the position of commander-in-chief. That this Congress did yesterday vote by thirty-six to three that the present commander-in-chief, George Washington of Virginia, be relieved of his post and the office be presented as vacant to the Baron Friedrich von Steuben and that he be requested to fulfil it and bring to a glorious conclusion the present conflict. Congress established a delegation of Messrs Samuel Adams, John Adams and John Hancock to converse with General Washington and then to proceed directly to negotiate with the baron, to report back on this day to Congress the necessary consequences of the aforementioned discussions. I will now call upon Delegate John Adams of Boston to apprise Congress of those deliberations.'

Adams slowly raised himself to his feet. 'Congress, we followed your directions and met first with General Washington. It was the most sympathetic of conversations. On your behalf, we effusively commended the general for his exertions on behalf of Congress and the people of the Thirteen Colonies over these long and difficult two years. He was greatly honoured by the high esteem in which Congress held him. We then expressed the desire of this house for an adjustment in the direction of the campaign.'

He was interrupted by a few grumblings of 'Hear, hear.'

'While understandably disconcerted by such an adjustment, General Washington, fitting in a man so virtuous, declared that he was but a servant of Congress and the people of the Thirteen Colonies and would support any adjustment deemed necessary by that body and the people it in turn served. He would, as a consequence, be content to step aside and allow such others as Congress deemed qualified to take on the role of commander-in-chief.'

The meeting broke into a spontaneous round of applause and some cheers, 'Good Old George!' and 'Most honourable of men'. Jefferson looked around him. He thought the overriding emotion of his fellow delegates was one of relief, relief that others had killed Caesar on their behalf.

'The delegation then proceeded to interview Baron von Steuben. We were most impressed with his plans for a swift cessation of the war. It would be impolitic for me to expand on those plans to Congress, for by their nature, they must remain confidential, as I am sure the delegates will understand, but you will be at rest when I say that the baron has already set in motion the next stage of the campaign. He is not a fellow who could be described as a prevaricator.'

This led to a large outbreak of laughter and further cheering.

'As you would have ascertained from these thoughts, the baron was both humbled by Congress's proposition and consented immediately. His only stipulation was that he be given the same powers as held by the previous commander-in-chief. I hope Congress will be content that I readily agreed with his request.'

There were cheers once again and almost frenzied chants of 'Yes! Yes!'

'Very well. I am confident that our small delegation fulfilled the obligations placed upon it by this Congress.'

Adams sat down, to further applause, with several members reaching over to slap him good-naturedly around the shoulders. Jefferson eyed it all with cynicism. The folly, the avarice, the weakness of men never failed to amuse him. He waited for the tumult to die down, ready to make his own speech, looking to catch President Hancock's eye. However, that moment never came. As soon as the commotion died down, Hancock cleared the marble from his throat in his tiresomely theatrical manner and announced: 'Delegates, recognising as I did your fervour for this change in personnel, I took the liberty of requesting that Baron von Steuben come to Congress this morning and address it. If it suits your mood, I will ask the ushers to alert the baron this moment.'

Again, wild cheers and shouts of 'Yes!'

Hancock tipped a nod to Charles Thomson who left his desk, opened the door of the assembly room little more than a crack and said softly to the waiting usher, 'The baron, now.'

Within a few moments, both doors were thrown open with a flourish and von Steuben strode in, closely followed by Reitsch, Conze and a retinue of a dozen smartly dressed Stormtroopers. He marched straight into the centre of the room, clicked his heels together and gave the raised arm salute Jefferson had seen the guards making an hour or so earlier, in the direction of Hancock. Far from being confused, some of Jefferson's fellow delegates replied with the same salute and no embarrassment that he could see. There were shouts of 'Bravo!' and 'Hurrah', and a general

311

frenzy of handclapping as the delegates rose to their feet to acclaim their new commander-in-chief.

All aside from two men: Jefferson and Sam Adams. The old Bostonian, the man whose Massachusetts Circular Letter back in 1768 had done more than anything to start the struggle, sat in his place, his hands affixed to his walking stick, watching aghast at the idiocy of his fellow Colonists. What he and his cousin had done was necessary. This idolatry was not. He caught Jefferson's eye and shook his head in disgust.

The Stormtroopers had taken up position behind Hancock and by the door of the assembly room, while Reitsch and Conze took two empty chairs behind the delegates. Deciding he had enjoyed the acclaim for long enough, von Steuben raised his hands up and down, imploring for quiet. Finally, the noise subsided and he made his speech.

'Delegates of Congress. I stand before you today, on the most humble day of my life. You have placed upon my troops and myself the most magnificent of responsibilities. We are obliged to serve you, to meet the expectations, the trust you have placed in us. The road ahead will be hazardous, but we, the Continental Army and the militias, will deliver you the victory that you and the people of these great colonies so long for!'

Again, an outpouring of wild applause, with the delegates rising to their feet as one, with the exception of Jefferson and Adams, who sat, politely applauding. Again, von Steuben called for quiet.

'However, the strength of the challenge ahead is ably demonstrated by the most monstrous plot we uncovered only yesterday, a plot that had it not been discovered by General James Ewing, then, well, I shudder to think of the consequences, but I believe they would have seen every man in this room bound in chains and thrown in a prison hulk to be transported across the Atlantic to face trial before that perfidious monarch George!'

The cheers were now replaced by gasps.

312

'Yesterday evening, in the first war council convened under this leadership, General Ewing revealed that there was a plot to secure a victory for Britain over these colonies. The first part of that plot was Howe's attempt to win this very city, where parties to that scheme attempted to have the Continental Army move north and leave Philadelphia unprotected. Those behind it were revealed by General Ewing to their faces, such was the strength of character of this great man.'

'Who were these traitors?' shouted a voice.

'General Ewing named the Frenchman Marquis de Lafayette as the leader. He had come to the Americas with the express intention of seeking revenge on the French court, from where he was banished. He was in the pay of the British and managed either to recruit or persuade a number of General Washington's closest advisers that the war was not winnable. There was, of course, personal advancement if they changed sides. Their most able recruit was,' he paused, 'General John Sullivan.'

There was uproar. Von Steuben had chosen well. Many in the chamber still held Sullivan personally responsible for the failed invasion of Canada in 1776 and had not forgotten the events following his capture by the British at Long Island the same year, which led to Sullivan being forced to bring a proposal for a conference to Congress.

'Decoy Duck!' shouted someone, a cry picked up by others until it ran around the room. Von Steuben looked on confused.

'Baron, the cry is "Decoy Duck" for that is the nickname our esteemed colleague John Adams gave Sullivan when he came before Congress last summer charged by the British with trying to persuade us to agree to a peace conference,' explained Hancock. 'It will not surprise many members that this Sullivan would be party to such a heinous plot.'

'Ah, Congress must excuse my ignorance of the past. The tragedy was that General Sullivan, uncovered in this very room, launched himself at General Ewing, stabbing him before slicing open his throat. We then witnessed the bravery of General Cadwalader, who attempted to subdue Sullivan, but was struck with such ferocity that he is still to regain consciousness. We were most fortunate that one of our men was present and was able to overcome Sullivan, who was killed in the event.'

The room was now quiet.

'During the course of this confrontation, which was witnessed by Obergruppenführer Werner Conze and Frau Hanna Reitsch, Ewing uncovered his fellow conspirators, who we were able to overwhelm. It saddens me to tell Congress that the other members of this cabal were Alexander Hamilton and Nathanael Greene.'

There were shouts of 'Shame' and shudders of disgust around the room.

'We were able to take them into custody yesterday and interrogate them to ascertain who else was part of this plot. At first they claimed there were but four members of the conspiracy – Lafayette, Sullivan, Hamilton and Greene – but then they gave us one further name.'

Von Steuben paused, looked down towards the floor. The room was quiet again. He raised his head, looked about him, tears in his eyes.

'The fifth member of the conspiracy . . . it breaks my heart to reveal this to you. I wish, as God is my judge, that I could give you any name but his. The fifth conspirator is General George Washington.'

Immediate uproar, screams, the air wild with curses and utter disbelief, tears from some, howls of outrage from others. Until finally Jefferson stood up and calmly said, 'Mister President, may I have the floor?'

Hancock, who had been dabbing his eyes with a handkerchief, nodded his assent and Jefferson started, slowly.

'Mister President, Congress, Baron. These are indeed grave

314

accusations. Yet, we live in such strange times. I have recently heard wild accusations levelled at others in this room, such terrible accusations that nevertheless should be heard. At New Brunswick, fifty unarmed, surrendered British soldiers were massacred and forty innocent women, children and civilians raped and slaughtered. Outside of Heidlebergtown, at a Jewish trading post, several families murdered, their houses burned to the ground. And an Indian village, along the Susquehanna River, seventy or more women and children killed, murdered, as they stood unarmed. Such incidents are what we expect of marauding British troops, men who have no respect for the people who escaped the tyranny of their country and carved out a new world from this wilderness. Or should we expect it from paid mercenaries with no loyalty to any country, only to their purse?'

He peered at von Steuben.

'Is this what we should expect from Hessian mercenaries who come here claiming to be our friends, these acclaimed Stormtroopers, who arrived with no prior notice in such mysterious circumstances, betraying one paymaster for another? For these atrocities were the work of these men you now look to bring to your bosom, who you now look upon to win you your freedom – but at what cost? You will excuse me my scepticism, but when I hear of outlandish plots involving some of the most honourable men I have ever met, I weigh up what I know and I ask myself who do I trust more: my friends or an imposter?'

There was uproar now, screams and shouts from both sides of the room, a maelstrom of accusation, taunting, jeering.

'An imposter! Yes, I say an imposter! This is no more the real Baron Friedrich von Steuben than I am King George. The real baron is a short man in his forties, a man thrown out of King Frederick's circle for improper relations with young men! The man before you is an imposter!'

At once the Stormtroopers at the door began to move, but von

315

Steuben in the midst of the pandemonium had the presence of mind to have them stop by raising his arm. Hancock attempted to regain control by hammering his gravel on his desk. And then, finally, von Steuben shouted, 'Be quiet, all of you!'

It had the desired effect; the room was silent once more. Jefferson stood, ramrod straight, facing down the accused.

'Thomas Jefferson,' von Steuben said. 'Let me say this to you. I know not of this other baron you speak of. I am who I am. My actions since my arrival here give proof of my virtues. I can offer no greater assurance for myself than that, nor should I wish to. As for these atrocities you talk of, I know nothing of atrocities. But I do know that the men under my command have shown themselves to be always ready to sacrifice their lives for the freedom of this country. At Trenton, at the Elk River and, yes, at the Susquehanna River, some did indeed give their lives for this great cause. For you to come here and besmirch their sacrifice is shameful. Shame on you, sir.'

'The shame is on you, Baron – or whatever your name is. What have you done with the Negroes who joined the Continental Army? They were removed from the camp at Lowantica, and the Negro units closed down, where are they?'

'I find sympathy for Negroes touching from a slave owner. Are you interested because you wish them for your plantations? I hear you have an uncommonly close interest in the welfare of your slaves, especially the girls.'

There was laughter throughout the room. 'You cur!' shouted Jefferson. 'Is there no level to which you will not stoop? Where are your witnesses to this supposed plot?'

'I was wondering when you would get round to that,' replied von Steuben with a slight smirk. 'It is time Congress met some old friends.'

FORTY-FIVE

It was a pitiful sight.

Alexander Hamilton, about twenty-two years old, was broken. They had done the best they could to cover up the bruises and the broken bones, with a clean outfit and what appeared to be rouge on his cheeks, but his mouth was swollen, and there were gaps where teeth had been pulled. However, it was not so much the physical condition as the mental state of the man. Behind his eyes, there was nothing, nothing but surrender. Whatever had happened over the previous twelve hours had shattered him utterly.

He was led into the assembly room in a daze, to gasps from the delegates. Behind him trembled Nathanael Greene, more than ten years older, his face ashen, his usual red lips as pale as his face, walking unsteadily, propped up by the guards who carried him in by his shoulders, no surprise, given that his ankles were cracked.

'Alexander Hamilton and Nathanael Greene, previously highly esteemed members of the Continental Army, you stand before Congress as traitors to your country. How do you plead?' barked von Steuben.

Neither man replied.

'How do you plead to the charges of conspiracy?' von Steuben barked again.

A tear fell from Greene's eye as he whispered, 'Guilty.'

'Louder, Congress needs to hear you admit your guilt.'

His head still bowed, Greene said a little louder, 'Guilty. We are guilty as charged.'

'I have in my hand two confessions, signed by these men independently of each other, in which they fully confess to their part in the cabal and of those others who joined with them, including George Washington.' Von Steuben brandished two handwritten letters and walked to the two men. 'Nathanael Greene, is this your mark?'

Greene slowly nodded his head. Von Steuben moved to Hamilton. 'And is this yours, Alexander Hamilton?'

The young man kept his head lowered, so no one could see his tears and shame. He simply nodded his assent.

'Congress, we have it there. You have borne witness to these traitors and their damnable plot. We shall publish these letters tomorrow, so all the colonies will know, and the British will understand we have foiled their scheme.'

'Wait!' shouted Jefferson, pushing his way past the front rows to the floor of the chamber. 'Look at these two men. Is it not obvious to all that they have been tortured? That these confessions are the product of torture? What have you done to these boys?'

'Whatever misfortune has occurred, they have brought on themselves. Thomas Jefferson, what world do you live in? Do you think criminals give up their secrets easily, willingly let the world know of their plots? Evil always tries to hide from truth. Yes, we had to use some force on these men, but no one forced them to sign the documents or give their assent today. You witnessed it yourself. If they were innocent, they could have said so before this room. But they did not, did they? They admitted to their guilt.'

Jefferson moved closer to the two men. Up close, it was even more shocking, the beatings they had endured.

'My poor boys, what dogs did this to you? I shall seek vengeance for you.' Close to Greene, he lifted his head, 'Dear Nat, this is all nonsense, isn't it?'

318

Looking up at Jefferson, his eyes full of sadness, Greene whispered, 'Tell Kitty, never forget me. I love her. And my babies – look after them. I beg of you, Thom. Protect them.' And he let his head drop.

Jefferson turned to von Steuben, furious. 'What threats did you make to these two men's families?'

Von Steuben laughed: 'What? None whatsoever. The only danger their families face is the danger created by their own treachery.'

'You and your Stormtroopers or whatever you call them are criminals. I will not forget this.' Jefferson turned to the members of Congress and said loudly, 'I dispute these charges. I no more believe in these accusations than I do in the man in the moon. Those of you who fall for this, you are either fools, ready to betray those who have fought on your behalf, ready to believe whatever nonsense comes your way, because it is easier than facing the truth. Or you are truly evil.' He looked towards the Adams cousins. 'For if you are knowingly party to this charade, then you are beyond contempt and will be judged so by your Lord on the day of reckoning.'

There was shouting from the members, paper flew in the air, threats and oaths thrown at Jefferson. Fearing anarchy, Hancock thumped his gavel several times and shouted, 'Order! Order!' until finally the room was quiet. 'We shall have a debate and then we will vote to determine the guilt or innocence of these men.'

There followed some small discussion from the floor, but all the speakers rallied against the treachery of the accused and against Jefferson's insults to them. Within half an hour, everyone who wanted to had spoken. The debate exhausted, Congress voted on the charge of treason against Greene and Hamilton and by a vote of three abstentions, Jefferson and Sam Adams against and thirty-seven for, Greene and Hamilton were sentenced to death that day.

FORTY-SIX

The prisoners were taken away.

Jefferson looked about him, fury in his eyes. He spotted an unusually quiet John Adams sitting stony-faced.

Walking across to his old friend, he said, 'You have been remarkably quiet over this plot, John Adams. You are the cleverest man in this chamber. You will have seen this pantomime for what it is.'

'As a lawyer, Thom, the case seems clear to me. Guilt has been proven. They admitted it themselves and their peers have agreed. In my experience of the law, it is most problematic when one finds those one has previously admired to be guilty of a crime. It can throw one's entire philosophy off balance.'

'Balderdash! You're throwing your lot in with these thugs and vandals to suit your own devices. Shame on you, John. Shame on you. I mistook you for a man of virtue. This is something I cannot comprehend. Our friendship ends this day. Goodbye.'

Jefferson walked towards the doors of the chamber, his way blocked by Stormtroopers.

'What, will you have me give you a false confession as well? Will you beat me senseless as well? Come on, have a go!'

From across the room, von Steuben shouted, '*Ihr Manner! Lassen sie ihn gehen!*' and the guards moved aside so Jefferson was able to walk out.

Conze sidled up to von Steuben and whispered in his ear, 'We should seize him. Treat him as we have that troublemaker Thomas Paine.'

Von Steuben replied almost inaudibly: 'Let him be for now. Should anything happen to Jefferson in the coming days and weeks, it will raise suspicion. We shall be magnanimous. He is likely to be a voice in the wilderness, listened to by no one. This is not a modern state, with political parties and an organised opposition, Werner. There is nowhere for him to go, no constituency who will want to hear his ramblings. Besides which, sometimes it is useful to have opponents by which others can measure you. Better for you to go and comfort Adams, he has sacrificed his friend to stick with us. Go to him.'

Werner went over to John Adams. He remained rigid in his seat.

'Mister Adams, condolences. At times like these, personal friendships may have to be sacrificed for the greater good.'

'And you would know, young man, would you?'

'More than you might imagine,' Conze replied. 'Over time there may well be a reconciliation.'

'No, there will not be,' sighed Adams. 'I have chosen one road and Thom will remain on his. Those roads will never meet again.'

'I call it *Realpolitik*.'

'*Realpolitik*?'

'A German word. A new word, for when we have to act according to the situation as it occurs, rather than on our preconceived morals or ethics. A pragmatic way of viewing the world, if you will.'

'Pragmatic. Is that what you called it when you beat those false confessions out of those two men?'

'False? They were not false, they were—'

'Do not, Herr Conze, take me for a fool. I know the game. I understand the game. I do not like it, but I understand its necessity. Do not let us pretend it is anything but what it is. It has won

321

us what we desired. But, let me make this clear to you and your baron: this is as far as it goes. There will be no more "plots" and conveniences of this kind, no more atrocities, murders or slaughtering of the innocent. Do we understand each other?'

FORTY-SEVEN

Jefferson hurried out of the State House. The crowds outside were getting still bigger, the open square outside the building was completely full, Chestnut Street blocked. As he pushed through the people, he felt nauseous. He turned off the main road and into a side street, held himself against a picket fence and retched. The horror of what had happened in the assembly room, the weakness of his fellow delegates, disgust at all that was occurring made his gorge rise again. He spat and wiped his mouth with the back of his hand. He needed a plan.

Asking locals for help, he found his way to Carter's Alley. Cromwell and Hand were inside the rickety smithy, leaping to their feet when the door opened, relaxing when they saw it was not Stormtroopers, but Jefferson.

'Tyranny, murderous tyranny!' screamed Jefferson.

'What's happened?' Hand asked.

'Where to begin? They have created a plot to secure their position, those damnable Hessians, and they have tied Congress up in it. Damn those fools!'

'A plot?'

'A plot. A plot of such simplicity that only a simpleton would believe in it. They have murdered John Sullivan, the French boy Lafayette, and will do the same to Alexander Hamilton and Nat Greene, who they have tortured close to death by the looks of things, securing from them confessions which claim that at the heart of the plot lies one George Washington.'

'This is insane.'

'It is indeed, Edward. That is the only word for it. Insanity. And Congress has gone with it. Washington has been toppled and they have placed von Steuben, or whoever he is, in his place. They have handed their army, our army, over to the Hessians. Insanity.'

Hand slumped into a chair. 'This is too horrible to imagine.'

'I felt fortunate to have escaped with my own head intact. There were guards there who would have arrested me on the spot, no doubt to drag me off to make a confession of my imagined sins. I do not mind telling you I felt quite frightened for my safety.'

Cromwell said softly, 'They will destroy everything precious in this country.'

Jefferson looked at him, 'That they will, Mister Cromwell. The question is how we stop them. They have the army, they have the people.'

'They have the people for now, Mister Jefferson,' replied Cromwell. 'But who are the people? The Negroes, the Jews, the Indian people, will they have them? Will they have anyone who looks different to them, thinks differently to them? Nah, they have some of the people, but they do not have all the people.'

'And this is just one city – Boston, New York, the smaller towns to the north, even Charleston to the south, they may not fall for this so easily,' Hand responded.

'Maybe not, Ed, but they have Philadelphia for certain,' replied Jefferson, his hands cradling his head. 'There is a madness about this city, a frenzy for the Hessians and their damnable swastika. Gentlemen, we may not be safe here. We should think about departing for the north, swiftly.'

'Where is George Washington?' asked Hand.

'A good question. I have no inkling. But they are after him, make no mistake, they . . . dear Lord. The scaffolding, of course!'

'The what?'

'In front of the State House this morning they were erecting a platform and on top of it what appeared to be a scaffold. They will look to hang Greene and Hamilton this afternoon and I suppose Washington with them. We have to stop them.'

Cromwell spoke up. 'The city is too dangerous for you both. They will tear Ed from limb to limb and you, Mister Thomas Jefferson, you may not be so lucky the next time. I will go. I may not be able to save your friends, but I will at least bear witness.'

FORTY-EIGHT

For the first day of September it was unseasonably hot, and even now with the sun long set, the heat was rising from the ground in shimmering waves. It seemed the whole of Philadelphia was in front of the State House, from society dames in their finest clothes to immigrants just off the boats in the rags they had travelled in, a vast throng of people pressed closely together, a hot, sweaty, sticky mass of bodies. Many had been standing there from mid-afternoon, determined not to lose their place. Several were carried away from exhaustion, but still more came and the others held their position. No one wanted to miss another momentous day in the history of their city and country.

The stage was now lit by flaming torches. At the rear sat the delegates of Congress, dressed soberly, all of those who had been present at the morning's debate with one exception: Thomas Jefferson. A band struck up a tune and then John Hancock made his way to a rickety lectern at the front of the stage to deliver the opening speech.

Behind the stage, out of sight of the crowd, von Steuben, Conze and Reitsch huddled together. Conze had organised the event, decided on the running order, planned the speeches, even designed the set, stealing everything from those rallies he had attended at Nuremburg in a far-distant time and place. He had decided on the drama of a night-time rally, when passions could be roused from

326

the darkness, inhibitions thrown aside, the crowd turned into a frenzied monster.

He deliberately had Hancock start the meeting. He cared not that the President of Congress would make a long, aimless speech that would glorify the role Congress had played in the events before and after Elk. Better for the lead actor to be preceded by a self-aggrandising, mediocre bore. No one would remember anything Hancock would say. There was one main actor on this day.

Finally, Hancock came to the substance of his address:

'After long and torrid discussion, Congress concluded that a change of leadership was necessary to achieve a swift cessation of the present conflict. Consequently, General Washington has stepped aside and in his place Congress has elevated Baron von Steuben.'

There was a sudden, remarkable outpouring of cheers and acclaim. From nowhere, flags and banners appeared in the crowd, all emblazoned with the swastika. Hancock barely had time to take in the scene before von Steuben marched across, invading the stage. 'I'll take it from here, I think,' he said to Hancock, then walked to the edge of the platform to a further round of cheers and screams.

Hancock, unsure of what to do at first, slunk off to the wings, while von Steuben stood, his arms outstretched, bathing in the approval of the huge crowd.

There was no certainty that the noise would ever abate. For five minutes or more he wallowed in it, lowering his arms to wave at imagined familiar faces in the crowd, walking a little to the left to receive hoarse congratulations from that side, walking to the right to receive even more frenzied cheers from there. Finally, deciding that even he had had enough, von Steuben raised his arms up and down and 'Shussed' the crowd.

Waiting a beat, he looked up and shouted firmly: 'Friends, fellow fighters for freedom, Americans!'

The last was met by a cheer even greater than those that had preceded it.

'Yes, Americans! How wonderful does that sound? Americans! A new people for a new nation! We are so close to triumph, so close to throwing off tyranny, so close to forging something new and wonderful that will be a beacon to the whole world.

'It has been less than a year since I first came among you, but I am overwhelmed by the way you have taken me to your bosom, so that I no longer see myself nor my men, as Hessians, as Germans, as Europeans. No, they and I are like you: Americans. Proud citizens not of a colony subjected to the whims and fancies of a foreign king, but proud citizens of a new nation.

'Your Congress has this day bestowed upon me the greatest honour I could ever imagine. Never has a man been more humbled than I when I received this calling. My only sincere thought is that I may prove equal to the trust you the people have placed in me and I can lead you to a quick resolution of this conflict. That I may bring you victory, peace and freedom!'

Uncertain that the mob was totally following him, he bellowed those words again – 'Victory. Peace. Freedom! Victory. Peace. Freedom! Victory. Peace. Freedom!' – until the crowd took it up as a chant and shouted it back to him several times: 'Victory. Peace. Freedom!'

Again, he raised his hand for quiet.

'We shall win that, we shall make this country great. The best. The very best. I have a plan. A plan to win the war and then win the peace. To win the peace for you, the people. We don't want a country like all the other countries of the world, do we?'

'No!' the crowd roared back at him as one.

'No, we want the best. When I see all the other countries – and I have seen many countries in Europe – I see what they have become. They have become weak. They have forgotten the people who made them great in the first place. People like you!'

Another roar from the crowd.

'But they keep power for the few. They look after the rich. They let anyone into their countries. Bad people. Weak people. Jews. Followers of Muhammad. Your fathers and mothers carved this country out of the wilderness. They worked hard. Worked hard for you. We're not going to hand that over to these other people are we? We look after our own and that's what I will do. I promise you, I will look after you. We will built a country on the basis of National Socialism. Do you know what that is?'

The crowd did not.

'It is a new way of building a country, where the government rules for all the people, not just for the few. A strong country. A country that protects its borders. A country that protects its people. A good country. Do you want that country?'

The mob roared that it did.

'Then you will have it!'

The horde wanted it.

'But listen, even as we can almost taste the sweet fruits of victory, we have learned how close calamity and disaster sit beside us. Many of you were surprised when the army took the decision to leave Philadelphia undefended and make for the north—'

Booing interrupted him.

'Yes, you're right. It was a bad, bad thing they did. But luckily, there were those of us who disagreed and stayed behind to protect you—'

Roars of approval once more.

'And we beat those British, didn't we, we gave them one hell of a beating—'

More and more cheers, screams of 'A hell of a beating!'

'Yes, we did. And we will do it again. We will do it until we have driven them off these shores, for ever!'

The crowd to a man, woman and child was now in a state of hysteria. The flaming torches illuminated the rage and frenzy in their faces, the air shook with the howling, passionate din that could be heard for miles around.

'Listen, listen. Please. Listen. We have uncovered a most terrible thing, a very bad thing. We have discovered that there were those in the command who were secretly plotting to secure a peace, a victory even, for the British! Rats. They were traitors, to you, to all of you, traitors!'

Screams of 'Traitors' ran around the throng and then, 'Who are they?' picked up until it became a chant.

'Who are they? Those names that will live in infamy, who are they? You want to know? You want to know the names of those who would look to destroy you? You want to see those men, those traitors, who would have thought nothing of having your children stabbed to death as they slept? The rats who wanted this new country destroyed while it was still in its crib!'

Roars of 'Yes!' and 'Rats', like enormous waves crashing on rocks, the hysteria growing larger with every yell.

'First, I want to tell you about a hero, about a brave man, a very brave man. His name was General John Ewing and when he discovered the plot, he looked to uncover those men. In doing so, he was murdered by them. A very brave man. He will not be forgotten. We will name roads, no, cities after him, such a brave man. So too, John Cadwalader – he came to the aid of General Ewing and he was injured too. He lies, unconscious still, in the Philadelphia Hospital. He may never recover. A brave man. But General Ewing killed one of the plotters, a French boy called Lafayette. Forget him, he is gone, but two more traitors are alive. We have them. We have full confessions from them. Would you like to see them?'

The largest shouts yet, cheers mixed with ferocious, bestial screams. Two guards dragged Greene and Hamilton on to the platform.

'Look at them. Look at them. Such bad people, such bad people. Nathanael Greene and Alexander Hamilton. These men argued that we should leave Philadelphia undefended, while they knew that Lord Howe would come sailing up the Elk and put this city to the torch and with it all of you good people. They knew. We have it here' – he brandished a wad of papers – 'their confessions. We'll publish this today so that all of you can read it and see these men for what they are. For traitors, bad people. Bad. Very bad.

'So, what shall we do with them?'

And again the crowd exploded, a volcano of spite, hatred, madness, incomprehensible screams, a torrent of noise, that rebounded off the buildings and echoed around the open plaza, painful to the ear, murderous in its intent. The flames of the torches shivered as the hatred rose up like warm air currents from the writhing, angry mass.

'What was that?' asked von Steuben of the crowd. 'You said what? You said, "Hang 'em up"?'

He had heard no such call, but suddenly that was the call of the swarming mass, their inarticulate screeches, barks and cries suddenly taking shape around a unified call: 'Hang 'em up!'

Greene and Hamilton, their bodies shaking, the terror of the hatred of the mob burning into them, suddenly started protesting their innocence, but their words were lost in the uproar. Greene attempted to struggle. A guard whacked him around the head.

'The people have spoken! The will of the people agrees with the will of Congress. Put them to the rope, boys!' said von Steuben, as the guards dragged the two men towards the scaffolding.

Greene and Hamilton were lifted on to the scaffold, ropes placed around their necks. The crowd grew quieter. The two men stood shaking on the edge of the scaffold. Von Steuben looked around the mob. The whites of their eyes, like thousands of fireflies, blinked in the balmy night, lips salivating, a drooling desire for vengeance running around the square. Von Steuben paused and then screamed:

'Let the people's will be heard. Let them hang!'

The guards pushed the two men off the scaffolding. Limbs automatically flayed as they flew forward at first and then downwards. The crunch of the snapping of their necks echoed around the arena, followed by the most extraordinary primeval roar of approval, men, women and children dancing in celebration at the death of the two men.

Von Steuben let the noise play out for some time. Throwing a satisfied glance at the twitching bodies, he said to the guards, 'Cut them down and throw the bodies away,' before walking back to the front of the platform.

'You did good,' he said to the crowd, 'You did real good. Bad people. Bad people. But there is one more person we discovered to be part of this group, one more person who was looking to destroy you all. And this one will surprise you. It will upset you. It breaks my heart to tell you this. It really does. For if there was one man I thought beyond such wickedness, but . . . I was wrong, I was very wrong. For the leader of this cabal of crooks was none other than General George Washington!'

There were gasps from the crowd, screams of 'No!', shrieking and even audible tears.

'No, no I didn't want to believe it either, but it is true. It is true. George Washington!' He looked over to the guards, 'Bring him on.'

And then on to the stage, his hands trussed together in rope, his clothes ripped, head bald, teeth removed so his jaw was sunken, came the once tall and proud, but now bent double, George Washington.

Again the crowd found its voice, first with hisses and boos and then a shout of 'Traitor!' that was picked up by all so that with voice they one insulted their former favourite.

'Now what to do with this one?' asked von Steuben. 'What to do with the leading rat?'

And immediately came back the single cry: 'Hang 'im up!'

FORTY-NINE

Cromwell arrived back at the smithy, breathless and frightened. He had watched the rally from its edge. He had felt uncomfortable throughout, the lack of any black faces noticeable. As the night wore on and the frenzy of the crowd grew, so too did Cromwell's unease.

After the hangings, the mood grew darker still. A group of youths, drunk and leering, had spotted him and shouted, 'Nigger! There's a nigger here! You ain't wanted here, boy!'

Despite Cromwell's evident size and strength, they pushed through the crowd towards him. While most of the crowd slunk away to avoid trouble, a few others joined the group until there were about twenty young men, jeering, jostling, spitting at him. Cornwell understood that any act of defiance on his part, no matter how small, would be regarded as provocation. He kept quiet and looked around for someone who might support him, but every other face turned away. He had never felt so lonely or terrified. He had fought for this country, or rather another version of this country, and even on the battlefield, he had never thought himself so close to death as he was at that moment.

He backed away, the group followed him for a few yards, but when he turned and walked more quickly out of the square, they stopped and loudly celebrated how they had run him out.

Soon after, von Steuben and the Congress left the stage and

eventually the torches were put out and the crowd dissipated. But as it moved out and into the streets, so the frenzy came with it. Bars and taverns reopened and the city became a sprawling, mewling carnival of debauchery, drunkenness and devilishness. Couples openly fucked on the streets, men fought with each other, gangs of youths ran wild, looking for 'Jews' or 'Indians' or simply 'foreigners'.

'It is madness out there,' Cromwell told them, but they sensed it, could hear the cacophony of shrieking madness that was rumbling through the streets and over the low rooftops of the city. He laid out what he had witnessed, ending with, 'They went to throw their bodies into the Delaware.'

'And what of Washington?' asked Jefferson, his tone as sombre as the words.

'Ah, they didn't hang him. The crowd shouted for it, but the baron said he had to be tried properly by Congress. They have set the trial for the day after tomorrow. They have taken him off to the city prison.'

'And they will malign another great man, traduce his memory and achievements, then throw him into the Delaware, as if he were no more than fish guts and slops from the shipping boats. These are dark times.' Jefferson put his head in his hands.

'We have to save him. If we can save Washington, there is a chance we can build an opposition, resist these Germans.'

'How can we do that, Edward?' Jefferson's voice betrayed his despair. 'There are but three of us.'

'Knox is still with Schuyler in the north. They will not believe these fabrications. If we can join them, there is a chance.'

Jefferson took it in, nodded his head

'Ah, sir, these people have it in for the Negroes,' Cromwell said. 'They will treat us worse than any slave master in history. Every free black man in the north will rise agin 'em. You will have

334

common cause with them – and inspire any free-thinking Negro on a plantation to rise and revolt.'

'Not easy for myself, sir,' Jefferson admitted. 'I inherited slaves myself. I still own them at Monticello.'

'Then you must set them free. If you show leadership, they will forgive you your past sins and embrace you as a changed man,' said Hand.

'I have for some time considered the moral impunity of slavery. Unfortunately, I have let narrow pecuniary interests outweigh my instincts. That and my fear for their welfare should they be freed. But . . . I accept that my hypocrisy on this subject is a stain on my character.'

'There are others who will join us, sir.' Hand was keen to stop Jefferson's philosophical musings and grasp the practicalities of the moment. 'These Germans will do for the native peoples. Chiefs like Akiatonharónkwen, of the Iroquois, who has fought alongside General Washington and knows the qualities of the man. He will see this calumny for what it is. Once they understand these Germans will seek to destroy them, he and his people, and with them the Mohawks and others, they will ally with us. I feel sure of that.'

'Some of those Indians support the British, Hand.'

'Aye, they do, or rather they did, but the British are not long for this continent. One thing is certain: von Steuben will see them off quickly. Then they will turn to slaughtering the Indians. We must make Akiatonharónkwen and the other chiefs understand that they will not have a future if they do not ally with others looking to halt the Germans.'

'We ally with savages?'

'I would rather ally with a noble man such as Akiatonharónkwen than allow this country to be governed by barbarians who have no time for truth or freedom. It was savages as you call them who rescued me and brought me back to health when the

Hessians had left me for dead. They are not the savages. The savages are these Germans who slaughtered those people and the Colonists who follow their philosophy, who want to destroy anyone not in their own image. We must find a way of bringing Akiatonharónkwen and General Washington together.'

'Washington. Ah, dear Old George. Did you not hear your friend Cromwell here? He is to be tried and then hung, tomorrow probably.'

'Sir, why accept his fate?' Hand asked. 'Surely we should be looking to rescue the man?'

Jefferson laughed. 'And how would we do that, Edward? Walk into prison and ask them to release him to us?'

'No,' said Hand. 'But there is one thing that we can use to win his freedom.'

FIFTY

The port was still. Even the bars and brothels were quiet at this hour, something close to three in the morning. At the front of the stockade were three guards, American Stormtroopers, who failed to see Cromwell, Hand and Jefferson moving quietly among the empty fish tables to their left. Within an hour the fish market would be alive again, with the oily catches of the day, the tables sprayed with marine blood and guts, the shouts of buyers and sellers. For now there was an empty quiet.

They found the hole in the stockade from their previous visit and slipped in. Now the giant furnaces were quiet, no workers hammering at the naked plates of iron, none of the hissing of steam as hot metal was plunged into vats of cooling water, no giant flames jumping up from the ground to the sky, none of the urgent moving of men and machinery. All was quiet.

In the giant shed, the machine sat. Jefferson gasped at its size and magnificence.

'That is their weapon?' he asked.

'It is,' said Hand. 'It is a cannon that moves. Look closely.' He led Jefferson to inspect the platform on which the gun rested. Whispering, he said, 'See the cannon is on this track. When it fires, it recoils back along this gauge, and then springs forward ready for further loading. And the circular platform, it can easily be moved around its circle. Much less cumbersome than a cannon on two wheels. And then sheets of metal around it, to give protection to the gunnery crew.'

'Ingenious. Simple ingenuity. The genius of invention always lies in simplicity.'

'Ah, but the real genius is with the rest of the carriage. It moves, you see, by steam power.'

'It moves?'

'Yes, we witnessed it in the yard yesterday. See at the front there is a grate for a coal fire. Behind the tank of water. Through some connection of the two, the machine moves. The pilot steers it by the wheel at the front. Look at those wheels it has, six wide metal wheels on each side, better to traverse all kinds of surfaces.'

Jefferson clapped his hands and laughed out loud. 'Of course, it is what is called a fire engine.'

'A fire engine.'

'Yes, I studied one at William and Mary.'

Both Cromwell and Hand stared blankly at him. Jefferson was caressing the machine.

'My college at Williamsburg under Thomas Small. He taught us the philosophy of the notion and then the practical implementation. We went to visit the first one in America, in a copper mine near Passiac. They use it to pump water out of the mine. It wasn't like this beauty, I must say, and by the time we saw it, it was much repaired and filthy, but by God, it worked. But it didn't move, of course.' Turning to the two men, he asked, 'And does she move fast?'

'Fast enough. You would not enter it for a horse race, but it moves faster than a man.'

'It bears close resemblance to the one at Passiac. Ben Franklin has spoken to me of creating a moving engine such as this. Although not on land. I believe he is planning a steam-powered ship with his friend James Watt. You've heard of Watt?'

Cromwell and Hand shook their heads.

'A genius. A real genius, but sadly an English genius. For such a revolutionary machine, the mechanics are actually very simple. The coal once lit releases energy, the heat from the fire boils the water – here,' he pointed to the water tank, 'which is turned into steam, the steam is captured there and turns those pistons below. That's how it works. As long as you keep the fire burning and enough steam, the machine will indeed move. A child could operate it.'

Cromwell and Hand looked doubtful.

'You don't believe me? We'll have this lady moving, let me assure you of that. And the piloting, well, no different to taking a boat out down the Delaware. Can you fire the cannon, Edward?'

'I think so. A child could,' he smiled at Jefferson.

'Very good!' he replied. 'If the cannon is prepared, ready to be fired, with one good shot we could cause enough damage and surprise to give us an opportunity. God willing, we might be able to then rescue the general and flee the city before the Hessians are aware of what has unfolded.'

'We will need horses ready for our escape. We will also have to be clever, if we travel up the north road to Trenton, we will easily be discovered.'

'That is why we should go across country, to the north,' said Cromwell. 'They wouldn't expect us to take such a trek. I can have four horses fed, watered and ready within the hour. If you both can have this metal horse moving and ready, I will be at the prison to meet you. If the Lord is on our side, we may prosper yet. Shall we sort those guards at the gate out? They appear to be sleepy fellows.'

The guards, sorted, trussed and gagged, were placed at the back of the shed. Cromwell went on his way while Hand and Jefferson made the carriage and cannon ready. First, they took half a dozen brass shells and a sizeable amount of gunpowder. Then they added further coal to that already on board the carriage. Happy with their work, they started the fire in the carriage's little furnace and waited for the heat to produce the necessary steam.

Within fifteen minutes, the carriage was moving. The night was still dark, the pulsating orange eye of its furnace and the slow rumbling as the carriage made its way through the docks startled the shadowy, early morning figures heading to begin their shift at the port.

'If matters were not so serious, Ed, I would say I was enjoying myself, guiding this carriage through these streets,' Jefferson said. 'See the wisdom in having these streets cobbled. This my friend is the future!'

As the machine made its way down the cobbles of Walnut Street, so it began to attract attention. The clanking and grumbling of the ogre along the street woke many from their sleep, no matter how deep. Baggy eyes pressed themselves to dirt-encrusted windows, many falling back in terror at the belching, banging beast, unable to believe what they saw. Some ran to their doors, several screaming at the apparition, shouting that the devil itself was among them. Some brave boys gave chase, hollering at the contraption, coughing as the plume of smoke laid over them. No one in Philadelphia had ever seen anything like it before. No one on the earth had ever seen anything like it before.

They arrived behind the jail. Cromwell came dashing over to them, shouting over the pistons, 'This machine is damnably nosy, it's waking everyone up, we have to be quick. The horses are awaiting over there.' He pointed to four horses tethered to a tree on the South-East Square directly opposite.

Jefferson stopped the engine. 'Let's get this gun lined up,' he said, jumping down and immediately turning the wheel around so that the cannon faced the back of the prison. As he did so, Hand tipped what he gauged to be enough gunpowder into the pan of the cannon, slipped the shell into its mouth and rushed to the back. 'Thomas, you aim the gun, Oliver and I will take up our places to the side of the jail. Once you have fired, we'll enter. You may want to think about some further explosions, but not, I beg of you, into the prison.'

'Of course. Good luck, gentlemen.'

'May the Lord shine upon us!' replied Cromwell, dashing off alongside Hand.

Jefferson lined up the cannon with as much accuracy as he could. The prison was a large target, he felt confident he could not miss. Dashing back to the front of the furnace, he produced a taper, lit it from the coals and then went back to the cannon and set the taper to the wick. Immediately, the greased wick began to hiss and Jefferson lurched to one side.

The sparkling fuse disappeared down into the hole. There was a momentary pause – for a split second Jefferson almost went to check – but then there was an ear-piercing explosion, so loud and powerful it threw him to the ground as the gun reared back, and then a further almighty explosion in the distance. Scrambling to his feet, the gun returning to its firing position, Jefferson looked out towards the jail. The sun was rising but the feeble morning rays were out-muscled by the red and orange flames that licked the edges of the hole his cannon had made in the side of the prison.

Hand and Cromwell had crouched down ready for the explosion. It was greater than they had imagined. Brick, wood, slate, dust all thrown back out by the impact of the explosion. Checking that each other was uninjured first, they ran towards the hole.

The shell had taken out most of the front wall and the first floor of the prison, opening up rows of cells. Inside, there was carnage. A group of sleeping troopers on the first floor were the heaviest toll, their scarred bodies hung from knife-sharp floorboards, scattered limbs dotted the floor, the painful moans of those who had survived the only noise.

On the ground floor, Hand and Cromwell found with ease what they were looking for: the iron bars of the cells. There were twelve in total. The middle cell's cage had been bent out of all shape by the impact of the explosion. Inside it, the charred remains of a prisoner. The shell had ended its life here, it seemed, and turned the man into charcoal. Had they killed George Washington?

Climbing over the debris, a second cell contained two men, screaming in pain, and in the third, as quiet as one could imagine, a dishevelled figure, hugging his limbs and shaking. It was Washington.

'General Washington, it's Edward Hand, I'm come to rescue you.'

Covered in dust, Washington slowly raised his head, shock giving way to a thin smile. In a cracked voice, he said, 'Thank God for you, Edward Hand. The keys to this cell and these chains are over there, hanging on that wall.' He slowly raised himself from the ground. Almost immediately, he appeared to regain the height and confidence of the war commander, his false teeth were in place and he reached for a dust-covered wig. 'Let us get out of here before these damn Germans capture us again.'

Hand collected a large round ring with several heavy iron keys. Turning towards the cell, he found his feet were stuck. Something was holding his right leg. From the grey debris on the floor, a huge, monstrous hand gripped Hand's ankle tightly. Under the dust, wood and bricks, he could make out the outline of a giant's body. A blond mop of hair coated in muck, blue eyes fixed and determined, and the face of Lothar Kluggman.

With an almighty tug, Kluggman pulled Hand to the floor, before rising from the ground, scattering rubble as he did so. Hand landed painfully on the floor, but was composed enough to throw the keys towards Washington. He looked up as Kluggman's boot

342

was coming towards his face. Hand's head jerked to the left and the boot crashed on a pile of rubbish. The Irishman reached out for a weapon, any weapon, scrambling about the floor as he did so. Before he could find anything, Kluggman had lifted him up from the waist, throwing Hand into a pile of broken chairs and tables.

From behind, Cromwell threw himself on to Kluggman, pulling at his hair, trying to punch his head. The blows seemed insignificant to the German, little more than an irritant. Reaching behind, he pulled Cromwell around and headbutted him square in the nose. Cromwell shrieked in pain. Now Kluggman punched him once, twice in the stomach, and Cromwell fell to the ground, before the German delivered a kick to the ribs. He stopped only because Hand was up, gripping a plank of wood that had once been the top of a desk. He struck Kluggman around the head twice with the wood. The giant stopped momentarily, slumping under the blows, but as Hand went to make a third strike, Kluggman seized hold of the plank and wrestled with Hand for it. Jerking it from side to side, he overpowered the Irishman, who let the wood slip and stumbled to his right. Kluggman threw the plank at Hand, who put his hands up to protect himself, as it splintered about him.

Before Hand could make his next move, Kluggman seized hold of him, putting his head under his left arm. Squeezing the Irishman tightly, he punched him in the face with his right fist. He was about to punch for the second time, when an enormous explosion rocked the prison. Jefferson had fired a second round into the jailhouse, aiming higher than the first; it brought down what remained of the roof. Bricks and slate rained down. Kluggman's enormous body protected Hand's head, but large fragments of brick and tile landed straight on the German's skull. Trying to protect his head, his arms released Hand. Dazed and stumbling, further debris knocked Kluggman off balance, and he fell backwards, slamming against the iron bars of Washington's cell.

The German tried to get to his feet, but he could not raise his head. He felt metal against his neck.

Washington had unlocked his chains during the fight and now had them wrapped around the German's neck, pulling him right up against the bars. Kluggman tried to fight back, thrashing about with his legs and body. Washington struggled to hold him rigid, such was the strength of the Stormtrooper, the general's long legs held against the bars as he sought every leverage to pull the chains tighter. Back on his feet, Hand started to kick the German in the chest, and now Kluggman tried to kick out at him. Pulling a brick from the rubble around him, Hand smacked it full into the German's face, not once but twice. At last the German began to weaken, the kicking and thrashing less intense. Washington pulled the chain tighter and tighter around his neck. Kluggman's face went bluer and bluer with each pull until, finally, he gave up the fight.

Von Steuben and Conze surveyed the destruction of the jailhouse and the broken body of Kluggman. Through the gaping hole in the prison, out on the road, lay the managed metal remains of the carriage and gun, destroyed by Jefferson before the quartet had fled the scene.

'We have sent a unit up the Trenton Road. They won't get far. We will soon have them back.'

'Don't be so sure, Obergruppenführer,' replied von Steuben. 'Whoever broke Washington out was organised. They executed their plan well.'

'Four men were seen riding away, just four men.'

'I cannot believe four men alone overpowered the guards at the docks, stole the tank and then did this, all this! Four men alone could not murder Kluggman. This is bigger than four men. There is a conspiracy. How could they have known of the tank, how to drive it and fire the cannon? There are those in the Continental

Army still loyal to Washington. Even in Congress, and now we see within our own forces. We need to root them all out. The traitors must be purged. Our mission, Werner, is not as simple as we may have thought. We have a long way to go before we have established the Reich in this land.'

FIFTY-ONE

Across from the lake, the wind blew through the trees and with it the last leaves of autumn fell. The chill breeze cooled the bronzed arms of the rowers who had brought Akiatonharónkwen, Tyonajanegen and her husband, Han Yerry Tewahangarahken across the water. Pulling their canoes up on to the pebbled shore of Lake Oneida, they formed a guard around their leaders as the rest of the tribes formed a large semicircle. The Oneida had come from all over their lands, west from Canandaigua, south from the Susquehanna River, from the St Lawrence in the north, but most had walked the seven miles from the town of Oneida itself.

The son of an Abenaki mother and African slave father, Akiatonharónkwen's birth name was Louis Cook. The French captured the family and gave the boy up to the Mohawk, who named him Akiatonharónkwen – 'he unhangs himself from the group'. The name suited him. He had spent years fighting for the French in the Seven Years' War and broke from his Mohawk brothers at the start of the Revolutionary War by leading the Oneida and Tuscarora in siding with the Colonists. In doing so, he wrecked the Six Nations Iroquois Confederacy, the other four tribes siding with the British. The Americans had come to call him Colonel Louis, a nickname won by his efforts in Benedict Arnold's Quebec expedition of 1775.

Now he walked up from the beach and towards a man he had first seen in 1755 when they were both part of a failed peace

346

conference on the eve of the Battle of the Monongahela. The battle in which he first fought the British and destroyed the Braddock Expedition.

The twenty-two years that had passed had aged both men. Akiatonharónkwen's naked torso bore the marks of many battles and a life spent living rough, moving from village to village as the British ate into his people's lands. The man he walked towards was grey-faced, his hair white, a troubled jaw jutting out in the wind. With him were three men he had never met, but he knew who they were. And behind them their troops.

'Father George, it pleases my heart to see you once more.'

'Colonel Louis, old friend, my spirit rises to see you and your people this day.'

'The war cloud rising in the east has made much trouble and brought a great distress upon the American people, which troubles my soul. War is a great evil to any nation or people. I know this by sad experience. The war between the English and France ended in the conquest of Canada by the English King George. It brought devastation to the French people of these lands, but also to the Oneida, the Tuscarora, the Mohawk, the Onondaga, the Cayuga, the Seneca. I rejoiced when you took up arms to defend your rights and liberties against the English. I came to you and pledged myself and the Oneida in your cause. That broke the Iroquois. And now, I am told that the American cause is broken.'

'It is true our cause is no longer united. The British are almost gone from America. King George has few supporters left. They are under siege in New York and by the end of winter they will be finished. But we allowed our cause to be perverted by others who did not share our values of liberty. If we allow them to succeed, they will prove themselves to be greater tyrants than even King George. They will enslave the Iroquois and all the native peoples of America. They will destroy the forests. Poison the lakes. Kill the animals. They will turn this land into a desert. We come here today to forge an undying alliance with the peoples of the Oneida and Tuscarora and hope it may lead to restoring the ancient bonds of the whole Iroquois people. For these Hessians – or Nazis, as they now call themselves – threaten the life of all the peoples native to this America.'

'Father George, we the Iroquois, are now in a feeble state compared to what we were once. We were once the lords of this soil, but we are now much reduced in numbers and strength. We once lived as free as the deer in the forest and fowls in the air. We will ally with you if you determine to live peacefully and no more violate the lands of the Iroquois or any people who dwelt here before the white face. If you agree to this, then we will treaty with you. We may build a Two Nation Army, of our peoples and yours. The war spirit, which is naturally in us, still burns in our blood. If you uphold such an alliance, then we will exert ourselves to our uttermost to aid you against the Nazis, your enemies. Your enemies will be ours and ours, yours.'

He stretched out an arm.

'Let us seal our understanding in the way of you Americans.'

Washington moved forward and took Akiatonharónkwen's hand.

'Great Akiatonharónkwen, the chief known and feared by all Americans as Colonel Louis, let us this day pledge to create a new nation, a nation of equals, where the white man, the red man and the black man all find common cause together. A cause to defeat the dark forces that would divide men, forces that aim to destroy all that is good and pure in the hearts of men. Let us build together a nation of liberty, freedom and tolerance.'

Washington pulled Akiatonharónkwen into his arms and, as the two men embraced on the shores of the lake, great cheers arose from the Oneida and Tuscarora people, cheers that were picked up by the blue-jacketed men, white and black faces, of the Sons of Liberty brigade, the new army established by Washington and his allies. Seizing the moment, Thomas Jefferson, Edward Hand, Henry Knox and Oliver Cromwell joined in to embrace Tyonajanegen and Han Yerry Tewahangarahken.

The wind rose again. Ripples became waves across Lake Oneida; the tops of the pine trees on its shores billowed and shook. Over the forests, towards the towns and cities of the east and the south, the wind carried the message: America fights on; we will fight to the death for liberty, freedom and tolerance.

ACKNOWLEDGEMENTS

A number of people were wonderfully supportive during the writing of this novel. In particular, thanks are due to Dan Jones, the world's foremost tattooed historian, for helping sort out the initial storyline and continual enthusiasm. My apologies for failing to deliver on your vision of a Panzer tank on an Elizabethan warship, but there's always next time. Celina Parker insisted on helping out and provided insightful comments on early drafts.

Thanks are due to the wonderful team at Unbound who got the pitch immediately and then supported the part-time author with minimal cajoling and maximum patience. So that's a large helping of appreciation to Philip Connor, Jimmy Leach, Georgia Odd, Anna Simpson, Caitlin Harvey and Imogen Denny; Justine Taylor for her superb, no-nonsense editing and Mark Bowsher for making the video which may (or may not) have helped the funding, and if it didn't, it was entirely down to the presenter.

To all those friends who responded by pledging money to help raise the funding, thank you for coming on-board and making this book possible. I can only hope it wasn't too painful and the read is worth it.

Finally, one person bore the brunt of it all more than others, so thanks to my darling wife Tess for her continued support, encouragement and love. Now write your book!

SUPPORTERS

Unbound is a new kind of publishing house. Our books are funded directly by readers. This was a very popular idea during the late eighteenth and early nineteenth centuries. Now we have revived it for the internet age. It allows authors to write the books they really want to write and readers to support the books they would most like to see published.

The names listed below are of readers who have pledged their support and made this book happen. If you'd like to join them, visit www.unbound.com.

Kenton Allen
Mike Anderson
Simon Andreae
Ash Atalla
Dominic Bettencourt Aveiro
Kevin Bachus
Charlie Baker
Jason Ballinger
Josh Berger
Hilary Bevan Jones
John Bew
Andy Bower
Martha Brass

Sarah Broughton
Len Brown
Rob Brown
Andy Bryant
Anthony Butcher
Marcus Butcher
Nell Butler
Meredith Chambers
Juan Christian
Meagan Cihlar
Ian Clarkson
Vivienne Clore
Clive Cockram

Courtney Conte

Brendan Dahill

Claudia Danser

Kathy Day

Nikki Despard

Thomas Dey

Carol Dixon-Smith

Kieran Doherty

Kevin Donnellon

Claudia Downes

Tara Duffy

Stuart Duthie

Sarah Edwards

Claire Evans

Greg Fenby Taylor

Matthew Forde

Kelly Forrester

David Fortier

Eugenie Furniss

Stephen Garrett

Amro Gebreel

Adam Glover

Hermann Goering

Nick Gold

Noleen Golding

Mark Gorton

Sally Greene

Mike Griffiths

Pippa Harris

Stephanie Hartog

Simon Haslam

Gill Hayes

Emma Hindley

Philippa Hird

Antonia Hurford-Jones

Daniel Isaacs

Johari Ismail

Nick Jankel

Ian Johnson

Alex Jones

Jenna Jones

Matthew Justice

Joanna Kaye

Marigo Kehoe

Ricky Kelehar

Peter Kelly

Adam Kemp

Dan Kieran

Doron Klemer

Anita Land

CBE Langan

Nick LaPointe

Rex Last

Sue Latimer

Thomas Latimer

Ross Nicholas Laver

Keli Lee

Teddy Leifer

Max Linton

Martin Loat

Dom Loehnis

James Longbotham

Tracey MacLeod

Caryn Mandabach

Alistair Mann

Laura Mansfield

Zoe Massey

Lucinda and Jon Masters

James May

James McConville

Jo McConville

John Mitchinson

Jochen Mosthaf

Jamie Munro

Carlo Navato

Kevin O'Connor

Rodney O'Connor

Georgia Odd

Michael Paley

Celina Parker

Shaun Parry

Katherine Parsons

Ian Paye

Arlene Phillips

Jon Plowman

Justin Pollard

Claire Powell

Elaine Pyke

Gary Pyke

David Quantick

Adeline Ramage Rooney

Andy Randle

Joshua Reeves

Erwin Rommel

Iain Rousham

Andy Rowe

Paul Sandler

Jim Sayer

Matthew Searle

Adam Sher

Nicola Shindler

David Sloman

Graham K Smith

Mathew Smith

Stuart Snaith

Quentin Spender

Andy Taylor

Matt Tombs

Bruno Tonioli

Jane Tranter

David G Tubby

Peter Van den Bussche

Craig Vaughton

Mark Vent

Sue Vertue

Gerd Fabian Volk

Richard Wallace

Faye E J Ward

Robert Webb

Ben Weston

Amanda Willmott

Tessa Willmott

Ben Winston

Andrea Wong

Adam Wood

David and Charlotte Yelston

Bill Yelverton

Mark Young